This is the second of the three novels—

Deep Summer,
The Handsome Road,
and
This Side of Glory

—which were later gathered together into one gigantic volume and published in eleven languages under the title *Plantation Trilogy*.

The Handsome Road

is a vivid story of the Old South on the brink of war and the total disaster that the war was to bring to the old systems and ways of life.

The New York Times says of Gwen Bristow: "Miss Bristow belongs among those Southern novelists who are trying to interpret the South and its past in critical terms. It may be that historians will alter some of the details of her picture. But no doubt life in a small river town in Louisiana during the years 1859–1885 was like the life revealed in *The Handsome Road*."

THE HANDSOME ROAD
was originally published by
Thomas Y. Crowell Company.

Other books by Gwen Bristow

Calico Palace
Tomorrow Is Forever

Plantation Trilogy

   Deep Summer
   The Handsome Road
   This Side of Glory

Published by Pocket Books

The Handsome Road

GWEN BRISTOW

PUBLISHED BY POCKET BOOKS NEW YORK

THE HANDSOME ROAD

Thomas Y. Crowell edition published May, 1938

Pocket Book edition published May, 1949

6th printing..........April, 1971

This *Pocket Book* edition includes every word
contained in the original, higher-priced edition. It is printed
from brand-new plates made from completely reset, clear, easy-to-read
type. *Pocket Book* editions are published by Pocket Books, a division
of Simon & Schuster, Inc., 630 Fifth Avenue, New York, N.Y. 10020.
Trademarks registered in the United States and other countries.

L

For Bruce

"Nigger pick de cotton, nigger tote de load,
  Nigger build de levee foh de ribber to smash,
Nigger nebber walk up de handsome road,
  But I radder be a nigger dan po' white trash!"

PLANTATION SONG.

The historical background material for this book was supplied by the author.

The Two-Edged Blessing

On the 14th of March, 1794, Eli Whitney patented his cotton-gin. It was one of the greatest disasters that ever fell on the United States.

The cotton-gin was bound to come sometime. Too many people were looking for it. But if it had been delayed fifty years, almost certainly by that time American slavery would have ended; the lords of cotton would have built their fortunes with laborers who worked for wages, and there would have been no Civil War.

In the 1790's most Americans thought slavery was on its way out. They had good reason for thinking so. At first there had been slaves in all the colonies, but now the system was dwindling away. There were fourteen states in the Union. Of these, Vermont had abandoned slavery during the Revolution; Massachusetts (which then included Maine) had followed in 1783, Pennsylvania four years later. Connecticut and Rhode Island had taken steps intended to lead to gradual emancipation. The census of 1790 showed only 158 slaves in New Hampshire. In the other states—New York, New Jersey, Delaware, Maryland, Virginia, the Carolinas, Kentucky, and Georgia—no laws had been passed against slavery, but everywhere sentiment was rising against it.

The fact was that over increasingly large areas, North and South, slavery was proving itself unprofitable. In most parts of the country there were long stretches of the year when there was not enough field work to keep the hands busy, and it was expensive to support them in idleness. In the strip along the Southern coast the slaves were still earning their way, but in the interior—what they called the "back country" of the South—few people had slaves or wanted them.

At this time Southern planters were looking for a new crop. Indigo was being squeezed out by competition from the West Indies; the other coast staples, rice and sugar cane, did not grow well in the back country. They planted some cotton, but not much. Getting the cottonseeds out of the fiber was such a long and costly process that it made cotton cloth too high priced for most people to wear. In those days there was simply no such thing as inexpensive cloth, which is why in old books we read so much about folks in rags and patches.

Cotton is a cobwebby white stuff that grows on seeds, as your hair grows on your head. A cottonseed is oval, slightly less than half an inch long and about a quarter of an inch wide. Before cotton can be spun into yarn these seeds must be taken out, and before the gin they had to be pulled out one by one, by hand. (If you have ever pulled a burr out of the coat of a long-haired cat you have an idea of what this was like.)

To get a pound of clean cotton fiber you must get out about seven thousand seeds. Enough cotton to make a bale (450 to 500 pounds) contains three million seeds. Today's power gin gets these out in about ten minutes; for a hand worker, the job must have been almost endless. And a worker who can seed only a basketful of cotton a day eats just as much as a gin operator who can seed it by the ton. So cotton cloth was too costly to be much used.

Then one day Eli Whitney visited the plantation of Catherine Greene, on the Georgia coast. Catherine was the widow of the Revolutionary general, Nathanael Greene, and since his death she had operated the plantation for her children.

Eli had recently graduated from Yale and was now studying in Savannah. He was ambitious, imaginative, handy with tools; and he was eagerly looking for a way to make his fortune. Catherine Greene introduced him to a group of men interested in cotton, who told him about the problem of getting out the seeds.

Eli set to work. After several weeks he produced his first model. This was a wooden cylinder covered with rows of spikes, turned by a crank. In front of the cylinder was a wire grid, the wires so close together that a cottonseed could not pass between them. One man would turn the crank while another man fed cotton to the cylinder from in front of the grid. The fiber caught on the spikes and went through, but the seeds, caught by the wires, were combed out and fell into a trough.

Elementary as it was, Eli's contrivance would seed cotton at the rate of four or five pounds an hour. This was so much faster than hand seeding that his friends were rapturous.

A year or two later the spiked cylinder was replaced by a series of metal disks, edged with saw-teeth shaped like hooks. As these disks turned, the hook teeth ripped out the cotton-seeds. (This is the principle still used in the great gins of today.) It did not take long to replace the hand crank with one that could be turned by mules. The great problem was solved. Cotton goods that had cost two dollars a yard dropped to ten cents.

It is hard for us today to visualize the revolution caused by the cotton-gin. Armies needed tents, ships needed sails, house-wives needed sheets and towels and tableclothes, everybody needed clothes. Now for the first time in the history of the world here was a cloth to make all these, which *did not cost much*.

The cotton-gin changed the realm of textiles as the automobile changed the realm of transportation. Now the whole world wanted cotton, and here in the American South the land and climate were ideal for growing it. Farmers in the back country had a chance for wealth such as they had hardly dreamed of. They cleared and planted thousands of acres; green hills turned white with what they called "Southern snow."

Rarely did a country change so richly or so fast. The year before the gin, such little cotton as Americans had raised had been used at home. Five years later they raised all that the mills of this country could spin, and exported 18 million pounds to Great Britain. In ten years more the annual export to Britain had reached 62 million pounds, besides what they sold to other countries. It seemed like an explosion of glory.

But behind the brightness came the storm cloud.

There were not enough workers for all these new fields. The mills were begging for cotton and more cotton. Here was land waiting for plows, bolls bursting with cotton waiting to be picked. The cotton growers needed workers. The slave traders had a new market. Thousands and thousands of slaves were brought in.

Several states had been hesitating to abandon slavery because the slaveholders protested that they had paid good money for their slaves and were not going to give them up unless somebody paid good money in return. Now the demand of the cottonfields took care of this. The New York law of 1799 was typical: there would be no slaves in New York State after July 4, 1827. This gave the slaveholders plenty of time to sell their slaves to the traders, to be taken South.

People had been saying slavery was dying of its own defects. They said so no longer. There were more slaves than ever and the number of them was increasing every year. The evils of slavery were still there, but in such a mighty wave of prosperity it was easy to overlook them.

Farsighted Southern leaders—Washington, Jefferson, James Madison—were appalled at what was happening. They fought it with all their might. Washington freed all his slaves by his will, hoping other men would follow his example. Jefferson, when he failed in his effort to curb the spread of slavery, exclaimed, "I tremble for my country when I reflect that God is just."

And the war came. *The Handsome Road* tells about some men and women who were caught up in that war.

*Deep Summer** ends in 1810, when the cotton-gin is still new but firmly established. *The Handsome Road* begins in 1859, when the country is coming close to the Civil War. The cotton-gin, that most excellent and innocent of inventions, has ironically done its fearful work.

Many of the people you will meet in *The Handsome Road* are descendants of those you knew in *Deep Summer*. Readers who like to have all details in order, may want the exact relationships. If you are bored by family trees, skip the paragraphs in italics; they are not necessary. But if you want to know the lines of descent, here they are:

Denis Larne is the great grandson of Philip Larne and Judith Sheramy. Chapter IV of Deep Summer *tells how Judith's first son, David, was born in the log cabin. Chapter XVIII tells how David married Emily Purcell, daughter of Gervaise and Walter Purcell. David's son Sebastian, mentioned as a child in the last chapter of* Deep Summer *was the father of Denis.*

*Available in a Pocket Book edition.

Ann Sheramy and Corrie May Upjohn are both great-granddaughters of Dolores, of Deep Summer. *You will remember that Dolores and Caleb Sheramy had one son, Roger (born in Chapter VIII). Roger married Martha St. Clair. Roger and Martha had a son, Cyril, who appears as a little boy in Chapter XIX of* Deep Summer, *and again in* The Handsome Road *as Colonel Sheramy, father of Ann.*

Dolores and Thad Upjohn had a son, Gideon, who worked on the docks. Gideon married a girl named Esther (Chapter XIX), and the son of Gideon and Esther is the father of Corrie May. Ann and Corrie May are therefore descended from the two half-brothers: Roger of Silverwood was Ann's grandfather, Gideon of the docks was the grandfather of Corrie May.

The Handsome Road tells how these descendants of Dolores, of Caleb Sheramy and Thad Upjohn, Judith and Philip Larne, met the Civil War. It tells how the great-granddaughter of Dolores, Corrie May, finally got a chance—not to claim a heritage, but to make one.

The
Handsome
Road

THE PEOPLE OF THE STORIES

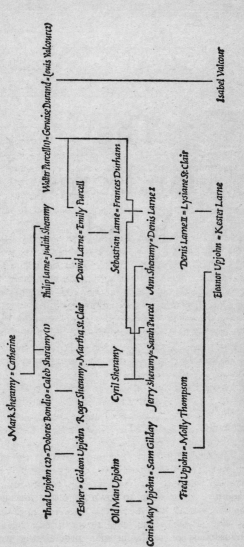

Less important characters have been omitted;
the reader will recognize that such minor figures as Bob Purcell and
Neal Sheramy are descendants of these families.

Chapter One

LEANING against a pile of cottonbales, Corrie May Upjohn watched the boats. Corrie May always enjoyed the
wharfs. Roustabouts heaving cotton and passengers coming
down the gangplanks of the floating palaces gave her more
excitement than even a show in a playhouse. She was waiting
for her beau, and she was glad he had told her to meet him
here.

Corrie May was fourteen. She had a slim young figure and
high-arched feet that hadn't lost their shape even if she did
have to go barefooted except in the winter time, and her blue
gingham dress matched her eyes and made a pleasant contrast
with her yellow hair and the sunburnt ruddiness of her skin.
Her lips were full, though they met each other in a straight
line, forming a kissable but very determined mouth. This beau
of hers, Budge Foster, was not the only young fellow who had
made eyes at her. Corrie May liked Budge best, but she
intended flirting around awhile so he could see she wasn't
taking the only chance she could get.

A wind from the river stroked her face. Corrie May took a
deep breath. She loved the river. From the wharf it was like
watching the whole world at once—fine steamboats curtseying
like great ladies as they docked, sassy little plantation boats
bobbing along the current and getting in everybody's way,
great steamers with foreign flags that came up the river for
cotton, slave-boats from which Negroes were led in long lines
to the market above the wharf, floating bawdy-houses that
moved jauntily from town to town as pious folk got after
them, showboats with big beflowered banners, shanty-boats of
peddlers who wandered up and down selling needles and
calico houseboats of medicine men proclaiming wonderful

1

remedies, ice-boats from up North, loaded with ice cut last winter from the frozen streams and brought down in summer to be sold to the rich households of Louisiana at twenty-five cents a pound. Corrie May had never traveled anywhere, but folks said you did not need to travel if you lived in a river town, for the world came to your door.

She felt secretly proud of the fact that though she was only fourteen she could already stand on the wharfs waiting for a beau. Budge had gone to pay his rent to the St. Clairs, the mighty landowning family from whom he rented the piece of ground he was working. He was a fine fellow, that Budge, setting out to raise himself some cotton and be independent in the world instead of living on uncertain wharf-jobs like Corrie May's brothers. And he was mighty fond of her. Not that he'd said anything right out, but she could tell. Budge couldn't be expected to say anything yet. That cabin he was putting up wasn't finished, and while he was building it he stayed on with his folks in Rattletrap Square, down below the wharfs. Budge wasn't one to be asking a girl to marry him before he had a house for her to live in.

It would be easier being married than staying around home. Her brothers were good fellows, hard-working when there was any work to be had, but now in the depth of summer when things were slow they had a hard time finding jobs, and Pa, of course, he never did anything but talk. In the winter Pa got on a houseboat with some other traveling preachers and they went up and down the river saving souls, and there wasn't a parson on the river could beat old man Upjohn when it came to sermons with rolling lines about Babylon and Sodom and hellfire and great white thrones, but in the summer time old man Upjohn didn't do anything, just sat on the stoop talking politics and religion and all like that. And while it was fine to preach, that didn't put victuals into anybody's belly. Corrie May was glad her brothers worked for their living, and left heaven and hell to Pa.

She looked around for Budge, but he wasn't in sight yet. At the land-office the men had to line up and wait their turns to pay the rent, and sometimes a fellow had to stand there an hour or more. The sun was getting hot. Corrie May thought of the park overlooking the river, where ladies took the air on pleasant afternoons. It would be cool in there. Crossing the wharf, she went through the gateway of the park and walked over to the little lake. She sat down on the grass in the shade of a magnolia tree, watching the swans gliding about the water.

It was drowsily quiet here, and the noises of the river sounded as though they came from a long way off. Except for children playing under the trees with their mammies the park was nearly empty. Not many of the great folk seemed to be about. But of course not; this was July, and they would be up North escaping the summer. But even as she remembered this she heard the soft thud of horses' hoofs and saw a carriage come into the park, and a young lady and gentleman get out. Corrie May recognized them—Mr. Denis Larne, who owned Ardeith Plantation, the richest and loveliest place in Louisiana, folks said; and Miss Ann Sheramy, whose father was the owner of Silverwood, the plantation that joined Ardeith at its north edge. Mr. Denis Larne was tall and slender and looked very fine in a black suit with long trousers buckled by a strap under his instep. He was bowing over Miss Sheramy's hand with deferential grace. Miss Sheramy looked pretty as a fashion plate in a great hooped dress of muslin, and pink bonnet with a plume. As they stood there by the Ardeith carriage they made such a picture of elegance that Corrie May smiled with admiration.

Mr. Larne went out of the park toward an office building on the wharf, and with a word to the coachman Miss Sheramy came toward the lake. Corrie May was seized with bashfulness and wondered if she should not move on, but apparently without noticing her Ann Sheramy spread her ruffled skirts on the grass and sat down, idly watching the swans. Corrie May nearly gasped at the sight of anybody's being so careless of such expensive clothes, but Ann Sheramy seemed to think nothing of them. She pulled off her gloves, and calling to one of the Negro marchandes who wandered about with trays of delectables for children she bought two molasses-cakes. Leaning forward on her knees in a fashion that was almost certain to get grass-stains on her skirt, she began tossing scraps to the swans.

Then, as she became aware of Corrie May's wide eyes on her, Ann impulsively held out one of her cakes. "Do you want this?" she called.

Corrie May could feel her face lighting with astonished gratitude. She moved nearer. "Why yes ma'am, thank you ma'am." She began to eat the cake, but stopped uncertainly, holding it with a crescent-shaped bite taken out. "Oh," she said, "did you mean it was for the birds, ma'am?"

Ann glanced up again, her hand full of crumbs. "Why no, you may eat it yourself," she returned smiling.

Corrie May had seen her often on the street, shopping or riding horseback, but she had never before been so close to her, and she was trying to decide now if Miss Ann were just naturally lovely or if it were her clothes that made her seem so. No, she was very pretty indeed, with light brown curls escaping from her bonnet, and large dark eyes, and a complexion that had been protected from even a tinge of sunburn. When she smiled a dimple appeared surprisingly under her right eye.

"These molasses-cakes sho is good," Corrie May said to her appreciatively.

"Are they really? I've never eaten one." Ann tentatively bit into the remnant of her own. "Why, they are," she agreed in surprise, and turning around she raised her voice. *"Marchande! Apporte-nous encore des gâteaux."*

Corrie May regarded her with increasing admiration as Ann concluded her purchase and offered another cake. "Thank you ma'am," said Corrie May. "You sho talks French pretty," she observed.

"I went to school in France," Ann said. She was eating with relish. Not a bit stuck-up, Corrie May thought. Though she was a planter's daughter and had traveled in foreign parts and all, she was really very nice.

"I ain't never heard nobody talk French but them gumbo niggers like that one," said Corrie May. She smiled, still shyly. "You's Miss Ann Sheramy, ain't you?"

"Yes. What's your name?"

"Corrie May Upjohn."

"Do you live here?"

"Oh yes ma'am. I live down in Rattletrap Square. I reckon you ain't never been there, is you?"

"No, I don't believe I ever have." Ann flung the crumbs of her last cake to the swans. What beautiful hands she had, long and white, with polished nails and not a shadow of dust under the edges. Corrie May twisted her bare toes around the grass, taking care not to touch the hem of Ann's fluttering skirt. "I ain't disturbing you, Miss Sheramy?"

"Why of course not. I haven't anything to do here. I'm just waiting for my friend."

"Mr. Larne's tending to some business?"

"Yes, he's arranging to have signs put up advertising for loggers to cut cypress."

"Loggers?" Corrie May repeated eagerly. "You mean he's giving out jobs?"

"Yes. Why?"

"Well ma'am, I got two brothers that ain't got no work. You reckon they could get a job in his cypress?"

"Why, I suppose so. I don't know very much about it—Mr. Larne just told me he was having timber cut in a swamp that belongs to his plantation. But they could apply at his office. It's the one that says 'Ardeith' over the door."

Corrie May blushed. "They ain't very good at letters, Miss Sheramy. But I reckon they could find it. I sho do thank you for telling me about it." She began to get to her feet, and having finished her own cakes she wiped her hands on her skirt. "I better be going. The boys is somewhere out on the wharfs, and I'll tell them about the logging job. Thank you ma'am, and thank you for the cakes."

"You're quite welcome," Ann said.

Not knowing what else to do with them, Corrie May scrubbed her hands on her skirt again. With a little curtsey to Ann Sheramy she turned around and ran out of the park. On the wharfs she started looking for her brothers Lemmy and George. If Budge showed up while she was gone he'd just have to wait. Getting work for the boys was important. She was mighty glad she had run into Miss Ann Sheramy.

She found the boys resting on a wheelbarrow in the shade of a pile of sugar hogsheads. Lemmy and George were big strong fellows, fair-haired and tanned like herself. They'd make good workers in a cypress camp. Corrie May told them Mr. Denis Larne was hiring loggers.

Say, that was great, the boys exclaimed. That sort of work would last all summer, at least till the plantations started moving this year's cotton crop. They hitched up their overalls and started looking for the Ardeith office. Corrie May went back to the pile of cottonbales where Budge had told her to meet him. He was waiting.

"I'm sorry I kept you standing," she apologized politely.

"Don't matter," he assured her.

"I was seeing about getting Lemmy and George a job," she explained. "Cutting cypress."

"Well, that's fine," said Budge. "Fine."

Corrie May smiled up at him. Budge was a right well set-up fellow and no mistake, big and strong, with a wide ruddy face. His shirt was open at the neck, and as far as she could see, his chest was thick with hairs, the skin under them burnt brickish by the sun. He wasn't charming and graceful like Denis Larne, but Miss Ann could have that one, Corrie May told herself contentedly; Budge suited her fine.

Their bare feet made tracks in the dust of the wharf as they walked along. Budge grinned at her. "Brought you somp'n," he said.

"Yeah? What?" she asked eagerly.

From a paper bag he took two confections of pink sugar each wrapped around a stick, and gave her one. "Ah, thanks," said Corrie May, glad she had not mentioned that Miss Ann Sheramy had given her the cakes. "You sho is sweet to me."

"Oh, 'tain't nothing," Budge answered airily. "Just a little thing one of them nigger women was selling."

Licking the candy off the sticks, they turned from the wharfs and walked around the Valcour warehouses toward Rattletrap Square. "You done paid your rent?" asked Corrie May.

"Sho," said Budge. He added, "That's a right fair little piece of land I got."

"Sho 'nough?" she asked with interest.

"You mighty right," said Budge. "Let's see. This here's fifty-nine." He counted on his fingers. "Eighteen-fifty-nine, sixty, sixty-one. By sixty-one I ought to be making out fine, if there ain't no floods or nothing to gouge me up so I can't pay the rent."

"You's a smart fellow," said Corrie May.

Budge grinned bashfully. Past the warehouses they descended into Rattletrap Square. It was hard to find your way around Rattletrap Square unless you knew it by heart. The alleys twisted around the saloons and crossed one another till anybody could get dizzy. But Corrie May and Budge had been born there and they walked fast.

"Reckon I better go give Ma this here cornmeal she told me to bring," Budge said as they reached the stoop of his home. "I'll be over to set awhile before supper."

"Come on over," said Corrie May cordially.

She turned toward her own stoop. Even before she reached it she could hear the drone of her father's voice, and she shrugged with exasperation.

Old man Upjohn was at it again. Sitting on the stoop before his lodgings, he talked and talked, underlining his most emphatic phrases with a spit of tobacco juice neatly shot from the space between his two middle front teeth. His neighbors lounged around, half amused and half agreeing. Not that you'd ever get any place listening to old man Upjohn, but it was cooler here than indoors where the womenfolk were getting up supper, and his complaints, being directed against civilization in general, made easier listening than the women's individually pointed whinings.

Old man Upjohn made a wide gesture. The wind ruffled his beard and lifted the tatters of his shirt.

"Tell you, fault of organization. Some folks got too much and others ain't got enough. No justice in this here country. Government sits up there in Washington and don't do nothing. Ain't I right, now? Tell me, ain't I right?"

Mr. Gambrell bit on a banana he had taken from his pocket. " 'Spect you is, Upjohn."

"Sho I'm right. And what do the rich care about? Tell you. Getting richer, that's what. No heart and no pity. You ride out on the river boat and see them people, living in luxury and sin. Ain't never seed the inside of a Bible. 'Woe unto you,' said the Lord, but do they listen? Not them."

He spat tobacco juice in a smart curve. It landed on top of a decaying cabbage leaf being investigated by an alley cat. She mewed and turned away.

"All fault of organization," continued old man Upjohn. "No evenness of distribution in this here country. State of Louisiana organized wrong. Whole South organized wrong. You think I'm just shooting my mouth? You, Gambrell, looking so smug, that what you think?"

"Not on your life, Upjohn," said Mr. Gambrell hastily. "Lot of injustice, all right."

"Injustice? Sho's you're born there is. You know who owns the land you all live on? Not you. Not a bit of it. Them St. Clairs. And do they live down here? Not them. They got to have more land on the river road to live on. I been reading a book. I can read good. me. You know who owns all the land in the South? Well I'll tell you. One per cent of the people owns eighty per cent of the land."

"Uh-huh. Ought to be some changes, that's so," mumbled Mr. Kelby, turning his head hopefully for signs of supper from his own stoop. Disappointed, he cut a quid of tobacco and let old man Upjohn ramble on.

"You know how many nigger slaves they got in this country?" droned old man Upjohn. "Four million. Four million nigger slaves in the South. And is you got a nigger, Gambrell? Is you got a nigger, Kelby? You mighty right you ain't. Not a nigger for y'all to bless yourselves with. You know who owns all them niggers? Three hundred thousand people. In the whole South, four million niggers and seven million white folks. And three hundred thousand people owning all them niggers. Ain't right. Ain't we all white as the next man? Ain't we got business having niggers same as them swells out on the river road? Fault of—"

"Oh Pa, for God's sake," said Corrie May. She had stood listening as long as she could. but his ranting made her tired. Him all the time talking with work to be done. "Is you cut that wood Ma said for you to cut?" she demanded.

Old man Upjohn coughed behind his hand. "I ain't been feeling so pert, Corrie May," he mumbled. "Got a misery in my leg " He kicked his leg forward to prove it, and winced. "Hurts back here."

"You's a fine one," said Corrie May disgustedly.

"Where you been anyway?" her father inquired. "Gallivantin' off with a young spark 'stead of helping your po' old ma dish up some victuals."

Humph. thought Corrie May. if everybody was like him there wouldn't be any victuals to dish up. She straightened her back defensively. "I been walking out with Budge Foster. He had to go down to the wharfs and said would I come along with him and cool off, it being so hot."

"Huh," said her father. "You better be getting in and helping your po' ma."

"Oh, all right," said Corrie May. She glanced around at the Foster stoop. Budge came back out to the stoop and waved at her as he came down the steps. He joined Corrie May and they started indoors together.

"What's your Pa ranting about now?" Budge asked her.

"Oh, the regular," said Corrie May as they went into the kitchen. "Politics and the government, and how nothing ain't being run to suit him."

Budge shrugged tolerantly. "Well, I reckon them as uses their mouths most gets least to put in 'em."

Mrs. Upjohn looked up to greet them. She already had the supper on, and was bending over a washtub in a corner by the stove, wringing out some shirts for the boys and hanging them on a line stretched near the stove so they would dry by morning. The kitchen was hot and thick with steam. The smell of soapsuds fought with the smell of supper.

"How're you, Budge?" asked Mrs. Upjohn hospitably.

"Can't complain, ma'am," he answered. Budge admired Corrie May's Ma. She was a good woman, though not much to look at. Her shoulders were humped and her abdomen stuck out in front, with the string of her apron cutting the protuberance in two. Her gray hair straggled damply over her ears and was sliding down from the pins that held it in back.

"I reckon you better chop some stovewood, Corrie May," said Mrs. Upjohn. "It ain't no use waiting for your Pa."

Corrie May shrugged and started toward where the hatchet hung on the wall.

Budge detained her with a grin. "Say, honey, ain't no point in a girl chopping stovewood. I'll do it for you."

"Oh now Budge." She blushed. "Ain't you tired?"

"No cause to be. I'm right tough, me. Gimme the hatchet."

She got it and went out with him to the back yard. "There's the wood. There ain't right much left. I sho hopes the boys picks up that job."

"No reason why they shouldn't," Budge said encouragingly.

"Uh-huh," said Corrie May. She stood by the woodpile, twisting the edge of a torn place in her sleeve. "Er—Budge?"

"Yeah?" He smiled flatteringly at her as he got down on his knees and set a stick of wood on end for splitting.

She felt herself blushing again. "How'd you feel about having supper with us? I could mix up some spoonbread."

"Sounds might fine," said Budge. "Don't mind if I do."

Corrie May hurried back into the kitchen. "Budge is staying for supper," she announced.

Mrs. Upjohn gave a gratified smile. "He's a fine boy, that Budge."

Corrie May smiled too as she got out the cornmeal. "Ma," she asked as she stirred the spoonbread, "how old was you when you got married?"

"Fifteen going on sixteen," said Mrs. Upjohn. "And I didn't take the only chance I got, neither."

Corrie May did not answer. Seemed to her Pa wasn't so much of a chance if there'd been others. But it wasn't her place to be saying so. And of course, Ma never did get as put out as she did about all Pa's ranting. Ma was good-natured, said it came from learning to read. Poor folks didn't have business reading. Just filled them up with notions too big for their heads.

Ma was reminiscing. "I met your Pa at a party we had down at the Sheramys' gin-house one Saturday night. I knew a fellow helped run the gins. They always let the hands have a shindig after gin-time and bring ladies. I had a pink dress with great big sleeves and a straw bonnet with ribbons and my hair was curled up with quince-juice. We danced the Virginia reel, and they said I was lightest on my feet of any."

Corrie May was silent. She felt silence pressing on her ears. She had to say something so as not to let on how astonishing was the idea of Ma dancing and being light on her feet. "What—what color was your hair then, Ma?" she asked.

"Kind of lightish, like yourn," said Mrs. Upjohn. "You favor me, the way I looked in those days. Your Pa said I was the prettiest girl he ever seed."

Corrie May thrust the spoon into the dish and turned around. Mrs. Upjohn was still humped over the washtub. Her face had the lined, weathered look of a piece of cloth left out in the rain. She breathed with a little hiss, for she had lost four of her upper teeth. The hot water had reddened and wrinkled her hands till they looked like pieces of raw meat.

Corrie May walked over to a cracked piece of mirror hanging on the kitchen wall. It brightened things up, her mother said, the mirror and the strings of red peppers she hung about. Corrie May looked at herself, the strong young column of her neck, her high firm breasts, the ruddy clarity of her skin. "Ma," she asked in a faint, frightened voice, "when was that? When you went to the party and met Pa?"

"Huh? That would be—about thirty-nine, I reckon."

Thirty-nine, forty-nine, fifty-nine. Twenty years ago. Then Ma must be thirty-five years old.

Something cold and dreadful came into Corrie May's bosom and moved up to her throat. From the back yard she could hear the chop-chop of the hatchet as Budge cut wood, and his clear young voice singing.

> *"I went to see Jinny when my work was done,*
> *and Jinny put the hoe-cake on,*
> *And Jinny put the hoe-cake on, my love. . . ."*

Corrie May's fists clenched involuntarily, in helpless fear. She stood in the middle of the kitchen floor, seeing herself marrying Budge, and then pretty soon getting to look like Ma. Her mind moved back to the afternoon, and she remembered Ann Sheramy holding her gloves in one of her exquisite hands and with the other tossing bits of cake to the swans. She thought of Denis Larne standing with her by the carriage, and she thought of Ann Sheramy twenty years from now, with her hands still exquisite.

Then, all of a sudden, she heard some of the words Pa had been shooting off as she came down the alley. She had hardly heard them then, she had only felt mad that Pa talked all the time instead of doing a job of work. But they must have gone into her ears and stuck in her head, for now she heard them.

In the whole South, seven million white people and four million slaves. Three hundred thousand white people owning all the slaves.

So—if you counted out the slaveowners' families—six million white people who owned no slaves. Six million white people who owned nothing at all. She was not so stupid as not to know that those who owned slaves owned everything else. The first sign of a man's rise in the world was his buying himself a nigger.

"Jesus," said Corrie May aloud.

"Corrie May Upjohn!" her mother exclaimed, horrified. "You quit that taking of the Lord's name in vain."

"The Lord ain't done so much for me," said Corrie May.

"How you talk!" Mrs. Upjohn hung out the last garment and wiped her hands on her apron. "Ain't you got a good home? Ain't you got a pair of fine brothers that brings their wages in? Don't you get victuals to eat and clothes on your back? Ain't you got a fine young man courting you already? You ought to be down on your knees thanking the good God Almighty. When I think of some—"

"Oh, all right," said Corrie May.

She felt helpless, as though something infinitely stronger than herself were beating her back against a destiny planned for her ages ago. They were all forcing her to it, her mother and father and Budge as surely as the great folk who owned the slaves.

"I seed that Miss Ann Sheramy in the park today," she said abruptly.

"Sho 'nough? Them Sheramys is all the time to be seed in the park. Only I don't get up thataway much these times." Mrs. Upjohn chuckled suddenly.

"What you laughing at?" Corrie May demanded.

"I was recalling your Pa. He sho can think up the tallest tales. He told me once he was related to them Sheramys."

"Related?" Corrie May's voice was thin with unbelief.

Mrs. Upjohn laughed. "He sho can think up things to say, he can. He's a one. Said his Pa told him. His Pa was named Gideon. Said Gideon's Ma was a lady from Cuba. Seems like she was married to one of them Sheramys and they had a fight or something and he throwed her out, and she came down to Rattletrap Square and picked up Gideon's Pa and married him. I declare, your Pa sho can talk."

"You believe that?" Corrie May asked wistfully.

"Lord no, honey. You got to go a long way if you believe half your Pa says. You better put in that spoonbread."

Corrie May turned around. She poured the spoonbread into the pan and put it into the oven. A lady from Cuba. Hell and high water. There weren't any ladies marrying men named Upjohn. But the story gave her a strange creepy feeling as she thought about Ann Sheramy, a feeling that if things had been started off a little bit different it might have been herself

wearing hoopskirts and riding in a carriage. Queer to know there was even a legend that she and Ann Sheramy had a spoonful of the same blood.

Budge came in with an armful of wood. "Here you is," he announced, evidently hoping Mrs. Upjohn would observe he wasn't too good to work for his girl. "That sho smells good on the fire. Mighty fine eating for a man, Mrs. Upjohn, ma'am."

Mrs. Upjohn wiped off a chair with her apron. "Now you set yourself down and rest your bones, Budge. Boys'll be along any minute. Just make yourself at home." She smiled upon him broadly, letting him know she was taking it proud her daughter had a fine one making up to her, and started dishing up the side-meat. "Now Corrie May, you set down too and visit with Budge. It ain't no trouble for me, dishing up."

Corrie May obeyed silently.

"I'm nearabout done putting up a shack on my piece of ground," Budge said.

"Sho 'nough?" Mrs. Upjohn prodded appreciatively.

"Yes ma'am. Move out there for good pretty soon. It's got two rooms and a good cistern in back. Me, I wouldn't be content doing everything in one room like some."

"Mighty highclass," said Mrs. Upjohn. "You got good ground?"

"I sho is. Raise right smart cotton out there. Pay the rent and some over." He cleared his throat and crossed his legs.

She helped him along. " 'Fore long you'll be needing a wife to help you, I reckon. Man can't keep things tidy all by himself."

"Yes ma'am, you's mighty right. I'll be needing a wife, that's so."

He sidled a glance at Corrie May on the chair by him. He was good-looking, she owned reluctantly, him with his curly hair and wide healthy face. And honest he was, and hardworking. He'd be good to her. Not get drunk of a Saturday nor beat her up when the crop didn't come in. But something in her had begun to writhe backward in rebellion.

"Good home girl you'll be needing to marry," said Mrs. Upjohn. "Don't you get caught by one of them too fancy to do nothing but frock up and make eyes at men on the wharfs. Good home girl, knows how to cook and clean and can help pick cotton in the fall."

"Yes ma'am," agreed Budge, his eyes on Corrie May. "Nice home girl."

Corrie May felt as if something heavy and invisible were closing on her so she couldn't fight. It was like the rising of the river in high-water years, creeping up and up against the levees.

"Hey, Ma!" said a voice from the door. "Got supper up?"

Corrie May jumped as though struck. She felt rescued. For the present anyway this was over. Lemmy and George stamped into the room.

"Just call your Pa and pull up your chairs," Mrs. Upjohn said heartily.

Budge got redder, like a brick.

"How're you, Budge?" asked the two Upjohn brothers.

"Oh, I'm making out fine, fine," said Budge.

"Did you get the job?" demanded Corrie May.

"Sho did," said Lemmy. "Tell you about it. Let's eat."

Corrie May went to call her father from the stoop. They all pulled up their chairs. Everybody was talking. The boys were in high spirits. The kitchen was hot, but Mrs. Upjohn propped open the door to let in some air. They were hungry and it was a good supper, collard greens with side-meat, spoonbread and molasses and coffee. "Now you just try this here spoonbread, Budge," Mrs. Upjohn urged. "Corrie May made it. I declare, that young un's a fairer cook than me. Don't help yourself so skimpy—we got plenty."

"Good thing you got plenty, Ma," said Lemmy, bringing up a scoop of collards on the blade of his knife. "Me and George, we'll be needing a big supper tonight. Got to go to work first thing in the morning."

"Good job?" she asked eagerly.

"Oh fair, fair," said the boys nonchalantly, their tone implying that such excellent workers as themselves were besieged with good jobs and had only to select the one most worthy their talents.

"That's fine," said old man Upjohn.

The boys grinned with their mouths full. They regarded their father tolerantly, grumbling about his laziness but secretly proud that he could spout all those big words and awe the neighbors.

"Y'all's good boys," said Mrs. Upjohn. "I wish I'd been

spared more like you, praise the Lord." She sighed. She had
had so many. But it was hard to raise babies down here below
the docks. The little things just took on and died.

Lemmy and George started talking together about the job,
but George yielded to Lemmy, who was older. "We's gonta
cut cypress down in a swamp between here and New Orleans," said Lemmy. "Seems like the swamp belongs to that
Mr. Denis Larne that lives out at Ardeith Plantation. And we
gets highclass wages." He paused impressively. "Seventy-five
cents a day."

"Seventy-five cents a day!" The echo went around the table.
The boys nodded. "Right fair wages, huh?"

"That Mr. Larne must be a fine fellow," Budge observed.
"Don't work his men to bones like some."

"Y'all better look out," said old man Upjohn. "Them
swamps is full of fever this time of year."

"Shucks," said George, annoyed that Pa had tried to
dampen their news. "Ain't no swamp-fever ever touched me
and Lemmy. I expect we's built too tough for the fevers.
Thank you for the 'lasses, Corrie May?"

Corrie May passed the molasses silently. Somehow all she
had been thinking of before supper had lessened her pleasure
in having found a job for the boys.

"Besides," said Lemmy, "I'll tell you somp'n, Pa. Some of
the men got ideas about the swamp-fever. And Mr. Larne said
sho, he knowed they had some fever sometimes in the cypress.
Said he wasn't no hard one making men go where they might
get sick. Said his swamp was healthy, but if any man took on
with the fever and died he'd pay insurance to his folks—fifty
dollars." He spoke the last phrase slowly to let it sink in.

"Fif-ty—dol-lars!" They repeated the words in awestruck
voices.

"Sho's yo're born," said Lemmy and George together, and
George added, "I reckon that shows how much Mr. Larne
expects there to be fever, don't it?"

Supper was a jolly meal. The boys went to bed early so as
to be up and ready next morning. Budge wanted Corrie May
to go strolling on the wharfs after supper, but Corrie May
said she didn't feel so pert. Her mother wasn't much pleased
at that, but Corrie May wanted to think. Budge went off, and
she washed the supper dishes. There really wasn't very much

to think about. Budge was a fine man, she couldn't do finer. But she felt within herself a resentment against everything she had been born to, rising stubbornly in spite of her telling herself to be sensible and not want things she couldn't possibly have.

She got into bed in the little cubbyhole behind the kitchen. She could hear her father snoring, and her mother too, the breath whistling softly through the place where her teeth were out. Corrie May turned over and buried her face.

Chapter Two

FOUR Saturdays came around, and everything was going well. It was lucky the boys were working for a gentleman like Mr. Larne. Mr. Larne didn't manage things all sloppy like some men. Every Saturday there was a fellow from the logging camp made the rounds of the loggers' dwellings, bringing half of each man's wages to his family. Half for the family, and half written down in the book to be paid the man when the job was done.

Corrie May was thinking gratefully of Mr. Larne while she got dinner. Today was Thursday, and Saturday the wage-man would be around again. It sure was comfortable to have money coming in regularly this way.

She made corn-pone and cooked a pot of collards with rice. Her father liked collards. Corrie May didn't like them. Her opinion was that they tasted like blotting-paper soaked in grease, but she was used to them and then as her mother said, did she think she was a rich man's daughter that could have green peas and asparagus on the table? Funny though, Corrie May thought as the pot simmered. Rich people out on the plantations raised collards, but they wouldn't eat them. They raised them in big patches, clusters of coarse leaves so dark green they were nearly black, and fed them to the niggers and sent the surplus to market to be sold cheap to poor folks. But no use breaking your head bothering, Corrie May decided as she put the heads on a plate and began cutting up the leaves. No reason to bother now, with things being so smooth.

When she had finished cutting up the collard-leaves she went to the front to call her parents. Old man Upjohn sat on a box smoking his pipe and haranguing, though there was

17

nobody to listen but Mrs. Upjohn, who was used to him and didn't hear what he said half the time. Let him talk, she said, she could do her sewing just the same and he didn't bother her.

"Dinner's on table, Ma," said Corrie May.

"Fine," said her mother. "Be right in soon's I knot my thread."

"You's a big help to your Ma, Corrie May," said old man Upjohn, rising and brushing off his pants.

Corrie May shrugged. That was more than he was. That man could think up more miseries when there was a job to do—

There was a sharp thin wail from down the alley. Corrie May started.

"Say, what's ailing Mrs. Gambrell?"

"Lord, don't know," said Mrs. Upjohn, looking down the alley with concern.

Mrs. Gambrell was out on her stoop. A man stood there with her. Evidently he had told her something. Mrs. Gambrell threw her apron over her head and began to rock back and forth on her heels, wailing.

"Oh my God! Oh, Lord have mercy! Oh, have mercy, ohhhh—"

Corrie May ran down the alley. Two or three other women joined to ask the trouble. Corrie May got there first and grabbed Mrs. Gambrell's shoulder.

"What's the matter? Ain't no bad news I hope?"

Mrs. Gambrell rocked and wailed. Her neighbors' voices mingled into her cries with eager sympathy.

"Heaven help us. Heaven help us all!" Mrs. Gambrell's apron fell off her head and waved from around her waist. "They done killed him. My man. In the swamp with the fever. Lord have pity on my young uns. I told him he hadn't ought to go. Oh Lord, oh blessed Lord."

Corrie May drew .back. The other women who had clustered around Mrs. Gambrell drew back too, their eyes wide in their weathered faces. There was an instant of shocked stillness, for now they were becoming aware of Mrs. Gambrell's visitor, and they recognized him as the man who came around so promptly every Saturday to bring their men's wages. They sprang upon him, all of them demanding to be told what had happened to their men, while other women came running up from everywhere with children who didn't catch what was going on but knew it was something exciting and wanted to hear it. The stranger regarded them with compassionate impatience, but pulled back to keep the sleeves from being torn out of his coat.

"Now just a minute, ladies. Just a minute, please. I'll tell you everything in good time if you'll just be patient. Please give me a minute to talk, ladies, if you'll be so kind. Yes ma'am, we had a little fever in the camp. Not so bad, no ma'am, not half so bad as you all think. Lots of the men ain't got it at all but is just as healthy as you ever saw 'em. Just give me a little room, ladies, won't you now please?"

He spoke from Mrs. Gambrell's stoop, a little way above them as they stood huddled around.

"That fever!" cried one of the women. "Dragging them down to a swamp in the depth of summer!"

"Now now, ma'am, you ain't got no right to say that. Nobody was drug down to the swamp. Every man that went to cut cypress went of his own free will and accord, now you know that just same as I do. Now just be a little calmer, ladies." He patted the air with his hand as though giving them collectively a pat on the head. "I'll read you the names of them that took sick and died," he went on soothingly. "But before I read anybody's name I want to remind you all that they was working for as highclass a gentleman as ever hired labor. Didn't Mr. Larne write out insurance for every man in case he took on with the fever? And he meant it too, let me tell you that. Any lady among you that's lost a man from her family can go right down to the Ardeith office on the wharfs and get fifty dollars in cash, besides all the wages that was owing him when he died. Now be a mite quieter and I'll read you out the names."

He took a paper out of his pocket. Corrie May stood so stiffly the backs of her knees began to hurt. She found herself putting an arm around her mother, who had huddled up close to her. Her father stood a little way behind. The man on the stoop began to read.

"John Gambrell. Felipe de Sola. Joshua Horton." Each name was greeted by a scream from the group. Poor Mrs. de Sola went down on her knees in the dust and began a sobbing

Spanish prayer, bowing her head to her knees and raising it up again in rhythm with the syllables. The others patted her shoulder vaguely, hardly looking at her while they listened to the list of names.

"Peter Creel. Yvon Picot. Jean Lapeyroux. Hernando Grima. Henry Wales. George Upjohn. Lemmy Upjohn."

Corrie May heard a long choking cry from her mother, not hearing any more names and only mistily aware of the other women's grief around them, except to wonder why they should scream like that when it didn't do any good.

"We better get indoors, Ma," she said slowly.

She guided her mother into the kitchen. There on the table was the hot corn-pone, with the dish of rice and collards steaming. Her father was already there. He sat in a chair by the stove, his head down on his chest and his hands swinging between his knees.

But as they came in he got up, groggily, as though he had just had a knock on the head, and he said to Mrs. Upjohn, "You better sit yourself down here, honey."

Watching them, Corrie May thought she could understand for the first time why it was her mother had always loved him and been so patient with his trifling ways. He was so tender with her, rubbing her hands between his own and getting down on his knees so he could lift her apron and dry her tears. He talked to her softly, in the tone one would use to a child. His words were beautiful, some of them lines like music out of Scripture, about how her children had been washed in the blood of the Lamb and walked the golden streets by the river of God.

Corrie May walked out and sat on the stoop, for he knew better what to do than she did. Presently the house was full of neighbors, for those who had no loss of their own came eagerly to comfort the rest. Corrie May was glad she had victuals on the table. Though her mother could eat only a little, for all their urgings that she must keep her strength up, the others were glad to take refreshment when it was offered.

Budge came over the next morning. He had gone to live in his cabin on his piece of ground and had only just heard the news. He asked if he could help. Corrie May was glad to see him, for she had realized that anything that had to be done she would have to do. Her mother was too stricken, and nobody but old man Upjohn was any comfort to her.

Well, said Budge, he was glad he had come. He'd go down and pick out the bodies and bring them home so the boys could have a good funeral.

"I'll go with you," said Corrie May.

"Now say, honey, you don't have to."

"I reckon I'd better."

"It ain't no business for a girl," Budge urged protectively.

"I expect," said Corrie May, "I thought more of my brothers than to let a stranger go look out for their corpses."

"I ain't no stranger," Budge protested. "Besides, sugar, that air spell of fever might not be over, you know."

"Supposing it ain't," she flared. "Ain't it better to be dead and gone to heaven than worrying along seeing men kill theirselves when they's just trying to make a living?"

Budge ceased arguing with her. He let her get into the wagon with him and they rode out of town, down the road, and turned on the bumpy trail that led to the swamp. The cypresses grew thick, with the frantic way things had of growing in the warm damp air when they were not checked by the hands of men. The trees were so close that the swamp lay in perpetual twilight. It was quiet in the swamp, a quietness that lulled not only the ears but the eyes—gray water, silver trees, moss like rags on the branches, dull green cypress leaves, lavender bayou-hyacinths—and in the hot swimming air the landscape looked thin as though it had but two dimensions. Down here the heat was strange, not like the heat higher up where the town was, but wet and thick, so that sweat didn't dry on you but ran down your back and between your legs and over your forehead to drip from your eyes like tears.

The bodies were in a tent near the road. Far away the rest of the loggers were cutting at the white trunks that stood out in the gray-green dimness. The man in charge was very polite, and told them it was too bad the young fellows had died. There hadn't been very much fever. Just a little, but too bad it had to be at all. He asked Corrie May if she was related to the dead men, and when she said she was their sister he gave her a paper. "Give that to your Ma and Pa," he said, "and tell

them to take it to the office on the wharf. They'll pay a
hundred dollars, fifty dollars apiece insurance."

Corrie May put the paper into her pocket. Give it to Ma,
huh. Ma in her sorrow would lose it. And as for Pa, he'd get
the money, but he'd spend it for flowers and wine and
something fancy for Ma to wear, to cheer her up. She'd take
care of it herself and see it was used to live on.

They put the bodies into the wagon and covered them up
with a sheet. Corrie May cried a little bit on the way home.
Budge was very sweet, putting his arm around her and telling
her how sorry he was.

The boys had a fine funeral. Mr. Upjohn preached the
sermon and folks came from all around. They said it was the
finest funeral anybody had had since they could remember,
and Mr. Upjohn was sure a mighty preacher.

II

The day after the funeral Budge brought his wagon for
Corrie May again and took her down to the office to get the
insurance money. He agreed with her she shouldn't give it to
her parents.

As they rode to the wharf she asked Budge if it wasn't hard
on him, leaving his cotton so much to help her out. Budge
was surprised that she should ask.

"Why say, honey, you know I think more of you than my
cotton. You see—well—"

"What?" asked Corrie May.

Budge cleared his throat. "Well, this ain't no time to be
telling you with black still tied to the doorknob and all, but I
reckon you know how I been loving you all this time." His
face reddened awkwardly. "You don't need to tell me nothing
till you's got over grieving, but I'd sho be proud to think you
and me could get married before cold weather."

Corrie May bit her lip and hesitated. But she felt something
warm inside her, something gentle and comforting. "I—I
don't know," she returned. "I ain't thought much about
getting married."

"But you can marry me, sugar," said Budge. "I'll look out
for you, honest. I got a right nice little place to live in now,

and the crops pay the rent, and we could raise all we'd eat. And I sho am crazy about you, honey girl."

His voice was urgent. Corrie May fiddled with her bonnet-strings. She had been so sunk with loneliness, and scared. She found herself beginning to choke with tears, and was ashamed.

"I reckon it would be all right," said Corrie May faintly.

"Oh honey lamb, you mean it?" Budge kissed her right there in the wagon. "You sho make me a happy man, Corrie May."

She wiped her eyes on the back of her hand, and smiled. He was so warm and secure. "You make me right happy too, Budge. There ain't many girls can get a fine man like you."

"Then—before cold weather?"

"Yes."

He looked at her lovingly, as if he was going to kiss her again, but she moved shyly along the wagon-seat. "Not here. People'll notice."

But she felt better, better than she had felt since the boys died. Budge would take care of her. Maybe it wouldn't be wrong to use some of the insurance money to get a dress and some shoes to be married in. She'd like to show people she took some pride about getting married, not standing up before the preacher barefooted like a nigger.

When she went into the office on the wharf she was so happy she felt sinful, because it was the insurance money for her dead brothers she had come to get. The man at the desk looked up at her and smiled, and she thought he must think she was a pretty heartless girl, looking happy on an errand like this. His eyes shifted from her to Budge, and he smiled at Budge too.

"Upjohn," he said, taking the paper from her hand and consulting a ledger. "Yes, that's right. You related to them mister?" he asked Budge.

"I'm engaged to be married to this young lady," said Budge, and Corrie May looked down bashfully. "She's their sister."

"Money to be paid only to a member of the family." He shook his head.

"I'm their sister," Corrie May reminded him.

He looked at her doubtfully, and his brows drew together. "You ain't of age, are you?" he asked. "How old are you?"

"Going on fifteen."

"Sorry, Miss, but that's my instructions. Insurance to be paid only to a member of the family who's of legal age. Ain't you got a mother that could come for this?"

Corrie May looked at Budge, but Budge seemed at a loss. She tried to explain.

"I got a mother and father both, mister, but my mother, she's all wore out grieving—don't you see how that is?—and my father—well, I tell you, he ain't no' count. He'd go offn his head with a hundred dollars. I thought as how—" she put out her hands, urgently. "I thought it would be a shame, I mean he'd spend it all in about two weeks—"

Her listener nodded understandingly. "Sure, miss, sure, I see. But it ain't my money. It's Mr. Denis Larne's money and I got to pay it out the way he says." He thought a moment. "I tell you what you do. You take this paper out to Mr. Larne. You know where Ardeith is?"

"Yes sir."

"Well, you get your young man to drive you out there, and I'll give you a note to give Mr. Larne. And if he writes on the back of this paper that it's all right for you to have the money then I can pay you. Understand?"

She nodded and sighed, thinking of that long tiresome way in the sun. But Budge said, "Sho, mister, that's fine. I'll ride her out there."

The man wrote the note. "And good luck," he said pleasantly.

She and Budge got back into the wagon and Budge clucked at the mule. It was hot, and they had had no dinner. Budge bought a couple of bananas on the wharf and they munched as they rode. Corrie May was thinking resentfully how hard rich people made it for you even to get what belonged to you.

"Say, that man was nice, wa'n't he?" said Budge.

"Uh-huh," said Corrie May.

"Right pleasant fellow, I'd say. You know, Corrie May, it's all wrong what your Pa says about rich people. They ain't so mean."

"That man in there wasn't rich. He was just a clerk."

"Sho, but I mean the real rich ones. Like this Mr. Larne.

Ain't no law making him give insurance to men on his jobs, is there?"

"I don't know."

"Anyway, it makes me right pleased to think about your Ma getting this money. It'll keep her good, and you and me can get married without wondering how she'll get along. Not that I wouldn't be glad to help out your Ma if she needed it, but it's fine of Mr. Larne to be paying this to all the ladies whose men got the fever, and some of them with young uns too."

Corrie May turned suddenly on the seat. "Mr. Larne hadn't ought to sent any men at all down there in the depth of summer. He knowed there would be fever."

"Oh now go on, honey, how'd he know it?"

"Well, there always is. It ain't right. He shouldn't have sent them."

Budge scratched his head. "Oh now, Corrie May, how you do take on. You was the one told the boys about this job, and I reckon Mr. Larne wasn't no more thinking of the fever then than you was. Course I know it's hard on you, your brothers gone and all—"

"Yes." Her voice caught in her throat. "I reckon I'm still all cut up with hearing Ma wake up at night to cry about them. It just ain't right."

Budge took a hand from the reins and drew her close to him.

"You po' little girl," he murmured. "I know it's hard on you. You talk all you want and cry if you feel like it. I understand how it is."

"No you don't," Corrie May said in a low voice, but she leaned on him. They were silent. Budge kept his arm around her as the wagon went on. He was sweet, he was gentle, he was good. But he didn't understand. He could understand her sorrow, but not her anger. Budge was used to taking things as he found them without reasoning out their causes. Maybe after she married him she would get placid like him.

They rode past the cottonfields, whitening now, and long fields of cane bright green in the sun. At last they came to the gates of Ardeith, which stood open at the end of the avenue that ran between the oaks to the house. Budge stopped the wagon, and Corrie May looked down the avenue.

Even seen dimly through the draperies of moss that hung from the trees, the home of the Larnes was glorious. A lofty wrought-iron fence divided the estate from the plantation fields, and within the enclosure lay a lawn like green velvet, studded with flower-beds and shaded with oaks that looked a century old. Beyond the oaks was the house, white and shining like a king's palace, surrounded by columns that rose to the roof. Corrie May had heard tales of its splendor— doorknobs and candlesticks of silver, a spiral staircase of almost legendary magnificence, curtains of brocade and satin, mahogany beds so vast that a whole family could have slept in one of them. She clambered out of the wagon before the manor gates. "Do I go in here?" she asked Budge.

"I don't expect they'd like it if you came in by the avenue," Budge answered dubiously. "Look. You see that road around the fenced-in part? It goes through the cotton around to the back gate."

"Oh," said Corrie May. "Well, you wait for me. I'll be back soon's I can see Mr. Larne."

"Want me to come in with you?"

"No, never mind. I'll tend to it."

She went by the road he had indicated. The truth was she wanted to go in without Budge because he would talk, and she wanted to be quiet and look at the beautiful house. It was hard to believe all she had heard about it, but she wanted to see, and this was probably the only chance she'd ever have.

Even around in the back the house was beautiful with those tall white columns going up to the roof. Corrie May went through the back gateway. On the galleries of the quarters built behind the manor for the house-servants, several Negroes were passing the time of day. How nicely the girls were dressed, in blue calico with fluted aprons and neat shoes Corrie May glanced down at her own faded dress. It had been clean when she left home, but it was soiled now with the summer dust, and her feet were dusty too, and hard with going barefooted all summer.

The odor of roasting meat came enticingly from the kitchen-house. How grand to have things like that every night for supper. Corrie May began to be afraid one of these Negroes would call and ask her what business she had amid their magnificence. She felt in her pocket for the letter the

clerk had written, proving she had a right to be here, and
went down the path and climbed the steps to the back gallery
of the big house. A Negro man sat on the gallery turning the
handle of an ice-cream churn. Ice-cream for supper too.
Imagine. And ice twenty-five cents a pound.

Corrie May paused hesitantly. "Is Mr. Larne home?" she
asked.

The man at the ice-cream churn glanced up at her. "What
you say?"

"Mr. Larne," said Corrie May. "I've got some business with
him."

"He come home awhile back. You knock on de do'."

She advanced to the back door and knocked. The door was
open, but the hall was dim after the sun outside. How
enormous it was. You could drive a mule-team right through
it and have room on both sides. Far down near the front door
was a white structure. That must be the staircase. The front
door was open too, and she could see the lovely columns of
the front and the oaks beyond.

Her knock was answered by a mulatto girl in a crisp blue
dress and a plaid tignon tied into a pert bow over her
forehead. Her collar was of stiffened muslin ironed into a
frill, and there were gold rings in her ears. Corrie May was
scared of anybody in such finery, but she remembered she
was white and this girl was just a nigger after all, so she took
the note out of her pocket and asked that it be taken to Mr.
Larne.

"Very well," said the girl. "You wait here."

As she disappeared beyond the staircase Corrie May
slipped inside. The knob on the door—Lord have mercy, the
thing was silver. She made a fingerprint on it and rubbed it off
with her sleeve. And the hinges too, silver, sure as you're
born. She crept a bit farther down the hill, leaving dusty
tracks on the floor. That staircase. Holy Moses, why didn't it
fall down? It just went up in the air and turned with no
supports that she could see. And all that carving on the
balustrades. She sure would hate to dust all those scrolls and
flowers every morning. But somebody dusted them, for they
were perfectly white and clean, every single crack of the
carving.

From the front she heard the rustle of a newspaper and

Mr. Larne's voice. "Thank you, Bertha. The girl's waiting in back?"

"Yes sir."

"I'll speak to her." He walked out from beyond the staircase and Corrie May could see him silhouetted against the light from the front door, a newspaper under his arm, reading the note his clerk had written. But at that moment a carriage came down the avenue and Mr. Larne hurried out to the front gallery with a shout of welcome.

"Hello! Come on in."

Corrie May had seen the carriage before, and recognized by the green silk curtains at the windows that it came from Silverwood. The coachman doffed his tall hat in greeting to Mr. Larne as the young gentleman from Silverwood, Miss Ann's brother Jerry, got out. Corrie May had passed Jerry Sheramy several times on the street, and she thought again as she looked at him that in spite of his elegance he was the ugliest man she had ever seen. His hair was sandy and his eyes were mottled; he was long and gangling, clumsily put together as though his Creator had left the sorting of his parts to a foolish assistant. His ears stuck widely out from his head, and when he grinned as he was doing now, his wide mouth widened till it connected his ears and they looked as if they were suspended on either side by a slack string that hung across his face. He and Mr. Larne exchanged greetings and Mr. Larne gave a hand to Miss Ann Sheramy.

"Are we the first?" Ann Sheramy asked.

"Yes ma'am. I'm glad you got here early."

Several Negroes appeared to take their things. How pretty Miss Ann was; she looked cool and crisp like a salad, in a dress of green-sprigged muslin so wide it nearly hid the steps as she mounted them, and a bonnet with green ribbons, and a white lace shawl. "How cool it is here on the gallery," she was saying. "It was so hot in the carriage."

"Let's stay out here," Denis suggested. "There's more air than indoors." He drew chairs for them and told a servant to bring some wine. Corrie May surreptitiously crept nearer. They looked so imposing, Miss Ann in her rustling muslins handing her bonnet and shawl to one of the maids, and her brother, in spite of his ugliness, no less grand in his mirror-bright boots and fine thin broadcloth and lemon-colored gloves. As he sat down Jerry glanced at the paper Denis had been reading.

"What's going on in the world? I haven't seen a paper today."

"Just the usual," Denis returned. "Mr. Buchanan says he won't be a candidate for re-election, there's still no luck with the Atlantic cable and South Carolina's seceding again."

"Again?" murmured Jerry, screwing up his monkeyish face. "Seems to me South Carolina has been seceding ever since I can remember. Do you think they mean it this time?"

"If they do," said Denis, "they're the only ones that know it. Nobody up North takes that seriously any more."

Corrie May wondered what seceding meant, but Ann enlightened her by saying as she sat down on the step and leaned back against a column, "I don't see how South Carolina can be a nation all by itself."

"They don't intend to," Denis explained. "Their idea is that if they started it the rest of the South would go out with them."

"Louisiana too?" Ann wrinkled her nose. "Then would we have to pay duty on things we ordered from New York? I think that's silly."

"It's not so silly," Denis told her smiling.

"Don't you really think so?" Jerry asked.

"No, frankly, I don't. We're virtually two nations now."

Jerry leaned back and stretched. "Father's violently against secession. Of course he would be, after having been all his life in the army, but he puts up some mighty good arguments. He says the North will fight before they'll let the Union split."

"I don't see why they should want to," Denis returned. "They don't like us."

Jerry laughed. "They don't like us, but they like being in the same country with us. The colonel's right about that."

Denis leaned against the column opposite the one by which Ann was sitting, and switched his eyes from her to give Jerry a glance of amused disagreement. "Oh Jerry, don't get sentimental. They're not going to war because of any pretty speeches about an indissoluble Union."

Jerry spoke coolly. "Certainly they're not. But they'll go to war because of their pocketbooks, which is the main reason anybody ever had for going to war. The North can't afford to have the mouth of the Mississippi in a foreign nation, and the Northern textile mills can't afford to pay tariff on their imports of raw cotton. Those are facts, and people concerned with those facts can whoop up enough emotion about the flag to start a war."

Denis shrugged.

"Men are so excitable," said Ann. A white collie trotted out from the far end of the gallery and came to her. She put her arm around it and stroked its back. "Let's talk about something amusing. Politics bore me stiff. Whigs, Democrats, hunkers, barnburners, woolly-heads, silver grays, softshells, hardshells, fire-eaters, abolitionists, filibusters—I don't know what half of them are and I bet the men who argue about them all the time don't either."

The gentlemen laughed at her good-naturedly. Corrie May didn't know exactly what they were talking about but she was interested in hearing them. They talked so differently from the people she knew. Her father used some of their words, but not as they did; they were so amused about things, as if all you had to do was go on being nice generally and everything was bound to settle itself all right.

There was a swish of skirts over Corrie May's head and a gray-haired lady came down the spiral staircase. She was a tall, commanding lady in a gown of white with black frills, and a widow's cap of black lace. With her was a little girl. The young folks on the gallery saw her and rose with a unanimous movement of deference.

"Good evening, Mrs. Larne."

"Good evening," she greeted them. The young gentlemen bowed and Ann dropped a curtsey. Mrs. Larne kissed Ann's cheek. "It's nice to see you, my dear."

But she said it a bit stiffly, as if it were only a courteous phrase with no meaning behind it. Ann responded with formal politeness. "Thank you, Mrs. Larne, it was good of you to ask us here." Then, as if relieved to have got that over, she bent to give Denis' little sister a hug. "And Cynthia, honey, how are you? You're getting to be such a big girl!"

"I'm ten," said Cynthia proudly.

"You'll be a grown-up lady before you know it. What a pretty dress."

Cynthia looked up at her with worshipful gratitude. "Do you really like it, Miss Ann?"

"I certainly do. Those dark red ribbons are so becoming to a girl with black hair. I never could wear red."

"Some day soon," ventured Cynthia, moving closer to her, "will you let me come over to Silverwood and see the dresses you got in Paris?"

"Why of course. Any day you like."

"Tomorrow? I've got a new pony. I can ride over there."

"All right."

"Goody goody—Mother, may I go to see Miss Ann tomorrow?"

Mrs. Larne smiled at Cynthia fondly. "Don't let her get in your way, Ann."

"She won't. I love children."

Miss Ann was really rather sweet, Corrie May reflected even if Mrs. Larne didn't appear to like her very much. How beautifully they all spoke, even the little girl. They didn't pronounce words like folks in Rattletrap Square. Mrs. Larne was asking,

"Denis, who's that white girl waiting in the hall?"

"Oh Jerusalem." Denis sprang up again. "I forgot about her. Excuse me a minute, will you?" He came into the hall and glanced around. Corrie May had withdrawn hastily into the shadow of the staircase, afraid they wouldn't like it if they knew she'd been listening to their talk, but she came forward again.

"Here I am, Mr. Larne."

"Oh yes. You're the sister of the Upjohn boys?"

"Yes sir." She twisted the end of her sleeve. "Er—Mr. Larne, I wouldn't have come today if I'd knowed you was having a party."

"Oh, it isn't a party. Just a few friends in for supper."

He smiled at her reassuringly. A Negro man passed them, carrying a tray on which stood a decanter and thin-stemmed glasses. "This note from my clerk explains everything, I believe," Denis said to Corrie May.

"Then it's all right for him to give me the insurance money?" she exclaimed gratefully.

"Yes, quite all right. Have you the paper certifying their decease?"

"Their what?"

"I mean saying they died of fever in the logging camp."

"Oh yes sir. Here it is."

"Thank you." He drew a chair out from the wall. "Sit down here—you must be tired after coming this long way. I'll write the authorization in a minute."

He went into one of the rooms off the hall. Corrie May sat down and smoothed her skirt and tucked her feet under the chair. What fine manners he had. Like Miss Ann, he wasn't mean a bit. Maybe her father was wrong about rich people. Cynthia Larne came into the hall, dragging Ann, evidently to show her some treasure after the manner of little girls adoring big ones. They came down the hall so fast they didn't notice Corrie May and nearly ran into her chair.

"Oh!" said Ann. Then she laughed apologetically. "I'm sorry."

Cynthia looked with curiosity at Corrie May. Evidently she was not used to the sight of girls with sunbonnets and bare feet. "Are you the girl that wanted to see my brother?" she asked.

"Yes ma'am." Corrie May stood up awkwardly. "Er—Miss Ann, if you and the little lady wanted to be here I could wait on the back gallery."

"Why no indeed," said Ann. "Stay where you are. Did you see Mr. Larne?"

"Yes ma'am, I seen him all right. He's writing the paper for me."

"What sort of paper?" asked Cynthia.

"About my brothers, ma'am. They got fever in his camp and died."

"Oh, what a pity," said Ann sympathetically. "I'm so sorry."

"Yes ma'am," said Corrie May. "Thank you ma'am."

The Negro man came into the hall again with the tray. "Miss Ann, the mistress says will you have some sherry?"

"Yes, thanks." Ann took the glass. "And Napoleon, pour a glass for this lady too."

Corrie May started with surprise, but the servant did as he was told—though he was evidently surprised too—and Ann held out the glass. "Here. You must be tired after coming all the way out here in the sun. I hope you didn't try to walk it."

"No ma'am. My beau's got a wagon. He brung me." Corrie May sat down again, holding the glass carefully. She tried to sip daintily and not spill any drops, like Ann.

"Miss Ann," said Cynthia in a half-whisper, "let me taste that."

"Oh my soul, darling, I don't dare. Isn't your mother frightfully strict?"

"Yes ma'am, she sure is, but Brother Denis lets me taste things."

"Brother Denis can do a lot of things in this house that I can't, honey. Still, it does seem cruel, and it won't hurt you. Here." She moved her vast skirt between Cynthia and the door. "Thank heaven for hoops," she said over Cynthia's head to Corrie May, as though their both being older gave them comradeship. Corrie May wondered what it felt like to wear hoops. She had never had any. They cost five or six dollars a set, and besides it took such an everlasting lot of cloth to go over them. Poor folks couldn't be wearing skirts eight yards around. Cynthia secretly took a sip from Ann's glass and offered to return it. "Do you like it?" Ann asked.

Cynthia nodded.

"You may drink it all if you won't tell your mother on me."

"Oh—but then you won't have any."

"I can get some more."

"You sure are sweet," said Cynthia, and she finished the sherry with such awesome delight that Corrie May couldn't help laughing. Ann laughed too as she caught Corrie May's eye.

"Haven't I seen you somewhere before?" she asked.

"Yes ma'am. About a month ago. You was feeding the swans in the park and you gave me some cakes."

"Oh yes, of course, I remember." Ann bit her lip at the reminder. "Why—I told you about the work in the cypress, didn't I?"

"You mustn't feel bad," Corrie May answered respectfully. "You was trying to do me a favor."

"But I'm terribly sorry!" Ann exclaimed. "Is there anything I can do for you?"

"No ma'am, thank you ma'am. Mr. Larne's tending to it."

"I see. But if you ever need anything, you'll let me know, won't you?"

"Miss Ann," begged Cynthia, "come on out and see my pony!"

With a last regretful look at Corrie May, Ann yielded. "All right, honey. But don't set the glass on the chair. It'll make a ring. Put it on the little table with the cover."

Corrie May heard their voices trailing off. Another carriage drove up to the front and several more young ladies and gentlemen got out. She heard Mrs. Larne telling them Denis would be out directly. In spite of his assurance that it wasn't a party Corrie May felt embarrassed at having come into all this majesty, and she was glad when he reappeared. He gave her a paper.

"Here you are. Now if you'll take this back to the clerk, he'll pay you the money. Can you write?"

"Not much, sir. But I can set down my name."

"That's all you'll need. I was going to say if you couldn't you'd have to bring a witness with you to certify your mark. When he gives you the money, put your name on this line."

"Yes sir, thank you sir."

"And give your mother my very deepest sympathy," Denis added.

"Yes sir."

"I was greatly distressed about the fever in the camp," he went on. "We do all we can to keep the men well, but nobody can prevent disease entirely."

"No sir, I reckon not." Corrie May stood still an instant, looking up at his face with its expression of real concern. He didn't look as it he'd ever want to hurt anybody. And if he hadn't been kind he wouldn't have offered to pay insurance for the men that died. A hundred dollars was a lot of money.

The Negro man who had brought the sherry passed them again. How well-dressed he was, she thought, and how contented he looked. None of that frowning strain that could be seen on people's faces in Rattletrap Square. She'd love to have somebody like that to wait on her. But that was absurd even to think about. A trained butler like him was worth about three thousand dollars.

Something clicked sharply in Corrie May's head. Mr. Larne's fields were full of Negroes. Even a fieldhand cost five hundred dollars at the market. Two dead white men cost Mr. Larne a hundred dollars. Two dead slaves, even cheap ones, would have cost him a thousand. It was less expensive hiring white men for dangerous work than sending slaves to do it because if a white man died nobody had lost very much but his folks.

Corrie May turned around and went out. She couldn't look at that man any more. She had crossed the gallery and reached the back gate before she remembered she hadn't drunk more than half of that nice sherry and heaven knew when she'd get any more like it.

Some Negro boys were lounging around the door of the kitchen-house, hopefully awaiting a handout from the cook. None of them came forward to open the gate for Corrie May. She opened the gate herself, and walked past the cotton storehouses. Outside the storehouses were some platforms for cotton, where several Negroes sat resting after their day's work. They were singing to the music made by one of them who plucked a banjo. They were having a fine time, singing plantation songs. They sure could sing, too. All Negroes could sing. They seemed to do it just naturally But when Corrie May drew near enough to hear the words they were singing, something turned over inside of her and she stopped short.

> *"Nigger pick de cotton, nigger tote de load,*
> *Nigger build de levee foh de ribber to smash,*
> *Nigger nebber walk up de handsome road,*
> *But I radder be a nigger dan po' white trash!"*

Corrie May stood around an angle of the storehouse and the Negroes had not noticed her. They were repeating the refrain, and the little boys were shuffling on the cotton-platforms while the others sang and swung with the rhythm, so familiar with the words that they scarcely thought about them at all.

> *"O Lawd, radder be a nigger,*
> *Radder be a nigger, Oh my Lawd,*
> *Nigger nebber walk up de handsome road,*
> *But I radder be a nigger dan po' white trash!"*

Corrie May started to run. She ran through the cottonfield as though something were behind her trying to catch her and crush her to death.

"Lawsy mussy!" Budge exclaimed as she reached the big road. "What you running so for, Corrie May?"

She stood by the wagon, panting too fast to answer. Budge's face suddenly became grim.

"He didn't throw you out, did he?"

"No, no," panted Corrie May. "He was nice to me. He said he was sorry."

She put up her hand to shade her eyes and looked back at the columned palace of the Larnes. "He said he was *sorry!*" she repeated.

"Well now," said Budge soothingly, "that was good of him. I told you he was a fine fellow." He got out of the wagon. "Here, honey, lemme help you in. There now. If we hurry up this lazy mule we ought to get to town before dark. Giddup, Nellie!"

Corrie May sat by him on the driver's seat, her mind reaching desperately for words. Budge was talking and she began to hear him. He was saying how fine it would be when they got married, living in their own cabin in their own cotton-patch.

"You have to work mighty hard in that cotton-patch of yourn, don't you?" she asked suddenly.

"Sho, honey, you can't raise no cotton if you don't work. But I don't mind. Ain't everybody can make enough crops to pay rent for a piece of ground." Budge spoke complacently.

"It's mighty tough," said Corrie May, "for you to have to work every day from can't-see to can't-see just to pay rent. And me too. Married to you, working all the time with nobody to help me——"

"Say, baby," Budge protested in a hurt voice. "Honest, there ain't such a lot to do. Just two rooms to be cleaned up."

"And cotton to be picked," said Corrie May," and corn to be hoed, and young uns to be raised——"

"Oh there now," said Budge. "You and me might save up enough to buy a nigger, even."

"A nigger?" she flung back at him scornfully.

"Well hell," exclaimed Budge with sudden indignation, "is it my fault I ain't rich?"

She answered more gently. "No, honey, it ain't your fault. I know you does the best you can."

"You better quit talking about things you don't know nothing of," Budge advised her sternly.

"All right," she answered wearily. "I'll quit."

"That's right, sugar." He patted her hand. "Now me and you'll get married this fall and we'll get along fine."

Corrie May felt her back stiffen. Her hands curled over the edge of the seat and held it so tight the board hurt her fingers. Her feet got stiff too and she felt her toes turn under as though with cold.

"I ain't gonta marry you this fall," she said.

"That ain't too soon," pled Budge. "Course if you'd rather wait, till Christmas, say—"

"I ain't gonta marry you no time," said Corrie May.

"You ain't—what? You done said—"

"Yeah, but I'm saying it over. I been thinking. I ain't gonta have to work hard and mess around my whole life. I'm gonta be somebody, Budge Foster, you hear me? I'm gonta be somebody and have me some clothes to wear and have folks speak to me on the street."

"After all you done told me—"

"I take it back."

"Me loving you and hanging around all this time for you—"

"Oh Lord, I'm awful sorry, Budge." There was a quaver in Corrie May's voice.

"Say, you look ahere," said Budge threateningly. "You'll get in a peck of trouble if you start carrying on like that."

"No I won't," she retorted. "You just see."

"You think you's too good for a man that wanted to marry you honest and look out for you—" his words caught and he became hurt and pleading. "Corrie May, honey, I been loving you so much. Don't you start going on."

"You shut up," said Corrie May.

"Say," he exclaimed, "you talk to me like I was a nigger!"

"Lord no," said Corrie May vehemently. "You ain't no nigger! You's so white you wouldn't touch a nigger. You's a heap sight different from a nigger, you are!"

"Sho I'm different from a nigger. What do you—"

"I'll tell you how different," she cried with sudden fury. "You get up at the bust of dawn and work cotton, like a nigger; you wear overalls with a patch in the seat of the breeches, like a nigger; you waddle home so tired you can't see, like a nigger; and when you dies you ain't got no more'n you had the day you was born, like a nigger. But you ain't a nigger. You's white. You get sick one day and can't tend to your cotton and who takes care of you? Your crop fails one year and who feeds you just the same? Who keeps your roof patched so the rain can't come in? Who cares if you starve to death? Nobody. And that's the difference in you and a nigger, Mr. Budge Foster, and you can't tell me nothing else."

Budge was too astounded to form an answer. Corrie May rushed on.

"Suppose I got married to you. Suppose I worked my hands off, cooking and picking cotton and raising young uns. Then suppose a mule kicked you and you died. What would I do? I couldn't pay rent so I'd get turned offn that piece of ground. And could I work for somebody? Could I sew or scrub or take in washing? Who do you know that's gonta pay a white woman for doing them things when there's niggers doing 'em for nothing? I ain't gonta marry you. I'll be double-damned if I am. I'd rather be a nigger than po' white trash."

Chapter Three

I

DENIS privately suggested to Jerry that he would like to see Ann home after supper, so Jerry, who had more wisdom in these matters than one would have guessed from his gargoylesque face, good-naturedly invented an errand in town. As they drove toward Silverwood Denis asked Ann for the fourth time if she would marry him. For the fourth time Ann lowered her eyes enough to let him appreciate the length of her eyelashes, and answered, "Honestly, Denis, I don't know. Please give me time to think. I can't dispose of my whole life in five minutes!"

Denis was both amused and exasperated. He was wise enough in the ways of women to be fairly sure Ann was going to tell him yes, but he was inordinately in love with her and wanted to be sure. He turned and looked at her. In the dusk of the carriage she was like a warm shadow, provokingly scented with vetivert.

"Ann," he said, "why do you keep teasing me so?"

"But I'm not teasing you!" Ann protested. "I really don't know."

It was too dark for him to distinguish the full expression of her face. He could not tell whether she was in earnest or not.

The carriage stopped before the steps of the Silverwood house. "May I come in?" Denis asked as the coachman opened the door.

"Don't be a goose," Ann retorted. "Of course you may." They laughed at each other and went up the steps.

The house had a white sheen in the darkness. It looked like a Greek temple; ten Corinthian columns supported the pediment, and beyond them a great double door led between two pilasters into the main hall. As they went in Ann gave her

39

bonnet and shawl to a servant and led Denis into the parlor. Like all the rooms to the left of the entrance, the parlor had a black marble fireplace, while the rooms on the right had fireplaces of white marble, a conceit characteristic of the romantically-minded Sheramys, who liked variety in all things. The doorknobs and hinges downstairs were silver, but the doorknobs on the second floor were made of Dresden china decorated with little pink and blue flowers. It was a lordly house and a beautiful one, though Denis had always preferred his own—a preference doubtless caused by the fact that he had been born at Ardeith and expected to die there.

Colonel Sheramy came into the parlor to greet Denis. He was a tall, reticent man in his fifties, with white hair and a grave face. Most of his acquaintances stood somewhat in awe of him. After a few moments he left them alone again, and Denis turned back to Ann. She had spread her great skirts about her on the sofa and was chattering about nothing in particular—how hot the weather was, and how dull it was at home this time of year. "I was so mad," she went on, "when Father made us come back from Saratoga."

"Had you meant to stay there all summer?"

"I'd hoped we were going to. But Father hired a new cotton overseer by mail, and said he wasn't going to trust an unknown to supervise the crop. And he wouldn't let me stay there by myself." She looked down, lacing her fingers in her lap. "Denis," she said.

"What, honey?"

The corner of Ann's mouth flickered, but she spoke demurely. "Maybe I ought to tell you—I behaved very badly at Saratoga."

Denis laughed softly. "I doubt it."

"Oh yes I did. I got talked about. The ladies called me that fast young person from the South."

"My dear," said Denis, "I've observed that when old ladies say a young lady is fast it generally means only that she gets more attention from gentlemen than their daughters do."

Ann chuckled. "You're very understanding. But I did think I should tell you. What have you got?" she asked, for Denis was picking up something from the carpet.

"This fell out of your pocket." He held out her smelling-salts, a little bottle in a filigree holder. His gray eyes were on her teasingly. "What's it for?"

His candor was disarming. "A stage-prop, Denis," Ann returned truthfully, and he laughed aloud.

"I thought so. Ann, you're immense."

"You're terrifying. I never dare tell you fibs."

"You shouldn't. You're not very good at fibs." He bent nearer as though about to kiss her, but she drew back.

"No. If you're going to behave like that you'd better go home."

"Can't I stay long enough to say you look enchanting?"

"Anybody can look enchanting by candlelight. Go on home."

Denis regarded her thoughtfully. With her great skirts billowing around her Ann looked like a big flower upside down. She had a luscious figure, small waist, sloping shoulders, high round breasts. The breasts were obviously real; Denis wondered if any men were really deceived when flat-chested girls sewed ruffles inside their chemises. He was not sure if the waves in her hair were natural, but the hair itself was genuinely golden-brown and abundant, and made a silky frame for her cheeks. His eyes went to her face. Doubtless intended by nature to be classic, it was a face as far from Greek serenity as the bayou-hyacinths from asphodel: a straight, disdainful nose, a mouth stubborn and voluptuous, and large eyes several shades darker than her hair. The chin was too abruptly square for beauty, but it was dimpled, and there was the other dimple that appeared under her right eye when she smiled. She was smiling now at his scrutiny, and the dimple was so delightful that he unconsciously smiled back at her.

"Now do you know exactly what I look like?" she challenged him.

He nodded. Then, in the casual way in which he often told startling truths, he answered, "You look, my darling, like a girl who's always fed on the roses and lain in the lilies of life and who'll be damned if she'll consider doing anything else. And I promise," he added, "if I can help it you'll never have to."

"Good heavens," said Ann. "No young gentleman should

analyze me like that. Roses and lilies—is that why your
mother doesn't approve of me?"

Denis laughed. "She doesn't approve of anybody of our
generation. She always says modern young people have no
modesty and no manners."

"She likes you," said Ann. "Still, though, you're her
firstborn, and besides—you know, Denis, I think she has a lot
of respect for you because you've never had a pain. She's
always been delicate, hasn't she?—and she seems to think
there's something awfully clever about you, never to have
been sick."

"You've never been sick either, have you?"

"No, not particularly, but—but really, she does dislike me
and I wanted to ask you if I'd ever done anything to offend
her. She's so dreadfully polite, as if I'd forged a check and
had repented and people had agreed not to refer to it any
more."

Denis took both her hands in his. "Ann, she has mighty
serious views of life and she prefers girls who are very
thoughtful and dignified. But there's no reason why that
should come between you and me. I prefer you."

"Thank you very much," Ann said. She smiled up at him
frankly. "I do like you. Denis. You're so honest—and so sure
of yourself. I wish I were as certain of everything as you."

Denis stayed half an hour after that, until Colonel Sheramy
sent a servant down to remind him of the time. Ann would
not kiss him good night.

II

To tell the truth, Ann found his kisses so thrilling that she
was afraid lest they befuddle what she intended to be a long
conference with herself after she went to her room. But
Mammy took so long brushing her hair that she got drowsy,
and dropped off to sleep before she had squeezed out more
than a thought or two.

She woke up to a day so hot and still that it produced a
feeling of annoyance while she was yet half-conscious. She
wished she were back at Saratoga, and she hoped the new
overseer would turn out to be a model of efficiency, for if he
did the colonel might be prevailed upon to take her to a

watering-place for September. Ann pushed up the mosquito bar and pulled the bellcord. "Good morning," she said as Mammy appeared with the coffee-tray.

"Good evenin'," said Mammy accusingly.

Ann chuckled. "What time is it?"

"It's mighty nigh bedtime. Not much use gettin' up now." Mammy set the tray on the bedside table and as Ann sat up to pour her coffee Mammy plumped up the pillows behind her. "Miss Ann, you got business to be up befo' de day is half wo' out."

"If you scold me," said Ann, "I'm going to set you to picking cotton and let Lucile dress me."

Having heard this awful threat before, Mammy paid no attention and kept on scolding. No matter how hot the day Mammy always looked crisp, in her starched blue calico and her tignon wrapped smartly around her head. "Is you gonta get up, Miss Ann?" she demanded finally.

"Right this minute. Get me a cold bath."

"Humph," said Mammy, and waddled out.

Setting down her coffee-cup, Ann thrust her feet into the slippers that stood waiting on the bedstep and crossed over to the washstand, where she tossed up a handful of water to clear the cobwebs out of her eyes. She stood a moment looking at herself in the glass. Jerry said she spent half her life before a mirror, an accusation that Ann laughed at without troubling to deny it. Undoubtedly she was a nice-looking person; even in a rumpled nightgown and with her front hair in curl-papers she looked well enough to believe Denis' admiring eyes. Ann drew back from the mirror. She really ought to be making up her mind. Next week she would have her twentieth birthday. Twenty was a horrid age, so final; it put a period to one's girlhood and dragged one across the line of being entirely grown up. She ought to get married. In her lifetime Ann had had very few decisions to make, and these she had made in whatever fashion seemed at the moment likely to cause the least trouble for herself. So far life had dealt with her very pleasantly, and certainly a marriage to Denis would be the best possible insurance against having to trouble her mind about anything whatever. As she stood before her mirror considering, it seemed an inviting prospect.

There was a knock at the door. "Yes?" called Ann, thinking it was Mammy with the bath.

"Howdy," said Jerry's voice. He pushed the door inward. As he came in Ann took up a dressing-gown from a chair and pulled it around her. Jerry was carrying a box. "You finally out of bed?" he greeted.

"I sure am," said Ann. She adored Jerry. He had been named Cyril for his father, but his mother had started calling him Jerry for convenience and nobody had changed it. Jerry was so delightful and so ugly, and he had so much good sense —she quarreled with him frequently, but she always respected his opinions.

"Present for you," he was saying.

"What is it?"

"How should I know?" Jerry dispersed himself over a chair, looking more ungainly than ever against its slender legs and upholstery of skim-milk blue damask. "Came by hand. Something Denis sent over."

"Oh," said Ann. She took the box and sat on the floor, struggling with the strings. The lid came off and showed her a pile of white roses.

"Mighty pretty," Jerry remarked. He asked abruptly, "Say listen, Ann, are you going to marry Denis or aren't you?"

She sat up straight, cross-legged on the floor. "I don't know. None of your business anyway."

"Sorry, ma'am." Jerry grinned and stretched his long arms. "Only I understand he's wandering about full of woe, hinting darkly of blowing his brains out."

"Oh, shut up. I wish people would stop laughing at me."

Jerry started to whistle, puckering his big mouth grotesquely.

"You look like a monkey's uncle," said Ann. She got up and laid the roses on the mantelpiece. Their whiteness shone against the marble, making its veins like black shadows. "Sure enough, Jerry," she exclaimed, "tell me what you think. Should I marry Denis?"

Jerry ceased whistling. He put his feet back on the floor and sat forward in the flimsy little chair, his hands laced between his knees. "Of couse you should. He's a grand fellow. I don't know what you're worrying about."

"Maybe—" She looked down, untying the girdle of her

dressing-gown and tying it again. "Maybe he's too grand. We've always been, well, rather informal over here—but at Ardeith—I mean, Mrs. Denis Larne will be as much a symbol as a person. It might be rather—difficult."

"I don't think so. Not for you."

She came a step nearer. "Do you think he'll expect me to keep that house the way his mother does, poking in the linen-closets and counting the silver every week and standing around when they cut the fieldhands' clothes to make sure they don't waste any material—"

Jerry began to laugh. "Hell and high water, Ann, Denis isn't utterly idiotic."

"I reckon you mean to imply that I am." Ann poked out her lower lip. "I know I'm not terribly clever but I'm not as empty in the head as everybody keeps saying," she exclaimed. "I can play the piano and I dance beautifully as you'd know if you'd ever danced with me, and Madame Bertrand said my French accent was mighty near perfect and that was a big compliment because she thought all Americans were savages riding buffaloes, and I can embroider, and I do know how to be a hostess."

"All of that," said Jerry, nodding gravely, "sounds to me as if the good Lord has destined you to be Mrs. Denis Larne."

Ann spread her arms along the mantel and rested her forehead on it. She wished her mother were alive to be consulted. Her mother had died when she was ten, and all she remembered was a lovable black-haired woman who scampered about with a merriment very unlike the quiet hauteur of Mrs. Larne.

At that instant the door opened and Mammy panted in, carrying two big jugs of water. "Massa Jerry!" she exclaimed. "Ain't you 'shame', comin' in here and yo' young lady sister got no clothes on?"

Ann and Jerry turned laughing. Ann was relieved that Mammy had come in; such deep thought as she had been trying to indulge in was difficult if continued too long. "She's got on plenty of clothes," Jerry was defending himself.

"She ain't neither. And I got to give her a bath. Go on, Massa Jerry. Ain't you got no business to tend to?"

"No business at all. You'd better leave me alone, Mammy. I've been a good boy, riding the cotton all morning."

"Did you see the new overseer?" Ann asked.

"Sure, I saw him. Name's Gilday. Big red face and got a Northern accent that twangs like a tuning-fork."

"What's he doing overseeing cotton if he comes from up North?"

"That wouldn't matter. He says he's been South quite awhile, and he does know about cotton. But I don't think we're going to keep him. He's got a mean way of doing. Mean with the Negroes, and that always goes with a fellow who's mean with the land."

"Go on out, Massa Jerry," Mammy ordered again.

"All right, I'm going." Jerry started to retire obediently. "What'll you be doing, Ann?"

"I think I'll ride down the road toward town."

"You'll bake your so-called brain in this heat."

"I don't care. I've got to do something, haven't I?"

Without answering, Jerry pulled the door shut and went off down the stairs whistling. Mumbling about the ways of the young, Mammy helped Ann out of her dressing-gown and nightgown and poured the cold water into the tub she produced from its hiding-place behind the armoire. Ann sat down in the water, shivered at the first shock of it and then stretched happily, sending teasing looks to Mammy's righteous countenance. Mammy grumbled incessantly, but she loved Ann very much; Ann had nursed at Mammy's bosom when she was a baby, and had been washed and dressed and scolded by her ever since, and Mammy would have cut the heart out of anybody who made such remarks about her white child as she herself made every day.

After she was finally dressed Ann looked herself over in the mirror again, hoping she might meet Denis on the road, for she looked unusually well. Her green riding-habit, spreading around her on the floor, gave her an elongated appearance like an image in the bowl of a spoon, but above the waistline it fitted her figure trimly. One reason Ann liked to ride was that she knew there was no severer test of one's figure than a riding-dress, and her own stood the test so well. Mammy had done her hair in curls on her shoulders, and she wore a pert little green hat with a plume that curved down to kiss her cheek just below where the dimple would be if she chanced to smile at somebody. Ann pulled on her gauntlets, accepted her riding-crop from Mammy's hands and tossed her skirt over her arm to make it short enough for walking.

The house was very quiet as she went downstairs. Evidently the colonel was still riding the cotton, and Jerry must have gone out too. Ann went across the back gallery to the kitchen-house. Half a dozen pickaninnies, clustering around the kitchen door in hope of handouts, shouted "Howdy, Miss Ann," as she approached. "Hello," said Ann, grinning upon them and reflecting that she'd at least make a nice mother, for she adored children. Going in to see the cook, she received an elaborate scolding for being unwilling to wait for dinner, but eventually was given some hot biscuits spread with peach preserves. Munching, Ann went back through the house to where black Plato waited by the carriage-block.

Plato helped her mount and got on his own horse to follow her. They rode to the end of the avenue, where the wide iron gates stood open. A plantation wagon was about to pass. As Ann approached, a white man astride a mule alongside the wagon yelled at the Negro driver.

"Hey, you dirty black nigger! Let the lady go by, damn your hide!"

Ann winced. She hated to hear people howl at Negroes. As she slowed her horse she spoke distantly.

"I can pass quite easily, thank you."

The white man gave her a searching impertinent look, his eyes going up and down her as if she were standing up at the market for sale. He had a flat red face and little nasty black eyes, like a side of beef with two raisins stuck in it. As he took off his hat she observed that his fingers were thick, and there were drops of sweat among the hairs on the back of his hand. Bowing with what was meant to be an ingratiating smile, he said,

"My respects, ma'am. Could I make so bold as to ask if I'm having the honor to speak to Miss Sheramy?"

His manner was oily, and he talked through his nose in the fashion of uncultured people from New England and upstate New York.

"Yes, I am Miss Sheramy," she returned, and tried to get by him, but he had moved his mule inconveniently in her way.

"Howdy do, ma'am," he said, bowing again. "I'm Gilday,

come to oversee your Pa's cotton. Pleased to make your acquaintance, I'm sure." He wet his lips, his eyes going over her again. Ann started and felt her nostrils quivering with disgust.

"Will you please let me get by?" she exclaimed.

"Why sure, ma'am. Always your servant, ma'am." He moved the mule a trifle, and without answering she struck her horse and rushed past. Though she was going away from him as fast as she could she still had a feeling that his eyes were on her, stroking her up and down. Ann shivered and felt nauseated. So that was the new overseer. Well, he wouldn't be here long. A suggestion to Jerry or her father of how he had examined her and Gilday would be off the plantation before they got in the crop.

As she went around a turn in the road she slowed her horse. The road lay between the cottonfields, with big trees edging it and hanging long streamers of gray moss above her head. Far away across the fields she could see the green slope of the levee curving with the river. How fast the cotton was growing! How fast everything grew here on these thick velvet acres under the levee. The cotton with its bursting bolls and dangling pink and white blossoms seemed so rich and still, so serenely untroubled by the lowdown ways of overseers. She felt her angry spirit relaxing before the quiet peace of the land.

As Plato caught up with her he spoke.

"Miss Ann?"

"Yes?"

"Dat new overseer. He ain't no 'count."

"Oh, don't talk about him," said Ann. "He won't last long."

"No'm." Plato dropped behind her again and she rode on. The highway wound like a sun-dappled gray ribbon under the trees. She felt pleasantly peaceful again, and she pushed Gilday into the back of her head to wait there until she could tell Jerry what a disgusting creature he was. In spite of meeting him, she was glad she had come outdoors. The abundant life of the midsummer fields always delighted her. The pomegranate trees that marked the division between Silverwood and Ardeith were flaming with crimson blooms. As she passed the line she heard a voice calling her name, and there was a flutter in her throat as she looked around and saw Denis riding through his cotton toward her.

Ann drew back on the bridle and waited for him to reach the highway. How splendid he looked as he rode among the high blossoming cotton plants. Denis was tall, with a body all compact bone and muscle, broad shoulders, narrow waist, long hard legs. He wore neither coat nor hat, and his reddish sun-bleached hair blew merrily in the wind above his strong aquiline face, the modeling of which was accented by the line of beard trimmed to razor-thinness down each side of his face and only widening a trifle where it met the jawline.

"This is luck!" Denis exclaimed as he joined her. "How are you, and where are you going?"

"Fine, and I'm not going anywhere," she returned. Denis regarded her with frank pleasure, and thinking how different this was from the lecherous look of Gilday she thought she had never realized before what a thoroughly decent person Denis was. He was saying,

"You look perfectly lovely, and cool as ice-cream."

"Thank you." She smiled with more admiration of him than she would have liked for him to guess. "And thank you," she added, "for the roses you sent this morning. They're lovely."

They were riding together at a leisurely pace along the road. "I looked out of the window and saw them as the sun was coming up," said Denis, "and they looked like you."

"What have you been doing?" she asked.

"Seeing to the cotton. It's opening faster than usual. How's your father's new overseer?"

"He's perfectly abominable," Ann said with an inward shudder. "I'm going to tell Jerry and father I don't like him. Are you—" she fumbled for a subject removed from Gilday —"are you getting your cypress cut in spite of the fever scare?"

"Oh yes. There wasn't very much fever, and it's over now. I was very sorry about it."

"So was I," said Ann. "I felt a little bit responsible in a way. I met that Upjohn girl in the park the day you stopped to order the signs put up, and I told her about the work, and yesterday when I saw her at Ardeith she told me her brothers had died in the camp."

"But that wasn't your fault, Ann!"

"No, but I felt dreadful all the same. I wanted to ask you if you knew where she lived. Maybe she's in want, or something."

"Don't bother about it," Denis said soothingly. "I know she's not in want. I paid indemnity to the families of all the men who died."

"You did?" she exclaimed with admiring astonishment. "Oh dear, you make me feel so much better! That's really marvelous of you, Denis. Not many men are so charitable."

But praise always embarrassed Denis and with a deprecating little laugh he switched the conversation. "Anyway, the fever's passed and I'll get the cypress cut before the fogs set in. I'm glad to have sold that timber. Now I can put the land into rice."

"You're very astute," she observed, thinking how few men of Denis' youth could be trusted with the responsibility of a plantation like Ardeith. Most of them would have been glad to let the banks take care of it while they put on airs at watering-places.

"Not astute," he returned smiling, "just ambitious. Here we are," he added, as they reached the gates of Ardeith. "Come on in for awhile."

She agreed, and their horses entered the avenue. Ann felt unreasonably happy. Denis' cool self-assurance was so refreshing compared to the formal insincerity of most young gentlemen. She looked with increasing approval at his lean young figure and patrician face. They reached the house, and he held her horse while she dismounted. The air was thick with the fragrance of gardenias blooming around the steps. Denis picked one for her and she thrust it into the buttonhole of her lapel.

"You're very lovely," he said, half under his breath lest Plato hear him.

She smiled. Denis called to Plato that he could get something to eat from the kitchen while he waited, and he and Ann went up on the gallery. "Shall I order us some lemonade?" he asked her.

"Why yes. And tell them to put in lots of ice."

"All right."

When he had left her Ann stood a moment on the gallery,

thoughtfully striking one of the columns with her crop. Though she had visited Ardeith a hundred times in her life, it seemed to her that she had never seen its legended magnificence as clearly as she was seeing it this morning, now that she was seriously considering the probability that she would spend the rest of her life here. Dalroy, the town below the plantations, was often referred to as a city of palaces, and the road leading from Dalroy into the countryside was one of the noblest residential streets in America, but there was no other house along its length that could equal this one.

A wrought-iron fence with wide gates at front and back divided the estate from the plantation fields. Many years ago the Larnes had brought a landscape artist from France to plan the gardens—mimosa, magnolias, myrtles, banana trees, a dozen kinds of palm, roses and azaleas and calla lilies and gardenias, fire-colored cannas and crimson hibiscus with long golden-feathered tongues, camellias, jasmine, oleanders, and lavender water-hyacinths with bulby stems. The house had been built of cypress beams cut from the Ardeith lands, for cypress is a wood that will outlast many lifetimes. Around its four verandas stood vast Doric columns. Over the double door in front was a cut glass fanlight, and the house stood with its back to the river so the fanlight would catch the morning sun like a rainbow. The great hall ran through to another double door opening on the back veranda.

There were thirty rooms besides the quarters for the house-slaves, built sideways at the back, and the brick kitchen-house, which joined the main house by an arcade. The Sheramys had brought from Italy nine white and nine black marble mantels; the Larnes had chosen theirs all white, and they declined the further variation of Dresden china doorknobs. Every hinge and doorknob at Ardeith was silver, and so were the candle-sconces on either side of the marble fireplaces. The curtains were crimson brocade lined with white silk. The furniture of the master bedroom was so massive it had had to be brought up the river in pieces, and its cabinetmaker came with it to put it together.

But the glory of Ardeith was its staircase.

Ann went into the hall and looked up at the staircase. She had heard the story of its building over and over again. When this house was being erected by Denis' grandfather, David

Larne, he had wanted something that should distinguish
Ardeith from every other house in Louisiana. Not merely
marbles and silver and brocade—for the rawest dock-laborer
given money to spend could have had those—but something
that should demonstrate the great tradition Ardeith embodied
for its people. Their ancestors had come into Louisiana when
it was a jungle, and they had cut Ardeith out of the wilderness. The Larnes would come and go, they would grow up
and marry and have children and die, they would know early
illusions and later disappointments, but they must always have
courage to go on. "For of course," David Larne had said to
his wife, "life moves always in a circle."

She had suggested, "I like to think it moves rather in a—
spiral, shall we say?"

So they had built the staircase. The architect had spent
months on the calculations that would make it possible, and
when the staircase was finished he had destroyed the plans. It
was a miracle of architecture, a self-supporting spiral staircase
with steps six feet across, making a complete turn in the air
before it reached the second floor. The balustrades were
hand-carved with a succession of floriated scrolls so deep it
took two slaves an hour every morning to dust them, and at
the bottom where the stairs flared the balustrades turned and
swept around white pillars. At night when the chandelier
between the door and the staircase was lit, the candle flame
threw long shadows across the scrolls. In most houses a
staircase is merely an arrangement for reaching an upper
floor, but at Ardeith the staircase was a monument, a creator
of legend and romance, and when the Larne women swept
their great ruffled skirts down the stairs and the Larne men
descended with their characteristic slim-waisted elegance, it
was evident that here was an edifice built not simply for the
convenience of fragile humanity but as the epitome of a
tradition more lasting than any small human life could be.

Ann stood at the foot of the stairs, looking around. Along
both sides of the hall hung the portraits of Denis' ancestors,
splendid souls caught in a moment of their splendor for
posterity. Most of their names she did not know, but she
knew one of them was related to her. She and Denis shared a
common ancestor. Ann scowled at the pictured faces, wondering if those men and women had known the burden they had

been creating. Only Denis never seemed to find it a burden. He accepted his family background as he accepted the country he was born in, something that had made him what he was, but always present so that one never needed to refer to it at all. Denis was not by nature very analytical.

But why, she asked herself, be so concerned about it? Her family was as old as Denis', and her blood as blue; the only difference was that the Sheramys had a habit of considering themselves as individuals rather than as parts of a race, and were accustomed to doing about as they pleased. She had heard with amusement that her own father had surprised everybody by marrying a perfect featherhead whose independent ways had shocked the river country, but she had no reason to think their marriage had not been happy.

Denis came down the hall. He looked tall and splendid, and Ann called herself a fool to hesitate before the chance of the most enviable marriage on the river. As he met her at the foot of the staircase he impulsively swept her into his arms.

After a moment Ann drew back a little. She looked up at him, feeling a sensation of pleasure at the nearness of his physical beauty. Denis did not say anything. He stood with one hand on her shoulder and his other arm around her waist, smiling down at her so urgently that Ann felt herself yielding as though his ardor were a command she had no power to disobey, and as Denis drew her to him again she put her own arms around him and pressed his lips down to hers. He whispered how much he loved her, and with her head against his shoulder and her hand ruffling his coppery hair, she nodded when he asked again if she would marry him. But even then Ann was aware of a puzzling, unsilenced corner of her mind asking if there was anything he could give her besides romantic adoration, and she was unsatisfied because she did not know.

But Denis had no doubts. His delight in her made him radiant, and when she said, "Marriage is really what they say, isn't it?—terribly solemn—how can I possibly know what I'm going to want thirty years from now?"—Denis laughed softly, deep in his throat, and picked up one of the curls from her shoulder and kissed it, promising, "Whatever it is, sweetheart, you'll have it if I can give it to you."

"You're such a dear," Ann murmured, and she put her

hands on his shoulders and looked up at him. She appeared breathless with happiness, but the thought actually crossing her mind was what a handsome couple she and Denis would make; with his good looks and her own taste in clothes and decorations they could have a wedding so beautiful it would be talked about for years.

After awhile they went into the parlor, and she sat on the sofa leaning against him, his arm around her, while they sipped the iced lemonade he had ordered against the heat of the day. They did not talk very much. Denis was happy in having at last won her promise, and Ann was feeling a pleasant sense of security. Everything was going to be so simple now that she had finally decided to marry Denis. She could see her life with him as clearly as if she were looking back instead of forward.

Maybe, she thought, if she had not been brought up all her life to expect just such a marriage she would find it more exciting. It occurred to Ann that perhaps she had received too much good fortune. That thought retreated, abashed at its own silliness, as soon as it entered her head, but she could not help being aware of it: the road she had traveled had been so very smooth that she had no standard by which to recognize either the peaks or valleys of experience.

III

The first week in October, Mrs. Larne had the servants begin their semi-annual cleaning of the Ardeith manor. When the work was well under way she made her inspection of the closets and storerooms to make sure everything was going ahead according to her instructions. The keys clinked authoritatively from her belt as she moved.

Mrs. Larne loved her house. The fragrant linen-closets, the shining floors, the wine-shelves with their rows of dusty bottles, the china and glass and silver gleaming in their places, all gave her a smooth, quiet sense of work well done. This was her kingdom and she ruled it with honor. Her servants, well-disciplined and fairly dealt with, worked without confusion, each having his own appointed tasks and leisure when those were finished. She had never understood how some women could be so careless as to trust their homes to hired housekeepers. Her own keys never left her hands unless she was too ill to quit her bed, when she reluctantly gave them to Napoleon. She had trained Napoleon carefully from his boyhood, and proud of his position as head house-man he supervised the lesser servants more sternly than she did.

In the linen-closets the girls were replacing the linens on shelves newly dusted and covered with fresh tissue-paper. Between the sheets they placed packets of vetivert root wrapped in mosquito netting, and the warm fragrance of vetivert drifted into the hall. Mrs. Larne reached toward a pile of tablecloths, and her hands went with pleasure over the heavy damask. Here and there her fingers touched a darn, so delicately woven into the fabric that its presence could hardly be detected. She had herself taught the girls to darn like that. Linens like hers were meant to last for decades, and they did if well cared for; she never bought anything but the best, and she used it till it fell apart.

On the back gallery the house-boys were spreading out the winter curtains and rugs, brushing them to get off the last fragments of the tobacco leaves with which they had been rolled up all summer to keep out moths. With a glance at them Mrs. Larne went back into the hall, unlocked the wine-closet and went through it to the door at the back. This door opened on a staircase leading down into the vault. Calling one of the girls to bring her a lighted candle Mrs. Larne descended into the vault alone. The air down here was musty. The walls were brick and concrete, four feet thick. On the shelves lay rows of ancient bottles hung with cobwebs, rare acquisitions of liquor that were irreplaceable and brought out only in celebration of some great occasion such as a birth or marriage. To the left stood the safe where were kept a few fine heirlooms too precious to be locked away upstairs.

Everything in the vault was in place. Mrs. Larne went back up the stairs and through the wine-closet, locking the doors behind her. In the hall she gave her candle to the girl and spoke to Napoleon.

"Let me know when they've done putting away the linens. I'll be in my study upstairs."

"Yes ma'am." With the wellbred deference characteristic of him, Napoleon bowed from the waist. "You dropped your handkerchief, Mrs. Larne."

"Thank you," she said. Napoleon turned to give the boys directions about hanging the winter curtains in the drawing-room. He had been born at Ardeith, as had his parents before him, and he took a deep pride in the house. Mrs. Larne glanced down at him thankfully as she rounded the turn of the staircase.

She went into her study. Her account-books lay on the table, but she did not immediately go to work. She stood looking around the room, with its light rosewood furniture and a bowl of dahlias on the mantel bright in a ray of autumn sunshine. There would not be much more sunshine; any day now the fogs might be expected to sweep down the river, and she hoped she could get the house in order before the gloom began.

Mrs. Larne pressed her hands together and listened to the voice of the servants downstairs. "The mistress says do this. This mistress wants that done. The mistress . . ."

She said aloud, "The last time." Her hands twisted in her cap-ribbons. Voicelessly she prayed, "Give me grace not to let them see how much I care!"

Ever since her husband died she had been schooling herself for the time of her own surrender. Of course Denis would marry. She had no wish to keep him forever under her tutelage. And she had vowed with all her strength not to be one of the interfering mothers-in-law who could not resign their authority with their keys. But her resolutions had not taken cognizance of the possibility that Denis would marry that goose from Silverwood with her appealing eyes and her fluttery mind.

Her thoughts went back over the years and she could see herself, a young girl who was long and slender like a lady in a tapestry, with a face that while not regularly beautiful had the grace of quietness. She had been born Frances Durham, daughter of the great steamboat family who had begun their fortune in colonial days by building keels and flatboats for the river traders. She remembered when she had married Sebastian Larne, thoughtfully and with earnest prayers that she would make him as dutiful a wife as he deserved, and the gracious competence with which she had stepped into her position as mistress of Ardeith. Her life had not been easy; her health was never good, and Denis' birth seemed to drain all the vitality out of her, so that the four children who followed him had been frail little things who died soon after they were born, and Cynthia, her sixth child, had barely survived a babyhood so precarious it left Frances' hair whitening. But as Denis grew to manhood it seemed to her that at least her life had one splendid reward. For Denis had the strength that had brought his forebears into the wilderness and the charm that wealth and security had enabled them to acquire. When his father died, though Denis was still young, Frances felt that the destiny of Ardeith had passed into hands strong enough to hold it.

Then Ann Sheramy came back from a Parisian finishing-school with a mountain of clothes and no noticeable interest in anything else except the number of young men who could be gathered to admire while she wore them. She was like her mother, who had been a pretty flibbertigibbet with a fondness for champagne; Colonel Sheramy had met her while he was on duty at any army post in Savannah, and Frances had never understood how so grave and earnest a gentleman as he could have married her. And now Denis had become infatuated with Ann, though as far as Frances could see Ann was a fool.

But they were engaged. They were going to be married right after the cotton season. In spite of herself, Frances had let a protest escape her when Denis told her of their betrothal. He had spoken to her more sternly than ever before in his life.

"I know you don't like her," he said. "But I do. And it's not your business."

"No," she answered. "I'm sorry, Denis."

He asked, "Mother, why do you object to her so?"

"I object to any girl," she exclaimed, "who thinks of nothing but clothes, men, and spending money!"

"That's not fair," said Denis harshly, "and it's not true."

Frances was silent. It might not be fair to say it, but it seemed to her it was entirely true.

Today she walked up and down her study, thinking of Ann as mistress of Ardeith with its thirty beautiful rooms and the order she had created there; she thought of Ann making straw out of Denis' property and heaven knew what out of Denis' glittering life. From across the hall she could hear Cynthia in the schoolroom engaged in a French conversation with her

governess. As though in answer to her thoughts she heard
Ann's name in Cynthia's chattering. The governess let her talk
about anything that interested her, as long as she expressed it
correctly in the French language.

"She's so beautiful, Mademoiselle Lenoir, and she is ordering such clothes for her trousseau! She'll make the loveliest
bride anybody ever saw. I'd go over to see her every day if
Mother would let me. Her wedding dress is going to be real
Brussels lace over a white satin petticoat, real lace, think of it!
—with hoops of rolled steel."

Real lace, thought Frances. A thousand dollars or perhaps
fifteen hundred for a dress she'll never wear but once in her
life. Colonel Sheramy would try to pull the stars out of
heaven if she wanted them to wear in her hair.

Denis came out of his room across the hall. She heard him
and turned toward the door of the study.

"You're going out?" she asked him, for he was drawing on
his riding-gloves and carried a crop under his arm.

"Yes ma'am, to Silverwood. I may not be back for supper."

"Brother Denis!" Cynthia called in English from the
schoolroom. "If you're going to Silverwood give Miss Ann my
love."

He turned grinning. "All right." Coming inside the study he
asked,"Are you busy, Mother?"

"No, this can wait. What is it?"

Denis closed the door. "I wanted to tell you we've decided
on the sixth of December. Ann wants to go down to the Gulf
Coast—it'll be too cold to go North."

Frances sat down by the table and ruffled the pages of an
account-book. "Very well. How long do you expect to be
away?"

"About a month."

"That's a long trip for this time of year. You'll hardly be
back for the sugar-grinding."

Denis smiled. "They can start it without me this once. A
man doesn't get married very often. Ann likes the Coast."

"I don't suppose it's entered her head that a shorter honeymoon trip might be more in line with a planter's responsibili-
ties."

As she said it she could have bitten her tongue, for Denis'

face darkened and he leaned nearer her, resting one hand on the edge of the table.

"Mother, I don't mean to be rude. But I've listened to about as much of that as I'm going to."

She sighed. "I'm sorry, Denis."

"You're always sorry after you've said it. I should think you could be more courteous, for my sake if not for hers."

"I hope," Frances said quietly, "I've never been discourteous, Denis."

"You're so distant she can't help being aware of it. She's asked me more than once why you treat her as if she had leprosy."

The phrase sounded like Ann. Frances lifted her eyes and laid her hand over his. She made herself smile. "Denis, all my life I've tried not to be a meddling mamma, but sometimes things do get the better of me. Loving you as much as I do I'm afraid I want my own idea of happiness for you, and it's hard sometimes to realize that it isn't yours."

"I understand," Denis returned, and he smiled tolerantly. Then he grew serious again. "But there's something else I've got to say, and I may as well say it now."

"Yes, Denis?"

He answered without hesitation, but slowly, as though chosing his words with care. "I don't know why you shouldn't admire anybody as charming and sweet-tempered as Ann. But since you do dislike her so much, it's hopeless to expect one house to hold you both in peace."

Frances started inwardly, but she said nothing. She had not expected this. But she could not deny that from Denis' viewpoint she had probably deserved it.

"If Father were alive," Denis went on, "Ann and I could take a house in town. But as it is I've got to be here on the plantation."

Frances stood up slowly, sending up a wordless prayer that she would be able to control her voice. She answered him steadily. "I understand, Denis." She looked straight at his clear gray eyes. "I want to take Cynthia abroad anyway," she went on. "Her French accent needs improving. We'll leave right after your wedding, and when we come back to America we won't come back to Ardeith."

He smiled at her again. "Mother, you have a great deal more sense than most people. Thank you very much."

"My dearest boy," said Frances. She took his face between her hands. "God help me to let you live your own life in your own way. Run along to Silverwood, and tell Ann I sent my love."

"You're rather a dear," said Denis. He bent and kissed her cheek.

She heard him clatter down the staircase. Frances went to the mantel and began pulling one of the dahlias to pieces. The petals fell on the hearth.

She had tried very hard to do her duty in the world. Nobody knew how hard it had been. Nobody but herself seemed to remember those four little graves in the church-yard. Frances felt a flutter in her bosom like a little flame. Her heart sometimes behaved this way in moments when an effort at self-control had been almost too much for her, though she complained of her own ill-health as rarely as of the pains her spirit had undergone. But now she wondered if those two glittering young things would ever have to learn by experience how hard it was, when one was being continually assailed, to keep one's character intact. In spite of her, a sob caught itself in her throat and she laid her forehead on the marble, grateful for its coolness. A tear trickled down her cheek where Denis had kissed her and splashed on the rich-colored petals at her feet.

Frances found herself striking the mantel with her hands. She had been so proud of Denis, watching him ride his acres with the imperious authority of one born to rule. But either he or she was wrong about this marriage, and she loved him enough to hope it might be herself. It was quite simple to say to Denis she would leave the house so as not to be one of the mothers-in-law of funny stories. He would love her better for her tolerance. And as for that canary-brained girl he was marrying, she would merely shrug and take it as her right that the older generation should bow itself out to leave her room.

IV

Denis and Ann were married in the period of mist and quietness that came to the plantations between the time of the cotton-picking and the time of grinding the cane. Ann stood by Denis in the great hall of Silverwood in a gown that had required forty-two yards of handmade lace, and a veil that looked, as Denis said, as if it had been made of river-fog. Her skirt was so wide that Denis almost had to lean over to reach her hand when she slipped her finger out of the slit in her glove and held it to receive his ring, a heavy gold band that had engraved inside it, "Denis to Ann, December 6, 1859." There were a hundred guests at the ceremony, and two hundred others who came to offer congratulations and speculate on the value of the wedding presents, while two trusted slaves wandered with owl-eyes about the parlors lest some inebriated wellwisher take a spoon for a souvenir of this the most brilliant wedding the river country was likely to see for years.

Half the party piled into carriages and rode after the bride's carriage to the wharf, where Denis and Ann were to take the boat downriver to New Orleans. They planned to spend the night at the St. Charles Hotel and go on to Pass Christian the next day. At the wharf Ann let Denis help her out of the carriage, and she stood arranging her skirt around her and pulling her fur cloak closer about her throat—for it was cold here by the river—reflecting that she was being very self-possessed for a bride and reflecting also that she had never looked better in her life. A wagon rumbled down with her trunks. Denis went over to speak to his boy about their proper disposal and Ann stepped aside, nearer the gangplank and away from the chattering guests, whose reiterated good wishes were beginning to be tiresome.

Her hoops brushed the carpetbag of some lowly passenger waiting for the crowd to thin so he could mount the gangplank. She glanced up, a word of apology on her lips, and saw that the man before her was her father's ex-overseer Gilday.

Ann started back as she felt his raisin eyes creeping over her again, but behind her was a line of Negroes carrying her trunks to the boat and for the moment she was prisoned where she stood. Seeing that she could not get away, Gilday took off his hat with a cool deliberate movement and looked her over.

Ann turned her eyes aside, toward the river. She was remembering what Jerry had told her when she complained

that she did not like having Gilday at Silverwood. Jerry said
the colonel would have got rid of him anyway, because he had
just discovered that Gilday had formerly been part owner of a
breeding-farm in Maryland and wanted no overseers of that
ilk on his plantation. Ann had never heard of a breeding-farm
and asked Jerry what such a place might be. Jerry did not
want to tell her; he was sorry he had let the word slip out. But
she insisted, and he finally explained that there were stretches
of cheap land in Maryland and Virginia where men established colonies consisting of a few Negro men and many
Negro women, where they forcibly bred infant slaves for the
market, and where women were advertised for sale at prices
based not on their training but on their fertility. When she
heard it, the idea horrified her so that after barely managing
not to be sick she buried it deep in her mind, and resolved
never to think of Gilday or his wretched ways again. Meeting
him here today gave her the same feeling of physical revul-
sion. She had a sickish sensation in her stomach. And this was
her wedding day, she recalled angrily. She could have wished
him dead for bringing her such thoughts at such a time.

"Howdy, ma'am," Gilday was saying greasily. "So you got
married." His lips stretched in a sleek smile. "Quite a fancy
wedding, I observe."

Ann glanced indignantly at the moving trunks. Oh, why
didn't they hurry? If this creature touched her she was going
to scream. But he did not touch her.

"Well, I'm going," said Gilday, mouthing his words slowly.
"You got no reason to be upset any more about me. But too
bad," he murmured, "I should just happen to take your
honeymoon boat, seeing as how you don't like me."

"I'm not concerned about how you travel," she said shortly.

"No ma'am, I expect not," Gilday drawled. "But I been
hoping to see you. They tell me it was you told your father
and brother I should ought to be sent off their place. Told
them you didn't like me. Now that warn't pretty of you, miss,
not pretty of you at all."

"Will you please be good enough to let me pass?" Ann
exclaimed.

"Sorry." But he did not move. "I just wanted you to know I
ain't thanking you. On your wedding trip at them fine hotels

you might think sometimes about poor Gilday, with no job because of you."

"Oh, be quiet!" she cried through her teeth. The Negro carrying the last of her trunks passed behind her, and she rushed away from Gilday, up the wharf to where her friends were. One of her bridesmaids, a merry red-headed girl named Sarah Purcell, ran to meet her.

"Why, here she is! Where on earth have you been, Ann?"

"I got caught behind the trunks," Ann said hurriedly, feeling as if Gilday's slimy eyes were still on her back.

"A fine bride you are," Sarah chided, "getting lost at your own wedding."

Ann tried to control her panting breaths. "Where's Denis?"

"Here," said Denis' voice. It had never sounded so welcome. She unceremoniously snatched her hand from Sarah's and caught his arm. "The trunks are on," he was saying. "We can board now."

She held his arm tight. They started toward the gangplank under a sudden shower of rice. Denis laughed, and Ann laughed too with almost hysterical relief. All this was so right and normal, running across the deck of a steamboat on her wedding day with rice falling on her bonnet and trickling down the back of her neck. They ran together across the saloon and into their cabin. Denis banged the door behind him and slipped the catch.

"There's tons of it on deck," he exclaimed, flinging off his coat and hearing the rice clatter on the floor. "Nobody'll be able to walk there till it's swept up."

Ann laughed as she shook the rice off her bonnet. Tossing the bonnet to one side she linked her arms around Denis' neck and looked up at him.

"Denis, I do love you so."

He put his arms around her. "I love you too, darling."

"I don't think I knew till this minute how much I loved you," said Ann. "But you're so *nice*, Denis. So—so inevitable. I always know exactly what you're going to do because it's always what you ought to do at the moment. I'm so glad I'm married to you!"

Denis kissed her. In his embrace Ann felt as if she had withdrawn into a citadel.

V

The slaves of Ardeith were curtseying and singing on the lawn when Ann came home. The whole clan of the Larnes, headed by Denis' mother, stood on the gallery to welcome her. Ann neither blushed nor fluttered, but received their kisses smiling, knowing perfectly well they were studying her for possible circles under her eyes that might indicate the shadow of the stork's wings and finding it amusing to keep them in doubt before her blooming countenance. She had no reason to expect the stork yet, but she knew they had too much delicacy to ease their curiosity by asking her.

She went in, changed from her traveling-dress into a gown of checkered blue challis with white lawn collar and under-sleeves, and a matron's cap of lawn and lace with blue ribbons and she presided for the first time over her own supper-table. There were twenty guests, including her father and Jerry and a confusing group of cousins of both families. Mrs. Larne, who was leaving for Europe tomorrow ("God be praised," Ann thought devoutly), sat remotely at the far end, at Denis' right hand, but Cynthia sat next to Ann, adoring.

As the ladies rose to leave, Mrs. Larne came down the length of the table and proffered Ann her keys. Ann said "Thank you," and kissed her forehead. Denis' uncle rose to give another toast to the bride. Ann waited, thanked them, and slipped the key-chain around her girdle.

The keys made an uncomfortable burden at her waist. These ceremonies were really a nuisance. That night as she was going upstairs with Denis, Ann caught sight of Napoleon putting out the candles in the hall. She leaned over the balustrade and called him, slipping the chain off her belt.

"Napoleon, I've engaged a housekeeper-lady and she'll be here next week. Until then I reckon you know more about where things are kept than I do. Suppose you take these."

Napoleon cupped his hands, but his expression was aston-ished. "You want me to carry the keys, Mrs. Denis?"

"Yes, until she gets here. Then give them to her."

She dropped the keys. Napoleon's eyes went to Denis. Denis laughed with loving indulgence. "It's all right, Napo-leon."

Ann tucked her arm into his and they went on up the staircase.

Standing in the open doorway of her own room, Frances heard their voices. As Denis and Ann came up the stairs she stepped hastily inside, but though they did not look in her direction she could see them. Denis opened the door of the master bedroom. As they went in he picked up the decanter on the little table just inside. "A nightcap, honey?"

"Yes, thanks," said Ann.

He leaned across the decanter and kissed her, reaching with his free hand to push the door shut. Behind them Frances could see the candles burning in the silver sconces, and the white marble mantel with a bowl of roses at either end, and the armoires ready for Ann's clothes, and the great crimson-curtained fourposter that had had to be brought up the river in pieces because it was so huge. She looked along the hall at the spiral staircase built by Denis' grandfather as the monument to a great race. Frances felt a helpless anger that was like pain. She closed the door.

Chapter Four

I

NOT even so vast a sum as a hundred dollars will last forever. Though she skimped the very best she could, Corrie May found it vanishing before winter was over. Pa made a lot of fine speeches but he was no better than ever about work. He was off on his houseboat again with a couple of traveling preachers and they were saving souls up and down the river and everybody said what a fine preacher he was when he got going, could make you feel hellfire under your feet and angels over your head, but that didn't put any beans in the pot.

Day after day Corrie May walked the wharfs, thinking. Budge was mad with her, and her parents were mad with her for the way she had done Budge. He was living tidily on his piece of ground. Now and then she was tempted to believe if she had married him it would have been an end to her perplexities, but all the time in the back side of her mind she knew it would have been no such thing. Marrying Budge would have done nothing but tie her to the hopeless life she was born into, and at least now she was free to climb out of it if she could. But there seemed no way to climb out. Rattletrap Square held her like a quicksand; every day it seemed that another piece of herself was buried in it. At night, lying on her cot in the cubbyhole behind the stove, Corrie May would stretch herself and feel the muscles underneath her firm flesh and think how young and strong she was, how ready to fight her way out of Rattletrap Square, but always there would rush over her the realization of how hopeless was the battle. You could not go ahead unless you knew where you wanted to go, and the world's possibilities were hidden from her like the west bank of the river in an autumn fog.

There was something, she knew, better than what she had. There were a few fortunate people like Ann Sheramy and Denis Larne. Corrie May had stood on the wharf when they were taking the boat for their honeymoon trip. That night while she was cooking supper she tried to imagine what it was like to live that way, but again she came up against the fog. It was not only having a lot of money that made those people different, it was something else, an assurance that came of being born in the right place. Their slaves had it—that bustling mammy curtseying as Ann passed, that tall coffee-colored manservant bowing as Denis climbed the gangplank, those coachmen sitting on the carriages—they had it, the unconscious certainty that they occupied a definite place in the scheme of things, and as long as they followed their destiny they were assured of material plenty and social goodwill. That was what she did not have, and unless one was born to it she knew no way to get it.

But meanwhile one had to stay alive, one had to eat and pay rent. Corrie May asked for work on the wharfs. She could wash office windows or sweep out the hotels. Always the answer was the same. They had slaves, no need to hire white girls. Sometimes men spoke to her on the wharfs or tried to take her arm. She shook them off, less from principles of virtue than because she knew that was no way out. She did get some work in the early winter, for that year the orange crop was heaviest just when the cane had to be cut, and the Ardeith overseer hired white girls to pick the oranges. They paid her thirty cents a day. She and her mother could live on a dollar and eighty cents a week—a quarti red beans and a quarti rice and an onion for lagniappe, and there was dinner for a nickel—but the work did not last long.

But one day, six or seven weeks after Ann's wedding, Corrie May saw her walking in the park with a young lady named Miss Sarah Purcell, and Ann dropped a glove. Corrie May picked it up and turned it over. It was doeskin, the color of an unripe lemon, and to her astonishment she saw that there was a tiny darn at the tip of the forefinger. Corrie May returned the glove and Ann thanked her and went on into a shop with Miss Purcell, but as Corrie May looked after her a new idea pushed itself into her mind. She had never thought rich ladies wore mended clothes. She had had some nebulous notion that if an article got torn they threw it away. But evidently they did wear mended things. And Corrie May knew that she could mend very neatly. Ann doubtless had all the servants she needed, but a lady who required as much waiting on as she evidently did could always find room for one more.

The next morning Corrie May came down early to the wharf. She had put on her shoes—for she had a pair bought with part of her brothers' insurance money—and she looked very tidy. She stood around till she saw a sugar-wagon labeled "Ardeith." When it had been unloaded of its hogsheads she approached the driver.

"I got business to do out at Ardeith," she said to him. "Give me a ride?"

He grinned, looking up from the orange he was sucking. "Sho, white girl. Get on."

Corrie May climbed up, wrapping her hands in her skirt to keep them clean. It was a long ride, but she enjoyed it, for it was a shining January morning and the sun sparkled on the fields and the sugar-mills spurting fire. At the gate of Ardeith she got out, thanked the driver and went around to the back door. To the girl who answered her knock she said her name was Corrie May Upjohn and she wanted to see the mistress.

Presently the girl came back with word that the mistress was waiting. Corrie May's heart began to bump timidly. Ann had been pleasant to her, but then she had never asked her for anything; maybe now that she came seeking a favor Ann would be less cordial. At least, though, she would have a chance to walk up that glorious staircase.

But she was disappointed. The servant girl led her across the back gallery to where a straight narrow flight went up the wall. Corrie May climbed obediently. This was no time to be fussing, but she did wish she could get to be good enough to climb those spiral stairs.

The upper hall, wide and high as the lower, extended to a great window in front looking on a little white balcony. There were several doors on either side, and Corrie May observed with a smothered gasp that these too had silver hinges and doorknobs. The colored girl rapped. "Yes?" Ann's voice called.

"It's that white girl that wanted to see you, Miss Ann," the servant said, and she let Corrie May into the room.

Corrie May stepped over the threshold. Her eyes moved around with wonder. She was in a lady's sitting-room, high and warm and intimate, its ivory-colored walls hung with prints and its furniture upholstered in damask the color of thick cream. There was a soft perfume in the air. From the windows she could see the magnolia trees and budding camellias on the lawn. On a sofa near the fire Ann was reclining against a pile of cushions. Her hair was down and she wore a white satin dressing-gown with wide, ruffled sleeves, and no stockings, her feet half out of little white slippers edged with fur. As Corrie May came in she looked up, lowering the fashion magazine in her hand.

"Why hello, Corrie May," she said, and to the colored girl, "That's all, Bertha." Glancing at Corrie May again she asked, "What did you want to see me about?"

Corrie May had intended to be apologetic. She had rehearsed her speech all the way out in the wagon. "I hope I ain't putting myself forward, ma'am." . . . But at the sight of Ann so warm and indolent, so luxurious that she need not even put on her clothes though it was already past noon, her resentment flared above her diffidence. She blurted angrily. "I'm sorry I come so early in the morning, Miss Ann."

"So early?" Ann sounded puzzled, then she glanced down at her attire. "Oh," she said, smiling a little. "I was up late last night at a fancy-dress ball, and I'm just out of bed. That's why I'm not dressed."

Corrie May noticed, on a little table beyond the sofa, a breakfast tray with the coffee-pot still steaming. Just out of bed, this time of day. Ann was asking,

"I hope you've been well?"

Corrie May clenched her hands together to keep them from following their impulse. She felt like dragging Ann's soft body off the cushions and pounding it blue and then hauling her down to see how most people had to live in the town of Dalroy, the richest town on the river, the city of palaces. She swallowed and answered, but instead of the sweet respectful answer she meant to give she said,

"I've been terrible. I don't mean I've been sick. But since

my brothers died in your husband's cypress there ain't been
nobody to work in our family."

"Oh," said Ann. She let the magazine fall to the floor and
raised herself on her elbow. "I'm so sorry for you. If you'll
pull the bellcord—"

She had the amiable condescension of a lady reaching for
her purse. Corrie May came nearer and gripped the table on
which stood the silver coffee-pot. "I ain't asking you for
charity!" she cried.

Ann was evidently puzzled. "Then what do you want?"

"I want to work!" Corrie May exclaimed. "Please ma'am
let me work for you! I know you's got plenty niggers. But I
want to work and take care of my Ma and—and be somebody
my own self—I mean, there's lots of things I can do. I can
mend your clothes."

"But I don't need—" Ann began, then paused as Corrie
May rushed on.

"I bet there ain't one of your niggers can mend your
clothes as pretty as me. And if I do it that'll leave them time
for something else. I can sew with little bits of stitches, Miss
Ann. And I got to work."

"I understand," Ann said kindly. "I'm sorry I made a
mistake at first. Of course I'll give you work if you need it.
Can you clear-starch muslins too?"

"Yes ma'am."

"I'm sure I can find something for you. You're a good girl
to want to take care of your mother. Come in here." She went
across the room to a side door, her dressing-gown rippling
over the rug behind her.

The door opened into a bedroom on the front corner. It
was the biggest room Corrie May had ever entered in her life.
Every one of the four posts of the bed was bigger around than
Ann's waist, and the bed-curtains hung in heavy crimson folds
from the tester. There was a fire burning here too, though it
was sheer extravagance to have a bedroom fire in the daytime.
The bureau and washstand had big mirrors, and there were
embroidered monograms on the towels, and on the bureau
were hairbrushes and flasks of scent and downy powder-
puffs with silken backs. A mulatto girl was picking up clothes
and things from the floor. Corrie May walked marveling

through the cloud of fragrances to where Ann stood opening one of the high mahogany armoires.

"Here," said Ann, taking out a petticoat that clattered as its starched folds fell apart. "I tore the frills on this. Lucile," she said to the maid, "get a needle and thread. Sit here, Corrie May, and when you've mended this I'll look at it. If you do it well I'm sure I can find some others for you."

Corrie May took the petticoat, diffident with pleasure. Working in a place like this! Heretofore, she had merely thought of it as a job that would enable her to live, but that was before she had actually walked through the grandeur and thought what it would do to her spirit to be surrounded by it —no dirt, no screaming children, nobody drunk next door, no cats prowling against her legs, no cockroaches, no bad smells. She looked up.

"Miss Ann, this here's just outen the washtub. I expect I better scrub my hands right clean."

"All right. There's the washstand." Ann went back to the door of her sitting-room. "Lucile, you may go down when you've finished. Some time today press the ribbons on my blue satin bonnet."

Lucile brought Corrie May a workbox with thread and scissors and a thimble, and then went out. Corrie May washed her hands, feeling almost sacrilegious as she dried them on one end of the towel and refolded it so from the front it would look as if it had not been used; and she replaced the cover on the soap-dish, emptied the water and rinsed out the basin. Then she sat down and began catching up the ripped frills of the petticoat, working so hard she felt little beads of sweat on her forehead.

When she had mended the torn places Corrie May leaned back luxuriously. What a lovely room, and how clean. For the moment she was almost glad she was not used to houses like this, for if she had been she would have missed this rich sensation of pleasure. Everything was so beautiful. At one side, between the windows, was a little table. The sun had slanted to shine on it, and Corrie May's eyes were suddenly dazzled with green and ruby lights.

She got up softly, folding the petticoat on the chair. They lay in a heap, bracelets and necklaces and earrings, the stones glinting under the sun. She wondered what they were. Her mind ran over the names of all the jewels she had ever heard of—diamonds, amethysts, pearls, topazes, emeralds—what a pile of glory!

Timorously she reached out and touched the heap. In the glass over the washstand she saw her reflection, and she wondered daringly how she would look wearing jewels like these. It wouldn't be any sin, not if she put them back. Pushing up her sleeves she clasped a bracelet around her arm, and held a necklace against her throat, almost shivering with delight as she watched the sun flicker across the stones and reflect highlights on her face.

The door opened. "Have you finished?" Ann's voice asked.

Corrie May wheeled around. The necklace fell out of her hand and rattled on the floor. Her dreams of security and quiet in this house went down with it. She felt her skin get hot under her clothes.

"Miss Ann—I swear to God I wasn't taking them!" Her voice was quivering with fear. She began tearing the bracelet off her arm. "Please, Miss Ann! I wouldn't steal nothing for the whole world—I never stole nothing in my life—I know they belongs to you and I just wanted to see how they looked!" She burst into tears. Her legs were shaking under her. She could see visions of herself in jail for attempted thievery. Sobbing, she flung the bracelet on the table and rushed to catch Ann's elbows in her hands. "Miss Ann, before the Lord God Almighty—"

"Why, you poor girl." Through her own sobs Corrie May heard Ann's voice. She felt Ann's arm around her shoulders and Ann's handkerchief drying her tears.

The satin of Ann's gown was cool under her cheek. "My Lord, Miss Ann, but you's a sweet young lady." Her voice choked. "I know they's worth a thousand dollars or something and I shouldn't ought to've bothered them. But I never had diamonds or nothing like that."

"Don't cry," said Ann. Suddenly Corrie May realized that Ann was laughing. She raised her head incredulously and looked up. Ann was really laughing. "Why Corrie May," she was saying, "that's not jewelry. The whole lot isn't worth ten dollars." Crossing quickly to the table she gathered the ornaments into her hands. "Here. Do you want them?"

Corrie May gasped. "You mean—" She was so amazed she

could hardly say it. "You mean you's gonta give them to me?"

"Why yes, you can have them. They're nothing but glass. I wore this stuff to the ball last night—I was masquerading as a gypsy."

Corrie May accepted the handful. Even if they weren't real they would look right elegant in Rattletrap Square. "Why thank you ma'am. I never had nothing so pretty. I sho thought they was jewels."

"Real jewels like that," Ann explained gently, "would be worth more than this whole plantation."

Corrie May smiled, bringing her head and her arm together so she could scrub the last tears out of her eyes with her sleeve. "Anyway, Miss Ann, even if these ain't sho 'nough, I hope you don't think I'd steal from you."

"I'm sure you wouldn't," Ann consoled her. "Don't bother about it, Corrie May. I don't think you'd steal from me any more than I'd steal from you."

Corrie May blinked.

"Now will you show me the petticoat?" Ann added.

Corrie May laid the ornaments back on the table and went to bring her work. She moved slowly, her mind fumbling with the fine impartiality of an ethical principle that forbade her and Ann to steal from each other.

But Ann, who evidently had never had any reason to be troubled about such matters, was examining the petticoat and saying,

"You did this beautifully."

"Thank you ma'am," said Corrie May.

Ann sat down, the petticoat trailing across her knees. "If you really need work, you can work here for me two or three days a week. You can ride out on one of the plantation wagons. They're always going to the wharfs and back."

Corrie May glowed, "You mean honest, Miss Ann? I sho do appreciate it, ma'am."

"Why yes, I'll save the mending for you, and perhaps some laundry."

"All right ma'am, that sho is nice. You want me back tomorrow?"

"Yes, you may come tomorrow."

"I reckon I better be going now."

Ann smiled. "You're very trustful. What about wages?"

Corrie May bit her lip. "Why I don't know, Miss Ann."

"Neither do I." Ann shrugged a little. "I'm not used to paying wages, and I've no idea what to offer. What do you get for a day's work?"

"Well ma'am, for picking oranges they gimme thirty cents."

"Thirty cents?" Ann repeated. "For how long?"

"From can't-see to can't-see, Miss Ann."

"Good heavens," said Ann half under her breath. Aloud she said, "Still, if that's what you're used to—I'll tell you. This in finer work than picking oranges. Suppose we say fifty cents a day."

"Oh lawsy, Miss Ann, that's big pay. Thank you ma'am."

"You're entirely welcome." But as Corrie May started out she added, "Wait a minute." She went to the bureau and opening a drawer she took out a purse made of gilt beads knitted on silk. "Here," she said, offering a quarter, "this is for the petticoat."

Corrie May shrank before such generosity, for she had not expected to be paid for the petticoat at all. "Oh Miss Ann, that wa'n't hardly worth two bits, you reckon?"

"Never mind, take it. I think if you'll go back to the field-road you can find another wagon going downtown."

"Yes ma'am."

"Don't forget the pretties," said Ann over her shoulder as she went back into her sitting-room. Corrie May put the quarter into her pocket and gathered up the ornaments Ann had given her. As she turned to go she caught sight of Ann through the open doorway leading into the sitting-room. Ann lay on the sofa, her chin resting on her cupped hands. She was looking toward the windows, but her eyes were blank, as if she got no pleasure from the gardens—as if, in fact, she were not even seeing them. She looked so bored that Corrie May was startled and made an involuntary movement. Ann turned her head.

"Did you want something?"

"Why no ma'am." Corrie May paused awkwardly. Now she had to speak and she didn't know what to say. "I'm sorry—I didn't mean to be butting in on your private room. Only you don't look right well. You ain't sick, I hope?"

"No, I'm quite all right." Ann turned over on her back and stretched her arms. "Nothing but the doldrums."

"Doldrums?" Corrie May repeated uncertainly. "What's them?"

"It means you're not very happy."

"Oh," said Corrie May. She looked around her at the encircling splendor. "My God. You got to be *happy,* too?"

Ann regarded her with such incomprehension that Corrie May was abashed, and she hurried out and down the back stairs as fast as she could.

II

While the answer was not entirely money, money was part of it. Corrie May found a square box that had been thrown away after having served to hold some silk flowers Ann bought for her girdle, and she mixed flour and water and glued down the cover and cut a slit on top. Every time Ann paid her she dropped a penny or nickel through the slit. The box she hid on the shelf where she kept her clothes, so when Pa came home from his religious meanderings he would not discover it: if he did, he would be sure to think up something he could not live without and she would have to spend her money.

It took a long time to get even so much as a dollar, but the rattle of the coins in the box gave her a feeling of safety. Money was so wonderful, it built a wall around you, shutting out fear and hunger and ugliness so completely that you even forgot they existed. Money let you be clean and dainty, it gave you grace of manner and charm of speech. It made people bow to you as if you favored them by being alive, instead of shoving past as if you cluttered up the street. It made you sweet-tempered. Until she came to work at Ardeith Corrie May had never dreamed how many pleasant traits of personality could be fostered with money.

She had thought she knew all about how married people acted. Nobody in Rattletrap Square had any privacy. Corrie May had heard women yelling at their husbands in the night demanding to be let alone because they had too many children already and yelling more when the men went out and picked up trollops on the wharfs. She had helped at childbirths and then helped lay out the babies when they died because their mothers' wasted bodies could not provide milk enough to keep them alive. In Rattletrap Square folks screamed at each other when they got mad, women threw sticks of stovewood at their husbands and men hit their wives on the jaw.

She had not expected Ann and Denis to be quite so crude as that, but she was unprepared for their courtesy, their pleasant compliments, the way they knocked on doors and asked, "Are you busy, dear? Or may I come in?" Working at Ardeith, she saw a good deal of Ann and Denis—though they seemed to see very little of her—and she watched them, fascinated by their difference from any other people she had ever known. They were neither of them blessed with angelic dispositions, but even when they quarreled they did it prettily.

There was the day Colonel Sheramy came to dinner, and he and Denis got into an argument in the library afterward. Corrie May had been sent down to ask the housekeeper, Mrs. Maitland, for some summer curtains that needed to have the lace repaired where it had been torn in the laundering. She could hear Denis and Colonel Sheramy arguing as she passed the library door.

Colonel Sheramy was saying vehemently, "You're entirely wrong, Denis. The fomenters of rebellion in South Carolina are menaces to our welfare as well as their own. Dividing the Union would be—"

"But how," Denis interrupted, "can you overlook the injustices the South had been enduring these twenty years? Encroachments by Congress—"

"What encroachments, you young hothead? It was Southern sentiment that nullified the 1850 Compromises! It was Southerners on the Supreme Court—"

Their voices got fainter as Corrie May went down the hall to the sewing-room. But as she sat working on the lace she could still hear them talking, and though she could not make out the words she could tell they were getting mad with each other. Finally Colonel Sheramy went angrily out to his horse. As Denis came out of the library Ann met him in the hall. She had evidently been waiting.

"So that's how you talk to my father!" she exclaimed. The two of them stood in the hall just outside the sewing-room.

"That's how I'll talk to anybody who calls me a misinformed young fool," Denis retorted. "Your father sounds like an abolitionist Congressman."

"He's not an abolitionist and that's got nothing to do with it anyway. If you can't remember the respect you owe him—"

"Since you don't know anything about politics you'd better not try to give opinions." Denis was evidently getting mad with her too.

"I'm not talking about politics," Ann flashed back. "I'm talking about manners. You're as uncouth as an overseer. I want you to go right after him and apologize for what you said."

"I'm not sorry for a word I said and I'll do nothing of the sort. It's time somebody told him a few facts."

"Yes you will apologize!"

"I most certainly will not. Be quiet."

"You insult my father and you tell me to be quiet! You won't apologize to him?"

"Certainly not."

"You insufferable boor!"

Corrie May heard footsteps and the rattle of starched petticoats as Ann ran upstairs. Oh Lord, she thought, now they're going to fight all afternoon. When she went to take the curtains upstairs she heard voices from their bedroom. The words were indistinct, but she could tell they were still quarreling. Miss Ann's really got a temper, thought Corrie May. But I hope he don't slap her. Please, Lord, don't let him slap her. He didn't have any business being rude to the old gentleman. Corrie May was frightened. They sounded ready to rip each other apart. Denis hurled himself out of the bedroom, banging the door, and ran downstairs. Corrie May slipped to the front window of the hall and saw him on a horse galloping furiously down the avenue. Oh my soul, she thought, now he's going off and get drunk and he might not be home till morning. It's going to be mighty unpleasant around here. She thought she heard more sounds faintly from the bedroom. Though she could not be sure, she guessed Ann was crying with rage.

It was nearly dark when Denis returned. Hanging the curtains in the spare bedroom across the hall, Corrie May saw him in the avenue. He was riding more slowly than when he

left, and his seat on his horse was steady. He did not seem to
be drunk.

She heard him come up the stairs and knock on the door of
the master bedroom. From inside Ann's voice called, "Yes?
Who is it?"

"It's Denis."

"Go away."

Denis rattled the doorknob. "Darling, stop being a dunce,
unlock the door."

"I'll do no such thing."

"Oh, for heaven's sake, Ann, come on. Open the door."

"I told you to go away."

"If you don't unlock the door I'm going to break it in."

Corrie May doubted his ability to do it. The door was too
heavy for any man's strength. But she trembled.

There was a silence. At last the key turned. "All right, what
is it now?" Ann demanded.

Denis laughed deep in his throat. "Honey child, don't you
think we've been quarreling long enough?"

"Will you tell the colonel you're sorry you yelled at him?"

"I'll make peace with him, that's not what I wanted to say.
I wanted to say I'm sorry I yelled at you. I do love you so,
Ann—how do you manage to make me so mad?"

There was a pause. There were more words, blurred
because they were half whispered. At length Corrie May
heard the door close. Creeping to the doorway of the room
where she was she saw that it had closed with both of them
inside. She heard the key turn in the lock again.

So they could make up as easily as that! What amiable
tempers they had.

She was having her supper on the back gallery when they
came downstairs. Ann sent for her, to tell her that since Mrs.
Maitland wanted the rest of the summer curtains hung early
in the morning she could sleep tonight in the little room off
the gallery. Corrie May almost gasped at the sight of Ann's
clothes, for she had not often seen her in evening dress. They
were evidently going out; Ann had on a creamy satin gown
with puffs of tulle around the skirt, and a jeweled pin in her
hair and jewels on her arms. As Corrie May received her
instructions and curtseyed Ann turned to look up at Denis

adoringly. She held up her arm and watched the light flash on a bracelet at her wrist.

"Denis, it's the loveliest thing I ever saw in my life. You're such a darling."

Denis chuckled. "Like me better than you did?"

"Oh Denis. I'm so ashamed of myself. But I'll get mad with you every day if you'll always make up with something as beautiful as this."

Corrie May looked thoughtfully over her shoulder at them as she went out to the gallery again. When she had gone into the little room under the back stairs she sat on the cot, thinking. No wonder rich people could be so sweet. If Ann and Denis had lived in Rattletrap Square there wouldn't have been anywhere for Denis to go while his temper cooled, nowhere but a saloon or a bawdy-house where he'd have spent the money they needed for food and so made things worse. And instead of resting peacefully to quiet her nerves Ann would have had to be washing clothes or cooking supper, getting herself all hot and tired and madder than before. And even if Denis was really sorry, he couldn't have brought her a bracelet to prove it. So folks in Rattletrap Square screamed and threw things and folks at Ardeith kissed and called each other darlings.

Money. But not entirely money. Something else too, this unconscious conviction of their own value. She observed this particularly when Ann had a baby.

Denis and Ann spent July up North at a place called Saratoga, and when they got back Corrie May observed that Ann was expecting. You still couldn't see it when she wore hoops, but when she idled around in her dressing-gowns it was obvious. Corrie May was not surprised, and to tell the truth she was not very much interested. For a young couple in good health to be having a child seemed to her the most ordinary of occurrences. Corrie May had always regarded having children as a disgusting necessity. She had no fondness for babies, who bawled and squalled and dirtied their diapers and made more work for everybody, and the processes of maternity were a thorough mess. Everybody she knew, men and women alike, resented the approach of a baby.

So the way they started carrying on at Ardeith amazed her. An heir to the dynasty! How wonderful. An heir already!

How proud you must be, Denis. And Ann, my dear, are you
sure you're feeling well? Let me get you a shawl—there's a
draft from that window. They brought out-of-season fruits to
tempt Ann's appetite and new books to while away her
enforced leisure. They made her beautiful garments so she
could watch her altering figure with as little distaste as
possible, for it was important that she be easy in her mind.
Corrie May could have seen some reason for such solicitude
if Ann had shown any sign of not being well. But Ann
flowered like a well-tilled garden, and anybody could see she
was simply basking in her own importance.

The Negroes didn't have any more sense than the white
folks. They beamed and grinned and sprang to wait on her as
though she'd faint if she crossed a room unaided. On the back
gallery they talked about it in happy voices. The servants in
the house had all been born in its shadow, most of them of
families that had belonged to Ardeith for generations. Not a
slave had been sold from Ardeith in forty years. They were as
integral a part of the clan as their masters. The approach of
an heir was an event to be mentioned with thanksgiving to
the Lord. The line was going on, and with the mistress' health
and spirits what they were the household would not dwindle
as in the days of her predecessor. The servants hung ruffly
curtains at the windows of the old nursery and polished up
the carved rosewood cradle where Mr. Denis had slept,
confident that it would not go back to the attic till it had been
occupied again and again.

The mulatto girl Bertha, Napoleon's wife, who expected a
baby about the same time as Ann, was appointed for the
honor of wet-nursing the heir; she was moved from the
quarters to a room in the big house and coddled with as many
luxuries as the mistress. Corrie May thought if it were herself
she would have felt like a milch-cow being petted for the
parish fair, but Bertha, a smart young woman of elegant
speech and manners, put on a multitude of airs.

The girls in the sewing-room cut and stitched such piles of
tiny garments as no baby could possibly wear out before he
outgrew them. They embroidered nightgowns and pillow-cases
for Ann's confinement, and fashioned her caps of lace and
ribbon. There were new bed-curtains provided, crimson satin
lined with white, for she would be confined in November and

there must be no drafts across her bed. Seamstresses were imported from New Orleans to be consulted about the newest fashion in christening-robes and to design a particularly lovely gown for Ann to wear when she stood up at the font. And how Denis walked around! You'd have thought from the looks of him he had been elected President, instead of having done something so entirely commonplace as beget a baby.

Nobody found it ridiculous or even surprising, except Corrie May. To save her life she could not see that the coming of Ann's child was a circumstance of such tremendous moment. Black and white, the clan felt blessed, but when she watched them she became more acutely aware that ever that she had no share in that mighty unit. She stood outside, saying nothing of her thoughts, for she had no wish to endanger her livelihood by a hint of sacrilege, but the whole business, though sometimes it made her want to laugh, oftener choked her with fury.

Corrie May thought how the women she knew took maternity. They went about their work as usual, cooking and scurbbing no matter how they felt, sometimes leaving a washtub of clothes when the pains started. If the babies were born in the summer they didn't wear anything but a diaper; in the winter they were wrapped in a shawl or an old blanket. This costly nonsense at Ardeith appalled her. Corrie May rode the cotton-wagon to Rattletrap Square and sat on the stoop of her lodgings. She saw it as though it were new to her, this region below the wharfs where women were old at thirty-five and decrepit at forty, and where half the babies born did not live a year. She watched the children lying in the mud-puddles for coolness, their taut bellies swarming with flies. She thought of the slave-women at Ardeith, carefully tended during their pregnancies because a little Negro was worth a hundred dollars the day it was born. Her hands clenched on her knees, and her thoughts made rhythm like a drumbeat. Poor white trash. Poor white trash. Nigger never walk up the handsome road, but I'd rather be a nigger than poor white trash.

She hated them all at Ardeith. She even hated the unborn baby, destined in his mother's womb to hold her and her people in the limbo where it would suit him for them to belong. Secretly she rattled her money-box. There was not much in it, but hearing the coins clink gave her a sense of delight. She rarely earned more than a dollar and a half a week, and the rent was a dollar and a half a month, but she could still save pennies, for besides her wage she got lagniappe. Ann gave her cast-off clothes, and the meals they served her were so plentiful she could nearly always put aside some food to take home.

One damp morning in November she arrived at Ardeith to find the house hushed like a church. At the back door Mrs. Maitland told her in an undertone the baby had been born in the night, and the mistress was asleep. There would be no work done today; they were halting everything that she might have complete repose. Corrie May could come back the day after tomorrow.

Botheration, thought Corrie May. All that long ride for nothing. And in such dismal weather. It was a heavy, colorless day, blurred with fog. As she walked around to the front of the house she shivered and wrapped her hands in the end of her shawl.

Dr. Purcell's buggy stood by the steps, and he was saying goodby to Denis. As Denis turned around to go back into the house he saw Corrie May.

"Why, good morning," he said.

She curtseyed. "Good morning, Mr. Larne."

He was grinning unconsciously. "Did they tell you our son was born, Corrie May?"

"Yes sir, I done heard about it," she answered politely. "Tell Miss Ann I sho hopes she gets on."

"Thanks," said Denis. He ran up the steps, whistling softly.

All of a sudden Corrie May felt like laughing, not in derision, but with a curious sympathy that surprised her. He was just like a little boy. In spite of their pompous carryings-on about the baby, Mr. Denis was really so young—queer, she thought abruptly. She was herself only fifteen, and he must be ten or twelve years older, yet he seemed so young. He and Ann both. They didn't know *anything*. She started, remembering her sensation of wrath a few minutes back. It made her feel guilty. Here she worked in the house, and she hadn't done a thing to express felicitations about the baby. Until this minute she had not thought of doing so. Hurrying out to the gate, she waited till a cotton-wagon came by and rode to town.

At home she took her box from its hiding-place and felt the weight of it in her hands. Never had she shaken a penny out of it. Even now, tearing down part of her little wall of defense was so difficult that once she put the box back on the shelf, then gathered her courage sternly and took it out again. There was no unsaying Ann had given her work when she felt desperate, and now she was going to prove her gratitude by getting a present for Ann's baby.

Setting her teeth hard, she turned the box upside down and shook it. A nickel and a penny fell out. Corrie May took a long stern breath and kept on shaking. A dime fell out, and four more pennies, then another nickel, then a penny. Every coin as it dropped gave her a feeling that was almost pain. She shook the box resolutely. Six more pennies clinked into her lap. Her hand faltered and she stopped. She simply could not make herself deplete her hoard any further. For thirty-two cents one could get something.

Her money in her pocket, she made her way to the square around the park, and walked along till she found a shop that sold dry-goods. She went in timidly. Though she had on a newly ironed dress and a woollen shawl and a pair of Congress gaiters, only slightly scuffed, she felt out of place. The clerk was busy with a young lady at the counter. He glanced at Corrie May, and said, "Just a minute," as though he saw that she was not going to be a valuable customer anyway. Corrie May recognized the young lady because she had seen her often at Ardeith; she was Ann's friend Sarah Purcell, a soft-voiced little thing, attractive in an odd way, with a freckled-peppered face and a cloud of glorious red hair. When Sarah Purcell finished matching some ribbon to a piece of silk she had brought with her, the clerk saw her to the door and came back to Corrie May. "Something for you?"

She got up from where she had been sitting by the counter. "I want to see some flannel. Some nice flannel like for a baby's shirt."

He showed it to her. Enough to make a shirt was twenty-three cents, and for eight cents she got a skein of embroidery floss. That left a penny over. Corrie May put the penny back into her pocket to be returned to her savings-box. She had an odd feeling of pleasure.

When she reached home she washed her hands carefully and spread a towel on the bed so as to keep the flannel perfectly clean while she cut the shirt. Telling her mother to get dinner, she sat by the fire, not even willing to add a stick of wood lest she drop some dust on her sewing. She worked hard, joining the seams with tiny stitches that could hardly be seen. With her thimble for a guide she drew little scallops around the edges. The embroidery for these had to be very smooth with never a knot, or it would scratch the baby's skin. She worked all day, straining her eyes as the light faded, till at last her head began to ache and she was afraid if she stitched any longer by firelight the embroidery would get uneven in spite of her.

The next morning she got up early and set to work again. She had to be so careful that the sewing went slowly, but by dark the shirt was done. It was really beautiful, better than some of those made by the sewing-girls at Ardeith. Ann couldn't help liking it.

When she went out to the plantation the next day Mrs. Maitland gave her a peignoir of Ann's, the sleeves of which were tearing loose from the shoulders. Corrie May sat down in the little boudoir next to the bedroom to mend it. Ann's room was full of friends and relatives, and Corrie May waited until Denis had taken the visitors down to dinner. Then, taking her parcel in her hand, she knocked on the door opening into the bedroom. Ann's Mammy opened the door.

"Could I please see Miss Ann a minute?" Corrie May inquired.

Mammy hesitated dubiously. "She's powerful tired."

"Please ask her," begged Corrie May. "Tell her I done brought a little somp'n for the baby."

Mammy still hesitated, but Ann called, "She can come in, Mammy."

Holding her package in both hands, Corrie May came into the bedroom and curtseyed. The room was so bright with flowers and firelight you'd never have thought the day outside was heavy with rain, and the crimson hangings made the bed look like what Corrie May imagined a throne would be. At the head of the bed Mammy stood like a bodyguard. Ann lay against the pillows in a nightgown crusted with lace, and over her shoulders was a shawl of white wool. Her hair was down in curls that must have cost an hour's siege with the irons. As Corrie May came in Ann glanced at her and smiled. "Hello," she said.

At the bedstep Corrie May curtseyed again, tongue-tied with embarrassment, for the bureau and tables were piled with packages not yet opened. But Ann was still smiling in a friendly fashion. "It was sweet of you to think of me," she prompted.

"It ain't nothing really, Miss Ann," Corrie May apologized haltingly, though she still had a headache from eyestrain. "I just thought as how—well, I mean I thought I'd make the little master somp'n to help keep him warm, him being born in the foggy time."

"You're very thoughtful." Ann took the package and undid the covers. "Why Corrie May, this is lovely. Thank you so much."

"Oh—you like it honest, Miss Ann?"

"Why of course I do. All this beautiful work!"

Corrie May blushed proudly. But Mammy, evidently thinking the interview had lasted long enough for the strength of her darling, interposed.

"You better take yo'sef some rest, Miss Ann honey."

"I will, Mammy. And thank you again, Corrie May."

"Well ma'am, it ain't nothing to brag of, but I sho do appreciate your liking it."

"You better get 'bout yo' work," Mammy said to her. "De missis been havin' company all mawnin'."

"I'm going," said Corrie May. She curtseyed again and moved toward the door.

"Goodby," Ann said kindly.

"Goodby, Miss Ann."

Withdrawing into the sitting-room, Corrie May sat down again to finish sewing the seams of the peignoir. She felt pleased at how much Ann liked the shirt. Miss Ann was really so nice, Corrie May told herself reproachfully, it wasn't Christian or even decent to feel hateful toward her just because she was lying under a satin curtain. She had not quite closed the door, and from beyond it she could hear voices. Ann said,

"You know, Mammy, I'm really awfully tired. Don't let anybody else come in for awhile."

"I sho won't, honey lamb," Mammy promised soothingly. "You better get yo'sef a nap right after you eat yo' dinner."

"Let me see little Denis before I go to sleep, will you?"

"Sho, Miss Ann, sho. I'll go get him soon as I brush off de hearth. But 'fo' I do nothin', lemme get dat thing offn yo' bed."

In the sitting-room, Corrie May started and her work slid off her knees to the floor. She listened.

Ann was protesting. "The shirt? But what do you want with it? It's so pretty."

"Yassum. But you give it right straight to me. He got plenty shirts made right here in de house."

"But he can wear this one too," Ann exclaimed. "See how even the scallops are."

Corrie May heard Mammy give a deep sigh. "Miss Ann, you ain't got no mo' sense dan if you was just now born like de li'l massa. Miss Ann, she made dis at her house, and you ain't never seen de places where dem people live. Dem folkses stay in nothin' but holes. Dey got bugs crawlin' all over. You ain't gon' put nothin' from dat Rattletrap place on yo' li'l lamb."

Corrie May stood up. Damn that nigger. Damn her. Living like a lady in the soft clean luxury of her white folks, what did she know of the sweat and dirt of the poor? How could you help it if bugs got in from the swarming alleys? Corrie May remembered her mother on her knees, scrubbing the corners to clear them out. She could hear Ann's voice, suddenly high.

"Oh my soul, Mammy, I never thought of that! Take it. Throw it away."

"Yassum, I'll put it right in de fire."

"Oh no you won't either. Wool smells to heaven burning. Put it in the wastebasket." There was a knock at the hall door. "Is that Napoleon?" Ann asked. "If they've sent me chicken soup again I'm going to be furious."

Corrie May could hear the rattle of dishes. She was trembling with rage. One more minute and she'd go tell those two what she thought of them, just as soon as she could stop shaking. She heard Ann say,

"I don't see why people can't live tidily. The poor can be clean."

The poor can be clean, Corrie May echoed in her mind. I wish you had to try it sometime.

Mammy said, "Yassum dey can, but dey mighty nigh always ain't. Miss Ann, I sho wish you'd send dat girl 'bout her business. It ain't right, her sewin' on yo' clothes."

"Oh, shut up. I wish you'd stop harping on that. She looks clean enough when she comes here, and she needs work terribly."

In the sitting-room, Corrie May sat down slowly on the little damask sofa. Of course she needed work. She needed it so much that even now she had to smile and curtsey and be grateful. One disrespectful word out of her and Ann would respond with hurt surprise, telling her with pretty words spoken in her cultured accent to go back to Rattletrap Square and starve.

Corrie May's mouth curled with helpless rage. She dared not say so, but she knew she had been grateful for the last time. Now she simply hated them all, their casual pleasantness and their dainty charity. "I'll work for you now," her mouth said voicelessly as she bent to pick up the peignoir. "But I'll be somebody before I'm dead. Some day I'll get to where I can tell you what I think of you." Her hands were trembling so that it was several minutes before she could hold the needle.

Chapter Five

WHEN the baby was a week old Denis brought Ann a medallion set in diamonds, to contain the baby's daguerreotype on one side and a lock of its hair on the other. He sat on the bedstep as Ann turned the medallion in her fingers to examine both sides.

"Lovely," she said. "I'll have it made up as soon as he grows hair enough to spare some, and I'll wear it as a breastpin."

Denis bent over and kissed her. "How do you feel?"

"Fine. Dr. Purcell says I can get up in a few days more."

"Don't be in too much of a hurry, sugar," he urged. "You've got plenty of time."

"But I haven't, really. There's our anniversary dinner."

"Not for three weeks."

"Yes, but I've told the girls not to run up the seams of my dress till I've tried it on. They cut it by my old measurements, and I want to make sure it fits." She raised a warning finger. "And I tell you right now, Denis Larne, if my figure doesn't collapse to exactly where it used to be you can sleep in the sugar-house, for I'll never have another baby as long as I live."

Denis laughed at her. Sometimes Ann wished he wouldn't laugh at her so much. But half his fondness for her sprang from the fact that he found her the most amusing person on earth. She had exclaimed to him one day shortly after their marriage, "You don't want a wife, you want to keep me as a pet!"—a remark Denis found so funny that he repeated it with great success at a party.

Ann stretched. "Denis, let's do a lot of exciting things this winter. I'll be so glad to move around without feeling as if I weighed a ton."

"I've been thinking," he suggested, "we might give a ball New Year's Eve."

"Oh yes, let's. We ought to do a good deal of entertaining to make up for my not having been able to give any parties this fall. There'll be a lot of winter visitors in town."

Denis agreed, but he added, "For the present, you'd better have a nap. The Purcells are coming to dinner with Jerry and your father, and they're all going to want to see you."

"I'm not tired," she protested.

"You will be," said Denis, getting up off the bedstep, "if you try to talk to all those people without getting any rest." He kissed her goodby. "I'm going down now."

"All right," she answered, finding it as usual easier to obey Denis then to argue with him. He called Mammy and ordered her to draw the bed-curtains.

Ann slipped the medallion under the pillow. With the curtains drawn the bed was like a little house. From outside she could hear the crackle of the fire and the patter of rain on the windowpanes. She wondered if little Denis were asleep. She hardly knew yet what he looked like, except that he was very tiny and red as a radish. They kept him for the most part in the nursery, lest what with his crying and her talking they disturb each other. She wished she could see him oftener. Before he was born she had suggested that she would like to feed him herself, but Denis had protested in astonishment. "Darling, it'll keep you a prisoner for months. We'll hardly be able to go anywhere." So she acquiesced and sent for Bertha. She didn't want to be one of these young mothers who became so obsessed with their babies that they neglected their husbands. But even though she had seen so little of her baby it made her very peaceful to know he was there, as if she had achieved something monumental and had nothing to do now but lie back and contemplate it. She thought, "Maybe now that I've given her a grandchild Mrs. Larne will like me better. That painful prig of a woman! I've never done anything to her. I wish to heaven she'd stay in Europe. Now I suppose when she comes home I'll have to call her Mother."

That idea grated on her nerves. Mrs. Larne was planning to live with Cynthia in a house in Dalroy this winter, and Ann knew she would have to see her frequently and pretend an affection she certainly had no reason to feel. However, she wasn't going to bother about it; she'd be polite, and that was enough.

Ann linked her hands behind her head and looked up at the tester, trying to go over in her mind the guests who should be included in a New Year's ball. She must find out what out-of-town people were at the hotels. Every winter there were Northern visitors down for a holiday, and she and Denis had received so much hospitality at Saratoga last summer that it was time they set about returning it. Ann made a face at the tester. The trouble with being a famous hostess was that you were so busy entertaining guests you had to entertain that it was hard to find time for the people you really wanted to see. It was very comfortable, but not, to tell the truth, very exciting, to be mistress of a great house. What was expected of you was so definite that you had very few decisions to make. Still it was good to know that if you followed a clear code you couldn't possibly mess up your life, and wise persons accepted their destiny—what was it Corrie May Upjohn had said to her the day she came to Ardeith asking for work? "You got to be *happy*, too?" Probably that was what Corrie May had meant, envying her for being comfortably provided for instead of having to stir about and take care of herself. She's a funny little thing, Ann thought with irrelevant amusement. So quiet; she doesn't seem to notice very much. Very likely she's a bit stupid. I suppose she's had a hard life, but then she's used to it. People like that don't expect much in the world.

What was that darky proverb Mammy was always quoting? "Blessed am dem what 'spects nuffin, for dey ain't gonta be disappointed." Ann felt a pang of remorse. That was her trouble. She expected too much. She wanted security and adventure both. But since she had chosen security, she had no reason to quarrel. Denis was courtly, generous and physically thrilling; and Ardeith—oh, she did want Ardeith and all it stood for, a life free of dissension and disorder, sure of itself and by its assurance given serene command over the emotions of the individuals who composed it. Ann could see herself merging from girlhood into the great lady of the plantation legend. She could do it, not everybody could. A great lady was music and moonshine, but she was also hard as steel. She was too frail to put on her own shoes and stockings but she bore ten children quietly; she had never an idea in her lovely head but she could make a hundred not necessarily congenial guests coalesce into a pleasant unit; she must always be sent upstairs to rest before the ordeal of getting dressed for a ball but she could dance till sunrise once she got there; she turned faint at the sight of blood from a cut finger but she could ride to hounds and be in at the kill; she was an angel of mercy toward the poor and afflicted but cruel as Nero toward any of her own clan who violated the code of gentle behavior; she obeyed her husband with docile respect but she got out of him anything she really made up her mind to have. Ann began to laugh. If that was what they wanted of her, that they would get. She resolved that as soon as she was up she would have her portrait done by the best painter available and hung in the great hall of Ardeith beside those ancestors of the Larnes who had helped create the legend. There was already a picture of one Sheramy woman in the hall, that quaint old portrait of Judith Sheramy who had married Philip Larne before the Revolution. That had been in the days when the archetype of the Southern lady was in the making. Now the tradition was made. One merely had to live up to it.

"You know," Ann thought drowsily, "I wouldn't own this out loud for worlds, but I believe I'm a coward. I believe I want to be safe more than I want anything else. Nothing very exciting will ever happen to me, but I'm so marvelously, beautifully *safe!*"

II

She was up as soon as the doctor allowed, for she had a thousand things to do. Once she got through the dinner in celebration of her wedding anniversary and the christening party for little Denis she had to get ready for the holidays. She wrote invitations for her New Year's ball till her fingers ached, and in her dreams she saw her hand tracing "Mr. and Mrs. Denis Larne request the pleasure of the company of . . ." She arranged with the overseers to have a Christmas barbecue for the Negroes in the field-quarters, and she ordered their Christmas tree set up in the cotton storehouse with tinsel and lights and a present for every Negro on the place, heavy knitted shirts for the men, dresses for the women and a toy for every child. She would distribute them herself Christmas morning. There would be a group playing banjos and singing by the tree, and then they would come up to the big house and sing for the little master's first Christmas before they went off to the barbecue. "It sho is good havin' a young missis on de place again," the darkies told her as she hurried around, and Ann laughed and told them to get lots of cane cut and thus earn their holiday.

In the midst of her preparations she heard news that South Carolina had seceded. Ann was surprised; she had heard secession talk all her life and had never believed anybody would really do anything about it. Now they said all the Southern States would go out and set up a government of their own. At first she was interested, but after a succession of dinners at which the gentlemen talked nothing but politics she found the whole subject a great bore. Though she tried to understand what all the fuss was about, to save her life she couldn't see why the same government they had had since before they were born wasn't still good enough. Some of the gentlemen tried kindly to point out that it was really no longer the same government, and when she exclaimed, "But it's still American!"—they smiled indulgently and told her she was too pretty to try to be a bluestocking.

Denis was enormously interested, but she still could not understand when he tried to make it clear. She knew nothing about the tariff, the 1850 Compromises or the Kansas riots, and finally concluded that while secession might sound ominous to politicians it was no concern of hers. Besides, she was too busy to think. After New Year's she ordered the gown for her portrait, a strikingly simple evening dress of light blue silk with little sleeves of figured lace and a lace kerchief crossed low on her bosom, so low that she saw disapproval in the eyes of her mother-in-law. But she ignored Mrs. Larne, as she was sufficiently proud of her bosom and shoulders to want them recorded for her posterity.

Denis liked the dress, and the artist, who had been imported from New Orleans, said gallantly that it had been long since he had had the good fortune to have so charming a subject. He painted her standing at the foot of the spiral staircase, her

hand resting on the pillar of the balustrade, and enough of the
stairs showing behind her to leave no doubt of the identity of
the famous structure. What with posing for the portrait,
supervising a new outfit for little Denis to wear when he
outgrew his prenatal wardrobe, and making up for the entertaining she had not been able to do in the fall, Ann was so
occupied she rarely looked at a newspaper and found it hard
to remember which states were in the Union and which out of
it. She hardly saw Denis these days. He was in town, he was
on the wharfs, he was down at the sugar-mill urging speed,
for Northern contracts must be filled while trade was still
unimpeded. Ann protested that she wished he would stay at
home more, but he told her that though Louisiana had
guaranteed free passage of the river this guarantee might any
day be revoked and tariff barriers thrown up between the
North and South, so she sighed and said she thought the
whole business was silly, just as if they hadn't been getting
along all right the way they were.

But in early spring the political dissension interrupted her
life in a manner that was seriously irritating. She went
shopping and was met with the announcement that the regular
spring openings had been indefinitely postponed. Ann was
dismayed: she cried, "But we can't wear woolens and velvets
after March!" The salespeople shook their heads dolefully.
Establishments from New York to New Orleans had counter-
manded their orders because of the crisis, they said, and they
showed her the fashion chit-chat in Godey's Lady's Book,
which was mainly a lament that there was virtually nothing in
the way of style news to report. Ann sighed in exasperation,
"Show me what you have anyway. I've got to get something
for hot weather."

The head salesman gave her a bow. "Yes ma'am, certainly.
What sort of materials are you interested in? Where do you
expect to spend the summer?"

Without thinking, Ann returned, "Why, I've always gone
North for at least part of the summer—" then she stopped,
sat down abruptly on the stool before the counter and said,
"Damn!"

With consummate courtesy the salesman turned away,
pretending not to have heard a perfect lady swear, and began
to take some bolts of goods from the shelves. Ann was so

wrathful she did not particularly care whether he had heard
her or not. She bought some yards of lawn and went home in
a state of profound annoyance, intending to finish reading
"The Curse of Clifton" and so relax, but the housekeeper met
her with a new instrument of tribulation.

It was the guest-list for a dinner she was planning. Mrs.
Maitland said the master had just come in, and he had told
her the order of seating the guests as directed by the mistress
would not do at all. Many of them were visitors from out of
town, and it seemed that when you entertained nowadays
diners must be seated in the order in which their states had
seceded, those from South Carolina in the places of honor.
Snatching the list from Mrs. Maitland Ann ran into the back
study where Denis was going over his accounts.

"This is the most absurd thing I ever heard of!" she
stormed.

Denis leaned back from the desk with amused agreement.
"You're quite right, honey. But everybody's seating them that
way, and they'll be hurt if we don't."

Sighing, Ann dropped into a chair and began to look over
the list. "My cousins from Savannah—shall they be seated
ahead of the local people?"

"Yes, Georgia went out before Louisiana."

"Well, I'm certainly glad it did. It would look very discourteous not to put visitors ahead of home folks. And the
Prestons—they're from Virginia."

"Virginia hasn't gone out. They'll have to be placed toward
the end."

"Very well. I don't see what I can do about it. And the
Delaneys. They live in Wilmington, Delaware. Is Delaware
still in the Union?"

"Yes, and it's probably going to remain there. Delaware is
a slave state, but it's more Northern than Southern. Put them
below the Prestons."

"But doesn't it seem rather offensive? As if we were sure
Virginia would go out and Delaware not? And Denis, what
am I going to do about Mr. and Mrs. Rendon? They live in
Philadelphia."

Denis whistled softly. "Lord, I don't know. Do we have to
invite them?"

"They're already invited. And they gave that lovely dinner for us last summer in Saratoga."

"I don't know," Denis confessed again. "I like them, too."

"So do I. I wish all this had happened in the summer time. Then the Southerners would have been North instead of the Northerners being South, and it would be their problem. It's all idiotic anyway and I don't see why President Buchanan didn't do something about it when it started."

He smiled ruefully. "My dear, President Buchanan was elected because he was an amiable old gentleman incapable of doing anything. I tell you—let's make it a dance instead of a dinner. That will eliminate the precedence question."

"All *right*," Ann rejoined heartily. "I can't stand being rude to my friends just because they were born somewhere different from where I was. But oh dear."

"What?"

"I've already sent the invitations and now I'll have to write a separate letter to everybody changing it. And I've already got writer's cramp. Next winter I'm going to look up a lady in reduced circumstances and engage her as a secretary. But in the meantime, what will we be doing this summer? Saratoga again, or just the Gulf Coast?"

"I can't promise. There's no way to make plans yet."

She got up crossly, untying her bonnet-ribbons. "I'm sure I don't know why a lot of politicians have any right to complicate my whole life!"

Denis chuckled. "Do go on upstairs. How can I check my cotton receipts?"

"You're about as much fun these days," said Ann severely, "as an angel on a tombstone. I'm going to play with my papoose. He's the only person I know who doesn't care any more than I do what happens to the country."

She kissed her hand to him. Upstairs in the nursery Bertha was rocking little Denis to sleep, caroling an old church hymn. Ann put her bonnet and shawl on a chair and held out her arms.

"Give him to me."

Bertha obeyed, and Ann rubbed her cheek contentedly against that of the baby, rocking back and forth as she took up the hymn. He was such a darling, no longer red, but pink and white and chubby, with dimples in every conceivable spot. Holding him in her arms made her feel tranquil, far away from such plagues as postponed fashion openings and the difficulty of mixing politics with parties. She sang happily.

> *"Shall I be carried to the skies*
> *On flowery beds of ease? . . ."*

Denis had said he was glad she had ordered her portrait now instead of a year ago, for motherhood had given her a bloom she had never had before it. Whether this was fact or Denis' flattering imagination Ann was not sure, but she liked hearing him say it, and the portrait was really going to be beautiful if only her present burdens did not put lines into her face.

It was done in April. Everybody said it was lovely, and Ann was ecstatic. She tried to picture herself a little old lady with white curls and a cap, coming down the stairs to tell her grandchildren, "My dears, in sixty-one I looked like that!" The idea amused her, and she begged Denis to have his portrait done too before M. de Launay went back to New Orleans. Denis said he was too busy to stand for any portrait now, but he promised to think it over; maybe when this political confusion subsided he would have more leisure.

Then, all of a sudden, as amazingly as if a flower had exploded in her fingers, Ann discovered that there was going to be a war.

She never remembered when she first heard war mentioned. It was as if one day she was going on with her normal life and the next day there were flags on the houses and troops marching and the band playing "Dixie." It was terribly thrilling. Shop-windows were suddenly full of guns, cartridges, military sashes and camp kits; dressmakers displayed fabrics of Confederate gray for ladies' gowns; in bookstores fiction and poetry were moved to back shelves to make room for biographies of generals and volumes on military tactics; and even the toy-shops put their dolls and kites on back counters to leave space in front for regiments of tin soldiers. The air rattled with patriotic speeches. It was all so overpowering that it was hard to remember there had ever been a time when there was not a war, when life was bare of this gorgeous adventure of roses, music, parades, gallant rebels and dastardly Yankees.

Ann was so stirred that everything else that had ever happened to her seemed dull beside this. And only a few months ago, she remembered, she had been thinking nothing exciting would ever happen to her! She gave parties for the officers at the camp near Dalroy and helped organize Soldiers' Aid Societies to knit garments and learn the new war-songs. It was such fun to practise them—

> "Then Florida and Texas they both got in the ring,
>   For they wouldn't have a government where cotton
>   wasn't king. . . ."

and her hands tingled till she could hardly strike the keys. The young gentlemen from the camp came to Ardeith magnificent in their new gray uniforms with gold buttons, doffing their hats to her with gestures so courtly that the brims swept the ground. They danced in the parlor with herself and her friends, and told them it was an honor to be called to defend such beauty and chastity as theirs. They sat on the steps, each one tying a noose of rope to the barrel-end of his gun; that was to catch a Yankee and bring him home to be yoked up to the sugar-mill in place of the mule. It was a grand war. It wouldn't last long, of course; the Northern soldiers were enlisting for only three months, and to go them one better the Southerners jauntily signed up for a year, but they agreed they'd be home free and victorious in time for the sugar-grinding in the fall.

But when Denis came in one afternoon and drew her out of the parlor to tell her he was joining the army, Ann was swept over with such a flood of mingled pride and fright that she burst into tears on his shoulder. She flung her arms around him, standing in the hall at the foot of the staircase, sobbing that she couldn't live without him. Behind them in the parlor Sarah Purcell was playing the piano and everybody was singing, but under it she could hear Denis' voice, insisting that he simply had to go in, she wouldn't want to think he would let other men defend his country while he idled at home. His head overseer was amply capable of supervising the plantation. Ann held him tight, and while Denis got out his handkerchief and dried her eyes she begged him please to forgive her for being such a coward and said how proud of

him little Denis was going to be when he was old enough to
understand. Denis stroked her hair and kissed her and told
her he would be gone only a little while, and women had to
be brave in times like these. Raising her head she looked at
him, tall and handsome above her, and glowed through her
tears. From the parlor they could hear a tramping of feet.
The young officers were drilling around the piano, and singing.

> *"Oh, we'll be back by grinding time, grinding time, grind-*
> *ing time,*
> *Oh we'll be back by grinding time,*
> *With a Yankee to pull the mill!"*

Ann laughed. She was thinking how exceptionally handsome Denis would look in a uniform, and praising heaven M.
de Launay had been detained in Dalroy by another commission, for now he must certainly paint Denis in his Confederate gray, so little Denis could always see his father as a soldier.
Her own father was already in the army. Though he had
always opposed secession, Colonel Sheramy agreed that he
could not make war on his own people and resigned his
commission as soon as the war began. He was promptly made
a colonel in the new Confederate forces and went to the
camp, leaving Jerry to manage the plantation in his absence.
Ann thought now it was not every woman who had the
distinction of being both a soldier's daughter and a soldier's
wife and the mother of a potential soldier as well, and she
could really say she had given all she had to her country. She
kissed Denis again and told him she had never loved him as
much as she did this minute, and then she hurried to call
Napoleon, for Denis was about to announce the news to the
others and they could not properly celebrate his enlistment in
anything less than champagne.

Chapter Six

I

"HEY, Ma," said Corrie May, "d'you reckon it'll be too warm for me to wear a shawl?"

Her mother was standing by the stove pouring coffee. "I wouldn't aim to wear no shawl," she said, wiping the perspiration from her forehead with the corner of her apron. "It'll be plenty hot before noon."

"Yes'm. But this here dress is kind of teased out at the armholes." Corrie May stood with her back to the mirror on the kitchen wall, trying to twist her head to see just how much damage her wearing the dress had done to it. It was a blue-checked tissue Ann had given her, woven of long-staple delta cotton that had a silky shine to it, and she wore it with a set of Ann's old hoops. The ribs of the hoops were cracked in some places, but after Corrie May tied the broken places with strings the breaks didn't show much. Corrie May knew Ann's dresses would never meet around her own waist, and she wore a sash to cover the diamond-shaped gap at the waistband, but there was no way to disguise the tearing at the shoulder-seams. "I just got wider shoulders than Miss Ann," she acknowledged sadly.

"I expect you got more muscles than her," Mrs. Upjohn suggested. "Ladies that ain't never had to do no work don't develop to be broad across the shoulders. Here, you better have some coffee before you go out."

Though she accepted the cup Corrie May still examined herself in the mirror. She did want to look well for the parade. When you cheered soldiers marching to defend your country you had to be stylish. Setting the cup on the table she got her shawl, a light brown silk-and-wool mixture Ann had passed on to her when it got torn. Corrie May had mended the tear carefully, and when it was folded inside the darn did not show. She draped it around her shoulders with the point neatly adjusted to drop in the middle of the back. She had put a new ribbon on her last year's bonnet, and by trying it on at varying angles before the mirror she had managed to give it the new tilt-back look fashionable this season. If she could only wear her gloves, now, she would look very elegant indeed, but though Ann discarded plenty of gloves there was no mortal way for Corrie May to squeeze her own work-broadened hands into them. So she carried the gloves in her hands, pretending it was too warm to put them on. Holding the shawl together in front, with the yellow kid gloves in her hand at an angle that would not disclose the broken seams at the fingertips, she went out to join the girls who were waiting for her.

With one look at their clothes she decided she was more frocked up than any of them. One of the girls was Budge Foster's sister Ethel, whom Corrie May had not seen for a good while, not since Ethel married a fellow who worked on the upper wharfs; but apparently Ethel was not self-conscious about being with her brother's old girl. She was a placid sort of person, who would just take it that Corrie May and Budge didn't happen to run together any more, and leave it at that.

"You sho looks like one fine lady," said Ethel as they walked out of Rattletrap Square toward the street above the park, where the parade would pass.

"Thank you kindly," said Corrie May.

"Corrie May's been working out at Ardeith," one of the other girls explained. "She sho is getting to be elegant, too."

"You mighty right she is," Ethel observed enviously. "That's a real handsome dress."

"It's delta cotton," said Corrie May complacently.

"Delta cotton? Sho 'nough!" Ethel exclaimed. "Well, my my." She fingered a frill around the skirt. "Them delta cotton goods costs fifty cents a yard, even. And you got on hoops too, ain't you?"

Corrie May nodded, then caught herself in the middle of a nod lest she displace the back-tilt of her bonnet. "It's seven yards around the bottom."

"My my," said Ethel again. "I sho would like to have some

hoops sometimes. But they takes so much cloth. Say, Corrie May, you sho gets up in the world, don't you?"

"Oh, no, not so much," Corrie May said airily. "Just some little things they give me for working at Ardeith."

"But how come you got to wear a shawl?" Ethel inquired. "Me, if I had a real delta cotton dress I wouldn't be covering up the top of it with no shawl."

"I'm sensitive to drafts," said Corrie May. That was a weakness she had discovered just lately, since old Mrs. Larne came back from Europe. The girls were always being sent to fetch shawls for Mrs. Larne when she came to dinner. Corrie May was uncertain what drafts did to persons who were sensitive to them, but it was evidently a susceptibility that only highclass people could afford. But Ethel accepted her explanation.

"Well now, I never knew that before. I sho hopes you keep well, Corrie May." Then, as if tired of admiring and thinking it was time she got some attention for herself, she remarked, "My man, he's in the army."

"Sho 'nough!" the girls exclaimed with interest. "When'd he join up?"

"Oh, a little while ago. He'll be in the parade today."

"Honest?" They turned from Corrie May to Ethel. Corrie May might be all dressed up, but she couldn't boast a soldier for a husband, nor any husband at all for that matter. The other two girls were not married either, and they gave Ethel the deference due one who was making success of her life. "You don't mind him going?"

"Of course not," Ethel returned proudly. "It ain't every man gets right out to fight for his country."

Corrie May, who disliked losing their notice, put in,

"My Pa, he's joined up with the army too."

"Oh, he has?" they rejoined with evident surprise. Old man Upjohn had a certain respect paid him in Rattletrap Square, on account of knowing all those big words and being a preacher, but you wouldn't exactly expect him to be a soldier. Corrie May, who had scant illusions, knew her Pa had joined up partly because of the promise of regular pay and mostly because marching and receiving the cheers of the populace was like wine to his soul, but she nevertheless returned,

"Well, he's stout and healthy, ain't he? And you wouldn't

expect him to sit home when there's men needed to fight for their country, would you?"

The girls whose fathers were still lagging along at ordinary civilian jobs became both apologetic and defensive. Corrie May linked her arm in Ethel's. With soldiers behind them they could walk proudly together.

The streets were so crowded their progress was slow, and Corrie May had to keep reminding the girls not to push, as she had to be careful of her hoops. At last they got places on the right street, in the shade of a wrought-iron balcony overhanging the sidewalk from one of the residences. Corrie May had adroitly guided them here, for this was the home of the Durhams, the family who owned the great steamboat line, and in listening to conversations at Ardeith she had discovered that before her marriage old Mrs. Larne was a Miss Durham. Since the parade would not pass the plantations it was reasonable to assume that the Larnes would watch it from the Durham balcony, and if Ann should happen to pass and speak to her it would be a greater distinction than being married to a soldier. Any man who wasn't sick could be a soldier, but she was probably the only girl in Rattletrap Square who could be recognized by one of the great ladies of the plantations.

Carriages were driving up, their occupants getting out to enter houses along the route of the parade, and there were policemen ordering the lesser folk aside from the entrances. Corrie May and her friends edged as close to the Durham doorway as the policeman would let them. The Durhams were evidently entertaining quite a party. Guests came and came. Corrie May whispered to the others from her superior knowledge.

"That's Miss Jeannette Heriot, the one in pink lawn with the high bonnet. Her father owns the Heriot woodyards. Say, did you know a big steamboat burns six cords of wood a day? Yes it does too, and they buy it from the Heriot woodyards. That's Mr. Raoul Valcour with her. He's been running with Miss Jeannette. Folks say there might be a wedding. And that's Miss Sarah Purcell, the red-headed one in green."

"Dresses kind of flashy, don't she?" murmured Ethel.

"They say she does it to show off her hair. That's her

brother Hugh, the big one with the thin face. And that's Mr. Jerry Sheramy, the ugly one."

"Him?" said Ethel incredulously. "Looks like——" she hesitated.

"Like a gorilla," said Corrie May, when Ethel paused for lack of a simile. She was unsure what a gorilla was, but she had once heard Ann say that.

"Funny," said one of the other girls, "he should come in the Purcell carriage."

"I understand," said Corrie May importantly, "he's making up to Miss Sarah Purcell."

The great folk smilingly thanked the policeman for making them a clear passage across the sidewalk. They did not appear to see the street-crowds; it was as though they were passing between bushes the policemen were holding back. Corrie May wondered if she would ever, even if she became rich, be so exquisitely unconscious of unimportant people. Was it possible they didn't know they were being examined, their clothes and manners commented upon, any trivial line of their conversation that drifted to the crowd remembered and treasured, that she and her friends might say, "I heard Mr. Sheramy tell Miss Purcell the soldiers were going to be mightily hot marching in those heavy uniforms"?

She started, concealing her eagerness with difficulty, for she caught sight of the carriage from Ardeith. She knew it by the matched black horses that drew it and the curtains of flowered white satin Ann had prevailed upon Denis to order after arguing down his preference for solid rose-color. Corrie May pressed close to the curb.

The coachmam halted the horses. While he held the reins the footman sprang down from the seat beside him and opened the carriage door with a bow carefully calculated to reach its lowest just as his mistress appeared. The mistress this time was Ann's mother-in-law, who descended just as an elderly gentleman came out to meet her, exclaiming,

"Come right in, Frances. Delightful to see you, I'm sure. The young ladies with you?"

They evidently were, for after her mother came Miss Cynthia Larne, very stylish in a gown of spotted muslin. Cynthia curtseyed, saying "Good morning, Uncle Alan," with poise that though she was only twelve reminded Corrie May

that she had spent all last year in France. Cynthia said she
would wait for Ann, and Mrs. Larne went into the house with
her brother. Corrie May saw a white-gloved hand approach
the white-gloved hand of the foot-man, as a vast expanse of
hoopskirt filled the carriage doorway. It was a skirt of fine
white lawn, the ruffles embroidered with little pink and blue
flowers with green stems, and Corrie May involuntarily
winced at the thought of the hours some seamstress had given
to decorating a dress that would hardly survive six launder-
ings.

"That's Mrs. Denis Larne," she announced in a whisper.

"I've seen her around," Ethel breathed with awe. "Them
Larnes is the richest people hereabouts, ain't they?"

"I wouldn't be surprised," said Corrie May.

"Is it true they got silver doorknobs in their house? And a
staircase that turns around with nothing holding it up?"

"It sho is," said Corrie May, omitting to mention that she
had never used anything but the back stairs herself.

"Lawsy me. Is it honest them ladies got nigger women to
dress them in the mornings?"

"Absolutely."

"Do tell," marveled Ethel.

Ann emerged from the carriage with some difficulty, as her
hoops were so large it required dexterity to get them through
the doorway. She had on, not a bonnet, but a hat, think of it,
a straw hat bigger than a parasol, with white tulle crimped
around the crown and a frill of lace dropping from the brim,
and two long pink ribbons dangling from the hat over her
shoulders and halfway down her skirt. Smiling at Cynthia she
held out her hand, unmindful of how careful she should be of
such spotless gloves. Corrie May waited apprehensively lest
Ann pass without noticing her. Jerry came out of the house to
meet them, but Ann was detaining Cynthia by the carriage-
block in what appeared to be a serious conversation. Corrie
May listened, and managed to catch it.

". . . I'm glad she's gone in, for I wanted to ask you if
there's anything your mother would particularly like for
supper?"

Cynthia considered. "She likes lamb, but you said you were
going to have that."

"Yes, Mrs. Maitland ordered that. Does she like ice-cream? There'll be time to freeze it after we get home."

Cynthia nodded vehemently. "I do too."

"We can't have ice-cream," Jerry told her.

Cynthia looked up at him, startled. "But why not?"

"The ice-boat didn't come this morning."

"No ice?" cried Ann. "But what's the trouble? Didn't the rivers up North freeze last winter?"

"Up *North*," Jerry reminded her.

"Oh—but they've got to send us ice! We can't live!"

"The mean things," said Cynthia.

Jerry grinned. "We aren't going to send them any cotton," he said to Cynthia. "See how they like that."

"Well, they can wear last year's clothes but we can't eat last year's ice-cream," Cynthia retorted crossly. "I wish the war would hurry up and be over."

A bowing Negro man came from the door toward them. "Miss Ann, would it be yo' pleasure to step inside?"

"Yes, we'll be right in," said Ann, then as she moved toward the door she saw Corrie May. "Why good morning, Corrie May," she said cordially.

Corrie May thought she must be beet-colored with pride. In that moment she was willing to forgive Ann everything. She curtseyed. "Good morning, Miss Ann. Nice day."

"It's a lovely day, isn't it?" Ann smiled, gathered up her skirt and went indoors, Jerry and Cynthia behind her. Corrie May tried to glance around casually, as if being spoken to by a great lady were a matter of no moment in her life. Ethel exclaimed,

"She's just like a friend of yourn, ain't she?"

"Oh, she's all right," returned Corrie May, forgetting for the instant that she hated Ardeith and everybody who lived there. She basked in reflected glory. With a little laugh Ethel remarked,

"Imagine them people. Carrying on like that about ice."

"Biggity," said one of the other girls. "You'd think it was death to do without ice-cream."

"I ate ice-cream once," said Corrie May.

"Did you? What's it like?"

"It ain't so much. The way milk would be if it had sugar in it and was froze over."

"Where'd you get it?"

"At Ardeith." She added, "Ice ain't so much anyway. You tie the milk bucket to a string and put it down the well and it keeps just as good as if you had ice."

The ladies came out on the balcony over their heads. Servants brought chairs for them. Fine gentlemen who were not in the army stood behind the chairs and handed the ladies glasses of wine. They were all chattering and waving Confederate flags over the balcony-edge. Far down the street Corrie May heard a band playing "Dixie."

She and the others crowded to the edge of the sidewalk. The big road was cleared of carriages. The men came marching toward them. Coming down the road they looked perfectly grand, the officers on horseback and the boys carrying great big flags. Corrie May couldn't remember the names of all the states that were in it, because she had never heard of some of them before she heard about secession, but it was a big war, and her Pa was marching in line with his fine uniform just like a gentleman, only he didn't have any stars on his collar. The band played "Dixie" and everybody sang.

On the balcony overhead the ladies and gentlemen were throwing roses for the soldiers to walk on. Here came Colonel Sheramy on a horse. He took off his hat and bowed to the ladies, and Corrie May heard Ann exclaim, "Oh, Father! He never looked so magnificent before!" and looking up she saw Ann throwing kisses. Colonel Sheramy bowed till you'd think he'd fall off his horse, and the ladies flung roses under the horse's hoofs. Then there was Captain Denis Larne on a horse, and the ladies threw roses at him, and then came several others she recognized from having seen them at Ardeith. It was going to be a gentlemen's war, all right, and Corrie May was proud her Pa was in it to have flowers thrown at him. At last she saw Pa, marching along proud as anybody, though he was in the ranks, and Corrie May sang "Dixie" till she thought her throat would burst, and Pa looked at her and grinned. The soldiers all had nooses tied to their guns, to catch Yankees. The ladies on the balcony flung flowers, and one of them hit Pa's shoulder, just like a gentleman's shoulder. There were bands and flags and bright sunshine, and Corrie May had on her best dress. It was a grand war.

II

Corrie May had never been so joyously busy since the day she was born. Days she did not work at Ardeith she spent in Rattletrap Square with her girl friends, knitting socks and mittens and sewing shirts for the brave defenders of her country. Some of the girls said they thought it was mighty noble of Mr. Denis to go right out and join up with the army just like everybody else. Corrie May did not think it was so very noble of him and said so. "It's his country same as anybody's," she retorted, "and if they come down here and burn up everything he'd stand to lose a sight more than most folks."

Well, there sure was something fine about a war all the same, the other girls said, the way it leveled people and made rich men and poor men just alike. Dixie land was everybody's country and a poor man could tote a gun same as a rich one and they were all friends together in the army.

Corrie May had to admit there was something to that. Once they got into their uniforms you couldn't tell the difference, and certainly the rich ladies were working for the soldiers with all their might. They organized knitting clubs and met at one another's houses to work and didn't seem to mind at all. When the knitting club met at Ardeith the ladies had the jolliest time you ever saw. They came in their carriages with pretty workbags on their arms and sat a long time in the parlor, laughing and talking at a great rate; and though they fussed because the dye from the yarns stained their fingers, and said this war was going to be the ruin of their hands, they were so patriotic they seemed to enjoy it. In the afternoon there was a clatter of horses in the avenue and up came a group of young officers from the camp, and other young gentlemen not in the army, and Ann and her brother Jerry took turns playing the piano so they could dance till supper time. They gathered around the piano and while Jerry played —for he could play any tune he had ever heard, and do it better than Ann for all her music-masters—they sang rebel songs till the wall rang.

> *"As long as the Union*
>   *Was faithful to her trust,*
> *Like friends and like brethren*
>   *Kind were we and just;*
> *But now when Northern treachery*
>   *Attempts our rights to mar,*
> *We'll rally round the Bonnie Blue Flag*
>   *That bears a single star!"*

The young ladies shed tender tears and the young gentlemen kissed them—not very secretly either—and at last they went in for supper, at which one or two of the soldiers drank enough to be very noisily patriotic indeed, but nobody seemed to mind. But at last when the guests had left, Napoleon came to Corrie May and told her the mistress wanted to see her in the parlor.

Corrie May went in and found Ann curled up in a big chair looking around with dejected irony at the threads and scraps of yarn littering the rug. Ann asked abruptly,

"Corrie May, do you know how to knit?"

"Why yes ma'am," said Corrie May. "Sure."

"Will you teach me?" Ann asked.

"Why Miss Ann, don't you know? I sho thought I seen you fooling with some needles."

Ann laughed tersely. "That's exactly what I was doing with them—fooling. I can knit a straight piece if I'm lucky enough not to drop any stitches, but I don't any more know how to set a heel or turn glove-fingers—we're a fine lot of patriots, we are. Look at this masterpiece Sarah Purcell left here." She pulled out of a workbag a shapeless gray object, put her finger through it and gave a jerk. The stiches raveled into a ladder down the middle.

Corrie May laughed too, in derision. "What's it supposed to be?"

"I don't know—a muffler, I think. Will you really teach me how?"

"Sho," said Corrie May, "I'll teach you. You got some needles handy?"

Ann took them out of her workbag, together with a ball of yarn, and told Corrie May to sit by her on the sofa. Corrie May set about giving her a lesson. In about thirty minutes she

ck behind a hogshead so he wouldn't see her. But Budge
d caught sight of her already. He waved his hoe, saying
ell, well, well," and came down the path to the road. The
ver, nothing loth to do a bit of idling, drew back on the
ns and let the wagon stop. Budge leaned on his hoe,
nning with welcome that was only faintly self-conscious.
f it ain't Corrie May," he said. "How you been making
t?"

He looked healthy and right well pleased with himself. His
ce and arms were so sunburned that he was reddish-brown
e an Indian in a picture book. He wore a blue shirt, open at
e throat and with the sleeves rolled up above his elbows,
d homespun breeches neatly patched at the knees. His bare
et were hard and crusted with good rich earth. Corrie May
und her eyes going from his face to the patches at his knees.
eedn't tell her any man could patch as neatly as that. There
as some woman taking care of him. Not that she should
ind, and she assured herself that she didn't, but she did.
"Hello," she said bashfully.
"Don't you look grand," said Budge, "riding in the Ardeith
agon. I heard tell you was working out there. How they
eat you?"
"Oh, pretty good," said Corrie May. She wished she could
eep her eyes off those patches. "You look like you was doing
retty good yourself."
Budge grinned proudly. "Oh, I'm doing fine, fine," he said
heartily. He swept his arm toward his field. "Look. Ain't it a
handsome place? It's a shame you ain't seed it since I got the
and working. Made half a bale to the acre last fall. Do better
han that this year. Is you in a hurry? Come on, I'll show it to
you. Got corn in the back, and tomatoes—"
Corrie May was looking past him. Her eyes had fastened
n the open door of his cabin. No, she wasn't wrong. There
as somebody moving around in there. Somebody in a skirt.
he asked shortly,
"Budge, who's that woman in there?"
Budge turned around and glanced at the door. He burst out
aughing. He laughed and laughed, striking the side of the
agon with his fist. He said, "Ain't you a one!" and laughed
ome more.
"I reckon we better be going," said Corrie May with

---

was so exasperated she had difficulty keeping her temper. She
had never in all her born days seen anybody so stupid as Ann.
Those dainty white fingers of hers seemed utterly unable to
perform any task at all, even one so simple as throwing thread
over a needle. She knotted the yarn, she dropped stitches, she
forgot to count and purled in the wrong places. And what was
worse, she didn't seem to know how to give her attention to
what she was doing. In the middle of an explanation she
looked out of the window and said how pretty the moon was
as it came up. Corrie May recalled her and started to explain
all over again, but before she was half done Ann had jumped
up to examine an unusual moth flying about the candle.
Corrie May did not dare call her a dunce, but she did say,
"Miss Ann, I can't teach you nothing if you can't set your
mind to it more than half a minute at a time!"

"Oh, I'm sorry," Ann apologized, laughing at herself. "I
don't seem to have any power of concentration at all. You
must think I'm very dimwitted."

That was exactly what Corrie May did think, but she said
tactfully, "Oh no ma'am, only I reckon a lady like you that's
always had things done for her has a hard time trying to do
anything herself. Now you just be quiet and listen while I tell
you, please ma'am."

After that Ann listened more attentively, as though
ashamed of herself, and though her head seemed very slow at
accepting instruction she did learn something before the
evening was over.

However, Corrie May did have to admit that for all her
foolishness Ann did have an astonishing power of persever-
ance. She knitted all the next day, pausing only for meals and
for occasional romps with little Denis, and though she had to
ravel most of what she accomplished, when Corrie May was
ready to leave that afternoon and came for her wages Ann
proudly held up an inch of wristband on four needles.

"Look, Corrie May! I've been around eight times and
haven't missed the purling once!"

Smothering her contempt for a lady who found such
difficulty in so simple an accomplishment, Corrie May came
over politely and examined it. "Yes ma'am, it's very nice."

"Is it really all right?" Ann asked anxiously.

"Yes ma'am," said Corrie May with some impatience, for

she was tired and wanted to go. "Except some stitches is slacker than others. You got to learn to hold the yarn always the same."

"Oh. I'll try." Ann carefully did six more stitches, counting each one with a little bob of her head. "I'll do it right if it kills me," she said half under her breath.

"It will if you work that hard at it," said Corrie May laughing. "The trouble with you, Miss Ann, is you ain't never learned to do nothing and so you think things is a lot harder than they are."

"I suppose that's true. But it *is* hard." She purled twice.

"Could I please ma'am have my money?" Corrie May asked.

"Oh yes, of course. Here it is."

She took her purse out of her workbag and handed Corrie May a couple of yellow bills. Corrie May turned them over doubtfully. She stood first on one foot and then on the other, running her tongue over her lower lip and examining the bills. Ann looked up from her knitting.

"What's the matter?"

"Er—Miss Ann," Corrie May ventured, "excuse me, please ma'am, but this here—is this *money?*"

"Why certainly it is! You don't think I'm trying to cheat you! Oh." She began to laugh. "That's the new money. Confederate money. Don't you see what's printed on it?"

"I ain't so good at reading," said Corrie May timidly.

"I see." Ann took the bills from Corrie May's hand. "This line across the top says 'Confederate States of America.' It's just as good as the old kind."

"You mean it'll spend just the same?" Corrie May asked, relieved but still hesitating.

"Why of course."

"It's just different because of the war?"

"That's right." Ann returned to counting stitches.

"Yes ma'am." Corrie May curtseyed and went out to the back where she climbed into the wagon on which she was to ride to the wharfs. The wagon was half full of molasses-kegs. She sat down in the back, and as the driver clambered into his seat he looked back to tell her he had to go out the side road on an errand before going to the wharfs. She sighed, and leaned back against the side of a hogshead to wait until it

suited his master's pleasure for him to take her
wanted to go.

The side road was bumpy, for people who live(
were poor and the road had no need to be l(
carriages. The plots were small and had a half-h(
pearance very different from the thriving neatness of
plantations. The houses were whitewashed cabins in
of repair. This was St. Clair property: instead of wor
land themselves the St. Clairs let it out to tenants an(
their rents. Corrie May had seen at Ardeith a youn
man named Bertram St. Clair and a young lady nar
Harriet St. Clair, and she had marveled that they see
such agreeable people, for their name was such a h
everybody she knew that she had pictured the St. (
greedy ogres counting with long yellow fingers the re
squeezed out of Rattletrap Square and their tenant far
all her glimpses of rich people at Ardeith, she had nev
it clear in her mind how they could be so ineffably c
at the same time so very kind. There was a wo
Rattletrap Square whose husband had been killed in
from a scaffolding, and she had been turned into th(
with four children because she could not pay her rent
St. Clairs, and yet the very next day Mr. Bertram St
came to dinner at Ardeith with his mother, and he
attentive to the old lady that he might have been held (
model of devotion. It was all very puzzling.

The wagon was passing a field of cotton. Corrie
looked at it with surprise, for this was good cotton, a
worked as the cotton of Ardeith. Whoever rented this
was a thrifty fellow, proud of himself and meaning
some place in the world. Near the road she could s
cabin, so neat it might have been built yesterday
bean-vines climbing up the front. Around the house
vegetable garden where a man was working. She t
there was something familiar about his back, then
turned to look at the wagon rumbling by Corrie May
and started, for the man was Budge Foster.

She had not seen Budge in a long time. He hardly
to Rattletrap Square these days. She felt her face get
she was remembering how she had talked to him w
told him she would not marry him, and she wished sl

dignity. "This nigger's got to go a piece up the road before he rides me to the wharfs. We ain't got time to be loafing here."

But Budge caught her arm. "Oh, you ain't going no place. What makes you be in such a hurry?" He started laughing again. "That ain't nobody but my sister Ethel. She's been staying out here with me since her husband joined up with the army. Ethel!" he shouted over his shoulder. "Come on out. We got company."

Corrie May suspected that half his pleasure in seeing her picayune what Budge did or didn't do, but all the same she felt so pleased she couldn't help laughing with him. Ethel came running down the path. She had on a clean gingham dress and her hair was down her back in a pigtail.

"Well, if it ain't Corrie May," said Ethel with welcome. "Come in and set a spell."

"You's right hospitable," said Corrie May doubtfully, "but I got to be getting home."

"Oh, come on in," said Ethel. "We don't get right smart of company out here. It'll be nice having you. Budge can ride you to the wharfs. Can't you, Budge?"

"Sho," said Budge. "Be an honor. Come on in. You ought to see my little place."

Corrie May scrambled out of the wagon. Ethel was saying she must stay for supper. "I was just mixing up a corn-pone," she said. "And we got some pork left from last hog-killing."

"I'll show you around," said Budge.

Corrie May suspected that half his pleasure in seeing her was caused by the chance to have her follow him around and listen while he enlarged on the excellence of his farm. And it was a good farm, too. His cotton was thriving, and his vegetables, and he had chickens and a sow with a litter of pigs. This fall when the cotton came in he was going to get a cow. And he was building a barn. He stood among the corn and grinned proudly down at her, like a fellow with a crown on his head showing off an empire. "How you like it?"

She smiled with wondering admiration. "It's just grand, Budge."

"Ain't it?" he said eagerly. "And there wa'n't nothing here when I come out. Just a lot of weeds."

Corrie May swallowed. She looked down.

There was a pause. Suddenly Budge put his arm around her and kissed her.

She started back. "Oh Budge—don't do that!"

But he still held her. His face was close to hers. "You think I ain't missed you all this time?" he asked in a low voice.

She looked up at him. "I—I reckon I've been missing you too. I made out like I didn't. I tried to make out like I didn't want to think about you at all."

"What you suppose made me work so hard?" he demanded. "You told me you had to be somebody. You said you'd rather be a nigger than po' white trash. You thought I was trash. I reckon I was born trash but I reckon by God I don't have to stay thataway."

He took a long breath. She felt his body press against hers.

"You going there to Ardeith and working in the house with all them niggers," said Budge. "Coming out here in wore-out clothes them Larnes gave you, and shoes in the summer time. Is that what you call not being trash?"

She pulled away from him and burst into tears. She felt like a bug being stepped on.

"I know," she got out, scrubbing her eyes with her sleeve. "I hate them."

"I thought you would," said Budge grimly. "I was aiming to get you and bring you out here one day so you could see my place. Honest Corrie May," he blurted, "wouldn't you rather be here with me than bowing and scraping to them Larnes?"

She looked up again, tears still on her eyelashes. "Budge," she said, "I don't know."

"You said you hated them."

"I do," she cried. "Tiptoeing around their house scared I'm gonta get mud on their carpets. Swallowing my tongue so I won't tell them what I think of them. Yes ma'am, thank you ma'am, I sho do appreciate it, ma'am—oh Jesus, I'd like to bust their jaws sometimes!"

"Then what makes you want to stay there?" Budge insisted. "Corrie May, I been loving you pretty nigh ever since I first laid eyes on you. Why can't you quit them people and come on out here with me?"

Corrie May twisted her hands together. "It's so warm there in the winter time. It's so clean and quiet and they talk with such pretty voices. They don't give me no hard work, I just sew and mend and they got flowers in the yard—"

Budge took a cornstalk in his hand and began to smooth one of its leaves. "You like that better than being here with me?" he asked her.

"I don't know," she said again.

Ethel's voice sounded from the cabin. "Hey, you all! Supper's on."

Budge looked down at Corrie May with a slow smile. "I reckon," he said, "there ain't no urging you till your mind's made up."

She followed him toward the back door. Budge paused to wash at a basin set there. Watching him, Corrie May began to realize how fastidious she had become since she first went to work at Ardeith. It irritated her to see Budge scraping the mud off his feet so as not to track up the cabin. He only washed his hands as far as the wrists and she could see the black shadow on his arms above the clean ring. The soap smelt sour and strong. It did not occur to him to clean the black ridges from under his nails.

She went inside, and saw Ethel disposing of a rat she had just killed. She was holding it by the tip of its tail. "How them varmints do get in!" Ethel exclaimed good-naturedly as she threw it out of the back door. She brushed off her hands on her skirt and sat down at table. The kitchen was low and dark, and had a heavy smell of food. Supper was corn-pone and pork and some tomatoes stewed with onions. They sat on rough home-made stools with no backs. Corrie May thought of the meals they gave her at Ardeith, roast beef with rice and cream gravy, vegetables cooked in butter, chocolate cakes with pecan frosting. She tried to make talk.

"How's your husband like the army?" she asked Ethel.

"Oh, he liked it all right, last time I seen him. Course I ain't had a chance to ask him how he likes fighting." Ethel laughed.

"But thirteen dollars a month besides your keep is a fine mess of money," observed Corrie May. "More'n he ever made on the wharfs, ain't it?"

"Except in mighty good times. I sure am proud of him. He went right in and joined up soon as the war started."

"I'd be proud of him too," Corrie May agreed. "I'm right

proud of my Pa. Southern men sure is brave. What about you, Budge? Is you thinking of the army?"

Budge paused in his hungry attack on his plate. "Not much, I ain't. Course I love my country and all like that, but I ain't got nobody to leave on my place."

"He ain't no coward," Ethel said hastily. "But he's right about nobody to raise the crops if he left."

Corrie May considered. She hated to think of Budge not going into the army. How would she feel if she married him and people asked her what regiment he was in? She'd be ashamed.

"Don't you think everybody ought to fight the Yankees?" she asked.

"No I don't," said Budge with decision. "Somebody's got to raise the crops. I'll quit cotton and raise vegetables if they say I ought to, but I ain't gonta leave my piece of ground to grow up in weeds." He pointed his fork at her. "I've got up before daylight and worked till I can't see no more, every day, to get this place cleared up and raise my cotton, and just when I've got it going good I ain't gonta leave it. Suppose I went off with the army? When I got home they'd have rented this land to somebody else and I'd have to take a new piece and start over. I'm patriotic as anybody," he ended, settling back on his stool, "but I just ain't gonta leave my piece of ground."

She smiled, though she was still doubtful about his being right. He talked about his ground as if it were his child. "I reckon I see how you feel," she owned. "Still—"

Budge grinned at her across the table. Apparently he thought it unnecessary to justify himself any further, for he began praising Ethel's skill at making an onion-and-tomato stew. Corrie May got the idea that he thought the war a needless interference with people's lives, too far off to concern a man who could occupy himself with anything so important as setting up a homestead on a piece of ground. But she was not going to marry Budge. Not yet, anyway. While Budge might be entitled to his own opinions she certainly did not agree with him about the war, and she wasn't going to marry anybody who thought anything more important than saving the country from the Yankees. On the way home that night she told him so.

"Look here, Budge, I reckon I get how you feel about your place. You been doing fine out there and you get good crops and all, and I don't blame you for being proud of it. But when there's a war a man ought to go out and fight."

"Ah, Corrie May," he insisted, "I'd lose all my work if I went off. Even if I could send them the rent with my army pay, it would all grow up in weeds while I was gone."

"Well, that's your business," she returned stubbornly. "I ain't saying I'm not fond of you, Budge. I guess I'm fonder of you than I ever knew till this minute. But I ain't going to have to apologize to nobody for my husband."

Budge sighed. For a long time they were silent. But when she got out of the wagon in Rattletrap Square he caught her in his arms and kissed her again, so urgently that Corrie May almost felt herself yielding. "I can't say I understand you a little bit," Budge said wearily. "But I just can't help loving you, Corrie May."

"I—I'll think about it," she promised. Her voice was not quite steady. She broke from him and ran into the house.

Chapter Seven

I

SHE thought about Budge a great deal in the months that followed. It wasn't hard to understand how he felt about abandoning his little place. But after all, this was a war, and everybody's plans were upset when the country had to be saved. Much as she disliked the Larnes she could not overlook the fact that Denis had gone right out and put on a uniform as soon as the first call came. To be sure, there were a great many rich gentlemen who were not in the army—Jerry Sheramy among them—but that didn't alter the fact that they ought to be. For though the air was ringing with news of Southern victories, for some reason the war was not over by grinding time. It just lasted and lasted, and the Northern army took New Orleans and sent gunboats up the river, so that for several days there was such panic on the levees that overseers couldn't make the Negroes do any work. But all the troops did was go up and march through Baton Rouge and then make a vain attack on the Confederate fort at Vicksburg. They retreated to New Orleans with abashed quietness, apparently finding it all they could do to stay there.

And the war went on. With its lasting so long, and with the dreadful Yankees meanacing everything, Corrie May didn't see how any man worth a corn-pone could stay out of the army.

Then one morning at Ardeith she overheard something that made all her opinions about the war turn somersaults.

Jerry and some others had come over for dinner and as they sat in the parlor they talked about the war, which was all anybody talked much about these days. Coming into the parlor with a shawl she had been sent to bring for old Mrs. Larne, Corrie May heard Jerry exclaim,

"But what do the Yankees think they're going to do with the Negroes if they do set them free? Do they want to turn loose four million people who haven't any more notion of how to take care of themselves than babies?"

"Of course," said Bertram St. Clair, "Northern people don't realize how ignorant the Negroes are. They think—"

Corrie May went out. She had given Mrs. Larne the shawl and knew she was not welcome to stand around listening to their conversation. But her ideas about saving the country had begun to totter in her head. She returned to her task of darning Ann's stockings. Presently Ann came to give her an order, for Mrs. Maitland had resigned her post as house-keeper to be a hospital nurse and Ann had to pay more attention to things these days, though she still left her house-keeping largely to Bertha and Napoleon. Corrie May embold-ened herself to ask a question. Ann was saying,

"When you've finished those, will you mend these dresses of the baby's? Aren't children hard on clothes!"

"Yes ma'am," said Corrie May, "they all is, I reckon. Miss Ann, excuse me for disturbing you, ma'am, but about this war—?"

"Yes?" Ann set the pile of little Denis' dresses on the chair beside her. "What about it?"

"If the Yankees should win it would they turn the niggers loose?"

"Why yes," said Ann, "that's one of their ideas. Throw that stocking away, Corrie May, it's not worth darning."

"Yes ma'am." Corrie May set the stocking aside for her own use. "Miss Ann, would the Yankees pay you folks for the niggers, or just turn them loose for nothing?"

"Of course they wouldn't pay for them. You can get dinner from the kitchen at half-past two, and when you've finished those dresses you may go."

Corrie May did not answer. After Ann had gone out she sat holding her needle in the air, looking through the window of the sewing-room toward the fields where the Larne Negroes were working.

She tried to calculate the value of the slaves at Ardeith. She didn't know how many there were, but there must be at least six hundred. A baby in arms was worth a hundred dollars, an adult fieldhand five hundred to a thousand depending on his age and strength. An expert cook or seamstress, a lady's maid or butler, two to five thousand—Corrie May whistled softly. No wonder Denis Larne had gone to war. No wonder rich people wanted everybody to fight Yankees. But why in the name of reason should a fellow like Budge go out and fight their battles for them?

She jabbed her needle into the cloth. Budge was a simple soul. He didn't think very much. But he just knew by some kind of instinct that this wasn't his war. What a fool she had been. Patriotism and the "Bonnie Blue Flag" and the band playing "Dixie"—"Damn their souls," said Corrie May. She clenched her hands, crumpling baby Denis' dress between them. What was she doing here among these people? She didn't belong to them. None of their ideals had any meaning for her; she envied their stately, gorgeous life without having any hope of sharing it. All she had experienced of them was their selfishness, their suave cruelty, their assumption that charm and grace made them so superior that they were justified in crushing their fellowmen in order to retain the way of life that had produced those pretty qualities. When they talked about defending the country they meant defending their own property and their right of exploitation—the insolence of them! What was she doing here, picking up crumbs from their abundance? They didn't care if she lived or died. And yonder was Budge, who loved her, to whom she, Corrie May Upjohn, was of particular importance as a human being —and she was spurning him because he wouldn't go out and offer himself as a sacrifice to save the wealth of the Larnes! Corrie May felt that she was reddening with shame.

Well, she was done with them. She was leaving. She was going to marry Budge Foster and help him work his piece of ground. The first minute she could get there she was going out to Budge's place and tell him she'd marry him. Only first she'd make him swear to stand by his resolution of not getting mixed up in their war. Then let the Yankees come on down and free the slaves, and the sooner they did it the sooner Negroes and white folks would both have to work for wages and there'd be no more of this having to work in competition with slaves who worked for nothing. That was the way to be somebody—make them give you the chance to earn your own right to walk up the handsome road and not be poor white trash.

That evening when she left for home she told Ann she didn't feel so pert and wouldn't come to work tomorrow. She doubted very much if she was ever going back to Ardeith as long as she lived.

But as she went through Rattletrap Square and entered her alley she heard some excitement. There was a bonfire burning in the street, and folks were roasting sausages around it and children singing the "Bonnie Blue Flag." Corrie May hurried toward the fire, and in the midst of the gathering she saw a group of soldiers in spanking new uniforms, boys from the neighborhood who had joined up with the army and were getting a fine sendoff from the home folks. "The poor fools," Corrie May thought furiously. Just then several girls ran to meet her and pulled her in to join the fun, and as she got close to the soldiers the firelight flared up and she saw that one of them was Budge.

Budge was grinning and munching a sausage somebody had roasted on a stick. He had on a gray suit with shiny buttons, and on his feet were big strong shoes. He looked sheepish, as if he didn't quite know how to behave with himself the center of so much going-on, but at the same time he appeared mighty proud of himself. Corrie May broke from her friends and ran directly to him.

"Oh Budge," she burst out. "Oh Budge!"

"Well, if it ain't Corrie May!" He slapped his chest. "How you like me in my new clothes?"

Her breath was coming short and fast. She gripped her hands around his arm and pulled him aside a little so they could talk with more privacy.

"Tell me, Budge—did you join up on account of me? On account of all them silly things I said?"

Budge looked down, shifting his weight from one foot to the other. "Well no, not exactly. Course I been thinking about what you told me. I thought about it a lot. About you being ashamed and all like that if you was to be married to a man that didn't think enough of his country to fight for it—"

"Budge, I don't feel like that no more." She pulled him into the shadows away from the fire. Her heel struck the step of somebody's lodging and she sat down, drawing him down beside her. "I'm all done with them notions, honest," she insisted. "I was coming out to your place tomorrow if I had to walk every step of the way, so I could tell you—"

"Why—you mean honest, Corrie May?" Budge's face was aglow in the light. "You mean you was coming to see me?"

"Yes. I'm crazy about you!" Her words tumbled out. "I reckon I've been crazy about you always. I'll get married to you and I'll make you the best wife I know how. Only you got to get rid of that damn uniform and get back to working our piece of ground."

"Why— But—" Budge floundered, and looked down at his shiny buttons and back at her. "Why, honey child, I can't get back. I'm in the army. The men came and got me."

"Came and got you? What you talking about?"

"The conscription officers. Said there was a new law that all young men had to be in the army."

She gasped. "You mean they made you come? Even when you said you didn't want to?"

"Well, I didn't exactly mind so much then. Not after I'd been thinking about all them things you said about being ashamed of me. Only—" Budge hesitated. He took a breath, and blurted, "Only I did pretty near bust out crying when I had to leave my piece of ground."

Corrie May got slowly to her feet. She could see what they had done. Budge had cleared out that patch of weeds and worked from dawn till dark to plant his cotton so he could be independent and get somewhere in the world, loving every bit of it, working proudly through heat and rain and backaches and mosquitoes, and now that he had it all planted and his cabin built, those officers tore him away.

"Them filthy bastards," she said.

"Now, Corrie May," said Budge with soothing admonition. "You mustn't say them kind of words. A nice girl like you."

"I'll say what I think" she flung at him fiercely. "Them taking you away from your place to make you fight for somebody else's niggers. I'll say it. I'll say it out loud to everybody. I'll say it this mintue and I'll slap anybody down that tries to stop me."

She started to run toward the bonfire. She ran half blindly, pushing her way through the crowd with furious haste. Let them fall down. It didn't matter. Somebody had to stop this.

Somebody had to shout out loud and tell these folks what they were fighting for. A child sat on a goods-box by the fire; she shoved him off, not heeding his yell or his mother's demand of what did she think she was doing. She sprang upon the box and shouted,

"Stop it! All you folks! Stop this yelling and singing! Go on back and mind your business and leave this war alone!"

Around her she heard gasps of amazement. "Who on earth is that?" "It's that Upjohn girl—her Pa's the preacher." "Oh, him. Kind of touched, ain't he?"

"You think my Pa's touched!" cried Corrie May. "Well, he is. If his head had been on straight he wouldn't be out fighting for them folks that own slaves. You shut up, all of you, and listen to me."

They listened, too astonished for the moment to do anything else. Corrie May jerked off her bonnet and pushed her tumbled yellow hair out of her eyes. She stood above them, mounted on the box, the light of the bonfire flashing on her as though she had drawn all its glow to herself, so that she was bright against the dark of the alley behind her as she shouted in her fierce ardor to tell them the truth.

"You know what this war's about?" she demanded. "I reckon you don't because ain't nobody told you. The Yankees want to come down here and turn the niggers loose. And suppose they do? Why should you care? You all ain't got no niggers. Let them that's got niggers fight to keep them! You po' halfwits strutting in them fine uniforms—ain't you grand! I could just bust laughing. Why ain't you all got nerve enough to tell them to hell with their war?"

"That there girl!" a voice shouted in the crowd. "Talking treason!"

"I ain't talking treason!" cried Corrie May. "I'm talking sense. I'm telling you the rich people want you to go out and get killed so they can keep their niggers! And if their slaves was free you'd all get better wages. Yes you would! You *want* the niggers to be free. You—"

A clod of dirt hit her in the stomach. She gasped. "You poor silly—"

"Shut her up!" cried another voice. "Put her in jail!"

Another lump of dirt hit her. She staggered but kept on shouting. "I won't shut up. I'm telling you what I know—"

She felt a stick of wood strike her head. "Shut your damn mouth," said a voice out of the dizziness. Corrie May felt herself falling down. She tried to scream. A blow in the mouth smothered her voice as the crowd surged around her, soldiers and older men and yelling women and children. They beat her and kicked her and dragged her across the ground. She fought like an animal, striking with her fists and biting their legs. From somewhere at an enormous distance she heard Budge crying out, "You folks leave her alone! She don't know no better!"

But she could not see Budge. She could not see anybody in particular; she only knew she was down on the ground and the whole mob seemed to be on top of her. They were tearing her hair out by the roots and blood was trickling into her eyes. Somebody's foot gave her a kick in the stomach. A pain shot through her insides and she began to vomit. Above and around her, a long way off, she heard them saying this was how they'd treat all Yankees and all traitors who were paid by Yankees to come talk against the war. By this time she did not care any more. She was sick and bleeding and they were beating her. She could not even scream now. She could only choke and beg them weakly please, please to stop. But they would not stop. They were like wild animals tearing their meat to pieces. Then she couldn't do anything but groan under the fists and feet, and then she could not do even that, for everything got black and there was a noise in her ears like thunder. She felt as if she were upside down and then right side up and then upside down again and something was pounding her body. At last she did not feel even that.

II

Deep in the pit of blackness where she was lying she slowly became aware of herself again. She shuddered, and her bruised mouth murmured, "Don't hit me any more!"

But to her amazement everything around her was silent. Corrie May thought they had pounded her ears into complete deafness. As her senses returned she felt pain all over her, in her head and arms and legs, pain gathering from everywhere and striking with increasing force as her mind awakened. She tried to open her eyes. They seemed stuck together. A long sobbing noise came out of her throat.

From somewhere in the vagueness above her she heard a man's voice. He was asking, "What's happened to you, lady?"

At that she became aware of what had roused her. Somebody was feeling her bruised body, trying to move her. With a vast effort Corrie May pulled open her eyes. On the ground by her was a lantern, and in its ring of pale light was a man in a policeman's uniform. Above her she could just make out the crazy angles of the tenements. The walls seemed to lean over her, harshly silent.

The policeman asked, "Can you get up?"

She said, "I don't know," but the words sounded strange, and it hurt her to say them, for her mouth was so swollen with bruises that it could hardly form words at all.

"I'll help you," he said.

The sound of a friendly voice was so sweet that tears welled up behind her sore eyelids. She managed to say, "I thank you, mister."

He put his hands under her armpits. "Steady, now. You got caught in that riot out there?"

"Yes," she said, trying to hold her breath hard so she would not scream, for the agony of movement hit her from a dozen angles at once.

"Too bad," he was saying. "Too bad. Them beating up a girl."

Corrie May cried out as he lifted her in his arms.

"There now," said the policeman. "I reckon you better not try to walk. Don't think there's nothing broke, but you's all cut up. Where you live? I can tote you—you ain't so heavy."

She managed to mumble some directions. He started off. The streets were mostly deserted, for the people of Rattletrap Square dreaded the police and ducked indoors at the sight of them. Every step he took sent a jolt of pain through her, but she was so glad to be alive and on her way home she hardly minded. At the door of Mrs. Upjohn's lodging he knocked with his foot. The door opened cautiously.

"Who might it be?" Mrs. Upjohn inquired in a timid voice.

"This here girl got hurt in the riot," the policeman explained. "Says she live here."

Mrs. Upjohn screamed. "Oh, my lawsy! Corrie May! Sure,

come right on in, Mr. Officer. Lay her down here. Oh Corrie May, honey, is you bad hurt?"

"I—I reckon I'll be all right," Corrie May murmured as he laid her on the bed.

Mrs. Upjohn was bustling around. "How on earth did it happen? I heard the racket but was scared to go out."

"Well ma'am, I can't say I rightly know just what did happen. Somebody started yelling sedition and the folks got to fighting. They sent some of us down to clear it up, but by the time we got here there was so much commotion we couldn't do nothing but pile a few of the rowdiest in the wagon and take 'em down to jail to cool off."

He stood around while Mrs. Upjohn began to wash Corrie May's cuts and bruises. "Terrible, terrible," she was murmuring, "to beat her up like this."

"Yes ma'am, sure is. I found her in an alley back a piece. Guess she just fainted in the middle of it and they went on fighting each other. This always was a tough part of town."

Though she could hear them talking, Corrie May did not pay much attention. Her mother bound up her wounds and brought her a cup of coffee. As she raised up to drink it she saw that the policeman was having a cup of coffee too. He sat in a chair by the stove.

"It sho was kind of you to bring me home," Corrie May said to him.

"Well now, that's all right. Always glad to help a lady in distress." He sipped his coffee gratefully. "How'd it all start, miss? Was you there in the beginning?"

Corrie May hesitated and swallowed a spoonful of soup her mother was offering her. His question had frightened her: the coffee had revived her sufficiently to make her understand that if she told this kind policeman she had started the riot he would be transformed from a kind policeman into an avenger who would take her off to jail for treason.

"Corrie May," said her mother reprovingly, "answer the gentleman. Ain't you got no manners in front of company?"

Corrie May wet her swollen lips. "Well—there was somebody talking against the conscription law."

"Oh," said the policeman. He blew on his coffee to cool it. "Some fellow scared to fight, I expect. Belongs in jail, them kind of men."

Corrie May swallowed another spoonful of soup. "They's really gonta conscript everybody?" she asked. "All the men?"

"Yes ma'am, I expect so. Except the old ones, of course, and them that ain't able to fight, and of course the big slaveowners."

She pushed the soup aside. The movement roused a pain in her shoulder. "Wait a minute, Ma." She turned her head to look straight at the policeman. "What was that you said about the big slaveowners?"

"Mind if I pour myself another cup of this mighty fine coffee, ma'am?" the policeman was asking.

"Go right ahead," Mrs. Upjohn said in hospitable gratitude. "Help yourself. Don't you want your soup, Corrie May?"

"No, Ma. I want to ask him—what was that you said about the big slaveowners?"

"Oh yes, miss. The law says any man that owns twenty slaves or more is exempt from conscription. Somebody's got to stay home and grow the crops, you see, and look out for the niggers."

"Oh."

Corrie May felt all the little strength that had returned to her flow out of her again. She fell back on the bed. The dingy room went swimming around her. Against the ugly walls she could see all in a whirl the silver doorknobs of Ardeith, the shining chandeliers, the marble mantels, the obsequious slaves, the columns behind the moss-hung oaks, and the triumphant faces of those patricians who in the moment of ordering a war to protect their luxury ordered also that they should not be required to wage it.

Mrs. Upjohn sprang up. "Lord have mercy, Mr. Officer, I do believe the poor child's fainted again! Will you help me tend to her?"

"Sure ma'am, sure. She tried to talk too much, I reckon. Shameful it is, them treating a girl so."

Corrie May began to mumble deliriously. Her mother had no time for awhile to pay attention to what she was saying. The policeman had to go back to his beat, and Mrs. Upjohn called in a neighbor woman to help her. Corrie May was feverish all night. She tossed and kept trying to talk. Now and then Mrs. Upjohn bent over her, hoping she was beginning to make some sense, but Corrie May kept beating on the bed and saying bad words, which her mother of course forgave her since she was clean out of her head, but she couldn't understand why Corrie May should be saying such ugly things about the Larnes, those kind rich people who had given her work after her brothers died.

III

It was two weeks before Budge could come to inquire. By that time Corrie May was sitting up by the window, looking out into the alley. On the stoop Budge explained to Mrs. Upjohn that he had done his best to get there earlier, but they wouldn't let him leave the camp.

"They made us go back that night before I could find out what had become of her," he said, "and then they made us drill extra time every day for getting mixed up in a riot. I sho hope she'll understand how it is."

"Sho, she'll understand," Mrs. Upjohn assured him. "I'm glad you came to cheer her up, Budge. She's been mighty low in her mind since she came outen that fever."

"How's she getting on?" he asked anxiously.

"Oh, she's lots better. But she's low in her mind. She don't say much, just sits there by the window doing nothing. I tried to get her interested in her knitting again, thought making socks for the soldiers would get her mind off her troubles kind of, but she wouldn't have none of it. I'm glad you came."

"Can I go in now?" asked Budge.

"Sho, walk right in. It sho will cheer her up, seeing you looking so find in your uniform." Mrs. Upjohn opened the door. "Corrie May you's got company."

Budge came in, his hat in his hand. "How you do, Corrie May?" he inquired heartily.

Corrie May sat by the window, a shawl over her knees. There was a patch on her forehead and she was thinner than he recalled, but otherwise she looked fairly well. Budge thought her eyes looked enormously big, but that was evidently because of the heavy black circles still under them.

"Lawsy," he said, "it was a shame what they did to you!"

"I'm mighty glad to see you," said Corrie May. "Sit down."

Budge took a chair, and began to explain why he hadn't been to see her before. "I tried to get you away from them that night, but some fellow knocked me down. My head hit a brick. Kind of knocked me silly for a few minutes."

"It's all right," said Corrie May. "I ain't blaming you. I ain't blaming nobody."

Budge understood what her mother meant by saying Corrie May was low in her mind. She seemed to be talking without much interest, as if she had been struck so hard she was still insensitive. He had come prepared to sympathize with her, to be very tender and make it clear that while it was hardly right for her to say such things about the war he was not angry with her, even if he did wear his country's uniform. But now he thought he had better postpone all that, and he rummaged in his head for something funny to make her laugh.

"Now you just set and be comfortable, Budge," said Mrs. Upjohn, "while I take my mending out to the stoop. It's right pleasant in the sun there."

"Yes ma'am," said Budge. He turned back to Corrie May. "Say, you oughta seen a fellow got brought into camp the other day," he started. "Come from some place in the sticks out a ways from Baton Rouge, didn't even know there was a war going on till the conscription officers come by to get him. He sho was a one. I declare, never had been to a town in his life nor had on a pair of store shoes. He didn't look right bright to me, had a big wobbly head like a jack-o'-lantern on a stick—"

He observed that he was doing well, for she had perked up a little and looked attentive. "Go on," she said. "What'd they do with him?"

"Well, he was so funny. He asked what these Yankees was we was going to fight—thought they was some kind of animal out West some place." Budge laughed at the recollection. "He looked so cork-headed they was scared to trust him at first, and then they asked him if he'd ever toted a gun. And holy Moses, did he turn round at that. Toted one ever since he could walk, he said, could shoot anything that ever was in the woods, and will you believe it, they stuck up the ace of spades and asked him could he hit that, and he walked off so far you could hardly tell the ace from a fly-speck, and he put a hole right through the middle. So they told him well, he was in the army all right, and then they dressed him up—" Budge chuckled with glee. "Well, Corrie May, when he walked out

in a uniform and army shoes and all, that was the proudest
white man this side the Mississippi. You should have saw him
strut. You'd have thought the whole war was just a fashion
show for him to show off his new clothes. Only thing
worrying him was that his girl friend back home couldn't see
him all dressed up. So along about that time who should come
strolling in but a fellow with one of them daguerreotype
outfits, said for four bits he'd take anybody's picture so he
could send it to the folks back home. This here fellow ain't
never heard tell of no daguerreotype. At first he wouldn't
come near it, thought the whole outfit was gonta explode on
him or something, but the fellows told him to come on, it
wouldn't bite. So when I left last thing I seed was him sitting
up there to have his picture took, proud as a king but still
kind of scared, holding that gun of his'n ready to shoot the
fellow if the box started doing any monkeyshines."

Corrie May started to laugh, and Budge thought he must be
cheering her up something fine, but all of a sudden her
laughter choked in her throat and turned into little smothery
sobs. Budge sprang up and bent over her.

"Corrie May, sugar, what's ailing you? Is you mad with me
or something?"

She shook her head.

Budge kissed her. "Honey child, sho 'nough tell me what's
the trouble. You know I'll do anything in the world for you,
Corrie May."

She looked up, tears still on her lashes. "Budge, you can't
do nothing. Can't nobody do nothing. They go get that po'
fellow that ain't never even heard of Yankees and send him
out to get shot! They get you off your piece of ground—"

"Well sho, honey," he answered dubiously, "but it's a war.
Like you said that time out at my house."

Corrie May sat forward, her eyes on him so intently it
almost frightened him. "Budge, sit down. I want to talk to
you."

"Yes, honey." He pulled his chair close to hers.

"I been wanting to talk to you ever since that night I got
beat up," said Corrie May. "But that night I tried to talk to
everybody at once. That was wrong. I reckon I ain't so much
of a talker, or they'd have understood what I meant." She was
not crying any more. She was talking very steadily as if this

was something she had been saving up to say. "Budge," she went on, "you said you'd do anything in the world for me. Will you?"

"Why of course, honey. Don't you know how much I love you?"

Corrie May put her hand over his. "Will you get outen that uniform and come off with me some place where they ain't heard of this war?"

Budge started. He stared at her unbelieving. "You mean— desert?"

"That's just what I do mean," said Corrie May.

Budge's jaw had dropped. "Honey girl, you don't know what you's talking about."

"Yes I do. I been thinking about it every minute since I got hurt. There ain't no hope in this country for folks like you and me. I'm getting out. I'm going across the river. Out West. Out where there ain't no rich people owning everything and treating poor folks like cockroaches. I'm going. If you'll come with me we can get married soon's we can find a preacher. If you won't come with me I'm going by myself."

Budge was dumfounded. He opened his mouth and shut it again. Finally he said, "You's wanting me to be a traitor!"

"Traitor to what?" she cried scornfully. "To a lot of rich people that send the band out to play 'Dixie' and get you so choked up in your throat you ain't got sense enough to think what you's fighting about. That's all." She flung the shawl off her knees and stood up. "Budge, in the name of the good Lord God, do you know what you's fighting for?"

Budge sprang up to face her. "Sure I know. I'm fighting for my country. And if you think I'm a coward that's gonta run away now I'm in the army—"

"Oh, squashes!" said Corrie May. "The Larnes' country and the Sheramys' country and the Purcells' and St. Clairs' and Durhams'. Your country! You make me laugh. But it ain't your fault. Ain't nobody ever told you."

"I ain't gonta listen to you," said Budge sternly.

"Oh yes you is." She came close and caught his arms. "Budge, they told you they wanted you to save the country from the Yankees. But do you know what the Yankees want to do? They want to come set all the slaves free. So men like you could make more money because there wouldn't be any niggers working for nothing."

Budge scowled. "They want to turn loose the niggers? Who told you that?"

"They told me out at Ardeith. Since when is it your business to fight so they can keep their niggers?"

"Well, well, well," said Budge. He sat down. He stroked his chin. "Still, though, I don't know as the niggers ought to be free. They'd get awful uppity if they was working for money like white folks."

"They couldn't be no more uppity," said Corrie May with slow conviction, "than them niggers at Ardeith is this very minute. I know, Budge. They won't even say good morning to me when I pass them, they're so stuck up. But I want to tell you something else, Budge. Maybe those folks is got a right to keep their niggers that they bought and paid for. But they made a law saying a man that owned niggers didn't have to fight for them unless he wanted to. Mr. Denis Larne joined the army of his own free will and accord. But they came and got you, because you was a po' man that didn't own no niggers."

Budge scowled, impressed but still hardly believing. "Corrie May, how come you say that?"

"Because it's a law. A policeman told me, and who'd know the law if it wasn't a policeman? If you'd been rich enough to own twenty niggers them conscription officers couldn't have made you join the army."

Budge got up. He walked to the end of the room and back. He said, "Corrie May, that's the meanest damn thing I ever heard of."

"Ain't it?" she asked him intently.

"And think," said Budge slowly, "the way I worked. The way I nearabout broke my back planting that cotton." He was quiet a moment. "You mean if I'd had niggers and just took my ease on the gallery drinking juleps they'd have let me alone?"

"Yes," said Corrie May.

Budge kicked at the leg of a chair so roughly that he knocked over the chair and scuffed his bright new shoe. Bending, he righted the chair and sat down in it, leaning forward with his elbows on his knees, and looking at the floor.

Corrie May sat down too. She waited. Her outburst had tired her, for she was still more weak than she had realized. After a long silence Budge asked,

"What you aim to do about your Ma if you run off?" He was still not looking at her.

"Pa gets his army pay," said Corrie May. "He's been sending her half of it."

There was another silence. A group of tattered children ran down the alley, chasing a cat. Their voices sounded loud. Budge got up abruptly.

"It ain't fair," he said to the wall. "Taking me off my piece of ground because I ain't rich." He turned around on his heel. "Where you figure to go?"

"I don't know of no places," said Corrie May. "But we could go up the levee till we came to a ferry landing and get over to the west side of the river. Ain't nobody over there ever seed you. They wouldn't know you was ever in the army. Then we could keep going."

"I wish I could read," said Budge. "I'd get a map."

"Map or no map," said Corrie May, "any place is better than this." She went up to him. "Budge, do you mean you got your mind made up to come with me?"

He started. "I ain't got my mind made up to nothing. It's a terrible thing, deserting the army in war-time." He doubled his fists. "But it ain't the same as if they had done me right. If they'd given me the same chance to go or stay they'd give a rich man."

"Well, they didn't," said Corrie May. "And I guess you notice there ain't no rich people sending their niggers out to get shot, neither. Niggers costs a lot of money. You don't cost but thirteen dollars a month."

"Look here," said Budge, "I got to be going. I ain't got but a little while off."

She smiled derisively. "You sho is scared not to mind them, ain't you?"

"Oh Corrie May, shut up. You don't know what you's asking me. Its a dreadful thing to do. I got to go."

"You'll be coming back to see me?"

"Sho, honey. Soon as they'll let me."

"It better be soon," Corrie May warned him quietly. "I

ain't staying here one day after I feel natural in my legs again."

"Oh, quit talking like that," said Budge. "I got to be going."

"Goodby," said Corrie May.

He put his arms around her so tight she winced, for she was still more battered than he knew. She buried her face against him. "Budge, please come away. I'm so crazy about you. I can't stand to think of them doing you like that."

Budge kissed her. He released her suddenly and rushed away without saying goodby.

IV

For another ten days she did not see or hear of him. One afternoon while she was mending a torn jacket the door burst open without a preliminary knock. She looked around, expecting to see her mother, who had gone visiting a neighbor, but sprang up in welcome when she recognized Budge.

Budge did not respond to her greeting. He stood stiffly, his hand on the closed door behind him, looking around the kitchen with eyes that were grim and apprehensive.

"Where's you Ma?" he asked.

"Gone to see Mrs. Gambrell. They been having a hard time ever since Mr. Gambrell died in the cypress swamp. Come sit down, Budge, I'll make you some coffee."

"I don't want no coffee." His eyes went over the room again, as though fearful of what they might see in the corners. His hand gripped her. He dropped his voice. "Corrie May, I'm leaving."

She jumped. "Budge! You mean it?"

"Yes. I been finding out things. It's true what you said. I see them bring the men into camp every day, po' fools like me, drug out to fight when they don't no more know what it's about than I did. It ain't human. I'm gonta break for the West tonight."

Corrie May's heart began to pound. "I'll go with you."

"It's an awful thing, what we're doing," said Budge.

"It ain't awful. I'm so proud you had the nerve."

"Are you, sho 'nough?" he asked wistfully.

"You're mighty right I am." She put her arms around him and kissed him. Budge held her tenderly.

"Corrie May, you got lots of spunk. It ain't gonta be easy."

"Since when do you think I been used to having things easy?" She slipped out of his arms and pulled up a chair. "Now sit down and tell me what you aim to do. How'd you get out?"

"I got permission to come see you. I'm supposed to be back by six."

He sat down. Their heads close together, they made plans. Budge told her he would hide in the gin-house behind the warehouses till after dark, when she would meet him and they would go up the levee until they came to the first ferry-landing, where they would cross the river. Neither of them had ever been on the west bank of the river, and once there they would be unrecognized. Corrie May promised to bring Budge her father's long black preaching-coat. The trousers would be harder, she thought, till she remembered an old pair of overalls that had belonged to Lemmy. They were badly torn, but he could wear his uniform pants under them. It would be a shame to throw away such a good pair of pants.

She was astonished at his grim determination. Now that his mind was made up, he was more firmly resolved than she was, and less apprehensive of possible dangers. Budge, she decided as she talked to him, had a head that could hold but one idea at a time, and she was grateful now for his simplicity. She promised to bring a package of food and her money-box when she came to the gin-house.

When Budge got up to go he put his arms around her yearningly, as though he hated the prospect of being separated from her for even so brief a time.

"Corrie May, honeybunch, you ain't scared?"

She shook her head.

"'Fo' God," said Budge, "you got more sand than any girl I ever did see, or any man either, I reckon. Oh I declare, Corrie May, when we gets West I'll pray the good Lord every night to let me make things easy for you like you deserve to have 'em. Rugs on the floor and shawls warm enough in the winter time and a good big stove that don't smoke."

"I'll love them things, but I'll love you anyway no matter how we get on." She pushed back a lock of hair that had fallen across his forehead. "You go on now. I'll be at the gin-house right after dark."

"And by morning we'll be across the river." He smiled proudly and kissed her goodby.

Left alone, Corrie May found her heart thumping and her knees unsteady. Her imagination, more flexible than his, began to present all sorts of frightening pictures—deserts, hunger, Indians. She had no idea how far one would have to go before reaching the West, and she found it hard to visualize a landscape with neither trees nor a river. But they'd get there, she promised herself. They need not go as far as the desert. The West had farms and villages. Other people got along there, so why not herself and Budge?

She wrapped the overalls and her father's preaching-coat in a paper, and made up another bundle of bread, cheese and side-meat. That done, she sat down and waited. Her thoughts went guiltily to her mother. It was going to be bad to leave her mother, who had no more children now. Somehow she must contrive to let Ma know she was all right. Yet there was nobody she dared take into her confidence, and she could not think how otherwise to leave a message. If she only knew how to write! Her father had taught her to recognize capital letters, but she had had little experience in combining them except to make her own name. And there was nothing in the cabin to write with even if she had known how.

But at last she decided to try it. She spread out a piece of wrapping paper and burnt the end of a sharp stick in the stove. Down on her knees she started to print, slowly and with effort. Before she was done she had to re-blacken the stick several times, and she was afraid her mother would come in any minute. However, she was not interrupted and at the end of half an hour she was through.

MA I WEL BEE ARIT DON WOREY
CORRIE MAY

Her mother could not read, but somebody could be found hereabouts to read it for her. She hid the note in her bed, and put the packages between the bed and the wall.

Getting through supper was dreadful. Corrie May kept telling herself she ought to eat a lot so as to have plenty of strength, but she couldn't make herself feel hungry.

Mrs. Upjohn fell to recounting a long story about Mrs.

Gambrell's troubles with her oldest daughter, who was always slipping off to the camp, where everybody knew a girl wouldn't be going if she was up to any good in this world. Corrie May twisted her ankles around the legs of her chair and sat stiffly. At least she wouldn't be disgracing her Ma. She would be married. Soon as they got to a town where there was a preacher she would get married, and she wouldn't let Budge touch her till then.

After supper Mrs. Upjohn had to patch an apron. Then she had to cover up the coals in the stove so she could start the breakfast fire without wasting a match. Corrie May could have screamed with nervous impatience. But after what seemed like endless delays her mother went to bed. Corrie May pretended to go to bed too. She lay stiff, feeling perspiration creep from her armpits down her sides. At last she made sure her mother was snoring.

She got up and set her letter on the stove where Mrs. Upjohn would see it first thing in the morning, and taking her bundles she crept out. At the door she paused and looked back through the dark to the vague lump of her mother's body on the bed. She wondered if she would ever see Ma again. But she must not think of that. She had to set all her mind on getting Budge safely out of town.

The alleys were dark and nobody paid much attention to her. One or two men jogged her elbow or spoke to her, but she brushed them aside and hurried on to the gin-house.

The gin-house was a black mass behind the warehouses. Moving uncertainly among the sheds, Corrie May looked for Budge. It was so black she had to walk blindly, holding her foot out in front of her before she took each step to feel for a possible box or wheelbarrow in her way. The silence pressed on her like a weight. Then suddenly she heard a movement on the platform. She halted. It might be a rat, or a pile of sacks settling down. She spoke faintly. "Budge?"

"Sh!" he said instantly.

Dimly she made him out, flat on his stomach, creeping toward her on his elbows. He whispered, "Here I am. You all right?"

"Sho," she whispered back. She knelt down by him. "Here's the coat and overalls. Put them on."

Budge kissed her wrist as she laid the package by him.

Corrie May went to the edge of the platform to keep watch.
But there was nothing around her but silence and the dark.
Budge came to her. "Ready," he said in an undertone.

They climbed down off the platform and walked around
the building. Budge whispered to her that they'd better take the
back alleys and avoid the wharfs, and not walk along the
levee until the town was behind them. Except for that they
went ahead silently. Already at the start they were compre-
hending the seriousness of their undertaking, and too
weighted by the knowledge to want to talk.

They walked around the park, and took the back ways
behind the residential streets. The roads were rough and more
than once Corrie May stumbled against loose clods of earth.
Budge helped her up gently. Few people passed them, and
those gave them scant attention. It was hard walking. Once
they stopped to shake the earth out of their shoes. Corrie May
ventured,

"We's past town now. And we'll make better time if we go
by the river road."

"Right," said Budge. "I wonder what time it's getting to
be."

"Nigh onto midnight, I'd say," she returned.

"Tired?"

"No," she said, though her knees were beginning to have
little aches in them.

He took her hand and they crossed a field to the smooth
oak-lined curve of the river road. As they plodded along
Corrie May was surprised to see how much traffic there was
on the river road even this time of night. Young gentlemen
passed on horseback, sometimes singing hilariously on their
way. Now and then a carriage came along, bearing a group
from a theater or a party. She was surprised too at how the
inhabitants of these fine houses sat up of nights. Half the
windows were still lighted, with senseless waste of candles,
just as though there wouldn't be plenty of light in the morning
for whatever they wanted to do. She heard another clatter of
hoofs and Budge caught her and drew her against a tree.
Down the road came five or six carriages together, evidently
bringing a lot of guests from some party. The horses were
trotting at a leisurely pace as though the passengers didn't
care whether they got home before sunup, and the ladies and

gentlemen called from the carriage windows to one another, laughing merrily. The voices were louder than necessary; they sounded half tipsy. Several of the young gentlemen waving from the windows had on army uniforms. The ladies had bare arms and bosoms, and flowers in their hair. Corrie May stared as the gorgeous cavalcade swept past, and trembled lest one of these officers see and recognize Budge. But they were too merry to notice anybody but themselves. As the last carriage went by the young soldier on the back seat pulled the lady by him into his arms and kissed her.

"Huh," said Budge, "they sure are enjoying the war."

"Well, it's their war," said Corrie May. "Let 'em have it."

They started trudging through the mist of dust the carriages had raised.

"I reckon we could get over to the levee now," Budge said presently. "We done got past where the steamboats are moored. And there's too much passing on the road to suit me."

"All right," Corrie May agreed.

They started toward the river, going by a path that led around the gardens of one of the big houses. It seemed a long way from the road to the levee, longer than Corrie May had realized. The river road got its name because it followed the river's turnings, and out where the plantations were you could look across the flat fields and see the levee. She was tired. The thought of all the miles she had to go before Budge would be safe made her tireder still. She tried not to think about them. At the foot of the levee she paused and looked up at the grassy slope, black against the stars. It had never looked so high before.

"You tired, sugar?" Budge asked anxiously.

"Not a bit," said Corrie May. She laughed. "You must think I'm a fine lady that can't hardly put her foot to the ground."

"You was breathing kind of heavy," said Budge. "And we been going a long time."

"Not long enough," she insisted. "Come on. Do we walk on top of the levee?"

Budge looked up at the lofty earthen rampart that held the river back from the fields. "No, it's easier walking up there, but if there was anybody in the field they would see us too plain. Let's stay here where it's black dark."

Corrie May leaned against a tree growing at the foot of the levee. "What's that bundle you got under your coat?" she inquired.

"My gray army coat and hat," said Budge.

"What you aim to do with them?"

"Throw 'em in the river. You wait." Budge climbed the grassy slope of the levee and crossed its broad top. She heard him scrambling down the slope on the river side, and a moment later she heard a faint splash as he flung his bundle into the water. He clambered over the levee again and rejoined her. "There now," he said with finality. "I hope that's the last I ever see of the Confederate army."

They started walking along the little strip of grass between the levee and the plowed fields. They were plodding northwards. At their right side the fields stretched away from them, dark and flat; at their left stood the levee, fifteen feet high, and behind it the river swept silently toward the Gulf. Corrie May thought yearningly of the west bank. Over there Budge would be so much safer. But it was foolish even to wish they could swim across. The river here was a mile wide, with a current so powerful it was a rare athlete who could make the crossing. She had never until tonight thought much about how vast the Mississippi was.

She was so tired! Budge was trudging doggedly beside her, and she wondered if his legs felt as heavy as hers. Her shoes were thick with soft earth. They were light gaiters Ann had given her because she had carelessly bought them too big, and though they were well made and of good leather, they had never been meant for such walking as this. She envied Budge his stout army shoes, built for long marches.

"There's a shed up here a piece, on the Ardeith land," she told him, "where they pile up the cane sometimes. If we can get to it by daylight maybe we can sleep there awhile. You shouldn't try journeying in the daytime."

"I'd feel safer if we was across the river," Budge answered. "Seems to me there's a ferry landing somewhere hereabouts. Only I don't know if the ferry runs at night."

If she got on a ferry-boat long enough to sit down, Corrie May thought, she'd go directly to sleep. She concentrated all her mind upon the work of putting one foot in front of the other.

Budge gripped her arm. "What's that?"

They halted. From further along the levee they heard men's voices.

"Just some niggers, I reckon," she whispered.

"Them ain't nigger voices," he whispered back. "It's white folks."

Corrie May listened, then laughed under her breath. "Why Budge, we's a pair of 'fraid cats. It must be that ferry landing you was talking about."

As she finished a man in the darkness cried, "Halt!"

They stiffened with terror. Some yards in front, horses' hoofs were padding in the grassy strip at the foot of the levee. In the darkness Corrie May could just see the outlines of three or four horsemen riding toward them. The starlight sent a pale streak along the barrel of a gun.

"What you doing out here this time of night?" called one of the men.

Corrie May whispered quickly, "You let me answer," and aloud she called back, "We's just walking, mister."

"Oh Lord, sergeant, one of them's a girl." There was low amused laughter. "What's that, sergeant? Yes sir, all right." He raised his voice again. "Sorry to interrupt you, sister. But we got to have a look at you and your young man." He flung himself off his horse. "What are you all up to anyway?"

There was another laugh from his companions. One of them asked, "Didn't your mother ever tell you the facts of life?"

"Oh, shut up. Give me that lantern." A match flared. "I hate this worse than you do, young folks, but it's orders. Patrol the levee and stop anybody prowling around." He walked toward them.

Corrie May's blood nearly congealed. As one of the men lit a lantern she saw that all the group wore Confederate uniforms. Wildly she thought what a hideous color gray was, and that never in her life would she ever wear a gray dress. She was trembling. But Budge was standing straight, and his arm around her was steady.

The soldier came up to them, and she saw thankfully that his face bore a good-natured grin. "Sorry," he said, "but you all got business to stay home nights, you know. What you got in that bundle?"

"Things to eat," said Budge stoutly.

"Let's see."

Budge took his arm from around Corrie May and opened the package.

"I see," said the soldier. "Where you going you need to carry your breakfast?"

"Up the river," said Budge. "To—to Baton Rouge."

"Hum." He raised the lantern to shine on their faces. "What's your name?"

"John. John Smith."

"Where you live?"

"Dalroy."

"What you do for a living?"

"Work on the wharfs."

"What you going to do in Baton Rouge?"

"Got a chance at a better job."

"But how come you got to start there in the middle of the night?"

Corrie May leaped into the breach. "It's on account of me, sir. We wants to get married. And my folks don't want me to marry him. So we had to run off."

"Oh, I see. Well, all right." He lowered his lantern. "Get along." Then he stopped abruptly. "Hel—lo!"

He was staring down toward the ground. As they started to pass him he grabbed Budge's arm. "Wait a minute, Mr. John Smith. Where'd you get those shoes?"

Budge swallowed. "Er—I bought 'em off a fellow was in the army."

"You did? What'd you pay for 'em?"

"A dollar and a half."

"Huh. Who was he?"

"Fellow named—" Budge's imagination was faltering. "Fellow named Budge Foster. Fifteenth Louisiana."

"What business he got selling his army shoes to you?"

"Uh—I don't know, mister. He just said would I buy 'em."

"So you bought 'em, did you? Well, suppose you just wait a minute, John Smith. Maybe you're lying and maybe you're not. But we'd better see."

Budge took a step as though about to run. But the soldier's gun was against his ribs. He was being shoved ahead toward the other horsemen. Corrie May cried out and ran after him.

The sergeant, still on horseback, was saying, "You might as well look him over. You never can tell."

They had a gun on Budge and had made him hold his hands above his head. The soldier took something from the pocket of the preacher-coat.

"What's that?" asked the sergeant.

"A Bible, sir."

"Oh. Well, give it back to him."

The soldier reached into the pockets of the pants under the overalls. Corrie May could have shouted with relief that he did not attempt to examine the pants themselves. He appeared, in fact, bored by the whole performance.

"And what's this?" he was inquiring. "A love-letter?"

He whisked the paper out of the pocket and glanced at it by the light of the lantern. His bored chuckle changed to a gasp of horror.

"Holy angels! You—filthy—rat! And you toting a Bible, too!" He wheeled around. "Keep that gun on him. Take a look at this, sergeant. Identification papers." He faced Budge again. "So, Private Foster, you thought you'd change your coat and head North, did you?"

Corrie May felt her legs crumpling under her. She did not know what Budge said or did. She went down against the levee side and with her face against the grass she began to scream. She didn't mean to scream. It just happened. She was so exhausted and so utterly conquered. In the midst of her despair she found herself thinking how dreadful it was not to know how to read, for if Budge had known what was on that paper he could have thrown it into the river along with his gray coat and hat.

She felt one of the soldiers giving her a shove with his foot.

"Get up, sister. And quit that damn yelling or I'll tie your face up. Do I bring her along, sergeant?"

"Sure. Helping a deserter escape? Sure."

He picked her up roughly by one arm.

Budge was fighting like a madman. He kicked and clawed and bit. But it was no use. One of the soldiers knocked him on the head with the butt of his gun and Budge collapsed on the ground. Corrie May cried out again, and breaking from the soldier she rushed to Budge. But the soldier dragged her away.

"Come on. He's not dead."

They threw Budge across a horse. He hung limply. They put her on another horse, with one of the soldiers holding her there. She had never been on a horse before. She slipped and slid and would have fallen off but for his support. Her legs ached, and pains began to shoot from her knees into her thighs. It seemed ages before they got to town.

They rode by the calaboose. The soldier got off from behind her and she fell on the ground like a sack of meal. Day was breaking around her. After awhile the soldier came back with the jailer and they dragged her up and made her walk inside. They pushed her into a cell. She fell on the floor and lay there. When she turned over a ray of sun was poking between the bars of the little window high over her head. She did not know whether she had fainted or had been asleep.

The days passed curiously. She did not know how many of them there were. Two policemen came and got her and took her into a courtroom where there were a lot of people and a judge sitting in a high seat. They said she had been helping a deserter. They seemed to be doing a lot of talking. She did not understand any of it very well. They took her back to the cell again. Sometimes her mother came to see her. Her mother always cried when she came. Corrie May did not pay much attention. It was as though she were half asleep all the time. But finally she did rouse herself enough to ask what had happened to Budge.

Her mother began to cry again. She said they had stood Budge up against a wall and shot him. The penalty for desertion was death.

Chapter Eight

I

ANN wondered mildly what had become of Corrie May. Her first assumption was that she might be sick, and it occurred to her that she ought to send and inquire, but though Corrie May had said she lived in Rattletrap Square that part of town might have been in China for all Ann knew about it. There was something in the paper about a private named Foster being executed for attempted desertion, but as Ann had never heard of him she did not think of connecting this with Corrie May's disappearance. She concluded that Corrie May must either have married somebody or found a job at better wages, and though she did not care she did think it ungrateful of the girl not to have given notice. In a few weeks Ann had virtually forgotten about her.

Her mind was occupied with other matters. Denis was at Vicksburg and Colonel Sheramy at Port Hudson, and though the river forts seemed impregnable she was frightened for both of them. The first shining excitement of the war had passed, and it had become terrifying. Everybody said those soldiers at New Orleans might be expected to storm back up the river any day, and for awhile Ann went to bed every night trembling with the fear of being wakened by guns. But the time passed and passed, and they did not come. Yet though nearly everywhere she heard of magnificent Southern victories, the war dragged on and on.

The newspapers contained nothing but accounts of battles and lists of dead. Ann felt revolted before such a mountain of death. The war ceased to be glorious; it became ghastly, it became sickening. The papers did not describe it, but one could not help hearing things. At Shiloh the first day of the battle the ditches ran with blood like water, and by the second

145

day it had clotted so thick the horses bogged in it. At Corinth there was a fence, and wounded men stumbled over it and hung there, their intestines dangling out of their bellies, and stayed hanging there screaming until they died. That was war. That was this golden adventure in which you threw roses at brave heroes marching off to fight for your country. Sometimes Ann sat for hours at the foot of the spiral staircase looking up at the portrait of Denis in his gray uniform, which she had insisted on his having painted before he went away. She looked at it, twisting her hands together till the fingers hurt. She stopped praying, "Please Lord, let them hold the river forts." She simply prayed now, a dozen times a day, "Keep him alive! Oh, God in heaven, don't let those things happen to *him!*"

Still it went on. The war lasted nearly two years before Denis even got a furlough. Ann waited for him tremulous with hope. She had not discovered until Denis went away how much she loved him and how childish their marriage had been. The war had made her feel lost and helpless. It had shown her an aspect of reality for which she had no preparation, and she longed to turn to him for a defense against it. And now Denis was coming home. He would make her understand the reason for all this, and when they had understood it together they would be married as they had never been before.

But when Denis came home, lean and grim, she found that he would discuss any subject on earth but the war. To her amazement she realized that Denis did not know she had heard those accounts. He thought she still saw the war as a march of drums and roses. Or if he did not quite believe this he wanted to believe it. He had been at Vicksburg, and Vicksburg was a blazing cauldron of blood and hell. While he was free of it he wanted to be aware only of Ardeith with its gracious halls and dreamy gardens, and of her, gay and delicate and perfumed, a lovely lady who would make him forget the war. He kept following her around as though the sight of her refreshed him; he would pass his hands over her arms and shoulders, feeling the soft texture of her skin and murmuring in a voice that was almost awestruck, "Ann, you're so *clean!*" He never mentioned what he had seen or how it had scarred him.

Very well, then, she would not ask him any questions nor tell him anything that would make him know she too had shuddered at it. She did not even tell him about the minor hardships of home—how soap was a dollar a bar and tooth-brushes two dollars apiece; how you had to go to shop after shop for the simplest necessities, hoping frantically they had managed to get something through the blockade; how careful you had to be with little things like needles and buttons, for once lost they could not be replaced. But she felt bitterly cheated. She had wanted so much from him. Now she could not ask for it. But she kept silent. There was not much she could give him to make the war more endurable, but at least she could keep the illusion of beauty and charm he wanted. As a last gesture she gave a ball, the night before Denis went back to Vicksburg.

In preparation for the ball Ann worked harder than she had ever worked in her life. This was to be as if nothing had happened, her last pretense that the war was the gallant adventure both she and Denis had thought it was going to be.

She spent money madly, buying wheat flour, coffee, vanilla, ginger, chocolate, rare luxuries that cost enormous sums in her yellow Confederate notes. She pled with the shopkeepers and cajoled them and flirted with them to make them open their priceless goods that were there only for the army. If Denis had had any idea how she was getting these things, she thought sometimes, he would have stopped her in dismay. But he did not know. He was still largely ignorant of the state of affairs at home. He must not be allowed to guess that the head of the commissary absolutely refused to part with one of his barrels of wheat flour, telling her they were to be sent to the hospitals, until she laid on the counter the diamond bracelet Denis had brought her in remorse after their first quarrel. She laughed as she rushed about with her preparations and he laughed too. He kept telling her she was so pretty, everything she said seemed so wonderfully clever, and he adored her. He protested he had never seen her so busy in preparation for a party—couldn't Bertha and Napoleon attend to it? But never, Ann insisted; this had to be very special because he was going away again, and besides she had got used to attending to things herself since Mrs. Maitland left, and she scampered off

again to search for the priceless delicacies that would assure
Denis she knew nothing about the war.

Only once her resolute merriment gave way, when Mrs.
Larne voiced disapproval of her wild extravagance, and Ann
exclaimed coldly, "I've thought of a new simile. As mean as a
person who's stingy with Confederate money." But this was
not in Denis' hearing. And she did not tell Mrs. Larne that
she had not only bribed the commissioner with her bracelet,
but in order to get the money she was spending she had
pawned a watch and some rings and breastpins for half their
value.

Some day Denis might ask her what had become of her
jewelry, but she crushed that possibility down into the general
confusion of her mind, though she knew she could crush it
down only because the confusion contained a stronger possibility, persistent in spite of her refusal to acknowledge its
presence, the thought that it did not matter because he would
not come back from Vicksburg to observe that so many of
her trinkets were gone. For the present, all she would let
herself think was that she had to have the usual refreshments
at the party supper because cornmeal cakes sweetened with
brown sugar would remind Denis of the war.

She had Bertha make her a new dress of sea-green velvet
obtained from a blockade runner at sixty Confederate dollars
a yard. To trim the bodice she ripped some of the lace from
her wedding dress. Mutilating her wedding dress gave her a
pang sharper than any the war had yet cost her. She had put
it away carefully in vetivert and tissue-paper, so that if she
ever had a daughter it could be her wedding dress too;
whatever the fashions then, this gown was so exquisite any
girl would love wearing it. She had begun to suspect that she
was going to have another child, and when she cut into the
lace it gave her a pain in her throat that made her want to
sob, for this child might be a girl and now she was cutting her
wedding dress away from her. It was the first time she had
ever realized how precious one's little secret dreams could be
and how painful it was to destroy them.

But she did not tell any of this to Denis, nor confess to him
that the lace on her ball-gown was not new. He had seen her
wear the dress only once, and then had been aware of her
only as a cloud of bridal loveliness without noticing the details

of her costume sufficiently to recognize the lace on the green velvet. She did not even tell him she had any reason to think baby Denis might be about to have a little sister. Why she was silent about this she was not even sure herself; she simply had an inarticulate feeling that he must have no cause to be concerned about her when he went back into battle. No matter what it cost, she must give him as her last and most desperately fashioned gift the picture of the pampered darling he wanted to remember.

So she went beautifully to her ball in her sea-green velvet trimmed with lace from her wedding gown and pinned at the bosom with the medallion that had baby Denis' daguerreotype on one side and a lock of his hair on the other; and never since the foundation of Ardeith was a more brilliant ball given there. Most of the gentlemen were in uniform, and there were several with empty sleeves or their arms in slings, and one or two who could not dance because they walked with crutches, for although they were not included in the conscription laws most of the men she knew had been drawn into the army by the same gallantry that had put Denis there. The ladies paid the wounded men particular attention, and pretended it was not awkward to polka with a man who had only one arm. Jerry was there in uniform too, for he had just joined the army and was going up to Vicksburg with Denis. He had been married to Sarah Purcell a month before. Ann was dancing with Sarah's brother Hugh, himself on furlough, when she suddenly noticed how magnificently all the ladies were dressed. Like her own, their gowns must have been unpatriotically procured from the blockade runners, for there was no other way to get such materials nowadays. There were men who talked angrily against the feminine passion for finery, which made it so profitable for the blockade runners to bring in silks and velvets that they did not bring the necessities of which the poor were in such dire need, and when she thought of this Ann smiled sardonically, half forgetting the music her feet were following. Did they really think it was mere love of display that made women go decked thus absurdly over the ruins? There had never in the history of the country been such mad gaiety as now. Ann knew this was true of the South, and she suspected it was true of the North as well. She had heard the phrase "laughing one's self to death," but it had never occurred to her that there were times when people actually did it.

"May I say, Miss Ann," said Hugh Purcell, "that I've never seen you more charming than you are tonight?"

"Thank you. I'm so glad your furlough lasted long enough for you to come."

"I'll be going back next week," said Hugh.

"Where?"

"Port Hudson."

"My father is at Port Hudson," said Ann.

"We need great soldiers like Colonel Sheramy at the river forts," he told her.

"But they're sure to hold, aren't they?" she asked. "There's no chance of the Yankees' getting past Port Hudson and Vicksburg?"

"Oh no," he returned with assurance. "We'll hold the river."

She thought, "And that's all you'll tell us. Maybe it's just as well you think we don't know any more than that."

But her own nerves were beginning to get taut, and she was glad when the dance with Hugh ended. She looked around for Jerry. He was always so honest; maybe she could talk to him about what she was thinking. She found him standing between the piano and a window, watching the ball with a look of ironic amusement. In his uniform he looked uglier than ever. That trim outfit seemed designed to emphasize strong regular features like Denis', but a badly-made man in Confederate gray simply looked grotesque.

"Are you having a good time?" she asked him.

"Delightful." The corners of his mouth were quivering with grim amusement. "You are a consummate hostess, my dear, the flower of Southern womanhood—"

"Please stop that!" she pled in a voice just above a whisper.

He lifted an eyebrow. "Then what do you want me to tell you?"

"Oh—something resembling the truth." She closed her hands tight around the ivory sticks of her fan. "I'm getting a little bit desperate, Jerry."

He gave her a slow smile and moved nearer the shadow of the window-curtain. The music covered their voices. "All right, you're being a very noble fool and you deserve a medal. I never saw Denis having a better time."

"Then—you do think it's right, don't you?—all this."

"Of course, honey."

"Jerry," she asked suddenly, "am I giving this party just for Denis? Or is it for me? Do you think I'd have been different if I hadn't married Denis?"

He looked up and down at her great velvet skirt, the lace on her bodice and the flowers in her hair. "I can't answer."

"Why not?"

"Why, because you would have married Denis. I mean, if it hadn't been Denis it would have been somebody else like him. I don't believe this nonsense about the impossibility of falling in love but once; a woman can fall in love a dozen times, but it's always with the same man."

Ann bit her lip. Her hands were around the fan so tightly that its sticks hurt her fingers. The waltz-music came to an end. She lifted her eyes to his.

"I'm afraid I can't reason that out. Or maybe I'm in no state to think very well. It's about midnight. Shall we start moving in toward supper?"

"Forgive me?" Jerry asked smiling.

"For what? Please let's go to supper."

Jerry stood aside for her to pass between him and the piano. "You're nervous as a witch," he whispered. "Be careful."

She became very busy again. In the supper-room she went about deftly, seeing to it that the older ladies had chairs, tactfully edging back those who had filled their plates so as to make room for the others, and managing to distribute the inadequate supply of gentlemen so that there should be no obviously neglected groups of girls. "This is what I was born for," she said to herself; "this is the only thing I can really do well. It's a crime to require anything else of me."

"May I bring you a plate, Miss Ann?" asked Hugh Purcell at her elbow.

She flashed her famous hostess-smile at him. "Thank you, but not yet. I can't stop that long."

"But you should take some refreshment. Here—a minute's pause anyway."

He took two glasses of champagne from the tray Napoleon was passing and held out one to her.

"The South, God bless her?" he suggested.

"The South, God bless her," Ann echoed obediently. She had a sudden feeling that none of this was real, or that if it was she was watching from a great distance and it had nothing to do with her. But the champagne had an invigorating effect and she was glad he had suggested it. Setting down the glass, she went off to corner one of the Alan Durhams and make him take care of the St. Clair girls, reflecting that the Durham family had very little imagination, the way they persisted in naming so many of their male members Alan. There was another Durham cousin sitting quietly in a corner by himself. He had one leg and a cane, a reminder of the defense of New Orleans. Ann glanced around for some nice girl to amuse him. She thought of Sarah, who was her favorite; but no, it would not do to give a mutilated man to a girl when her husband of a month was just before going up to Vicksburg. Cynthia Larne came up to her. "Are you looking for somebody, Ann?"

"Yes," Ann said, "I—" She hesitated, glancing down at Cynthia. Cynthia was nearly fourteen, a thin, wiry young girl with a pale face and a heavy cloud of black hair. She would never be pretty, but she had a quiet dependability about her that Ann had begun to admire. "Cynthia," she said in an undertone, "do you think you could help me out with that Mr. Durham who's lost a leg?"

"Why of course," Cynthia returned with cool assurance. "What shall I talk to him about?"

"Anything but the war."

Cynthia smiled a little. "I see. All right."

Ann took a breath of relief. The rooms were crowded, and the closeness was giving her a headache. Grimly she ordered her nerves to be quiet and went on about her work of being hostess. Now and then one of the gentlemen offered her a glass of champagne, and she was glad of it; she had no time to eat and was becoming aware of a jittery exhaustion that was growing harder and harder to fight. She gripped herself after she had taken champagne with Bertram St. Clair. She must be careful, for that stuff was insidious, and this was Denis' last party. No matter how she felt it would not do to let her famous charm give way now. She began again.

"Have you tried the jellied chicken, Mrs. St. Clair? Oh, but you must—my cook is very proud of it and I'm sure she'd run away to the Yankees if we left any behind us. Napoleon, will you fetch some of the chicken, and some wafers? How do you do, Dr. Purcell? Thank you, I'm feeling very well indeed, no need of your ministrations. I'm so glad you like the cakes—have you tried a piece of that fluffy chocolate one? It goes very well with coffee. Miss Valcour, may I present Lieutenant Chauncey? The lieutenant's from Virginia, down here doing something important and mysterious about the river defenses."

At last she got herself to one side and stood still, watching them—the flowers and lights, the billowing flounces and white shoulders, the shining epaulettes, the crutches and scars. "I wonder how many of them will be alive a year from now," she thought. "And I've got a child in the nursery upstairs and I'm sure I'm going to have another one. Imagine any woman's having the cruelty to bring children into a mess like this."

She saw Denis, his fine head and shoulders visible as the center of a group of flowered coiffures. He caught sight of her, and let a smile flicker in her direction. She lifted her hand and kissed her fingertips in a little secret gesture.

As her hand moved down she touched a flask on the sideboard. Almost automatically her fingers closed around it. Then all of a sudden Jerry was beside her.

"Stop that, Ann."

His voice was low, but so sharp and stern that she looked up at him in astonishment. "Stop what?"

"Getting drunk," said Jerry.

"Why—"

"Come in here," said Jerry tersely. He drew her through a nearby doorway into the back study. Ann stood staring up at him, surprised and resentful.

"Jerry, I'm not drunk! I've never been—"

"Look here," he said. "I know the signs. You've been pouring down champagne all evening. You were just about to start again. Stop it."

"I don't know what you're talking about!" Ann exclaimed. "I'm shaking all over as it is, trying to get through this—"

"Yes, I know." He was suddenly very gentle as he put his hands on her shoulders.

She sank down into a chair. "Jerry, I've been going through

fire and brimstone in my mind. If I don't do something I'll go to pieces."

"Do you think you're the only one?" he asked her almost fiercely. But as if afraid to voice his thoughts he added more quietly, "I'm not going to read you a lecture. I just wanted to warn you. And by the way . . ."

"Yes?"

"Er—be rather specially nice to Sarah, will you? She doesn't like my going."

"How can she? I don't see why you're going. You don't have to. I wish to heaven Denis had had sense enough to stay out of it. Maybe father was different—he'd been in the army already, and Mexico—but not you and Denis!" She was talking vehemently, finally turning loose what she had not said to Denis in these past weeks. "Why do you suppose they exempted men like you from conscription if it wasn't to save the sort of people who are really important to civilization— the sort who have culture and ideals—and—everything?"

"We won't be able to save ourselves forever," Jerry returned shortly. "Besides, it—gets you. I can't explain. Let's go back."

Ann got reluctantly to her feet.

It was after four in the morning when they said goodby to the last guests. Denis went to the door to see them out, and came back to meet her in the hall. He pulled her into his arms.

"Darling, it was a grand party!"

"It was fun, wasn't it?" Ann agreed.

"I never enjoyed anything more in my life. *Look* at this house!"

She glanced around at the gay disorder. "It doesn't matter. The girls can clear up tomorrow."

"Are you tired?"

"Practically dead," she returned laughing.

Denis did not know her hands were tight fists, buried on either side of her in the folds of her green velvet skirt.

"It takes a lot of doing, a party," she added.

"I know it does, sugar. You were a dear to have it. Come on then, let's go to bed."

"I'm so sleepy," she murmured.

"Let me carry you up. Put your arms tight around my neck."

"Can you?"

"Try me and see."

She laughed. Denis hoisted her up. "How do women walk with so many clothes!" he exclaimed as her skirts billowed around them both. He added, "You looked mighty pretty tonight." She held to him as he mounted the spiral staircase. At the head of the stairs he paused, and she turned and kised him, feeling his arms tighten adoringly around her as their lips met.

Afterward she thought she would always remember Denis like that, mounting the stairs with her in his arms for their last night together. She was glad he had gone from her in such splendid strength. For she would always have that memory of him, and she grasped it like a changeless refuge when Vicksburg had fallen and they learned that Denis had been killed during the siege.

II

It was not until July, after the fall of Vicksburg, that they learned of the death of Denis, for during the siege no word could be had from the garrison. To Ann the news came hardly as a shock. It was merely an intensifying of the pain of loneliness that had been growing upon her ever since he went away. It had been like living on an island, with no news from outside but the vaguest rumors; and now Denis was gone too. Denis to whom she had looked to stand between her and everything she did not want to face. She felt deserted and full of terror. She had one child and was shortly to give birth to another, and the thought of her children, defenseless but for herself in a world gone mad, frightened her to the limit of endurance. If there were only somebody she could talk to, she wished frantically, but she discovered to her surprise that there was nobody she knew well enough. She had never needed other people very much, and so she had never gone to the trouble of establishing intimate relationships.

Certainly not with Denis' mother. Not long after Denis left, the government had asked for the use of Frances' town house as a military headquarters and Ann had felt duty bound to

ask Frances and Cynthia back to Ardeith, but during the
months that she and Frances had occupied the same house
their acquaintanceship had never ripened. Now, watching the
courage with which Frances was facing the loss of her son
Ann admired and envied her, and wished with all her heart
for an offer of support in her own trembling weakness. At
night when she was alone she lay in bed with her hands
pressed over her eyes, thinking, "If she would only come *talk*
to me!" But Frances did not come, and Ann did not dare to
seek her. Frances went about with her face white as a bone,
so silent and stricken that Ann ached to go to her, but the
thought of being repulsed was more than she could bear, so
she could only emulate Frances' silence and lock herself in
her own room to shed her tears.

But she astonished herself by the decision with which she
acted. With Vicksburg fallen and the Federal fleet no longer
divided between two forts, she suspected it could not be long
before Port Hudson must go too, and then the army would
come swarming down the river unchecked. She got Cynthia to
help her, and working in the hours between midnight and
dawn for secrecy they buried the more important pieces of
silver in the gardens and set out nasturtiums and oleanders
above the treasure-troves. Other valuables they hid in the
vault, and one night they moved a set of portable wine-shelves
across the door leading down to the vault from the wine-
closet so it would look as if there were only another solid wall
at that side. The effort left Ann so exhausted that she crumpled
panting at the foot of the staircase and finally crawled up on
her hands and knees. Cynthia, who was doing the best she
could with a dogged obedience that roused in Ann more
admiration than in her present weariness she could express,
whispered scared protests.

"Ann, I don't know much about ladies in your condition,
but I'm sure this is bad for you. Couldn't we get somebody to
help us? We can trust Napoleon."

Ann shook her head. In her present state she was afraid to
trust any Negro. The fieldhands were drifting away from the
plantation, and though the house-servants had stayed on this
far, she was unsure whether that was from loyalty or from
their inbred contempt for joining the fieldhands in anything.

She hardly remembered getting into bed. As soon as she lay down, sleep dropped over her like a blanket.

She woke up toward the middle of the morning, so aching with weariness that it seemed too much of a task to ring and summon Mammy to bring the brew of burnt corn and sweet potatoes they had been drinking since the coffee gave out. She simply lay where she was, staring up at the darns in the mosquito bar. The squares of sun moved across the floor, and it was nearly noon when the door opened softly and Cynthia tiptoed in.

"Ann, are you awake?"

"Yes. What is it?" Ann raised herself on her elbow. Cynthia was carrying a tray. "Here's your breakfast. Sarah's come over from Silverwood to see you. She wanted to say she's had word about Jerry. He's all right."

"Oh." Ann shivered with thankfulness, for though Jerry's name had not been on the list of those killed at Vicksburg she had hoped and dreaded to get news of him.

Cynthia pushed back the mosquito bar. "Sarah and Mother came up to your sitting-room so you wouldn't have to go down the stairs. I told them you weren't feeling so well—I figured you wouldn't be after shoving things around all night. How do you feel, anyway?"

"Terrible."

"I thought you would." Cynthia set the tray on the bedside table. "Well, I reckon you'd better eat."

Ann surveyed the tray, where there were hot cornbread and butter and preserves, and a cup. She lifted the cup. "Why—Cynthia!"

"Chocolate," Cynthia told her proudly.

"Where on earth did you get it?"

"I found a little bit in the back of the kitchen safe. Left over from that party you—I mean, I thought it might be good for you."

Ann drank it hungrily. "Cynthia," she said, "I like you."

"Do you? Thanks."

"No, I mean I like you because you're so different from most people. You don't go around giving me a lot of worthless sympathy. You manage to be practical about it."

"I can't make pretty phrases," Cynthia retorted. "Mother

always said I had less tact than any other young lady she ever saw. Do you feel like getting up now?"

"Yes, I feel a lot better. Where's Mammy?"

"Out in back washing the baby's clothes. Can't you get dressed without her?"

"I'm not even going to try. I'm too tired." Slipping out of bed Ann went to the bureau. She gave her hair a stroke or two with the brush and put on a dressing-gown Cynthia brought from the armoire. One of its seams, she noticed, was beginning to tear out. She must have it mended. Then she thought fiercely that she would mend it herself; at school in Paris they had taught her to do exquisite embroidery, and anybody who could embroider could sew up a seam. She opened the door and went with Cynthia into the sitting-room.

Sarah was there with Mrs. Larne. Cynthia sat down on the floor, her arms around her knees, watching a ray of sunshine play on Sarah's torch-like hair. Sarah was very white. She had the delicate skin characteristic of red-haired women, and with her present pallor it looked waxen, like a magnolia petal. As she talked she sat with her hands laced tight in her lap as though afraid if she loosened her fingers they would quiver. They talked about Vicksburg. Ann said very little. Sometimes these days she felt if anybody said anything more about the horrors of Vicksburg she was going to turn into a screaming maniac. Maybe that would be easier than keeping sane. Sarah said Jerry had survived the siege; she had received his letter only this morning.

"He's in prison somewhere?" Ann asked at length.

"Why no," said Sarah. She spoke with her mouth tight, not looking directly at any of the other three. "I thought I had told you. He's in a hospital in Natchez."

"Oh," Ann said thinly. "Starvation."

Sarah nodded. She looked out of the window. "They got— you know—scurvy, and things like that."

There was a silence. Ann could not look at Mrs. Larne. "Jerry," she thought, "Denis, starvation, scurvy. I hope whoever started this war roasts in hell forever." She looked out of the window at the lawn where a gardenia bush was blooming above the silver coffee-service that had been one of Frances' wedding presents.

"I'm glad," Cynthia said slowly, "we didn't know how hideous Vicksburg was till it was over."

"Sometimes I think," said Sarah, "the men who got killed, like Denis, were more fortunate than the ones who lived through it."

"They ate rats," said Cynthia.

"They ate all the dogs and horses," said Sarah. "They dug up a mule that was dead and buried and ate that."

"They starved for months," said Cynthia. "They got down to a biscuit and a piece of bacon a day before they started eating the horses."

"When the garrison surrendered," said Sarah, "some of the men couldn't keep in line. They fainted when they tried to march out."

"Will you two girls leave the room?" said Mrs. Larne.

Sarah and Cynthia gasped. She had been so silent they had forgotten she was with them.

But Ann had left already. As Frances sprang up Ann had rushed into her bedroom, slamming the door behind her. Frances stood looking at the shocked faces of the other two.

"My darlings," she cried, "haven't you any pity?"

"Oh Lord," said Cynthia, "I reckon I never will get any sense."

"But I thought she knew," cried Sarah. "I thought everybody knew now."

"I suppose we all knew," said Frances. "But do you have to tell it all over again?"

"I'm sorry," Cynthia said contritely. "I'm so sorry. But I just can't think about anything but Vicksburg. All the time, no matter what I'm doing, I'm thinking about it. Hoping Denis got killed before they had to eat the rats."

"Will you be quiet?" her mother screamed.

Cynthia ran to her. "Oh darling, I'm really a fool!" she cried. It was the first time she had ever seen her mother exhibit anything but self-control; even her tears at Denis' death had been quietly shed. Cynthia flung her arms around her. "I'm so terribly sorry! I'm sure he got killed early. You know how Denis was—up in front of everything—I'm sure he got killed early!"

For a moment none of them spoke. Frances had buried her

face on Cynthia's shoulder. Sarah stood at the window with her back to the room.

At length Frances raised her head. "I'm going to see how Ann is."

"Can't we come?" Cynthia asked penitently.

"No. I'll take care of her. But please, both of you, remember her delicate state of health." Frances put her hand on the knob of the door. "And don't ever, ever mention Vicksburg again where she can hear you."

She went into the bedroom. Ann was lying across the unmade bed, both arms around the pillow, and she had caught a corner of the pillow between her teeth and was biting on it in an effort to gag the long choking sobs that were shaking her body. The bedstep had fallen down on its side. Frances righted it and mounted to sit on the bed by Ann.

"You poor girl," she said gently. She slipped her arms around Ann's rigid shoulders. Ann clenched her fist around the pillow-case, so tight that there was a ripping noise as the cloth tore away from her teeth.

"Let me alone," she jerked out. "You—made out of ice and vinegar—"

Something fiery moved in Frances' chest at the place where her heart was. She was used to her heart's fluttering, but it had never given her such a thrust of pain. "Oh my dear," she said weakly, "don't you know I loved him too?"

Ann's face was nearly buried in the torn pillow. Her words were muffled till Frances found it hard to distinguish them, and they came in a rush as though dammed too long. "I loved him more than anything else on earth. And he never knew it. I did so want us to be married the way some people are—one flesh and one spirit the way it says in the book—but all he ever wanted was for me to be a sweet little thing that amused him. Now I've told you and you know and you can go away and gloat over it because I think it was you that did that to me. You thought I was such a fool he couldn't help believing you even when he didn't know he was believing you. So you needn't be jealous any more, because now he's dead and you can remember you had him as you wanted him, and all I've lost is the chance for something I never had."

Though the fire was stirring again in her bosom Frances paid it no attention. She gathered Ann up into her arms like a child and kissed her. Her heart felt as though there were a fist closing on it, but it seemed unimportant by the blaze of remorse that was forcing its way through the ice of her long denial. She held Ann's head against her breast, stroking back the hair that had tumbled over her face. "Ann," she whispered, "are you ever going to forgive me?"

Ann was silent. After a long time she looked up, unbelieving. As their eyes met Ann began to cry softly, and she buried her face and dried her tears on Frances' collar. "You did think I was a fool, didn't you?" she asked at length.

"Yes," said Frances simply.

"But why? Am I, really?"

"No, darling. I think—" Frances spoke slowly, for even now she found confession difficult—"I think you never had a chance to be anything else."

Ann drew a long breath. "I think nearly everybody is a fool. We don't tell each other anything. We go around so terribly alone."

"How did you know that?" Frances asked in wonder.

"I've been so lonely. And now that I've noticed I think other people are too. We talk and talk and we don't say what we think, and we never get to know anybody. I'm glad I'll have my children. All I've thought of these past days is that they'll have everything they ought to have no matter what it does to me to give it to them. That's why I've been hiding the silver."

"You've been doing that? When?"

"In the middle of the night. I'm terribly scared. If anything happens to me Cynthia knows where the places are. All those heirlooms mean something—I mean, don't you see, they stand for what Denis would have given his children."

Ann was speaking with the undecorated simplicity of a little girl. Frances said,

"You are a very brave woman, Ann."

"Brave?" Ann raised her eyes, uncomprehending. "No I'm not. I'm just scared—and so disappointed."

Again they were silent. Ann was relaxing wearily in Frances' arms. After awhile Ann said, "Thank you for being so good to me."

"I'm sorry I haven't been good to you before."

"That doesn't matter. It didn't bother me. I never needed you before."

Frances smiled a little. It seemed to her it had been a long time since anybody had needed her. Denis had not for years, and Cynthia was so independent it was hard to imagine her being aware of a need for anybody.

Ann was thinking that for the first time since the war impinged on her life she was feeling a sense of security. She looked up at Frances again. It was the most regal face she had ever seen, with its straight mouth and hard chin, as though its calm were an achievement after storms. But you could trust anybody with a face like that. Now she would be all right. Denis was not here, but his mother would take care of her.

There was a knock on the door. Frances said, "I'll answer it," and Ann lay back on the bed wishing their peace had not been disturbed. She heard Cynthia's voice at the door.

"Mother, how is Ann?"

"She's all right. Why?"

"Well, I've got to tell her something. Maybe you'd better tell her."

Cynthia evidently meant to speak in an undertone, but she had one of those incisive voices that are hard to lower. Ann sat up and her foot felt for the bedstep. "What's happened, Cynthia?"

A crumpled newspaper in her hand, Cynthia stood with Frances in the doorway. "Oh dear, I reckon I should have waited. I don't know how to do these things. It's—"

"Port Hudson!" cried Ann. She stood up and put her arm around the bedpost.

"Yes," said Cynthia. "It had to surrender."

Frances took a step forward. "And—Colonel Sheramy?" she asked in a low voice.

"He's dead," said Cynthia shortly. She looked from Frances to Ann, and then at the paper she was twisting into a rope in her hands. "Oh Lord, Ann, I knew I'd make a mess of telling you. I guess I'd better go."

The door closed behind her. Frances sat down slowly on the sofa near the door. Ann stood still, her arm holding the bedpost. There was a silence. Ann walked across the room. A daguerreotype of the colonel was in her bureau drawer. She took it out and looked at it, and thought how quiet and gentle he had always been, and how indulgent of her extravagances. He must have loved her very much.

Strange, she thought, that this should knock her right in the middle of herself this way, when she had known all the time that with Vicksburg gone Port Hudson would almost certainly follow, and when she knew anyway that in the natural course of events she would outlive her father. Her voice overflowed.

"The colonel," she said incredulously, her eyes on the picture. "It's not right. It's not even heroic. It's just fantastic and stupid. Because—oh, I don't suppose it matters if I tell you—he didn't even die for something he believed in. The colonel never did believe in secession. But he was in the army, and he had to take one side or the other, and I reckon he couldn't turn guns on his own people." She looked out at the flowers, blooming so lavishly in the sun of this dreadful summer.

"Yet, you know, after the war started he never said anything to suggest he didn't believe in it. We were all so amazed and excited then, I don't suppose there would have been any point in his trying to talk to us anyway. But it must have been pretty dreadful for him. After Mexico, and being so proud of the army, as he was. Yet I never thought of it. I don't suppose I was ever much use to him as a daughter."

There was a rustle of skirts as Frances stood up. Ann turned around. Frances was standing with her hands clenched in front of her, looking ahead as though she were not seeing anything.

"No, Ann, it's not heroic," she said in a strange voice. "We try to pretend we believe it is. But we know all the time it's nothing but stupid butchery."

She spoke with such vast weariness that it seemed as if it took all her strength to bring out the words. Ann had a curious sense of being afraid of her; it was as though this last message of death had startled Frances out of the still agony she had been enduring since she heard Denis was gone, and now the horror of the whole war had rushed upon her at once, so that in her own mind she was aware of it all.

Then suddenly Frances put both hands over her heart. There was a sound in her throat halfway between a scream and a sob. Ann rushed to her.

"Please let me help you!"

But Frances, still holding her hands tight on her bosom, managed to answer, "It's no use, dear. I can't go on."

As Ann reached her she crumpled up on the rug. Ann cried out, and it was more by instinct than with any hope of finding a heartbeat that she pulled loose the fastenings of Frances' collar.

Later, all she could say to Cynthia was, "I'm going to miss her so. We had just begun to be friends. I feel so forsaken!"

She remembered her moment of security in Frances' arms and wondered if she would ever again experience such a sense of peace. But she could not help realizing that even then she had been mistaken, for though Frances had offered her help, she had had no strength left with which to give it. It seemed to Ann that everything had gone away from her, leaving her nothing but loneliness and fear, and now she began to wonder if she would ever have anything else. She felt that she was living in a world where she would never understand anything any more.

III

Ann's second child was a girl, born at noon on one of those heavy blue October days when the summer heat, after receding before a cool wind from up the river, suddenly came back and lay over the countryside merciless and stifling, until the plants drooped as though they had bloomed themselves to death and were resigned to wither. Ordinarily Ann had enjoyed the summers and wondered why Northern visitors should find them so trying, but this year she had drooped like the plants, so listless that the very thought of any physical or mental effort tired her. Though she tried to tell herself her lassitude was due to her condition, she could not help knowing that much of it came simply from the fact that she felt herself facing more than she had any power to cope with, and she was afraid. She did not want to read papers or hear news. She simply wanted to be let alone, with a dull feeling that she did not care what happened as long as nothing else happened to her.

Dr. Purcell and every other doctor in the neighborhood had long since gone to attend wounded soldiers, so when her child was born there was nobody to care for her but Mammy and

Bertha. When Mammy at last brought her daughter to her, Ann was lying in such spent exhaustion that it required all the strength she could muster to open her eyes and look at the wee creature wrapped in the blanket. But when Mammy would have laid the baby in the old carved cradle that stood ready by the bed Ann murmured, "No, no, give her to me." She folded her tired arms around the baby, and as she laid the baby's tiny hand against her own cheek she felt a sweep of love such as she had never felt for any living creature before. She had loved her first baby very much when they brought him to her, but that had all been so simple, like the working of a long-planned destiny. But about this child there was something wonderful and miraculous—Denis' last legacy, a legacy he did not even know he had left her, born into the wreckage of Denis' world. As she felt the baby warm against her and thought of her other child it came back through her weariness like an inspiration that no matter what happened she somehow had to give that world back to her children. Her mind felt a release like the cessation of pain in her body. She smiled as she heard Mammy drawing the window-curtains to darken the room, and dropped off to sleep.

Down in the depths of sleep she began to hear noise. It was not definitely identifiable as any particular kind, it was just noise, stabbing pitilessly into the unconsciousness that had come to rest her after her avalanche of pain. As she felt herself being forced awake the baby woke too and began to cry. Instinctively Ann reached for it and tried to soothe its little wails. There was such a racket, banging doors, heavy footsteps, the shouts of men's voices. Between the drawn curtains was a line of sunlight. Ann glanced at the floor and by the position of the sun on the rug knew she had been asleep only an hour or two. Oh, why couldn't they be quiet, whoever they were, when she was so tired? Mammy should stop them, or Cynthia or Napoleon or somebody. Who were they, anyway?

She tried to raise up and fell back, her forehead damp with the effort. The door burst open. She saw a soldier in a blue uniform shove Mammy aside, paying no attention to her protests, and then suddenly the room was full of them. Nobody seemed to notice her. One of the men picked up a candlestick, exclaiming, "Say, this looks like silver," and another one stumbled against the empty cradle and knocked it over. Two of them threw open the doors of her armoire and then her clothes were all over the floor, being examined and kicked around as though they were dividing her dresses in such haste they had no time even to care whether or not they stepped on them. Ann lay quivering with helpless rage, her arms around the baby as though in spite of her own weakness she could somehow protect it. She was not protesting; she was simply crying, softly and weakly, into the pillow. Suddenly cutting through the hubbub she heard Cynthia's sharp voice at the door.

"I tell you, go into that room and make them stop! They'll kill her—aren't you even human?"

A man in a captain's uniform elbowed his way through the mob in the room. He took one look at the bed and turned around.

"Get out," he ordered. "Can't you see that girl was telling the truth? Get out."

The other soldiers began to drop the articles they had picked up. He spoke to them again. Unwillingly and resentfully they began to file out of the room. The captain stood by Ann's bed.

"When was that child born?" he asked her.

She tried to stop the tears that were spilling over her face, and gathered her voice. "About an hour ago."

She heard him take a quick breath. For an instant he stood there uncertainly. He laid his hand on her arm. "I'm very sorry, madam," he said.

Ann could not answer. All she could do was keep on shedding those weak silly tears. Shoving a petticoat aside with his foot the officer made his way to the door. He went out and closed it. Left alone, Ann put her hand over her eyes and tried to stop crying. She was not thinking at all; she was simply angry and exhausted, and very glad nothing had happened to her baby. She did not know how long it was, but the noises that had wakened her began to subside, and at length Cynthia came in. Taking one look around the tumbled room she burst out, "Oh, the brutes!" and dropped on her knees by the bed. "Ann, did they hurt you?"

"No," Ann murmured. After a moment she managed to ask, "What were they doing here?"

"They just appeared," said Cynthia. "I was playing with little Denis in the front, so he wouldn't disturb you. They just poured down the avenue—it was almost as if they'd sprung up out of the ground. I don't know all they did. They drove off most of the mules and they took lots of hams and chickens and got all over the house. I tried to tell them about you. I said the shock might kill you. They wouldn't believe me. Finally I dragged that captain up here. When he saw you he got them out."

"Are they gone?"

"Yes. Don't bother any more. Go back to sleep."

"Where's little Denis?"

"Mammy has him."

"You're sure he's all right?"

"Yes, honey. Please go to sleep again."

"Bring Denis up here so I can see he's all right."

Cynthia obeyed her. But when she brought little Denis Ann saw with relief that he was not only unhurt, he was crowing with delight and his dress was sticky with jam. One of the soldiers had given him a piece of chocolate and another had opened some preserves-jars and let Denis regale himself on all he could eat.

Cynthia assured her the men had not reached the vault, though they had got as far as the wine-closet and were happily stuffing bottles into their pockets when the captain ordered them to leave the house. She leaned over the bed and whispered, "You were smart to insist on burying the silver."

Ann nodded. With a great effort she murmured, "Please leave me alone."

She dropped off to sleep again with her next breath.

The weeks after that she remembered only as a bewildering daze. Items of information drifted past her ears without making much impression on her mind. Dalroy was under martial law. Nobody could walk down the street without a military pass. All the servants were gone but Mammy and Napoleon and Bertha, and Bertha's little boy Jimmy, born just before little Denis. "I don't care," Ann repeated. "I don't care about anything. I just want you to leave me alone."

Her recovery was slow, but at last they said she was strong enough to come downstairs. She came carrying the baby in her arms. Ann had named her Virginia, because it had always been her favorite name, the one she had most frequently as a little girl given her dolls. She sat down near the bottom of the stairs, looking around the hall.

"Cynthia, where are the portraits?"

"In the back attic. I had Napoleon hide them there. Some of them are valuable."

"Oh," Ann said with relief. She wanted them back in the light. She wanted to look up at those pictured faces and remind herself of the great folk who had created the greatness of her people, the legend her children must grow up in and renew. Heretofore she had thought lightly of tradition, but now that it was all she had left, she understood and thanked heaven for it. And she wanted visible symbols to remind her. She glanced down and kissed the baby's head, and as she did so her eyes fell on a mark on the bottom step. "Why Cynthia, what's that?" she exclaimed, pointing. "It looks like a horse-shoe."

"It is," Cynthia returned crisply. "One of our guests that day rode his horse into the hall."

Ann looked up at the staircase. Life must move in a spiral, even if the spiral had the hoofprint of an invading army.

But her determination was hard to keep before her. For the war went on and on and on, as if there never had been anything but the war, there never would be anything but the war. Ann rarely talked about it. She was becoming by habit very silent. She simply went about doing what had to be done, taking care of her baby and trying to get Bertha to teach her to do housework, for three servants could not even keep the house dusted. Her clumsiness was annoying to Bertha and disgusting to herself. "What a helpless fool I am," she said to herself over and over. But she did not even say this out loud, any more than she talked about the desolation and the smoking ruins. At least somebody in the house had to pretend to have courage. If it would only end! But it went on, draining men out of the country; they killed and killed till she thought the continent must tremble under their fury.

The others praised her for her bravery. She let them think she was brave. She never confessed to anyone that she had nightmares where she saw pieces of men flung about with all their crazy killing, and those ditches running with blood at Shiloh. Nobody knew how often she woke up in the middle of the night and sat up in bed with her hands pressed over her temples, crying out in the dark, "Oh please, please, God, make them stop! Give them anything they want, but only please make them *stop!*"

Chapter Nine

CORRIE MAY stood on the wharf, eating a banana she had filched from the back of an army wagon and feeling the heat of the sun on her head. After this long time in jail the sun was good, and the tumult of the river was good, and so were the sun-warmed boards of the wharf under her bare feet and the river-wind rushing her hair. She felt strong, and though her clothes were falling apart and she had to slip a banana off a wagon in order to eat, she was not frightened. The war was over and everything was going to be different, and though she could not see ahead she welcomed whatever was coming.

The time in jail had been awful. The food they shoved at you was garbage and the women they put in there were a strange bunch, mostly drunks and prostitutes picked up for soliciting. Still, once they sobered up they weren't so bad to talk to. They had a vast encompassing sympathy. Yes, they said, the world was a tough place, but you might as well get along the best you could and not bother about it. They listened to Corrie May's story about how the army men had shot Budge and they always cried about it. She had never known any women who could cry so easily and so lavishly. But they were not moved to anger by it. They were just sorry.

Corrie May could not understand how anybody could reach such a bland attitude of acceptance. She had no intention of accepting anything. The news of Budge's death had pierced her numbness with a shock that was at first grief, then anger, then bitter resolution: when she got out of this place she was going to start over, and she wasn't going to be caught walking the wharfs, either. So when a blue soldier appeared one day and said sharply, "You girls clear out of here—we need this place for a hospital," she scampered out without asking him any questions.

Tossing the banana-skin into the river Corrie May turned and started toward the square to see about getting a job. What was going on these days she didn't know, but the square had always been the center of town. Maybe she could get some work cleaning in the courthouse.

The streets were full of blue soldiers. Corrie May made her way along till she neared the courthouse. But the lawn in front of the courthouse was packed with Negroes, overflowing till they packed the street too. They were cheering a man in a black suit, who stood on the courthouse steps making a speech. His words began to drift toward Corrie May.

". . . the gr-r-reat eagle, my dear-r friends, who like Moses has led you from this land of bondage and who now spr-r-reads his protecting wings about you. . . ."

He waved his arms toward heaven and the Negroes shouted, "Yay boss!"

". . . that noble eagle, my friends, who guar-r-rds the flag of freedom. . . ."

Corrie May followed his gesture upward, but though she saw the flag she didn't see any eagle. The only place she had ever seen an eagle was on the back of money. Thinking of money reminded her she was looking for a job, so she started pushing her way among the Negroes.

"You quit dat shovin', white girl!" a big black man exclaimed to her.

"Huh?" asked Corrie May.

". . . free under the flag!" bawled the man on the steps. "Free and equal. . . ."

"Yay, hooray!" shouted the Negroes.

"You quit dat shovin'," the black man repeated to Corrie May. "Don't you know we's free'n' equal? Free as you and good as you?"

"Well, that ain't saying much," Corrie May retorted. "Why don't you let me get by?"

He glared down upon her. "Den you walk in de big road. Sidewalks is foh cullud gen'l'men dese days."

"Colored gentlemen?" said Corrie May. "My lawsy me."

But she turned around and walked in the big road. She was angry, but at the moment she had no time to bother about it.

He was bigger than she was, and she had been beaten up once already in a street fight; besides, she had set her mind to getting a job. You had to eat before you could concern yourself with your right to use the sidewalk.

Making her way around the black throng she got to the side of the courthouse steps and paused to look up at the shouting speaker. He was lean and tough-looking, with a red face. His mouth was wide and thin and he had little mean eyes. He was lowclass, because his suit needed an ironing and his hair was too long; and he came from up North as you could tell by the way he talked through his nose and grabbed hold of a final *r* and curled it around the word like a tail. But he was smart; he was beating the air with his fists and flapping his coat-tails and putting on a fine performance for the darkies. Reminded her of the way Pa used to preach. She wondered where Pa was. And Ma. She hadn't heard of either of them for a long time. Her ideas about time had got all jumbled while she was in jail, but probably it was at least a year since the last time Ma came to see her. That fellow sure reminded her of Pa. He had the same way of rolling syllables, the same memory for lines out of the Bible, the same violent attraction for a crowd. And the folks listening believed every word he said. "Yes Lawd," the Negroes shouted. "Sho is true. Amen, boss!"

He was promising them milk and honey, corn and wine. Next thing you knew he'd be promising them great white thrones. Just like Pa, only this fellow wasn't telling them the Lord was going to provide these luxuries; it was the flag and the eagle and the government. But about how one was to start getting them he was as vague as Pa. Only, like Pa, he thrilled them with his sweeping arms and rolling words, and they shouted amens, forgetting to ask questions.

"I wonder what he wants from them," Corrie May asked in her mind. When Pa carried on like this he wound up by passing the hat for a collection. This guy wasn't doing that, but you could see he had a head on him; whatever it was he wanted of these poor believing Negroes he was mighty likely to get it. Corrie May burst out laughing.

But again recalling what she was here for she went on around the courthouse to the back door. The soldier on guard there told her if she wanted a job she'd have to see Mr. Gilday.

"Thank you kindly," said Corrie May. "Where's he to be found?"

"Front office on the left of the corridor." The soldier leaned sideways against the wall. "What you want a job for?" he inquired conversationally.

"What for you reckon?" she retorted. "I got a habit of eating."

"Well, you needn't be so snappish about it," he said back at her. "I got it myself." He grinned slowly. "You're kind of skinny, though. Looks like you ain't been keeping up the habit."

"I ain't been fed nothing fit for a pig in quite a time," said Corrie May. "Take your hand off my arm."

"Sorry. I didn't mean nothing," said the soldier. But as he obeyed and turned aside from her she saw that his left sleeve was empty.

Corrie May felt remorseful. "I'm sorry myself, mister," she apologized. "Er—that arm of yourn—it's a shame. Was it in the war?"

He nodded. "Mansfield."

She began to observe him. He was not tall, but he was thickly built, with muscles in his remaining arm that bulged under his blue coat, and a thick black beard creeping through his face. "I'm sorry I talked mean to you," said Corrie May.

"Ah, shut up," he returned without rancor. "It's all right."

"They should have sent you home," she said.

He shrugged his good shoulder. "For what?"

"Why, so you could go back to doing whatever it was you did before the war."

"Fine chance," he responded dryly. "I was a blacksmith."

Corrie May sighed. "This here war sure was a mess."

"Yeah." Then recalling his uniform he added, "But well, the Union is saved and the niggers are free."

"Uh-huh," said Corrie May. But she looked up with a fresh interest. The Union was none of her concern but she had been wanting to inquire about the slaves. "The niggers is really free then?" she asked. "Free sho 'nough, for good and all?"

"Why sure," said the soldier, giving her a look of wondering condescension. "Where you been?"

"None of your business. But tell me—they'll have to work for wages from now on?"

"They'll have the *privilege* of working for wages," he corrected her patriotically. "They're free. They got the priceless blessing of liberty."

Corrie May chuckled. "Say, mister, you don't have to read me no speech. I know what you mean."

"But you better get it right in your head," he told her, "you and all the rebels. The niggers are free."

"Well, I ain't got no complaints," she replied. "I'm glad of it."

"Glad?" He stared. "Ain't you a rebel girl?"

"If you mean was I born in these parts, sure. But I expect I'm a Yankee in my mind. I don't reckon you'd understand what I mean. But—" she hesitated and looked down, stroking the floor with her toes. "I—I don't just know how to say it—"

He smiled at seeing her blush. "Go right ahead, miss."

"Well," said Corrie May, "I'm sorry you lost your arm and all, but I think it was mighty fine of all you Northern gentlemen to join the army and come down here and set the niggers loose—I mean anyway, thank you."

She started to run into the corridor, embarrassed, but he put out his arm to detain her. "Well say, miss, that's kind of you," he said. He sounded not only surprised, but wistful, as if he had been wanting somebody to talk to. She paused and looked up at him. "Er—there ain't—" he floundered too. "I expect you're the first rebel girl that's spoke to me pleasant since I been here."

Corrie May glanced at his empty sleeve and glanced away again quickly. "You mean they act stuck-up?"

"Yes, though I guess you can't exactly blame them, can you? Still, it makes it awful lonesome."

"I reckon so," said Corrie May.

"I'd kind of enjoy seeing you again," he suggested bashfully. "What's your name? I ain't meaning nothing wrong."

"My name's Corrie May Upjohn," she acquiesced.

"I'm Jed Lindsay. Twenty-first Indiana."

"Pleased to meet you." said Corrie May. There was an awkward pause. She added, "Well, I reckon I better look up that Mr. Gilday. Who's he anyhow?"

"Government agent. Down here to keep things orderly and look out for the niggers." Jed Lindsay shuffled his weight from one foot to the other. He looked down and then up again. "And say, Miss Upjohn, I hope you get the job."

"Mighty good of you. Well, goodby."

"Goodby," said Jed. They smiled at each other and Corrie May went into the courthouse corridor.

The office to which Jed had directed her was at the front, its torn curtains flapping against the green view of the park. The room was occupied by a big untidy desk, a bookcase, some chairs, a large brass spittoon and six or eight men, mostly with their feet on the desk, smoking and passing a bottle. As she entered they looked around and regarded her with interest.

All the faces turned to her were good-humored, as if somebody had just told a funny story. Corrie May advanced past the door.

"Which one of you is Mr. Gilday?" she inquired.

"Me," answered the man in the main chair behind the desk. "What do you want?" He smiled at her. It made her think maybe she had some prettiness left even after being in jail.

Mr. Gilday was the man who had just been haranguing the Negroes outside. Corrie May felt encouraged. From her knowledge of Pa she figured this one wouldn't be hard to get along with. And heaven knew his office needed a doing over, papers and cigar-ash all over the floor and nothing looking as if it had been dusted in a week. She went over to the desk and told him she'd like a job cleaning up the place.

Mr. Gilday let his eyes travel up and down her in a way that made her feel self-conscious. Not that it bothered her; she was used to being looked at on the wharfs and you needn't tell her the male half of the human race had changed its ways any while she was in jail. "So you want to go to work, eh?" said Mr. Gilday.

"Yes sir," she returned.

He grinned, narrowing his mean little eyes, and leaned across the desk. "Well, sit down a spell. Move your feet for the lady, Dawson."

The man addressed as Dawson good-naturedly removed his feet from the desk. Corrie May lifted herself to sit on the muddle of papers. "Thank you sir," she said.

"Well now," said Mr. Gilday. "Shame for you to have to work. Pretty girl like you. Ain't you got no husband to work for you?"

"No sir," returned Corrie May. "I ain't got no husband."

"Well now, well, well," remarked Mr. Gilday. "Don't know what all these good-for-nothing Southern men are about. What they mean by none of them marrying a pretty girl like you?"

"I was just before getting married," she justified herself and her countrymen. "But he's dead."

"Too bad," put in Mr. Dawson. "Killed in the war?"

"Well, more or less," said Corrie May.

Mr. Gilday sighed at that. "Too bad," he remarked. He leaned nearer her. She caught a whiff of whiskey on his breath. He put his hand on her knee, and stroked it. "Too bad," he repeated.

His hand was thick and hairy. Corrie May closed her fingers firmly on his wrist and lifted his hand to place it again on the desk. "You might find a better use for that," she said coolly.

The others laughed with appreciation. "Got you there, Gilday," one of them exclaimed. Corrie May began to laugh too. Mr. Gilday joined in. Comrade-like, he reached to the floor for the bottle.

"Want a drink?" he inquired.

Corrie May accepted the bottle. She didn't want it, but to be sociable she lifted it and let the whiskey touch her tongue before she set it down again. "Well, Mr. Gilday," she insisted, "do I get a job?"

"Don't see why not," Mr. Gilday returned genially.

"Oh, thank you!" Corrie May cried. "Thank you. I'll work good, Mr. Gilday. I'll get this place all cleaned up. It sho needs it, too."

They all began to talk clubbily. "Guess we do need a female to shine things up," owned Mr. Dawson. "How much you work for?"

"Well, I don't know," said Corrie May warily. "How much you reckon?"

"Five dollars a week, say?" Mr. Dawson suggested.

Corrie May caught her breath with delight. Five dollars a week! Nobody had ever paid her that much money. But before she could say anything Mr. Gilday interrupted.

"Stingy," he said to Dawson. "We'll make it ten."

"Ten?" Corrie May echoed in wonder. Things sure were

going on in the courthouse now that these Northern men were in charge. Maybe that was the kind of wages they'd paid up North where there hadn't been any slaves working for nothing. She felt Mr. Gilday's hand on her knee again.

"Ten," he was assuring her.

Corrie May smiled. She lifted his hand and looked straight at him. "Let's say I work for five," she suggested, "and you keep your hands in your pockets."

Everybody kept laughing, including Mr. Gilday; apparently they had reached the mellow stage where almost anything seemed funny. "Ah, make it ten anyway," Mr. Gilday agreed jovially, and he opened a big ledger. The pages were ruled for names, and at the top of each page was a colored picture of the flag. He dipped a pen into a bottle of ink. "What's your name?"

"Corrie May Upjohn."

"Age?"

"Twenty."

He wrote, mumbling the words as he did so. "October third, 1865. Corrie May Upjohn, twenty, cleaning courthouse, ten dollars per week." He reached into a drawer for a Bible and held it out to her. "Put your hand on here. Do you solemnly swear to uphold the Constitution of the United States and faithfully abide by all laws passed by Congress and all proclamations of the President unless reversed by the Supreme Court?"

"Why sure," said Corrie May, "but what's that got to do with me cleaning up the courthouse?"

"Ah, get along with you," Mr. Gilday exclaimed in high good humor.

Corrie May slid off the desk. "Want me to start today, or do I come around in the morning?"

"Now, now," murmured Mr. Gilday sympathetically, "you ain't even got no shoes."

"It's warm weather still," said Corrie May.

"Better get some," said Mr. Gilday. From his pocket he drew a roll of bills about two inches across and peeled off one of them. He laid it on the desk by her hand. Corrie May chuckled. It was like a game. With her thumb and forefinger she flicked the bill back toward him.

"Never mind, Mr. Gilday," she said. As the men kept on

chuckling, she added with amusement, "After it gets dark you take a stroll along the wharfs, headed downriver. And if you don't like what comes along you keep going till you get below the Valcour warehouses, and if things ain't changed since the war you turn in at the third street below the last warehouse. But," she continued, pleasantly but clearly, "that ain't where I live. Well, goodby. See you all in the morning."

Followed by their laughter, she went out and shut the door behind her. She didn't know who they were or what they were doing down here, but she liked them. They were all right. As for keeping off that funny Mr. Gilday, that was no trick; she had been doing that sort of thing successfully since she was about twelve years old. To be dressed so low class, he sure had a lot of money. Ten dollars a week, imagine. And he'd written it down in a government book, so it must be right. Corrie May began to whistle as she went toward the back door.

"Get the job?" a friendly voice asked as she emerged.

She looked up at the broad pleasant face of Jed Lindsay. "I sho did," she returned. "Go to work in the morning."

"Well now, that's fine," said Jed. "Expect I'll see you then."

"You on guard duty here every day?" she asked.

He nodded. "Can't do much else with one arm. Just tell folks where to find the men inside. They paying you fair?"

"Mighty fine. Ten dollars a week."

"Holy—jumping—Jehosephat!" marveled Jed. "They sure pitch money around, them government agents, don't they? Wish they'd give me a job."

"That better than the army?"

"Humph. Nineteen dollars a month."

That was puzzling. If the government could pay ten dollars a week for a cleaning-girl, it would seem they could pay at least that much to a maimed soldier. Jed added,

"Where you suppose they get so much money?"

"I reckon they's rich," suggested Corrie May.

"They don't hardly look it. Must be the government in Washington gives it to them." He studied the back street and the people passing. "Want an apple?" he offered.

"Thanks," said Corrie May.

He took a couple of apples from his pocket and they sat down on the back steps.

"We don't see apples much around here," said Corrie May. "Where'd you get 'em?"

"My mother sent them. We got some trees in our yard."

There was a pause as they munched. Corrie May liked him. His simple directness reminded her of Budge. She looked regretfully at that empty left sleeve of his. Jed began telling her about his home. Just a little place in a village, he said, but it was tidy. He and his mother lived there, and he had had his smithy. No, he didn't know what he would do when he went back. Couldn't shoe horses. But he expected he'd think of something. Yes, it was fine up North, he told her proudly. No slaves. Some places up North used to have them, old folks had told him about it, but they found out it was wicked and so they passed laws setting all the Negroes free. Ever since he could remember, everybody had been free up North. In Indiana, now, where he lived, everybody was free and equal. Sure, some people were richer than others, but that didn't make any difference. Everybody was the same before the law.

"It must be a grand place, the North," Corrie May said wistfully. "It ain't never been like that down here."

"But that was what the war was for, miss," Jed explained. "To make everybody free and equal down South like they are up North. That's the way it'll be."

She smiled with hope. "I sho will be happy if I live to see it."

"You'd like it better up North," Jed told her, "where things is already that way."

Corrie May sighed. "I reckon I would."

But as the shadows began to lengthen she told him she had to go. It would be dark as soon as the sun was set. Jed said yes, that was something that always astonished him, the way it got dark all of a sudden in Louisiana. Up where he lived it took a long time to get dark. Corrie May laughed and said she couldn't see that it made much difference one way or the other, and he said no, he expected not; anyway, he'd see her in the morning. She thanked him again for the apple and started off.

As she had no place to sleep she made her way down to the Valcour warehouses, where she got under a shed and curled up on a cottonbale. In the darkness of the shed she lay and thought. Things had been dreadful, but they were going to be different now. The South was going to be like the North, everybody equal. Jed had said so, and who should know what the war had accomplished if not a Northern soldier? As for her, she'd probably get married and have some children to bring up into this new order of things. She would tell them from the beginning how different it was now from what it had been when she was growing up. Nowadays if you worked and stayed honest and minded your business you could get some place in the world.

II

The job turned out to be splendid. Corrie May did her work and Mr. Gilday paid her every Saturday. Of course the government agents pestered her some, and that Mr. Gilday, he was just one of these fellows that couldn't keep their hands off any woman that happened to be around, but she didn't really mind, for she was adroit at keeping herself to herself. She rented a good room to live in, with a woman who had lost her husband in the war and was glad to give lodgings to a good girl who paid her regularly. It wasn't in Rattletrap Square, but in one of those modest respectable streets above the wharfs. And on her wages she could buy neat clothes and look tidy.

She went down into Rattletrap Square to ask about her mother. But Mrs. Gambrell said why, didn't she know, her mother was dead. And as for old man Upjohn, he just hadn't turned up since the war. Maybe he was dead, maybe not. You know how it was, in those battles there was so much confusion they didn't always keep up with the private soldiers. There were lots of men that just hadn't been heard of. Corrie May shed a good many quiet tears about her mother. It was a shame, Ma had never had anything, and now that she was getting such high wages and could have made things a little easier, Ma was dead. It just seemed as if everybody was gone from her as well as everything that had any connection with those years before the war; it was almost like being without any past.

Nothing was as it used to be. Even the familiar streets around the wharfs were somehow different. The whole town had an air that was at the same time festive and sullen. There were flags about everywhere, the same striped flag you used to see before the war, only then it had been displayed only in front of a few public buildings, but now it streamed all around so common you got plumb tired of the sight of it. When folks from the great houses came downtown they'd walk around the block to keep from passing it, for the law said every time you passed it you had to salute, and how they did hate that—a circumstance that amused Corrie May mightily. They had lost their war and lost their slaves and they were taking it with a bewildered resentment, just as if they had always thought they had a private agreement with heaven that nothing would ever happen to them and now the Lord had cheated them.

There were soldiers all over the place all smartened up in their blue uniforms, only it was kind of silly, for the war was over and they had precious little to do but hang around and they were sick of it. They kept saying yes, they'd saved the Union all right and now why the bloody hell couldn't they go on home? Some of the soldiers in the Union army were Negroes, and they sure did strut. What they were intended for she didn't know, unless it was to show off and remind the slaveowners that they'd lost the war in a mighty way. And of course there were the other Negroes, all over the place too, acting uppity and too good to work and just being an infernal nuisance. The blue army had a camp for them out of town where they tried to keep the poor things fed and orderly, but the Negroes didn't like staying there; their heads were bursting open with fool notions about now that they were free the government was going to give them carriages and big houses and champagne. It all made Corrie May want to laugh. For while she didn't pretend to know much about it, any halfwit could see the agents around the courthouse didn't have any such intentions in the back side of their minds. The Northern soldiers and Northern government men talked about the Negroes fine, sure, but they didn't like them as folks and they didn't want to touch them.

Well, it wasn't any of her business and she didn't care what they did. She was concerned with getting along herself personally. As the months passed she felt more at ease than she ever had.

She was making a good living and enjoying herself; she

liked Jed, and several other soldiers he introduced her to, and they had picnics in their time off and sometimes went to see a show. And in the courthouse there were the government men, making jokes and keeping things lively. Mr. Gilday got very entertaining sometimes, and often when she was cleaning up his office he'd stop writing in his books and pass the time of day with her. Sometimes he invited her to a show or a party, but she always declined, and though he laughed at her for preferring the company of Jed and his fellow-privates, who had so little money to spend, Corrie May merely laughed back at him.

She and Mr. Gilday got to be on rather friendly terms after awhile. There was very little pretense between them; she understood perfectly well what he wanted, and though she was flattered by his persistence she was also amused by his self-confidence. She continued to prefer Jed, who had been brought up to have some respect for a good girl. She kept at her work, and remembered to make a proper curtsey every time she passed one of those flags.

The government men liked having the flags up, for they enjoyed watching that wave of cold silent anger that crossed the aristocrats' faces when they had to stop and make obeisance three or four times in the same block. "Why don't you take down some of them stupid flags?" Corrie May asked Mr. Gilday one morning when she had been working for him about a year. She was brushing up the floor in his office. "It's just a nuisance," she added, "making the people stop so often."

He knocked out his pipe so the ashes fell on the floor. "Oh, don't hurt to keep 'em reminded they lost the war," he told her easily.

Corrie May smiled a little. She got on her knees to brush up the ashes, and lowered her head so he wouldn't observe her smile. But he had seen it, and he bent nearer her.

"What's so funny?" he inquired

"It ain't none of my concern," she replied, brushing unnecessarily hard at the floor.

"No, go on. You're not going to make me mad."

She sat back on the floor, her brush in one hand and her dustpan in the other. "Mr. Gilday, I ain't got no love for them that was the big slaveowners before the war. God knows they kicked me around like I was a stick of wood. But you can make them salute your flags and you can let niggers shove them off the sidewalk till the Judgment Day, and they'll still be *them,* if you know what I mean."

"Well, go on," said Mr. Gilday as she paused. He was thoughtfully stroking his chin.

Corrie May hesitated, but she remembered that everybody was equal now and she could say what she pleased, so she continued, "Mr. Gilday, you ain't really going to get at them people till you hit them in the place where they keep a little private contract with their private God that they're better than other folks. They got education and manners and I ain't saying them things ain't fine to have, I wish I had some, but them Larnes and Sheramys and their sort, they honestly think the reason they're like that and you and me ain't is that the Lord God made them out of a different kind of dust from us. It ain't never been in the back side of their mind that if you and me had been started off like them the day we were born we'd be elegant as them now."

Mr. Gilday's little black eyes narrowed as he studied her and his mouth stretched in a sort of smile that he made without parting his lips. After a moment he asked, "Where'd you ever learn so much, Corrie May?"

She was getting to her feet. "I ain't never been accused of having nothing the matter with my head, sir."

"Nor have you," said Mr. Gilday. He looked her over as she stood whisking the trash from her dustpan into the wastebasket. "You sure are getting to be a nice-looking young lady, Corrie May," he remarked.

"Mighty kind of you to say so," said Corrie May without turning. She got out her dustcloth and began wiping off the chairs. She did look well, she reflected, in her blue gingham dress and white apron, with her yellow hair brushed and braided. Wearing nice dresses and shoes she had bought herself was far more pleasure than it had ever been to dress up in the patched magnificence of Ann's cast-offs. Mr. Gilday added,

"You satisfied with your wages, Corrie May?"

"Yes sir, thank you," she responded without raising her eyes from the chair-rungs.

"Well, maybe before long we can be giving you a raise."

"Don't put yourself out. I'm getting on."

He chuckled. "I won't be putting myself out. It's the government you're working for. Just like me."

"The government sure pays us fine," Corrie May observed.

"Ah, get along," said Mr. Gilday pleasantly. "The government don't care about us, Corrie May. You got to look out for yourself whether you work for the government or anybody else. But you now, you got brains in your head, like me."

"Thank you sir. You're right smart."

"Smart?" repeated Mr. Gilday. "Sure I'm smart. Smart enough to do—well, maybe not quite what you said, but hit the rich where it hurts, all the same. See this here book, Corrie May? Come read what it says on the cover."

She went on dusting. "I ain't much good at reading, Mr. Gilday."

"Well, well," he said. "But I expect you know more than some that is. This here's a tax book, Corrie May."

She raised her eyes. "I been hearing you government men put up the taxes. Only I ain't complaining. I don't pay no taxes."

He laughed. "No, and you won't either, if you stay around here and act pretty. It's the folks you were talking about, the Larnes and Sheramys and St. Clairs and Purcells and them, they're doing the paying these days."

She chuckled involuntarily. "Well sir, all I can say is it's about time."

"Sure, somebody's got to pay for the war. And they started it, didn't they?"

"Why of course," said Corrie May. She paused in the dusting. This was beginning to sound like a reasonable conversation.

"Sure," repeated Mr. Gilday. "Three cents tax on every pound of cotton that goes to the gins, for instance. Who pays that?"

"Why, the plantations," she returned. She began to smile, wonderingly.

"And two cents a pound on sugar?" persisted Mr. Gilday.

"Well, well," said Corrie May with admiration. "That's a fine idea."

He nodded. "Right. And that ain't all. Land taxes—who pays them? Sure, Corrie May, and it's about time."

Corrie May stood up slowly. "But Mr. Gilday, don't that tax money go to Washington? What do you and me get out of it?"

"Why Corrie May," he returned, his eyes on her intently, "you get a job at the best wages you ever made, and me—"

"Yes sir?"

He opened a drawer and took out a paper with a seal on it. "And me, I get a big fat contract to work the river road."

"Why yes sir, that's just fine. You deserve to get paid good for working the roads."

He settled back in his chair and started filling his pipe. "Ah, Corrie May, that there river road don't need working."

"But it does!" she exclaimed. "They say it's full of ruts."

"Well, who uses it?" Mr. Gilday inquired coolly. "I ain't got no reason to go out to the plantations. Nor you. The folks that use the river road are the folks that live in houses along it. Let them fix the ruts if they object to 'em."

"Why Mr. Gilday!" she gasped. "But that—it ain't honest! You getting paid and not doing the work."

"Give me one of them matches on the table," said Mr. Gilday.

As she brought it to him he looked across his pipe into her eyes. "Corrie May, I'm just telling you. You got no reason to be standing up for those people. And me, I'm gonta be a right rich man if this keeps up. And you and me, we could get along fine if you'd quit acting so uppish."

Corrie May moved backward from the desk. "Mr. Gilday, I ain't never had nothing, but I been raised honest. And you're just a thief."

"Well now," he said, "I don't know why I don't fire you right out of this here courthouse."

She didn't know why either. She hadn't meant to say that, but it just said itself out of her astonishment. But he was still watching her with that look of amused summing-up.

"You better get along," he said, "before you make me real mad."

"Yes sir." She picked up the wastebasket and dustpan, but at the door she paused. "People come to call on that lady I rent a room from," she said. "They talk about you and the other Northern gentlemen around the courthouse. And they call you names."

"Tell me," he prompted without resentment.

"They call you carpetbaggers," said Corrie May.

Mr. Gilday blew out a puff of smoke. "Well now, ain't that rude of them. What makes them call us that?"

"They say there ain't one of you government agents down here that had more than what could be put into a carpetbag when you came," said Corrie May, "and now you're getting rich."

"Hm," said Mr. Gilday. "Damned if they ain't right, I expect."

He did not seem at all annoyed. He seemed to think it was funny. She added, "I didn't know what they meant till you just told me that about your contract. Are all the Northern agents doing such things?"

"Oh no," he replied genially. "Just the smart ones."

Corrie May went out.

She was glad when she had some leisure to go sit out on the back steps with Jed. She couldn't complain to Jed about the carpetbagger gentlemen, because Jed came from up North too and it might not be tactful, but he was so simple and jolly that it was refreshing to be with him. He gave her some more apples his mother had sent him. She was liking Jed better all the time.

"Your mother sho sends you a heap of apples," Corrie May commented.

"She ain't got much else to send, poor old lady," said Jed. "I'd sure like to do something for my mother sometime. She ain't got nobody but me."

"I wish I could have done something for my Ma," Corrie May said regretfully.

"Where is she?"

"She's dead. All my folks is dead."

"That's a shame. But it's smart of you, taking care of yourself so good."

"I ain't smart," said Corrie May.

"Yes you are," said Jed. "I sure do admire you, Corrie May. I ain't very smart myself."

Corry May glanced sideways at him. No, he wasn't very smart. The smart ones were fellows like Mr. Gilday. It was the simple honest folks like her and Budge and Jed that never got any place. "Jed," she asked, "do you reckon good people really go to heaven when they die?"

"Why to be sure," said he. "Of course they go to heaven."

"Well, I sho hope they do," said Corrie May. "They ought to get something somewhere."

"Corrie May," he ventured after a silence, "I been thinking. When I get back to Indiana, I think I'll open me up a store. Congress has voted that partly disabled soldiers like me is to get pensioned fifteen dollars a month, but a man can't hardly live on that, and besides, I don't want to just sit around all my life."

"That's right," she approved. "You know how to run a store?"

"Well, I know them farmers around there and what they need. I mean a store where you sell everything, you know, ribbons and pins and plows and feed for the stock. Sometimes you can get the postoffice at one side, if you know your Congressman. They don't seem to have stores like that around these parts."

"No, I ain't never seed one where they sold pins and plows both. But I reckon things is different up North."

"Everything is different up North from what it is down here," he said stoutly. He looked down and flecked a scrap of mud off his shoe. "Er—Corrie May—" he hesitated and got red.

"What was you about to say?" she inquired politely.

"Er—you want another apple?"

"Why yes, thank you kindly. You's right nice to me."

"You're a nice girl," said Jed. "I mean—well, you sure are a nice girl, Corrie May."

She looked down too, turning her apple in her hands. "It's mighty handsome of you to say so," she said.

"You sure would like it up in Indiana," said Jed.

"I reckon I would," said Corrie May shyly.

Jed shuffled his feet on the step.

At that moment Mr. Gilday came out of the doorway with one or two of the other agents from up North. Mr. Gilday greeted her in as friendly a fashion as if she hadn't just called him a thief.

"Why hello, Corrie May. How're you doing?"

She turned her head. "I'm doing all right, thank you, Mr. Gilday."

"Thought we might go down to Pailet's and pick up some dinner," said Mr. Gilday. "You like to come along?"

"No, thank you. I ain't got time."

The other gentlemen chuckled as they glanced at Mr. Gilday. He laughed too, a short little laugh. "Well, that's too bad. Thought we might get some bouillabaisse." He pronounced it bullybass. "Sure you can't come?"

"No sir. I got to work."

"I get it," said Mr. Gilday. "Well, come along, you fellows." It seemed impossible to make him mad. He just laughed at everything, as though he was having so good a time here down South he couldn't be ruffled. Corrie May got to her feet.

"I reckon I better be getting back to my work, Jed."

Jed got up too. "Er—Corrie May."

"Yes?"

"That Gilday fellow. Don't you let him start no funny stuff with you."

"Oh Jed, he don't bother me none."

"I hope not," Jed said uneasily. "But he's just a lowdown cuss, Corrie May."

She smiled. "He ain't so bad. Just out to get anything he can. I know how to look out for myself. Don't you worry."

"It ain't right," insisted Jed, "a nice girl like you having to work for them men."

"Oh, I don't mind," said Corrie May. "Well, I reckon I better be getting in."

She went back indoors and began sweeping the corridor. It required sweeping three or four times a day if it was to be kept anything like clean, what with Negroes and the carpetbagger men throwing papers and cigars and banana peelings all over the floor. They sure were a messy lot. But she was glad to be busy. It gave her a chance to think.

She thought hard. Jed. Indiana. There was no denying Jed was getting fond of her. He'd been about to get very serious when Mr. Gilday appeared. But when Mr. Gilday did appear she had had a sense of relief that surprised her, and now she went on from there; it had dawned upon her that if she gave Jed any encouragement she could probably marry him, and

she wasn't sure she wanted to. He was a good fellow very much like Budge, honest, thrifty, hardworking, and arm or no arm he'd always make a living and not ask charity from anybody, and she could probably boss him around the way she realized now she had always bossed Budge. She was just brighter than either one of them, that was all there was to it. Mr. Gilday had said she was smart, and she was too.

That evening she avoided Jed on purpose when she was leaving, and made her way home. After her landlady had given her supper Corrie May went to her room. She wanted to be alone and figure things out—did she, or didn't she want to marry Jed?

She lay across her bed, her head on her hands. Marrying Jed would mean security. They would live in Indiana and open up that general store and in her spare time between doing the housework and bringing up children she would sell things over the counter. They would send the children to school so they could get education. It would be good to live up North where there was justice for rich and poor alike, and where you wouldn't have to wait for the transformation that was coming in the South. And Jed would be a good husband. They could doubtless get along, though in verging toward affirmation she knew she was being more attracted by the golden equality of life up North than by Jed's personal charms.

But she decided to marry him if he asked her. It would be good to have peace and quiet after these stormy years.

When she went to work the next morning Jed was on duty at the back door. He stopped her.

"I brought you a little thing," he said shyly.

"Honest?" she exclaimed. "Well now, ain't that sweet of you."

It was a piece of blue ribbon to tie up her hair. She thanked him, and almost felt tears coming into her eyes as she bound the ribbon around her braids.

"Say," added Jed, "the boys from the camp are going to have a barbecue Sunday. Come with me?"

"Don't mind if I do," said Corrie May.

"That'll be fine," said Jed.

He smiled at her with a touch of possessiveness, as though he had already proposed and been accepted.

Corrie May felt a glow as she went in and set about her morning's work. He was so very good. It was comforting to feel that somebody was going to belong to her again. She hurried into Mr. Gilday's office to be done with her cleaning there before he came in, him with his smirks and thievery.

But he arrived while she was still dusting his desk. "Hello." he greeted her airily as he spun his hat toward the rack. The hat fell on the floor and she picked it up and brushed it off and put it where it belonged.

"Nice morning," he said as he sat down.

"Kind of chilly," she responded, without pausing in her work.

"You're mighty busy," observed Mr. Gilday.

"I got lots to do."

"Well now, no reason to be in such a hurry."

She glanced around at him, noticing what fine clothes he was beginning to wear, highclass broadcloth like the gentlemen who used to call at Ardeith. Mr. Gilday had laid a parcel on the desk and was undoing the strings.

"Look here, Corrie May. Like this?"

He was shaking out a shawl, wool printed with big red and brown flowers and edged with knotted silk fringe.

"Oh!" she exclaimed. She advanced toward the desk and felt the fine texture of the cloth. "It sho is lovely."

Mr. Gilday smiled across it at her. "Like it, do you?"

"It's just beautiful," Corrie May said wistfully. "A present for a lady?"

Mr. Gilday nodded. "For you."

"Me?" She started. The shawl fell out of her hands to the desk. Mr. Gilday leaned back.

Corrie May picked up her duster again. "No thank you, Mr. Gilday."

He reached across the desk and stroked her hand. "Oh, come on. Try it around your shoulders."

"No thank you," repeated Corrie May. She turned around and went to the door. "I don't need it, Mr. Gilday."

Before he could answer she had shut the door behind her. She ran to the back entrance, and stood there a moment holding the duster. Jed was giving directions to a group of Negro men who wanted to see one of the government agents.

She looked at Jed's ruddy honest face, and when he saw her and grinned it was as if somebody had lit a lamp.

"Gee, you been running?" he inquired. "You're all flushed up in the face. It's right becoming."

The Negroes were ambling into the courthouse. Corrie May stood where she was. She had several more offices to clean. but she wanted to talk to Jed; it didn't matter what about, but just to get a reminder of his friendly respectfulness. It didn't matter either if she neglected her work. She was probably going to lose her job anyway.

"I got a letter from my mother," Jed was saying. "She says it's mighty cold up home now. Snowing."

"Sho 'nough?" said Corrie May. "I ain't never seen it snow."

"It's right pretty," said Jed. "Gets all over everything, and freezes. We ride in sleighs."

"What's a sleigh?" Corrie May asked.

"Well, it's like a carriage, only it's got runners instead of wheels, and bells. It's fun. You'd like it."

She leaned back against the wall. "You make it sound so nice. I reckon I'd like everything up there. Don't you miss it?"

He smiled and sighed at once. "I sure do. Been about three years now since I left home."

"Then you wasn't in the army from the beginning of the war?"

He shook his head. "No. Truth is, I didn't see much use for me to be in it at all. I didn't know nothing about this part of the country, and I had to make a living for my mother. But then, you know how it is." He grinned sheepishly. "They got me in the conscription."

"Oh, they had conscription up there too?" She was surprised. With their wonderful ideal of freeing the slaves and making the country liberal she shouldn't think they'd have needed any conscription for Northern soldiers.

"I expect they always have conscription when they have a war, don't they?" Jed asked. "But of course it was for the right, saving the Union and all."

"Yes, I guess so. But they worked it right up there, I reckon, didn't they? Up there where everybody is equal."

"What you mean, worked it right?"

"I mean, took all the men regardless."

"Oh yes, except they made exemptions for men with young children, and them as wasn't well." Jed's eyes went to the blue ribbon in her hair and he smiled admiringly. "And of course," he added, "them as could pay for exemption."

Corrie May dropped the duster. Jed bent to pick it up for her. She felt her mouth fall open. But it must be she just hadn't understood.

"What you mean, Jed, them as could pay for exemption?"

"Why I mean, if a man was conscripted and didn't want to go to war, if he had money he could pay three hundred dollars and they'd let him stay home."

"You mean—the rich men didn't have to fight?"

"Well, not if they was rich enough," said Jed. "Of course it got hard after awhile, for with every new draft they made it tougher. I hear some men that had lots of money paid over and over so as to keep out of it."

"That was up *North?*" said Corrie May in a strained incredulous voice.

"Why Corrie May, what's the matter with you? You look like you got a pain."

"I ain't got no pain. Why didn't you pay to stay home and keep your arm where God put it?"

He gave a short laugh. "Why Corrie May, where you think I'd ever get so much money?"

She drew a long breath. "You wouldn't," she said slowly. "You never will, either. You ain't smart."

"Lord, child," said Jed, "I ain't never made out to be very smart." He patted her arm. "But I'm smart enough to know a pretty girl when I see one. You do look dressed up with that ribbon in your hair. Be sure to wear it to the barbecue Sunday."

She wheeled around and faced him. "Jed, I ain't going to no barbecue. And here's your ribbon. You better give it to some girl that ain't no smarter than you."

"Why Corrie May!" He took a step away from her, astonished and hurt. "What did I say to make you mad?"

"Oh, nothing. I couldn't tell you if I talked a thousand years. God just makes some people stupid, I reckon, so they can do the dirty work for them that's smart. And I'm getting to be smart. So you keep your ribbon and you keep your snow and your sleighs with bells on and your blasted North.

Free and equal! You make me laugh. You're gonta make the South like the North! Well, you needn't bother, mister, because the South is already like the North. There's just two kinds of people in both places, and one kind gets what they want and the other kind wander around believing what they're told about flags and getting their arm shot off to lay it on their country's altar. Hell and high water. *You!*"

She started to rush in, but Jed barred the door. He had heard her with such incomprehending amazement that even now he spoke breathlessly and his mind could grasp only the obvious fact that she was furious. "Corrie May, please tell me what I did! I didn't mean nothing!"

"Oh, you never will mean nothing. You better go back home to Indiana and pray God to take care of you, for there ain't nobody else ever gonta do it. And let me in."

She threw the ribbon on the floor and rushed past him. Her blood inside of her was boiling and waves of anger were beating in her head, anger not at anybody nor any circumstance, but at herself for having been so foolish as once more to have been taken captive by those rusty traps of duty and honesty in which the rich ensnared the poor. Look at the people who believed them—her brothers who had died in the swamp, Jed who had to start over because he couldn't pay for exemption and thus had lost his arm and his trade, her mother who had died old and stricken while she was still young in years. And the people who were too clever to believe them, like Mr. Gilday, dressed in broadcloth and carried in their pockets rolls of bills two inches thick. Corrie May put her hand on the doorknob of Mr. Gilday's office and went in.

Mr. Gilday was talking to a scrubby, faded man in a Confederate uniform so worn you could barely tell it had ever been gray. It had no buttons, for the law said no man could appear on the street in a Confederate uniform, and when it was pointed out that many men had no other clothes the law was amended to read that all insignia and buttons must come off. If a man who hadn't heard of the decree appeared on the street the carpetbaggers amused themselves by sending Negroes to rip the buttons off. The man at Mr. Gilday's desk was listening to some orders with the hangdog gratitude of a man who had been knocked around more than he could stand. As Corrie May closed the door she heard him say,

"I am very grateful, Mr. Gilday. It's good of you."

"Well, get along now," said Mr. Gilday. He twisted his finger in the gold watch-chain that hung across his vest. "Mind you go every day, weather no excuse."

"Yes, I understand."

The stranger bowed politely. He was highclass, you could tell that by the way he spoke his words and the cleanness of his pitiful uniform. Corrie May's lip curled with contempt. Slavedriver. Let him take the consequences of his damned war. Good for him.

She watched him go past her and out of the doorway. Mr. Gilday turned, his eyes sweeping her up and down with that look that always made her feel as if her clothes were transparent.

"You want something?" he inquired, with that little twist at the side of his mouth that could only be called a smile and yet wasn't like a smile.

"Yes," said Corrie May. She went up to the desk and leaned across it. "You still got that shawl, Mr. Gilday?" she asked.

His thick eyebrows tilted slightly in surprise. "Sure," he returned, "I still got it."

"I been thinking," Corrie May said clearly. "I got an awful hankering after that shawl. It sho is a pretty thing."

Resting his elbows on the desk, Mr. Gilday folded his hands one on top of the other and put his chin upon them. "Well, well, well," he commented dryly. "So you're beginning to get some sense."

"Yes," said Corrie May, "I'm beginning to get some sense."

Mr. Gilday began to chuckle softly. It was less in joy at her presence than in triumph for having conquered something.

"Sure," said Mr. Gilday, "you can have that shawl. I kind of thought you'd take it, after you thought about it awhile."

Corrie May began to laugh too. She made a dodge of her head toward the closed door. "Who's your friend?" she asked.

"He's going to carry the mail."

"Oh," she said. It was as though they were talking over a conspiracy. She felt a sense of amused pleasure.

"I got a contract to carry the mail," said Mr. Gilday. "Get a hundred dollars a month."

"That's a lot for just toting mail," she remarked. "But how come he's gonta take it?"

"I pay him forty dollars a month." Mr. Gilday reached out

and stroked her neck down to where it met her collar. "That's the idea, baby. Let the damn fools do the work."

Corrie May smiled and glanced at the door. She felt completely at ease. But Mr. Gilday had sobered. He was watching her with that intent regard of his, as if he could look through her eyes and see everything on the inside of her head.

There was a pause. Corrie May raised herself to sit on the desk, her hands laced in her lap. Gilday reached out and laid his hand over hers. She smiled at him. For a little while they sat there, looking at each other with comradely interest. It was as if they had been friends for years and had such mutual understanding they had no need for talk to clarify it. At length Corrie May inquired,

"Mr. Gilday, was you in the army during the war?"

He gave a little chuckle. "Lord no. Didn't you think I had more sense than that?"

"I thought you had," said Corrie May. "How'd you get out of the conscription?"

"Paid for exemption," returned Gilday. "How'd you think?"

"That's what I thought. Folks that's got money enough can do practically like they please, can't they?"

"Sure," said Gilday. He nodded pleasantly.

"But go on," urged Corrie May. "How'd you get so much money? Was you rich before the war?"

"Not a bit of it. Truth was, I got fired out of a good job down in these parts just a year or so before the war broke out, and I was pretty bad off. But lucky as it happened, when I went back North I got in with a fellow that ran a clothing factory—cheap men's suits, and all that—and we got a contract to supply some army uniforms. Right at the beginning of the war practically any man that manufactured anything could get a contract to supply it to the army."

"Oh," she said, with increasing respect. "So even then you was making money out of the government?"

"Sure thing," Gilday assured her. He laughed at the recollection. "Corrie May, I tell you those were times. Everybody was bewildered at the thought of war, the government most of all. Men were being dragged in from everywhere to be soldiers, and no clothes, no shoes, no guns, no saddles, no blankets, no nothing was ready for 'em. So the factory men took orders to supply the stuff, and of course there wasn't that much wool or leather in the country—" He laughed again and slapped her hands merrily.

She leaned forward. "So how did you do it?"

"Why, we made 'em uniforms out of shoddy."

"Shoddy? What's that?"

"Well, baby, it's practically anything you can lay hands on. It's old rags you buy for junk and ravel up and weave again into cloth, it's floor-scrapings, it's croker-sacks, it's flour-bags, it's anything. You weave it up, you dye the cloth blue and you glaze it and iron it out shiny, and that damn fool of a United States government pays you better prices than they ever paid before for good woollens, and you go home and kneel down and thank the good Lord that put so many trustful halfwits on earth."

"But didn't the cloth fall to pieces?" she asked in astonishment.

"Of course it did. Soon as the troops got rained on, or even if it didn't rain some of them uniforms wouldn't stand two days' march. But by that time they're a long way from Washington and who cares anyhow? They were brought out to fight, not to complain because they wasn't quite comfortable."

Corrie May laughed out loud. "You're a fine patriot, you are."

"Why baby," said Gilday in a voice of mock-injury, "I'm one of the finest patriots you ever did see. I bought government bonds and I gave money to young ladies that came around asking subscriptions for hospitals, and I went to Soldiers' Aid bazaars and bought pincushions and penwipers and crocheted antimacassars and all like that—" He joined the laughter he was not even trying to suppress. "Why Corrie May," he added, "if I hadn't been known as a fine patriotic citizen do you think the government would have appointed me to come down here to look out for the niggers and see to it them aristocrats paid their taxes?"

Corrie May shook her head awesomely. With admiration that was almost reverence she said, "Mr. Gilday, I reckon you are the *most* lowdown man I ever did see."

Gilday smiled. His eyes moved over her. He repeated that mean, triumphant chuckle she had learned to know so well. "I expect I am, baby," he agreed. He took his hands off hers and folded them on the desk as he continued to regard her with steady amusement.

She asked abruptly, "Mr. Gilday, who are you? Where do you come from?"

Without moving his little eyes from her he answered, "If you mean where was I born, it was on a farm in Ulster county, up in York state, near Kingston."

His eyes seemed to get narrower still. Then he was not looking at her. He was looking past her, as if he could see through the wall to that place in Ulster county of which her question had reminded him. His mouth became tight, as if he had been about to say something and had thought better of it.

"Funny about you," said Corrie May musingly. "Everything you do is wicked and yet it seems like you somehow ought to do it."

"Ought to?" he repeated. "Sure I ought to."

He was still looking past her as though at Ulster county up in York state. There was a long silence. From beyond the window she could hear the blurry voices of Negroes on the courthouse lawn. After awhile Gilday began to speak, though his eyes still looked past her.

"There was thirteen children in our family and my mother raised four of them to be grown up. Seemed like there was always a kid dying at our house. And did we have to work! By the time I was nine years old I was getting up at four in the morning to tend to the stock. It was so cold. My God, them winters. The milk used to freeze in the pail sometimes. You ever try to walk with chilblains, Corrie May?"

"Chilblains?" she echoed. "What's them?"

"I thought not. That's why I came South in the first place. I had to get away from them winters. I don't know why I'm telling you all this. I ain't talked about it in quite a long time."

"No, go on," said Corrie May. She was surprised at how low and intent her voice was.

He stood up. His fists in his coat pockets, he strode over to the window.

"First I helped tend to the cotton on a plantation in Virginia," he continued, still without looking at her. "The man that owned the place didn't live there much, spent his time mostly in New York or traveling around Europe. He was mean as hell. Always borrowing more money than he could afford and raising Cain with us overseers because we couldn't make big enough crops to pay his debts. Too mean to spend a dime for fertilizer and he was starving his land mighty near to a desert. So pretty soon me and another fellow could buy a piece of land he had to sell cheap. There was one stretch in Virginia and another up across the Maryland line. We raised niggers for the market. Just put 'em there and made 'em grow what they'd eat, and we could sell all the little niggers that got born. We were doing right well, too, only I got to playing around with speculations and when the crash came in '57 I lost what I'd made. So I had to go back to overseeing cotton. Worked for a planter in Georgia. Then in the summer of '59 this here Colonel Sheramy that lived out at Silverwood needed a cotton overseer and I came to work for him."

"You worked for Colonel Sheramy?" she exclaimed.

A crooked little smile flicked across his mouth. "Not for long. He had a daughter. She took a disliking to me."

"Why—you mean Miss Ann Sheramy that married Mr. Denis Larne?"

"The very same. I looked at her hard or something and she was too refined. My Lord, the way those people fixed up them doll-babies they called women, making out they was too flimsy to pick a flower and God knows keeping 'em too stupid to do much else. I met her at the gate one day and she was on a horse. Blazing summer and me half dead from being in a cottonfield since six that morning and no chance for even a drink of ice-water till night, and here she comes, prancing down the avenue cool as a waterfall and looking past me so goddamn superior. I started bowing and scraping like I was supposed to do, and looked her over and started noticing her corset. She wasn't more than seventeen or eighteen inches around. I thought about my mother slopping around with nothing tying her waist but her apron-string. I looked up the road after her. And then the next thing I knew I was even losing my job, her having complained to her brother that the new overseer wasn't properly respectful."

Corrie May clasped her hands in front of her and leaned across them. "Go on. I remember when she got married."

"Hell," said Gilday, "so do I. I spoke to her on the wharf. She didn't like that either. I rode down on the same boat, only

I rode below the decks. I thought about the things I'd been seeing happen all my life and about the lucky people who just thought we shouldn't mind because we were used to it. And I said, 'Gilday, some day there's some bastards gonta pay for this.' " He turned around. "And Corrie May, now I got my chance to make them do it."

She stood up slowly. "It's mighty right you are. I know, because at that same time I was thinking the same things you were. I worked for that woman."

"You," he said. "You got more sass in your left thumb than she'll ever have." Then he grinned. "Well, now I'm down here. They can call me any pretty names they like. I'll get in a lot of good stealing before I'm done. Damn it, Corrie May, ain't it our turn?"

"Yes," she answered quietly. "I reckon it's our turn."

Corrie May walked over to where he stood by the window. Gilday turned and put his arm around her. She looked up at him, his thick untidy hair and his shrewd little eyes and his lecherous mouth, and his jaw set square like that of a man who knew just what he wanted and was damn well going to get it. For the first time in her life she wanted to speak and was aware of the clumsiness of her vocabulary. For she had no illusions about him. He was a lowdown sneak, and there wasn't a soul in the parish who wouldn't be better off if he were dead, and yet he had what she had known all her life she needed, that completely frank determination in his dishonesty and that certainty of knocking aside anything that stood in his way without remorse or pity. She felt herself pushed toward him by a force so much vaster than herself that she could not even pretend to resist it. It was a feeling compounded of awe and admiration and wondering discovery.

"Well—for God's sake," said Corrie May. She spoke slowly. "You—Mr. Gilday—I mean, what's your first name?"

"Sam," he said, smiling down at her.

"I think you're kind of wonderful," said Corrie May.

He began to laugh again. This time she could feel his laughter, a deep quivering mirth of his body. "You and me," he said, "we'll have a fine time."

"You're mighty right we will," said Corrie May.

Chapter Ten

WHEN Gilday offered to take a house for her Corrie May felt a thrill that ran from the back of her neck down to the end of her spine. The balconied home of the Durhams, in front of which she had watched the soldiers pass on that long-ago spring day when the war was young, had been advertised for rent. Steamboat trade was scant, and property taxes had climbed to such heights that the Durhams could no longer afford to keep up their residence.

Gilday said he'd take it if that was the one she wanted. She drove her buggy to the house and sat looking up at its graceful front, and she trembled with pleasure. That she, Corrie May Upjohn from Rattletrap Square, should live in one of the palaces that had given Dalroy its famous designation! But when she went in and looked around she was disappointed. From the outside the house looked pretty grand with its wide galleries and long windows, but inside—why, even in the parlor the walls were just plain white, with only a tiny border of painted vines under the ceiling. Corrie May asked Gilday if she couldn't fancy it up a little bit, and he said sure, go right ahead; he thought like her it was too simple.

So she went to work, gleefully. In the front rooms she put up wallpaper with a design of red and purple roses climbing over a golden lattice, and in the hall blue paper scattered over with gilt bouquets tied with long pink bows. She draped the windows with red velveteen hangings looped back with gold cords, and hung pictures of cupids flying about among wisteria-laden arches. She hung a gilt-framed mirror over the parlor mantelpiece and placed a red plush sofa between the front windows. To spur folks' appetites she hung pictures of fruit and fish in the dining-room, and set up cabinets containing knobby tumblers of pink glass and a set of chinaware painted with ponies.

Gilday paid for everything, half with satisfaction and half with amusement. He enjoyed seeing the pleasure she got from spending money. "This sure is marvelous," she exclaimed breathlessly to him over and over, and he laughed and pinched her cheek. "Go right ahead, baby. Ain't I said it was your turn?"

Yes, it was her turn, Corrie May said joyfully to him and to herself, and she bustled up and down, laying a green carpet on the stairs and placing long vari-colored candles in the sockets. But though she gloried in her grand house, this glory was faint compared to that she found in buying clothes. At first it was hard to realize she could walk right into the shops and turn over bolts of goods with the assurance of a great lady. At first she went in timidly, murmuring, "If it ain't too much trouble, sir, I'd like to see some poplin, please sir," and shivered when the salesman's glance informed her she was not the type of customer he had been used to waiting on. But times were hard, the shops needed customers more than she needed clothes, and it did not take her long to find it out. It was only a little while before Corrie May learned to walk in confidently, flirting her train and tossing the stylish false braids pinned in loops to the back of her head, and say, "Tarletan? Huh, I'd as soon wear mosquito netting! Ain't you got none of these shot velvets I been hearing about?"

She loved seeing the salesmen cringe before her demands. She loved seeing some woman who had been rich come into the shop attended by her brother or an old servant who had remained faithful in spite of the times—for these days it was hardly safe for a lady with the look of resentful gentility upon her to venture unprotected into the street—and carefully choose a few yards of cheap percale, while she herself flung down her rolls of greenbacks in payment for satin. And how she enjoyed bossing the dressmakers! They mildly suggested that one did not decorate brocade with embroidery nor have street-dresses made with long trains; Corrie May demanded, "Look here, you, who's paying for these clothes?" There had been a time when they would have told her they were too pressed with previous orders to accept hers, but not now.

Their old customers were staggering under the weight of carpetbagger taxes and they were grateful for any customer who could pay. They made her gowns as she wanted them, and though they might shiver at her taste they eyed her porte-monnaie stuffed with bills and held back their protests, even when she demanded that they work all day Sunday to finish a bonnet. Corrie May reveled in it all. She gathered up her florid skirts and swept out to her carriage, singing to herself, "It's my turn! Now I'm walking up the handsome road!"

She had servants too, for though most of the liberated Negroes refused to work, there were a few of the more intelligent class who had sense enough to know the government wasn't going to support them and were glad to have employment. Not many of their former masters could pay wages for house-servants, but Corrie May could. She paid good wages, too, for she knew they despised her. She who had never bossed a servant before was harder to work for than the patricians for whom having servants had been no adventure. But on Saturdays when they lined up to receive their high wages she distributed the money with gleams of triumph in her eyes. "Times have changed," she reminded them. "When y'all was slaves the law said your missus had to keep you and feed you whether you did your work good or bad. But now you ain't slaves no more, and I can fire you if you don't do just like I say. So you'd sho better be good."

And they were good. These aristocratic Negroes were as bewildered by the new order of things as their masters.

Corrie May's life was radiant these days. Besides clothes and servants and a fine house, she was buying other things, more vital. She was buying a sense of her own importance in the world, and she was buying the knowledge that she was beautiful.

That came to her slowly as she turned before her toilet-mirror. She had no more sunburn, and with face-creams and sheltering her complexion was acquiring a pale delicacy; having no more work to do she could rub her hands with milk and polish the nails with chamois skin. She had learned how to darken her eyelashes, and the effect was to make noticeable the fact that instead of being just ordinary blue her eyes were large and dark, almost violet. And now she had leisure to wash her hair and brush it till it had a rich glitter. Folks used to call it "lightish," but now Gilday's friends who came to her parties exclaimed, "What beautiful golden hair you've got, Miss Corrie May!"

Though it was too late for her to achieve really close lacing, she did discover that she had a good figure, and Gilday said he'd never admired women laced too fine; in fact, he was joyfully astonished at how well she looked when for the first time in her life she put on a really good crinoline. "Maybe it's a good thing for a girl to work a few years, baby," he told her. "You develop yourself the way God meant you to be. And," he added with increasing satisfaction in his own good judgment, "maybe God ain't so wrong, the way he makes women."

Corrie May laughed softly. But she could not explain to any man the joy she found in her own discovery of herself. And she could not explain to anybody, man or woman, the glory that descended upon her when she stood before her mirror and knew with the honesty bred in her from a lifetime of facing facts that she was more beautiful than Ann Sheramy had ever been.

It came to her one evening when she came upstairs after passing drinks to several of Gilday's friends who had dropped in after supper. Gilday was still down in front helping the company to their carriages, for some of them were unsteady on their feet. Corrie May came into her room, and as she dropped her train she saw herself in the long mirror. Her hair caught the candlelight as though it had been brushed with gold and silver, and above the fluff of tulle her shoulders had a shimmery whiteness. With a sudden breath of joy she stepped nearer.

Holding up her arms, she watched the light quiver from her wrists to her shoulders, and noticed the firm strength of her muscles; she turned and looked sideways at her corsage tapering to where it met her skirt and saw how gracefully her figure had developed, so that she carried the great bunch of folds in the back as though it were a pleasant decoration instead of a burden. She looked at her shining eyes and her clear strong profile, observing that air and exercise had given her not only grace but a complexion that had the bloom of a well-nurtured flower. She remembered Ann's milky delicacy and her soft little skeleton that yielded without resistance to any fashionable corset. And suddenly Corrie May's pleasure in herself became so intense that it was like pain. A quivering ecstasy went through and through her, and she covered her face with her hands and crumpled on the bed, sobbing in an anguish of delight.

When Gilday came in and found her he was alarmed. He took her by the shoulder and asked her what on earth had happened. "Did one of them drunks say something not polite to you?" he demanded.

"No, no," sobbed Corrie May. "Didn't nobody say nothing. I'm just crying because everything is so wonderful."

Gilday laughed at her. "You're such a sweet little damn fool," he said.

She did not try to explain further. Gilday was not much interested in her intimate reactions, and Corrie May was too schooled in reality to expect him to be otherwise. But he liked her, and she worked too hard to please him for them ever to quarrel.

They had lots of friends and the house was full nearly every evening. The gatherings were hilarious, for the callers were of the group that was stepping high these days—revenue agents and supervisors of the Freedmen's Bureau, and a lot of Northern men who weren't even nominally representing the Federal government but who had come down to get themselves elected to state offices—and they brought along girls who, like Corrie May, were stepping high too. Mr. Dawson came with his new wife; her name was Laura, and where he had picked her up nobody knew, but she had contrived to stand him up in front of a justice of the peace one day when he was drunk and now they were married and Laura was putting on highclass airs, and how she did love to be called *Mrs.* Dawson. Corrie May regarded her with envy-tinged amusement. Gilday was a better patron to have, for he was smarter than Dawson and had twice as much money to spend, but by that same token he was too shrewd to get drunk. Not that it mattered very much. All the folks admired Gilday a sight more than they did Dawson, and they liked Corrie May better than Laura with all her airs.

Gilday said he wanted to give a really big party in August. Corrie May planned it happily: jellies and salads, cakes and cream-custards and liquor enough to make everybody tipsy; and for herself a costume so gorgeous that the planning of it fairly made her dizzy.

For if your imagination had been starved of splendor, this summer of 1867 was really the time to turn it loose. The country was relaxing from war-strain, and to match the excitement of release clothes had gone wild. Dresses were so loaded with decorations they became a burden to carry, and after sixty years of flat-soled shoes heels had shot up four inches high. The vogue for having a wire bulge in the back of the skirt and a bow half a yard wide just below made it almost impossible to sit down, while the new heels made it almost impossible to stand up; a false chignon that weighed a pound pinned to the back of the head produced shooting pains in one's neck; bracelets were so heavy one felt like a shackled criminal, and the long frilled trains swept up whatever of dirt and cigar-stubs happened to be underfoot. If you followed the fashions you could neither stand, sit, walk nor breathe without aching, and with every garment you put on you looked more barbaric; but the war was over and you had to riot in foolishness lest you remember you were dancing over a million graves. By midsummer bows and flounces had ceased to be enough and there appeared a yet more extravagant decoration, peacock feathers.

You thrust bunches of peacock feathers into your bosom. You banded your skirt with overlapping lines of them, you bought parasols made solidly of peacock feathers, you hung them around the brim of a hat or put one at each end of the strings that tied on a bonnet; instead of a rosette on your slipper you wore a peacock feather, and you put peacock feathers into your hair to nod above your flowing false curls. You bought a breastpin in which a peacock feather was imitated in colored glass stones, you cut bits of brilliant velvet and appliquéd them on your dress in a design of feathers; you had fans of peacock feathers, you embroidered them on your handkerchiefs, you even found them in the designs for bedspreads and curtains and dish-towels.

And if you gave a party in that peacock summer you ordered ice, quantities of Northern ice brought down to Louisiana on the boats, and you had it crushed and colored and packed in more ice to be re-frozen into designs that would turn out of the molds to be peacock feathers melting on the plates.

Corrie May thought that a wonderful idea. Four days before the date of her party she went down to see the head of the ice-company. Could he make up the peacock molds for her? Why of course he could, only the price—

"Damn the price," said Corrie May. "I'm having fifty-four people at my party and I guess you'd better make up two apiece. And then of course I'll be wanting more ice for the drinks."

That would be a lot of ice, the man said doubtfully, for he'd have to send up the peacock molds packed in buckets of ice, and to keep them solid he couldn't pack more than eight to a bucket.

Corrie May took out her porte-monnaie and began counting greenbacks before him. The ice-man eyed the money with eyes that stretched involuntarily.

"Mm," he breathed. "Times have been kind of hard hereabouts lately. We don't sell ice like we used to. The boats don't bring so much."

"Well, can't you order me a few pounds special?" she demanded.

"I sure can," he exclaimed eagerly. "I tell you, ma'am. Suppose I say right now you've ordered all the ice I'll get in from now till next Tuesday, and I'll order you a hundred pounds extra, special."

"That'll be all right, I reckon," Corrie May returned grandly. She picked up a newspaper from the table and began to fan herself. It was unusually hot, even for August, and though she had come from home in her carriage she felt as wilted as if she had walked. "Only you better make it a hundred and fifty," she told him. "Looks like we're in for quite a spell of weather."

"Yes ma'am." He spoke with reverence. "Only—I mean, for a special order it should ought to be paid for in advance."

"Sure," said Corrie May. She laid a bunch of green-backs on the table. Her counting was sometimes vague, so she added, "You count it out. Them bills soil my gloves."

"Yes ma'am, certainly, ma'am. Anything to oblige. Er—if I ain't making too bold to comment, ma'am, it's mighty fine to have a good cash customer these days, and I sure do appreciate it, ma'am, yes ma'am."

Corrie May observed him with disdain. She recognized the hungry way his fingers closed over the bills. It reminded her of herself when she used to get her wages at Ardeith. "Was you in the army?" she inquired.

"Yes ma'am. Only—" he caught his breath. "Only I mean I ain't a Confederate no more," he assured her hastily. "I'm real reconstructed I am, I mean you could look a long way and not find as loyal a Union man as me, yes ma'am, truth was, I got conscripted—"

"Ah, go on," she said laughing. "All you men now want to make out like you got conscripted. The way you talk when anybody comes around spending Northern money, a person'd think there wasn't a volunteer in the whole Confederate army."

"Yes ma'am," he said meekly, and turned red. When he had counted the money and given her back the remainder he ventured, "I expect you come from up North, ma'am, don't you?"

Corrie May smiled. She took the bills from him and put them back into her porte-monnaie. As she fastened the clasp she glanced down at herself. She had on a white muslin dress over a pink silk petticoat; the skirt had nine flounces and a train a yard long. Her gloves were pink kid embroidered with peacock feathers in purple and gold, and her sash was blue velvet. Her bonnet was made of pink roses, small so as not to interfere with her looped braids, and tied under her chin with blue velvet streamers.

"No," she said slowly, "I ain't from up North. I ain't never been up North in my life. Folks up there get chillblains when it snows. Me, I like the South all right."

"I beg your pardon, ma'am, I really do. But I mean—" he floundered. "You being dressed so elegant, begging your pardon for being so free, ma'am, and there ain't many Southern people got any money left these times, I expect you know how it is, even the pawnshops ain't taking no more spoons—"

Corrie May stood up. "Yes, I know, but if I was you, mister, I wouldn't worry about it. There's plenty of good times to be had right here where we are. Now you'll hold all that ice for me?"

"Yes ma'am." He grinned broadly. "I ain't forgetting it's paid for. I'll be holding every pound."

Corrie May went out and got back into her buggy. She drove to the courthouse. There were things still to be attended to and she needed some more money. The dressmaker had promised to have her gown ready this evening, and she wanted to go by and see that it was satisfactory before it was delivered, but she would have to pay for it. Gilday wouldn't let her run any bills. It was going to be a splendid dress with a long feather-edged train. At the courthouse she got out of the buggy.

Gilday was in his office with five or six other men. They greeted her amiably.

"Well, well, if it ain't Corrie May," said Mr. Dawson. "Dressed up like a Christmas tree. Where you going diked out so fine?"

"Why, I was coming right here," she returned pleasantly. "Wouldn't come call on my friends in a calico apron, I hope."

Gilday sat behind the desk. He reached out and pulled her to sit on the arm of his chair. "What you after, baby?" he asked her.

"What you reckon?" she countered. "I'm out of money again."

"Heaven help us," said Gilday with a certain pride. "This woman, she costs more'n a carriage and pair."

Everybody laughed. "Well, I hear they're offering a bounty for Ku Kluxers," said Dawson. "Only you got to bring in the scalp with the hair on."

They chuckled again at that, and Corrie May shrugged. "I always say if the niggers is fools enough to have the breath scared out of 'em by men in white sheets, leave 'em alone. It amuses the population and a good time is had by all. Look here, Sam Gilday. If you ain't got sixty dollars, say so, only if you ain't I can't get my gown and I won't be able to give no party Tuesday because I won't have nothing to wear."

One of the men named Cockrell, who was literary, began to murmur,

"Miss Flora McFlimsey, of Madison Square . . ."

The whole crew took it up. Corrie May listened impatiently. Seemed to her somebody was always quoting that doggerel. Gilday, who to her private annoyance often read books, came out with the lines,

*"Well, having thus wooed Miss McFlimsey and gained her,
With the silks, crinolines, and hoops that contained her—"*

Corrie May interrupted, "Are you devoting your time to poetry these days, Samuel, or are you gonta give me that air sixty dollars?"

"Well, I'm a fool," Gilday announced to the company. "Every time I lay eyes on Corrie May she's got on a different dress. But now I got to give her money because she ain't got nothing to wear. Lord have mercy on my sinful soul."

The others laughed again. Corrie May sensed proudly that their laughter was less to express amusement than to cover envy. The carpetbagger gentlemen were combing the South for women to satisfy their suddenly expensive taste. But the beautiful women were likely to be the sort who stood shabbily disdainful behind their magnolias, and not many of these men had Gilday's talent for discovering beauty under gingham aprons.

"Say listen," said Corrie May. "It's after four o'clock and I ain't got all day."

Gilday indulgently pulled open a drawer of the desk. It was full of money, the collections of land-taxes. Gilday had a way of altering the books to make it appear that the land had been appraised for less than its worth and consequently that the taxes paid were less than the sum he actually collected, and he spent the difference. He gathered some bills in his hand.

"Let's see," he said. "This here seems to be a hundred and ten dollars. Need it?"

"Sure," said Corrie May.

With a smile he handed it to her. As Corrie May stuffed the notes into her porte-monnaie she heard the door open, and there was a faint rustle of petticoats. She glanced up, and saw Ann Sheramy Larne standing just inside the room.

For a fraction of a minute Ann stood where she was, hesitating before approaching the desk. In that flash of time

Corrie May saw her more clearly than she had ever seen anything before in her life. It was the first time she had laid eyes on Ann since her last day at Ardeith, nearly five years ago, and her first thought was one of astonishment that anybody could have changed so much and so curiously.

Ann's face had grown so thin and hard that it looked like something cut out of a rock. Her whole person had a rigidity that reminded Corrie May of a carved figure on a monument. She wore a dress of the plainest gray poplin with narrow white bands at the throat and wrists, the skirt made scant as though there had not been cloth enough for fashionable puffery. Between her gray-gloved hands she held a purse. As Ann advanced toward the desk Corrie May observed that she wore only her own hair, rolled into a bun below her bonnet—a sure sign either of poverty or disdain of the fashions, and she knew Ann well enough to be sure it was not the latter.

Ann was so intent on her errand that she did not notice anybody in the room. She went directly to the desk and stood before Gilday, but evidently she hardly saw him, as if he were not a person but a symbol. In an expressionless voice she said,

"I have come to pay the last installment of this year's land-taxes on Ardeith Plantation."

"Well now," said Gilday. He leaned forward, and removing his arm from around Corrie May he rested both elbows on the desk. He smiled slowly, his odd mirthless smile that was merely a stretching of his lips. "Don't tell me I'm meeting up with an old acquaintance. Miss Ann Sheramy, as I live and breathe."

With a flicker of astonished recognition Ann's eyes went to his face. She said coldly,

"My name is Larne."

"Sure, now, my mistake," said Gilday. He spoke with deep satisfaction. "Just like me to forget a lady changed her name when she got married. Don't say you've gone and forgot me, now."

"I believe your name is Gilday," said Ann. She spoke with so slight a movement of her lips that her face looked more than ever like something cut out of a rock. Corrie May observed that her hands had tightened on her purse till the knuckles stood out under the cotton gloves.

"Right, right the first time," said Gilday expansively. "Now ain't this a pleasure, us meeting again after all this time. Must be seven or eight years, think of that. Pleased to see you, I'm sure." He held out his hand.

Ann's chest rose with a quick intake of breath. Corrie May nearly laughed out loud at the thought of one of these furious aristocrats shaking hands with a carpetbagger. With a helpless rage that was no less evident from its boiling behind its white mask of self-control, Ann took one of her hands from her purse. As it moved from the purse to meet Gilday's Corrie May triumphantly observed that two of the glove-fingers were darned, not the sort of little darns she used to be paid to put at the fingertips, but heavy woven darns that implied decency maintained at the point of desperation. Gilday clasped Ann's hand lingeringly.

"It sure is a pleasure to renew old friendships, ain't it?" he was saying. "Let me make you acquainted with these here gentlemen. Mrs. Larne, folks, old friend of mine before the war. Mr. Dawson, now he's a bridegroom, think of that, and Mr. Cockrell and Mr. Reed and Mr. Farnsworth and Mr. Higgins, and this young lady I'm sure you remember, old friend of yours."

"How do you do?" said Ann coldly. She had regained her hand. The glove was strained with perspiration from Gilday's palm. Gilday was beaming with sneering pleasure. Ann's eyes fell on Corrie May.

"Hello," said Corrie May.

Gilday's arm had fallen around her shoulders again, possessively. Corrie May smiled. A flicker of expression moved across Ann's frozen face. Her eyes took in Corrie May as quickly and as completely as Corrie May had seen her. Corrie May knew Ann was aware of her train and her flounces and her blue velvet sash and her false braids. It happened in an instant: Ann's eyes narrowed and the corner of her mouth curled in understanding contempt. Then it was gone, and Ann's face was again like a rock, and her eyes were back on Gilday as if he were the remotest stranger.

"I have brought you the tax in full," she said. "Will you take it, please?"

"Sure, sure," Gilday responded easily. He reached for his record book. "Only ain't no use to be in such a hurry. Mighty hot day. Would you sit down and be sociable?"

"No, thank you," said Ann.

She stood motionless while Gilday ruffled the pages of his ledger. Corrie May's eyes went over her searchingly. She observed the smoothness of Ann's plain coiffure and the immaculacy of her dress. Such instinctive gestures toward the past struck her for an instant as pitiful. But she smothered the feeling at once. She wouldn't be sorry for her, not after that curl of her lip. How she would like to do something to pay her back for that! Not merely watch Ann pay taxes. But something that should take place between the two of them to demonstrate that at last it was herself and not Ann Sheramy who fitted the scheme of things.

Gilday found the page.

"Right here," he said easily, speaking slowly as though to prolong the pleasure he derived from this performance. "Ardeith Plantation. Property of Denis Larne, Junior, a minor. In custody of Mrs. Denis Larne, Senior, mother of the owner and guardian during his minority. I expect that's as it ought to be, now?"

"Yes," said Ann. She unclasped her purse. "I have the statement sent me by this office," she continued. "The statement says the plantation still owes one hundred and ninety-eight dollars, payable today."

"Right," nodded Gilday. There was a greasy look about him. "Right as rain. A hundred and ninety-eight dollars. This sure is the last day, too. If you hadn't turned up here before six o'clock we'd have had to put some of that fine sugar land up for a tax sale, and we sure would have hated to do that, now you know we would."

"I have the money," Ann said quietly.

"Well, if you've got it," said Gilday, "let's see it."

Ann took a roll of bills from her purse and handed them to Gilday. Corrie May observed that she moved the bills toward him endwise, so that he took them without touching her.

Gilday's hairy fingers went slowly through the bills. He moved his lips inaudibly as he counted. At last he looked up.

Ann took a folded paper from her purse. "Will you sign the statement, please?"

"Well now," said Gilday. His finger fluttered the edges of the greenbacks.

She pushed the paper toward him.

"Hm," said Gilday. "Hm." His little eyes went up to meet hers. "Dear lady, I sure would like to sign that statement. I'd be glad to sign it if you had paid the full tax. But this ain't the full tax. Now lady, dear lady, you know I can't sign a United States government receipt till I get all that's owing."

Ann's throat moved as she swallowed. Her shoulders gave a little involuntary shiver. But her voice was even as she said.

"I believe you are mistaken. Mr. Gilday. I am sure I gave you one hundred and ninety-eight dollars."

Gilday smiled. "Now Mrs. Larne, really now you're a friend of mine and I'd like to make things easy for you, but I'm an officer of the government. I got responsibility. You know there ain't but a hundred and eighty-eight dollars here. I ain't one of these fool niggers that can't count, and you wouldn't expect me to cheat the United States out of ten dollars, now would you really?"

Ann drew a deep inaudible breath. She said with terrible steadiness,

"Would you oblige me by counting it again?"

Gilday chuckled. At the warm pleased sound of it Corrie May began to feel a little soothing of her own resentment. He pushed the bills back across the desk.

"Suppose you count it, lady."

Ann caught up the notes and went through them. She made a little gasp in her throat. She started again, counting slowly this time, her lips moving as his had. She laid down the roll and looked in her purse. It contained nothing but her hand-kerchief and a bunch of keys.

"I'm sorry," she said at last. "I must have dropped a ten-dollar note on the street."

"Well now," murmured Gilday. "Ain't that just too bad."

"I'll get it somehow," Ann said breathlessly. "I'll bring it to you tomorrow."

Gilday shook his head with lingering enjoyment. "Ain't it a shame, now. You know, this is the last day to pay them taxes. That statement you got says six o'clock today, plain as writing can be."

Ann's eyes went to the clock on the wall. "Mr. Gilday," she urged desperately, "it's half-past four. To drive from here to Ardeith in a carriage takes two hours. It would be two hours

back. I couldn't possibly bring you that ten dollars before six
o'clock."

"Well, well," said Gilday. He leaned back in his chair. His
fingers began to play with the watch-chain across his middle.
"That paper says six o'clock today, right out in the English
language."

Corrie May would not have thought it possible for a face to
get whiter than Ann's already was. But her skin got like chalk.
Gilday smiled insolently. He jiggled his watch-chain.

Ann gripped the edge of the desk. "Just what does that
mean?" she asked.

"Well now, we got orders to put tax-delinquent property up
for sale."

"The Ardeith sugar land—for sale—for ten dollars?" The
words came out almost like a scream. One or two of the other
men, who had been listening with a mild interest, began to
chuckle.

"That's the government's orders," said Gilday. He had
twined the chain about his thumbs and was rocking back in
his chair.

Ann was taking off one of her gloves. She drew her
wedding ring from her finger. "I suppose you'll allow me ten
dollars for this?" she asked.

The ring clattered on the desk. Gilday picked it up. He
turned it in his thick fingers.

"Why, it's got writing in it," he remarked. "Such little bits
of letters. Wonder could I read 'em?" He held the ring up to
the light. "Why sure, I can read 'em. 'Denis to Ann, December
6, 1859.' Such little writing, now."

There was a pause. Ann's ungloved hand gripped the desk.
Corrie May saw that it was reddened as though with work,
and where the ring had been was a streak of white.

"You sure this is real gold?" queried Gilday.

"Of course," Ann returned with more scorn than she had
yet let herself display.

Gilday flung the ring back on the desk. "Oh now, I tell you.
We've been really weighted down with this junk. Everybody
wanting to give rings and breastpins instead of money for
taxes. If it was old-time gold money, now, we'd know. But
how're we gonta tell which of this stuff is gold and which
ain't? We got no time to be pouring acid over everything. I

expect, tell the truth frankly, I wouldn't be able to allow you more'n five dollars for this thing."

"You—" said Ann, and she swallowed the last word into violent silence.

Gilday waved his hand. "Not me. The United States."

Ann stood up straight. "Yes, I know," she said slowly. "The United States." She took a deep quiet breath. "The United States."

Gilday twiddled his thumbs in his watch-chain. Dawson nudged one of the others and they both grinned with amusement. Cockrell tilted a bottle and refreshed himself with a drink.

In Corrie May's head an idea exploded. It was like stars and songs and banners of victory. She could feel a quiver of joy run through her.

She opened her porte-monnaie. Slowly and deliberately, she extracted a ten-dollar bill.

"Here it is," she said. "Put on your ring."

For the second time that day Ann looked at her, this time incredulously. Corrie May put her arm around Gilday's neck. With one hand she patted his thick greasy hair, and with the other she tossed the bill into Ann's insufficient pile.

Gilday began to ask "What's the idea?" But Corrie May paid him no attention. She said clearly to Ann,

"You take it. I got plenty more where that came from."

For a second Ann did not move. Then, very slowly, she picked up her ring and put it on. As though weighing the Ardeith sugar land against her own humiliation she closed her fingers on Corrie May's ten-dollar bill. Without looking up she said,

"Thank you. I'll send it back to you."

"You needn't bother," Corrie May returned casually. "You need it more than me, I reckon."

"What's the matter with you?" Gilday exclaimed. "That's my money."

"Shut up your noise and sign that receipt," Corrie May ordered in a low voice. "I wouldn't miss it."

Gilday frowned, puzzled, then gave her a one-sided smile as he obeyed. Ann put the receipt into her purse. She looked at Corrie May.

"You are very kind," she said with a strained attempt at graciousness.

"You're welcome," said Corrie May.

Ann picked up her glove. She turned around and went out.

As the door clicked shut behind her Gilday burst out laughing. "Gee, baby, that was funny," he exclaimed to Corrie May. "I didn't get the idea at first. But did you see her droop her feathers?"

Corrie May did not answer. She had begun to stare at the closed door.

"I couldn't have sold more than a few acres of that land anyway," Gilday was chuckling. "Only she didn't know it."

Corrie May slipped off the arm of his chair and stood up, "I reckon I better go get my dress," she said.

"All of you," Gilday reminded the others, "be sure to come around to our house Tuesday night. It's going to be some party."

Corrie May went out. On the courthouse steps she stood still a moment. She saw the Ardeith carriage, with Napoleon in the coachman's seat, go around the corner. Corrie May doubled her fists under her chin. She did not feel at all as she had expected to feel. She had resented Ann so deeply for so many years; she had thought when she threw that ten-dollar bill at her that her own reaction would be one of unmarred triumph. But it wasn't. She felt ashamed of herself. For the first time in her life she had deliberately done something mean and horrid, and for the first time since she had begun her association with Gilday she had discovered that she could not make herself be like him. She stood on the steps uncertainly, until she remembered she was going to the dressmaker's. She tried to recapture her earlier pleasure at the thought of her gown and its train edged with peacock feathers, but her whole party seemed suddenly like something that just had to be gone through with whether she felt like it or not.

Telling herself not to bother about what was over and done, she got into her own carriage and started for the dressmaker's. But she could not rid herself of the wish that when for the first time she had had a chance to act like a great lady, she had had the grace to act like one.

Chapter Eleven

I

LYING back in the carriage while Napoleon drove it along the bumpy road to Ardeith, Ann covered her face with her hands and pressed back the sobs that rose with little shoots of pain into her throat. "I am not going to cry," she told herself angrily. "It doesn't do any good. And they'd enjoy it so if they knew I was crying."

But she was so tired that fighting any sort of physical battle was too much for her, and her tears slipped between her fingers and ran down her wrists. Though she was used to it by now there came times, like this, when her desperation swept over her as though she had never felt it before. She was so tired! She was so tired cooking and scrubbing floors and doing the laundry and hoeing the vegetable patch; cutting up an old petticoat to make a dress for her little girl, raveling a shawl to knit gloves for Denis, covering a frayed hem with a flounce from another dress so she herself would not be ragged; hoarding for taxes and having Negroes elbow her off the sidewalks and hearing the tax-gatherers make obscene remarks at her as she passed. She was so tired of this whole battle to maintain decency and self-respect in a world where those qualities seemed to have no more existence. It was hard to remember that there had actually been a time when such things were taken for granted. Her memories of those lost years had withered up, like old flowers in an attic; it was almost as though that vanished world had never existed at all.

As soon as she could get her hands on so much money she must send ten dollars to that girl. Ann shivered as she recalled her, wondering how Corrie May, who had always seemed like a nice little thing, could possibly have descended to her association with that wretched creature Gilday, and wondering even more what she herself had ever done to merit the sneering condescension with which Corrie May had flung the money on the desk. She had given Corrie May work out of pure kindness, and she could not recall ever having spoken to her in an impatient voice, yet Corrie May had not offered that bill in the manner of one prompted by the gratitude the poor ought to feel for those who had befriended them. Her first impulse had been to throw it on the floor. Then there had swooped over her the knowledge of her own helplessness, and Gilday licking his lips at the prospect of offering the Ardeith sugar land for sale, and her children with nobody but her to care what became of them. So her hand had closed on the money, though while she heard her voice saying "Thank you" her mind was crying out, "But what did I ever do to make them hate me so?"

Heaven only knew where she was going to get ten dollars. The tax had taken the last dollar she could scrape up, and she had no prospect of more until she could sell this fall's cotton. But she could not have it ginned without pawning something to pay the gin-tax, unless Jerry could take it down to one of the secret gins the Ku Klux members were erecting in the swamps. Secret ginning was done at the risk of their lives, but unless they could dispose of their cotton heaven knew what they were going to live on. It was next to impossible to get any money from the pawnshops these days. Hugh Purcell had dug up some of the silver his mother had buried during the war, and he had been offered fifteen cents apiece for the spoons. Most of the Ardeith silver was still underground; it was not worth digging up.

The carriage had reached Ardeith. Ann gave Napoleon the key to the gates and he climbed down and unlocked them, led the horse in and locked the gates again. In old times the gates of Ardeith used to stand hospitably open from one year's end to the next, and when she first ordered them fastened after the invasion the day Virginia was born the lock was so rusty it had required oil and effort to make the key turn. But now, with the countryside swarming with marauders and half the food-crops stolen before they were ripe, Ann always kept the gates locked and carried the key on her chain. She looked around at the weedy yard. She used to be proud of the grounds, but now she simply could not do anything about them. She had nearly broken her back pulling up enough summer weeds to keep the avenue clear.

In the smothered light under the trees little Denis was playing with Napoleon's boy, Jimmy, both of them seemingly oblivious of the heat. As she got out of the carriage Denis ran up and summoned her to see a house they were building out of sticks and some boxes. Denis was bare-footed, and he wore a suit of plaid gingham she had put together from the skirt of an old dress. It did not fit him very well, for her sewing was clumsy and Denis was growing fast. But even in makeshift clothes Denis was an attractive child, prettier and sturdier than his little sister Virginia. Virginia had always been a delicate little thing, with a sober air about her as though she already knew she had been born into a stricken world. So far Denis knew nothing about the world except that he enjoyed it. He looked very much like his father, and he had the older Denis' gift for accepting what he saw without too many questions. Ann guessed already that Denis would never think deeply about anything unless he had to, and she had found forced thinking so painful that she could not help hoping he would never have to. She admired the toy house, and then asked him, "Did you write the copy I set for you?"

"Yes ma'am," he assured her virtuously. "I copied it ten times and put it on your bureau like you told me."

"As I told you, darling."

"Yes ma'am." Denis sighed. Ann brushed her hand lingeringly over his tumbled hair. Probably she corrected him too often. But there was so little she could salvage out of the ruins for her children that such economically gratuitous subjects as good English had assumed unprecedented importance in her mind.

Nobody was in the hall as she entered. Ann stood there a moment looking at the dust on the chandelier and along the scrolls of the staircase balustrade. She and Cynthia did as much as they could, but there was so much they could not do. Napoleon and Bertha and Mammy had stayed devotedly with them, but Napoleon had to spend most of his time supervising the few fieldhands she could afford to hire and Mammy was too old to do much. There was no way for herself and Cynthia with only Bertha's help to accomplish the tasks that used to occupy thirty servants. They had taken up the rugs and rolled them up with tobacco leaves in the attic, for it was easier to sweep bare floors, and the non-essential rooms they had locked up, since dust gathered more slowly if the doors were never opened. The house had the air of a neglected old man. As she went upstairs Ann ran her hand along the balustrade and looked at the dust on her fingers. "The poor can be clean!" she said bitterly under her breath.

In her own room she locked the door and rested her head a moment against the bedpost. A basket of worn clothes stood on her bureau next to Denis' writing-lesson, but she hardly glanced at it; after her visit to the courthouse her nerves were still twitching so that she did not feel capable of anything. But she roused herself to change her dress, for it was the only one she owned fit to wear on the street. As she took an old summer percale out of the half-empty armoire she marveled at what had become of all her things. Her racks of shoes, her piles of petticoats and chemises, dresses and shawls and bonnets, her dozens of pairs of stockings—they had simply fallen apart and disappeared, most of them, patch and remake them as she would. It had never occurred to her in the old days to buy clothes for durability. Nobody had warned her they were going to have to last forever.

While she was buttoning her dress her free hand reached toward the top shelf of the armoire. She hesitated, moved her hand down and reached up again to take the bottle of Bourbon standing there. A dozen times she had resolved to stop keeping whiskey in her room. The temptation to drink it was too strong when it was there under her hand and the door was locked. But what, in God's name, she asked herself angrily as she half filled the glass on her washstand, were you to do when your body and soul were screaming for relief? The liquor supply of Ardeith seemed inexhaustible, and in these despairing days she had often wondered how she would have gone on without it. Whatever they preached about liquor, these moralists who had never been made to face what she was facing, it did give you a strange courage and it did provide release on nights when you were too tired to sleep.

The sun was gone, but though the room was smoky with twilight the heat was still oppressive. The whiskey seemed to flow just under her skin and create a furnace within her to meet the heat outside, and it began to bring also the sense of peace she wanted. But not for long. There was a knock on the door.

She did not answer and the knock was repeated. She heard Cynthia's voice calling her. Ann roused herself, irritated. Cynthia was eighteen. Everything about her was sharp. She had a cutting voice and irregular features and a figure that was all angles—except for her clear skin there was nothing pretty about her—and she moved fast and had no delicacy of manner whatever. Sometimes Ann did not like her, though she always admired her.

"Ann!" Cynthia called again.

Slowly Ann got to her feet. "Yes! What is it?"

"Open the door."

Replacing the whiskey bottle in the armoire Ann reluctantly obeyed her. If Cynthia observed that she had been drinking, she did not say so; she had a rare talent for minding her own business. She simply said, "I'm sorry to bother you. But Virginia's sick again."

"Again?" Ann sighed. That poor darling was so frail, and the summers were hard on her. "What is it now?"

Cynthia's face was graver than usual. "It's not just a little attack, Ann. She's awfully sick. I came to call you as soon as Denis told me you'd come in."

"I'll go to her." Ann hurried to the nursery. As she went in Mammy sprang up from where she was sitting by Virginia's bed.

"Oh, Miss Ann, I'm sho glad you's come. De baby been so low!"

Ann bent over the bed. Virginia would be four years old in October, but she was small for her age. Her face was flushed and she was whimpering. At a glance Ann saw that Cynthia had not been mistaken; Virginia was very ill indeed. With a start of fright she put her hand on the child's burning forehead, murmuring, "Here I am, darling. Mother'll take care of you." She looked up at Cynthia, who had followed her in and stood at the foot of the bed. "When did it start, Cynthia?"

"Not long after you went out. She started screaming and grabbing her stomach. She's been dreadfully nauseated. It must be something she got at dinner."

"It's the milk." As she spoke Ann thought her voice

sounded rough as sandpaper. When this heat-wave struck several days ago she had thought yearningly of ice. But she had not seen a piece of ice in so long she had almost forgot there had been a time when she had found it necessary, and there was that land-tax in front of her. Buying ice would have seemed as foolish as buying diamonds. She held Virginia up in her arms and laid her cheek against the flaming cheek of the little girl.

Cynthia went on. "She can't keep anything down, not even a drink of water. I did everything I knew, but—" her voice lowered. "Ann, I never did see a child in such torment! I'm so glad you came!"

"Stale milk is like arsenic," Ann said tersely. She let go the child and got up, turning to Mammy. "Don't give her anything to eat. Water in a teaspoon if she can take it. Make a cold compress for her forehead. That might reduce the fever."

"Miss Ann," Mammy said sadly, "dat water in de pitcher is wawm as my hand."

"Tell Napoleon to draw some fresh from the well. It will be cooler." She bent over the bed again. "Virginia, sugar, try to be a good girl. I'll get something to make you well." Drawing Cynthia with her she went out into the hall, asking, "Do you suppose there's any ice in town?"

"Ice?" Cynthia frowned. "Why, I don't know. I think the ice-boats have been running since the war. But have you got any money?"

Ann shook her head. Twenty-five cents a pound, and the pitchers of lemonade she used to drink on hot days! "I paid the last cent I had to those vultures in the courthouse. But we've got to get ice somehow. That child's poisoned. I wouldn't give her anything out of the kitchen safe now for a thousand dollars."

Cynthia held out her hands helplessly. "I never heard a child scream the way she did. Is there anything you want me to do?"

"Take care of Denis. If I don't get down to supper don't let him eat anything but vegetables. No milk or meat. And tell Napoleon I want to see him right away."

She hurried into her own room for her keys and went down the stairs, through the liquor-closet and down into the vault. The big safe at the side stood like an armored sentinel, its dark sides blinking in the light of her candle. Ann unlocked it and turned over the trinkets she still had left. They were not many; she had pawned more than she cared to remember until the pawnbrokers began allowing so little for jewelry it was hardly worth offering. There was the medallion with little Denis' daguerreotype and baby hair. She had held on to that grimly, but now she picked it up, wondering what it would bring. Not much in these times, but perhaps enough to provide ice-packs for Virginia's forehead and keep her food fresh until this heat-wave passed. Ann slipped out the picture and lock of hair, and leaving them in the safe she locked the doors behind her and ran back upstairs. Napoleon was waiting for her in the hall.

She told him to take anything he could get for the medallion, and buy ice. He shook his head sadly and went off. Ann told Bertha to scrub out the old refrigerator. She went back to Virginia.

The child's fever was rising. Ann tried to cool her forehead with wet cloths. It was all she could do, and it seemed to be of little use. She thought of a doctor, but she had nobody to send for one, and even if she had, she doubted if he could tell her anything but that food ought to be kept on ice in this weather. The night hung hot and smothering over the house, the sort of night when well people with untroubled minds tossed and mumbled in their sleep. It was murderous weather for a sick child. Ann sat by the bed, or sometimes to ease her own restlessness she walked up and down the room, wiping rivulets of perspiration off her own face with her sleeve.

It was an hour past midnight when she heard Napoleon unlocking the front door. She rushed downstairs to meet him.

But his errand had been fruitless. He gave her back the medallion.

"I got one pawnbroker out of bed," he told her. "He says he's shut up indefinitely—he can't advance any cash on anything. Then I found the man who keeps the icehouse and got him up. I thought maybe he'd take the jewels and hold them for the ice until you could redeem them. But he hasn't any ice for sale; it was all bought and paid for by a woman who's giving a party next week."

Ann dropped into a chair, feeling as if her bones had gone limp.

"Napoleon," she said at last, "I know you're tired but you've got to help me. Go over to Silverwood and get my brother. He'll think of something I can do."

Napoleon went off wearily, and Ann remounted the stairs. Virginia was tossing and mumbling incoherently. Ann had never seen a child in such fever. So there was ice in town, plenty of ice. But some woman was giving a party!

Toward morning Virginia sank into a sleep that was like a stupor of exhaustion. It was after sunrise when Napoleon came back with Jerry. Ann hurried out into the hall.

"Have you got any money?" she asked Jerry breathlessly.

He put his hand into his pocket. "Three dollars."

"Go look at her," Ann said.

Jerry said nothing as he looked down at the bed, but turned abruptly on his heel and came back to her. Jerry was thirty-one years old, but he might have passed for fifty; scurvy had grizzled his hair, and Reconstruction was leaving deep tracks down his face. He wore a suit of butternut homespun and an old frilled shirt he had worn before the war to go calling on Sarah Purcell. He closed the door behind him and spoke in a low voice.

"Yes, Ann, she's very ill," he agreed.

"Can't you do *something?*" she cried.

"I don't know," he returned frankly. It was not Jerry's nature to hold out false encouragement. "If I had enough money I might be able to bribe the workers at the icehouse. Napoleon told me all they expected to get in from now till Tuesday was bought and paid for in advance. Some woman named Upjohn."

"Upjohn!" She twisted her hands together, blazing with rage. "And because that wretched little harlot wants to give a party I'm to stand here and watch my child die?"

Jerry took her clenched hands in his and made her sit down in a chair by the wall. "I'll go to town and see her. Do you know her?"

"She used to work here. You must have seen her around." Ann reached into her pocket and took out the medallion. "Find her, Jerry, and tell her she can have it if she'll let me be supplied with ice for a week."

He nodded understandingly. She heard him rattling down the spiral staircase. Ann went back to Virginia's room and lay down by her on the bed, spent with weariness. The sky had clouded over and the air was like steam.

II

Jerry's horse was tired, and he was tired too, and hungry, for he had stopped only for a cup of coffee and a piece of yesterday's cornbread when Napoleon brought him Ann's message. It took a dozen inquiries to discover where this Upjohn woman lived; he knew the Durhams had had to rent their home to a carpetbagger, but he had no idea of the names of the persons who had taken it. At last he was ringing the doorbell.

No, said the colored girl who answered the door, Miss Corrie May wasn't home. She might be at the dressmaker's or the baker's or almost anywhere. She was getting ready for a big party and was mighty busy. Mr. Gilday wasn't home either. He'd most likely be at the courthouse this time of day.

Jerry went to the ice-house. The man in charge was mannerly enough, but stubborn. He didn't want no jewelry. How'd he know if it was real or just glass? That lady that had bought the ice, that Miss Upjohn, she'd paid in real sure enough money, and real sure enough money was what folks wanted these days.

Looking at the man's lean body and hungry eyes, Jerry could not blame him. Since the war too many wretched people had tried to sell glass ornaments as jewelry, and persons unused to jewelry couldn't tell the difference. They were tired of being taken in.

Tying his horse to a hitching-post to rest, he walked to the courthouse. After an hour's waiting he managed to see Gilday. Behind his desk, Gilday leaned back and surveyed him, his thumbs in the side pockets of his vest. "Seems like old times, I swear it does, seeing all you Sheramys. Don't tell me you want something, now."

Jerry tightened his big mouth before he answered. Being deferential to these people was harder than paying their taxes. "I only wanted to ask if you knew where I could find your friend Miss Upjohn."

"Lord no," said Gilday, "I don't know where she is. I don't

keep up with all her goings-out and comings-in. What's the idea anyway? Here it's Saturday and I'm a busy man."

"My sister wants to buy some ice," Jerry said desperately. Exhaustion and hunger were beginning to tell on him. "Her little daughter is very ill, poisoned by stale food."

"Oh hell," said Gilday, "I ain't got no ice. You're just like one of these fool niggers hanging around the Freedmen's Bureau, thinking we're giving away anything they happen to want. What you think I'd be doing with ice around here?"

"Miss Upjohn has bought all the ice in town," Jerry pled. "And my sister's child is likely to die without it."

"That's so?" Gilday inquired. He pushed his chair back further so he could rest his feet on the desk. "Kids sure do take on and die, don't they?" he went on conversationally. "Seems like when I was a boy, hearing about how easy young uns die. My mother used to moan about it all the time. Said she didn't know why the Lord had to make so many, seeing they was gonta die anyway." His little eyes narrowed and his upper lip stretched and lifted away from his teeth. "You know, I expect, tell you the truth now, if Corrie May's bought up all that ice it must have been she wanted it for something important. And I guess your sister can get plenty more kids where that one came from."

Jerry felt his fists doubling. Without any conscious prompting of his own he reached across the desk and banged Gilday on the jaw.

Gilday's chair toppled over, but he was up and over the desk in an instant. Jerry felt a blow at his temple that sent him sprawling on the floor. Since he had had scurvy at Vicksburg he was not as strong as he looked.

A couple of Negro policemen pushed the office door open. "You havin' some trouble, Massa Gilday?"

Gilday brushed off his coat. "Take that white fool to cool off in jail tonight. Attacking an officer of the United States government in the peaceful exercise of his duties. And hurry up, will you?"

III

Jerry didn't come back and didn't come back. The clouds broke into a shower, and when it was over the sun blazed out again and the dampness rose in clouds from the earth. At last the sun went down in a crimson and purple glory that was tauntingly beautiful, and the stars hung low and big like gold coins. Ann sat at the window. These resplendent summer nights—she and Denis used to watch them, telling each other the stars were so near they seemed to brush the moss on the oaks. But she and Denis had both been so healthy they had never realized that these nights could be as dangerous as they were beautiful.

She turned from the window and looked through the starlit dark at Virginia. Earlier in the night Virginia had been screaming with delirium, but now she was quiet again. Ann bit on her fist to choke down the sob that came into her throat. Oh, where in God's name was Jerry?

As the day broke she fell asleep from sheer weariness, lying on the bed by Virginia, but she was wakened by her crying out again. It was another of those merciless days. She sent Napoleon to town to find out what had become of Jerry.

She was afraid to give Virginia anything to eat, and she was tormented lest in spite of his vigor little Denis be made ill too by food that could not be kept fit to eat in this weather. But Denis, though he protested at being put on a diet of sun-warmed vegetables without milk or meat, continued well. Ann left him in Mammy's care and stayed with Virginia. If only Jerry would bring that ice! People afflicted with dreadful nausea could sometimes ease it with melting ice on their tongues. As it was now, Virginia had a hard time keeping down even the cool water drawn up from the bottom of the well.

At last Napoleon came back to tell her Jerry had been locked up for striking Gilday. Ann had run downstairs when she heard him come in. At his news she sank down on a step of the staircase, resting her head against the dusty balustrade. She covered her face with her hands. "Please God, let her get well anyway!" she whispered desperately. "Don't do this to me. I can't stand any more."

Behind her closed eyes she could see Gilday's sneering mouth and Corrie May in the gaudy finery she had seen her wearing in the courthouse. It was as though they were laughing at her. "You can't stand any more? Oh yes you can. We're not done with you yet."

She went back upstairs. Cynthia met her at the nursery
door.

"Ann—" she began, but with one look at her Ann thrust
her aside and rushed into the room. Cynthia had drawn the
sheet up over Virginia's face. Unbelieving, Ann tore it off
again, but she saw Cynthia had not been wrong, though
Virginia's little body was still hot with the fever that had
consumed it.

She buried her face in the pillow beside Virginia's head.
Nobody had ever told her what this was like. Even in the past
days when she had been so frightened, she had not dreamed
what the suffering would actually be. Virginia was dead, and
she was such a little girl. Ann thought, "It won't really make
any difference to anybody. Nobody will even remember her
but me."

She thought of Corrie May Upjohn giving a party. There
would be molds and bottles packed in buckets of ice. Blocks
of ice and small lumps of it and chips of it, glittering under
the candles, like diamonds.

IV

In the weeks after that she felt so beaten that there were
long stretches when she really did not care what became of
Ardeith or of her, and all she wanted was to smother her
consciousness under a weight of black velvet oblivion. She
thanked heaven there was enough in the liquor-closets for
that; it was all she ever felt thankful for.

Jerry took her cotton down to a swamp-gin. But for his
taking care of her that fall the taxes would have swept
Ardeith out of her hands. Sometimes when he remonstrated
with her she roused herself, but after a week or two her
resolutions slipped out of her hands again. There didn't seem
any possible end to this. What was the use of fighting unless
you could see something ahead to fight for? She remembered
how Denis' mother had died, and began to understand why so
many of her acquaintances were dying now of mysterious
ailments for which the doctors could provide no pills or
plasters. It had never dawned on her before that there were
times when death was simply a matter of giving up before a
world too hard to bear.

Chapter Twelve

I

THOSE men who went galloping around at night all dressed up in sheets, scaring the daylights out of the Negroes, Corrie May thought they were funny. They were just lazy aristocrats used to partying their lives away and night-riding gave them something to amuse them. It was a scary awakening she got at the discovery that the Ku Klux was made up of desperate men risking their lives to fight the Reconstruction terrors. She had thought it was fine to tax every pound of cotton that went to the gins. Those planters had started the war and now let them pay for it. When she heard they had set up machinery in the swamps to seed their cotton so they could ship it tax-free down the river, she thought Gilday and Dawson and their friends were right to say they would find the hidden gins and kill any Ku Kluxer bringing in his cotton.

They did find a gin, away down in a swamp across the river. They hid there and when a line of sheeted men came up with several wagonloads of cotton they started firing.

But in spite of the laws against firearms for ex-rebels, the Ku Kluxers had guns too, and they fired back. And while Gilday was too smart to get hurt, hiding behind some machinery as he was, that fool Dawson got himself killed.

Well, it was too bad, for Dawson was a pleasant fellow. Corrie May went decorously in a black dress to his funeral. There in church was that woman Laura, all decked out in widow's weeds with a veil reaching to her knees. At the sight of it Corrie May nearly laughed out loud while the choir was singing "Asleep in Jesus." That woman being a widow and carrying a black-bordered handkerchief for her husband!

It was not until some weeks later that she was made

frighteningly aware of the fact that Laura's widowhood was not destined to remain indefinitely amusing.

Some nights now, Gilday just didn't come home. At first Corrie May was not concerned. She accepted it when he said he had been writing up records at the courthouse or playing poker with the boys. But one morning when she asked him where he'd been Gilday lost his temper and told her roughly to hold her noise. She swallowed the angry reply that came to her, thinking herself very clever to know enough not to nag at him, and before Gilday went out again he had become as genial as ever. Then, that afternoon, when she dropped by the courthouse to ask him for some money, she went through the outer office and looked through a half-open door into the inner room where Gilday kept his private records. He was sitting behind the desk and Laura Dawson, her widow's veil thrown back from her face, was half-lying across the desk, supporting herself on an elbow while she showed Gilday some papers she held in her hand.

Corrie May turned around and went out softly. She wanted to go home and think.

That woman, she thought fiercely when she got there. Whatever Laura Dawson was doing at any time you might know she was up to devilment, but just what kind of devilment was she up to now? Those papers. Whether or not Laura could read Corrie May did not know, but Gilday could.

Gilday did not come home that evening. Corrie May sat alone in the dark. This was something that had to be figured out. Laura might be smart, but the puzzling part of all this was that Gilday was smart too. Gilday had no conscience and no heart, and he would take what he wanted, but trying as hard as she could to be honest, Corrie May could think of no reason why he should want Laura. Why should he? Laura was neither very young nor very pretty, and Corrie May knew she was both.

"Oh please God," Corrie May began to pray, and it was the first time she had said a prayer since the men shot Budge, "please God blast that woman's sight out of her and make him come back so we can be nice and peaceful like we was. God, I know I been wicked. But if you'll make him like me as much as he did I swear to you I think I can get him to marry me. Don't punish me like this. I never hurt nobody in my life.

I'm sure I can get him to marry me if you'll give me a chance to try."

She opened her eyes. Yes, she had been very sinful and not troubled by her conscience at all. So now God let her know the dreadful thing it was to be a bad girl. You wanted your man and you didn't have a single thing to hold him by.

Oh you didn't, didn't you? Yes you did. You had your complexion and your figure, and the pretty ways you'd learned, and your new fall clothes. When she got up the next morning Corrie May brushed her hair till it shone, and put on her new dress of lavender-spotted black silk. This was Saturday and Gilday might come in early.

But he didn't come. Sunday morning she dressed herself fancy again. But again he didn't come. It was Monday afternoon when he finally showed up.

She sprang to meet him, flirting her train across the carpet as he entered the parlor. "Why Sam honey," she exclaimed, "how are you? Is you had your dinner or do you want some?"

Without answering, Gilday took her by the shoulder and put her into a chair. She sat there dumbly, wondering if he could possibly be drunk. She had no idea how he would act if he were, for she had never seen him take more than two or three drinks in an evening. But there he was, sitting across the parlor from her, and not saying a thing. Corrie May looked sadly at the big flowers of the wallpaper, thinking how beautiful she had made this house for him and now he didn't seem to appreciate that or anything else.

There was a silence, while she watched the sun on the wall move from one rose to another, and she could not think of any pretty things to say. She could only think, "Oh please God, please. Please!"

Finally Gilday asked, "You been waiting for me to come in, Corrie May?"

"Why sure," she returned cheerfully. "I didn't have nothing better to do. Can I get you a drink or something?"

"Ah, shut up," said Gilday. "All the time trying to be nice to me. Because I'm such a cuss."

She tried to laugh. "Why Sam, sure you's a cuss. I been knowing that. Is you all of a sudden getting religion or something?"

"Oh, get out," said Gilday.

She stood up slowly and started to leave the room. But he recalled her. "No, go sit down. I got to tell you something. I declare, Corrie May, I never thought it'd be so tough to tell you."

Corrie May sat down. "What you mean, Sam?"

He said, "Corrie May, I got married Saturday morning."

She gripped the arms of the chair till she thought the gilt must come off on her hands. She got out, "Samuel Gilday, are you losing your simple mind?"

"My mind ain't so simple," he returned with a short laugh. "That's why I got married." He braced himself and sat upright. "Now look here," he said sternly. "You got no right to be reproaching me. You knew how I was from the start. I got to get places, Corrie May. You knew it. Sure, you knew it all the time."

"Sam," said Corrie May, "did you marry Laura Dawson?"

"That's right." He laughed awkwardly. "Pretty smart of me, don't you think?"

Corrie May's heart was pounding till she felt as if it were about to knock the sense out of her. "That woman," she said. "Been on the street half her life."

"She'll be good from now on," said Gilday. "I can handle women." He leaned forward. "Now Corrie May, I'll tell you how it was. I didn't think I'd tell you. Just thought I'd say for you to pack your duds and move. But I got to make it plain. You're a nice girl. You got more sense than any other girl I ever did know, and if I got to marry somebody I'd a sight rather it'd have been you."

"What about you and Laura Dawson?" she asked harshly.

"Well, it was like this. That fellow Dawson, I never did give him credit for very much brains, but he was brighter than you and me ever knew. He was aiming to go to New Orleans. That's a big town and a rich town too. Even with the war they still got plenty money down there. And that Dawson, he had contracts to build levees at New Orleans—"

"What about you and Laura?"

"She's got all his contracts," said Gilday, "with his name written right on 'em. I couldn't get hold of them unless I married her."

"Your name ain't Dawson."

"Well," he exclaimed, "don't nobody in New Orleans know that."

The sun shone brightly on the wallpaper flowers. "Yes, I see, Sam," said Corrie May. "I see."

Gilday got up with evident relief. "Sure, I knew you'd see soon's I told you. Mighty nice of you to take it calm like this." He came over and fondled her arm. "Corrie May, I think a lot of you. I didn't want to do nothing to make you feel bad. It's a big load off my mind, your taking it like this."

She could not answer. She stared at him, nodding like a halfwit.

"But this is goodby," said Gilday. "It's got to be. I expect you'd better pack your things and be out of here by tomorrow so I can give up the house. I'm leaving next week for New Orleans." He pulled a roll of greenbacks from his pocket and peeled off several bills. "There's a hundred dollars."

She said stupidly, "A hundred dollars."

Gilday chuckled. "You'll get along. Well, baby, I got to be going. Goodby."

Then he was gone. She sat in the parlor among the cupids and roses with the bills in her lap. For a moment she could not think of anything except that it was the second time she had been left to face the world with a hundred dollars. Only this time she knew it was not very much money.

But as she heard his footsteps dwindling she sprang up. He could not go. Not this way. She rushed out to the front gallery and saw him getting into a carriage. Yes, he was going, he was disposing of her as coolly as he had taken her, and she would never see him again. The carriage turned the corner.

II

Corrie May went back to the woman from whom she had rented lodgings while she worked in the courthouse. The woman looked her over with distaste, but told her she could have a room if she'd pay for it in advance. Corrie May paid and moved her things in. For the next few days she sat on her bed bleakly, trying to tell herself things that would get her mind adjusted to what had happened.

That Gilday was a lowdown sneak. She'd been mighty fond

of him, too. But she wasn't going to think about that now, she told herself as the weeks began to dull the shock of his desertion. She knew by experience that rent and food could play havoc with a hundred dollars, and she had to do something. She'd worked before and she could work again if she had to. Only she might not have to. She had a trunkful of clothes and she wasn't bad-looking, and there were plenty of men around the courthouse who had looked enviously at Gilday when she was with him. But just as she had straightened out her thoughts to this point there came to her a revelation that sent every plan inside her head toppling as sandbags toppled when the levee broke. She was going to have a baby.

At first she would not believe it. After nearly a year! In the beginning she had been apprehensive, but then as time passed she had ceased bothering about it. And now that she was stranded alone, with Gilday gone, this had to happen to her.

Yes, they had been right, all those people who had looked askance at her and at whom she had laughed. They had known God would punish her. So God had punished her, even though she had promised she was going to try to make Gilday marry her, because God knew that if only Gilday hadn't left her she wouldn't really have cared whether he married her or not. God did all the things Pa in his preachments used to say he would do. She hadn't believed Pa, and now God was proving Pa had been right.

She had plenty of friends, or thought she had. They had come to her parties. But now that she could give no more parties they obviously didn't care if she lived or died. As for her old friends in Rattletrap Square—why, when she went down there she found out most of them could hardly eat, and they had a "serve-you-right" look about them when they spoke to her. She hadn't been near Rattletrap Square when she was prosperous, so why come back there now?

She had her clothes, but in these hard times second-hand clothes were hardly worth selling, and her ornaments had been nothing but showy glass to begin with.

She moved out of the house she was living in, down to a shabby place that was cheap. The winter rains came and the fog crept in till even her heaviest shawls failed to keep her warm at night. She hoarded the little money she had left, afraid to buy food till she was so hungry she couldn't bear it any longer, and then when she did eat it made her sick. She got pasty-looking, with bags under her eyes like an old woman, and her clothes wouldn't meet any more around her waist. When she went out she tried to hold her cloak around her to hide her figure.

On these cold nights when the fog was so thick that from her broken windowpanes she could hardly see across the street, she thought she had been a gilt-edged fool ever to imagine she knew what trouble was. With all that had happened to her, at least she had had the thoughtless self-confidence that came with a healthy body. But now she did not have that any more. She was sick, so sick that for days on end she huddled up on her sheetless bed shivering with nausea and weakness. It seemed just too much trouble to drag herself out to hunt for a place where her pennies would buy a few red beans. For days she would not eat at all. The less she ate the sicker she got.

So, she thought, she would lie here on this dirty mattress and have her baby all alone, and then God knew what would become of her. Probably the baby would die, and she would not care very much if it did, but she shivered at the thought that she might die too. She did not want to die. With all the beatings she had taken she did not want to die, though she could not think of any reasons why she should not want to.

One morning in April the woman who owned the house came into her room. She said the rent was three weeks overdue. Corrie May sat up and shook her head dully. "I ain't got no money," she said.

The woman retorted, "I ain't neither. I got to have my rent. What you think I rent rooms for—charity?"

She went and opened Corrie May's trunk. The dresses were still enticing. She grinned desirously. "I'll keep these here on account," she said. "Now you clear out."

At any other time Corrie May would have yelled back at her. Now she felt so ill it seemed less trouble simply to do as she was told. She dragged herself up and went out silently into the street.

The weather had brightened and the air smelt like spring. Corrie May stood on the street watching people pass. None of them noticed her. She just stood there, feeling sick and too heavy to walk. After awhile she sat down on the curb.

There was a ticklish feeling in her stomach. She tried to remember when she had last eaten anything. Yesterday, maybe. Or the day before. No, yesterday. She remembered slipping down to the back of the house and finding some cornbread and an old cabbage head in the garbage bucket. Maybe that was why she had this funny feeling as if she wanted to be sick and yet couldn't be. She was so miserable she could think no further. She was only aware of her misery.

A Negro policeman passing by shoved her with his foot and told her to move on. She got up obediently, glad the weather had grown mild, for her dress was no good for warmth. It was a plaid silk that had looked very fine when she had bought it, but she had never learned to tell the difference between silk that was really fine and silk that merely looked it, and this had begun to split with its third wearing.

The policeman had told her to move on, and she was moving almost mechanically. Without paying much attention to where she was going, she turned toward the wharfs. In the bright spring sunshine she stood watching Negro laborers load the boats. There weren't nearly as many boats as there used to be. Corrie May looked around, remembering how she used to enjoy standing on the wharfs to watch the world go up and down the river. Funny how when you lived on the river your whole life centered on it. If she was happy and wanted to celebrate she came to the wharfs, and in her moments of deepest perplexity she came to the wharfs, as she had done now without thinking, as though the wharfs were sure always to provide what she needed. Whatever happened, the Mississippi went on and on, heaving its golden waters to the sea unchanged and unconcerned. It seemed to her now that the river was the only thing in the world that had not changed in her lifetime.

Everything else had changed, and everybody, and now here she stood sick and tired and hungry with nobody in the world to care what became of her. But she cared. Oh, she did care, and standing here in the familiar sun by the familiar river Corrie May knew she cared in spite of herself, as if there were a little something inside of her that kept shouting through her despair that she didn't have to be beaten even now. You weren't beaten as long as you were so determined to stay alive that you'd do anything, anything in the world, to keep going.

Only now there were two people that had to be kept going, herself and her baby. She was startled to recall that she had even imagined she would not care if her baby died. She hadn't wanted it; she had hated it because it belonged to Gilday who had deserted her, but after all it was her baby too. Why, maybe it was her child who was going to be somebody, basing its rise in the world on its mother's knowledge that if you made up your mind to it you could stand anything. That would be something to leave a child. If you couldn't give it a big house and a plantation you could give it the ability to stand anything.

She was leaning against a box of freight, watching a Negro man load some empty hogsheads into a wagon. He climbed in and turned the mule toward the road that led out to the plantations. It reminded Corrie May of the day she had been so sunk in discouragement and had ridden out to Ardeith to ask Ann for work. Ann had been very sweet that day. To tell the truth, she always had been. With all her silliness and her exasperating luxury, she had been kind-hearted—and it occurred to Corrie May that of all the people she had ever known, how few there were from whom she had never experienced anything but kindness.

The driver of the wagon stopped a moment to lean out and chat with another Negro lounging about the wharf. Corrie May shuddered. No, she couldn't. After throwing that ten-dollar bill in Ann's face like that, she couldn't ask her for a meal now. She couldn't even ask for the ten dollars, for she had already received it, enclosed with a single sheet of paper with writing on it. She couldn't read the writing and had shown it to Gilday. He read it to her: "To Corrie May Upjohn, in payment of loan, Ann Sheramy Larne." She remembered how Gilday had laughed when he read it, and how she had turned red, ashamed. Today it seemed to her that she would rather jump off the wharf into the river than ask Ann for a piece of cornbread.

But what was it she had been thinking?—that she could stand anything. Lord, this was harder than being hungry. But if you were going to tell your child that the main idea was to stay alive and keep going, you must be able to say too that there were times when you gathered up your pride and swallowed it like a pill and pretended you didn't care. The wagon-driver wasn't noticing her. She climbed up and huddled into a knot behind the hogsheads. He finished his talk with his friend and started the mule.

"I'm going to be sweet," Corrie May told herself grimly as the wagon bumped over the rutty road. That thieving Gilday should have fixed this road. It was as rough as a forest trail. "I'm going to be nice and proper. I'm going to apologize for acting so stuck-up that day, and I'll tell her I want to work. I could do field-work if I had a good dish of victuals every day. And even if she's poor she's got victuals growing on the place. I'll work for my eating."

The thought was already making her feel better. Oh sure, she was going to have a baby. But she didn't have to whine like one of these fine ladies that acted as if they couldn't do a thing but sit around and be waited on. She remembered how Ann had lounged about in her frilly dressing-gowns before little Denis was born, and she laughed derisively.

The wagon stopped before a storehouse about a mile from the gates of Ardeith. As the driver started to unload the empty hogsheads he caught sight of her.

"Why hey, white girl," he demanded, "what you doin'?"

She smiled at him. "I just wanted a ride out the road. I wasn't hindering you."

"Well, you better get off now," he told her. "I got my work to do."

"You ain't going no further?" she asked hopefully.

"No, I ain't. Got to go in my house and have my old woman fix my dinner."

Dinner. Corrie May's stomach gave a jump. "Where you live?" she inquired.

He pointed to a cabin a long way out in the field, toward the levee. "Say, get along wid you, white girl," he urged good-naturedly. "I got to be gettin' home."

"All right," she acquiesced, and climbed down.

Ardeith was up the road. If she could keep walking long enough she could get there. She started to plod. How strange the fields looked. Here and there were a few laborers working, but not many. Half the ground was grown up in grass. But she had very little energy for noticing. She had to keep walking. No matter how tired she was, she had to put one foot in front of the other and keep doing it. If she could do it long enough she'd get there.

At last when her legs were aching and her head throbbing, she came to the gates of Ardeith. She'd go in by the front gate. Maybe it wasn't respectful, but around to the back was such a long way.

But the great iron gates were shut and locked. Odd. She had never known they had a lock on them. Corrie May put her face to the bars and looked in. Away down at the end of the oak avenue was the manor, its white columns shining through the moss as they always had, but between the iron fence and the house was a jungly growth of weeds, some of them shoulder-high. Here and there she could see flowerbeds not quite grown over, and oleander and gardenia bushes struggling bravely against the encroachers. Only the avenue was clear, though it was grassy between the carriage-tracks. Up near the front steps a little white boy and a little Negro were throwing a ball. That little boy must be Denis Larne. Why, he was a big child. Seven or eight years old. And husky too, by the way he was running around. If he'd been her child, Corrie May thought, she wouldn't have let him play with any ball, she'd have set him to pulling up weeds. These idiotic aristocrats! Not even war and poverty could put any sense into them. Probably it hadn't entered Ann's head that a healthy little boy could be taught to make himself useful.

The ball bounced in a wheel-track on the avenue and rolled down toward the gate. The children ran after it. As Denis caught the ball and tossed it to his companion, Corrie May called.

"Please, little boy! Denis!"

Denis turned toward the gate and saw her through the bars.

"Come here a minute, will you?"

He came up to the gate. "Ma'am?"

"You's Denis Larne, ain't you?" she inquired.

"Yes, ma'am," he answered politely, "I'm Denis Larne."

"Could you please let me in?" asked Corrie May. "I got some business to do with your mother."

"I'm sorry, ma'am, but I haven't the key to the gates. My mother has it." How precisely he spoke, with the same beautiful inflection she had listened to and envied before the

war. "My mother is in the kitchen, around behind the house,"
said Denis. "Maybe if you went back there she'd let you in."

"Oh, all right," said Corrie May scornfully. She started
around the estate, forgetting in her contempt how tired she
was. That young one and his exquisite syllables and all those
weeds around the house. Just like her, and all of them, putting
fine manners ahead of good sense.

Some of the fields were being worked for cotton. They all
had a neglected look, but it seemed to her she'd heard talk
about how folks were putting in more cotton now, since
Congress was going to take off the cotton tax. It had been
impossible to collect it. Lord, but she was tired. She paused
and took a deep breath. It wouldn't do to look too tired. Ann
wouldn't give her work if she didn't look strong enough to do
it. Here was the back gate, but it was locked too

The back yard was laid out in a vegetable garden, and a
young girl was working there, training some bean-vines over
the wooden supports set up for them. Near the door of the
kitchen-house was a washtub, and the clothes were hanging
out to dry on a line stretched between two fig trees.

"Please, miss?" Corrie May called.

The girl in the garden turned and came toward the gate.
She was tall and thin, with a knot of black hair at the nape of
her neck, and she was dressed in an ancient blue calico
darned at the armholes. Corrie May thought she had the
sharpest face she had ever seen. "A mean woman," was her
first opinion.

"What did you want?" the girl asked as she reached the
gate.

"I'd like to see Mrs. Larne," said Corrie May. "Could you
please ma'am let me in?"

"What do you want with her?"

"I want to ask for a job of work, please ma'am."

"I'm afraid we have no work to offer." The girl spoke
shortly, as if she had been bothered this way before.

"Please ma'am let me see her," urged Corrie May, remembering that she must be humble. "I need work something
awful. Please let me ask her myself."

"Oh—very well." Taking a key from her pocket the girl
unlocked the gate. Corrie May looked up at her, marveling
that such a young girl could have such a bitter face. She

began to remember—the day she had stood in the street to watch the troops march, the Ardeith carriage driving up, and an elegant child in a gown of spotted muslin dropping a curtsey as she murmured, "Good morning, Uncle Alan." It must be Miss Cynthia Larne.

She went up to the door of the kitchen-house. There was a fire going in the stove, and by the table Ann sat cutting a head of collards into strips like shoestrings on the plate. At her elbow was a plate of muffins. For an instant Corrie May stood there and looked at her. Ann's face was flushed from working at the stove, and her hair had slipped in little damp tendrils over her forehead. She had on a dress that had been some kind of print, but it had faded till the design was nearly gone, and at the neck it had lost a button and was held together with a pin. And cutting up collards. Good heavens above. Slave-rations.

As Ann became aware of the shadow in the doorway she raised her head with a puzzled expression.

"Why Miss Ann," said Corrie May, advancing a step, "don't you know me?"

Ann laid down the knife and fork and stood up. "Corrie—May—Upjohn," she said slowly. Then she exclaimed, "What do you want with me? Who let you in?"

"Miss Cynthia let me in," Corrie May answered. "I wanted to see you." Though she had meant to be very deferential and ask for work properly, the odor of the collards came to her nostrils and there on the table was that plate of muffins, and behind Ann she caught sight of a wire safe full of food, milk and a slab of side-meat and oranges piled up on the shelf. Her head got light and something twitched at the bottom of her stomach and she dropped into a chair on her side of the table, gasping. "Miss Ann, for God's sake give me something to eat!"

Ann came slowly around the table. When she spoke her voice was thin with amazement.

"Why—do you mean you're hungry?"

Corrie May nodded. She sat with her elbows on the table and her suddenly damp forehead in her hands. "I ain't had nothing to eat since yesterday I got some scraps out of a garbage can."

There was a silence. It lasted so long that the lightness passed away from Corrie May's head and her stomach righted itself and she was able to look up. Ann still stood by the kitchen table, looking at her, and not moving at all. On a shelf at the side was a bucket of water with a dipper in it. Corrie May asked,

"Could I please ma'am have a drink?"

As Ann still did not say anything she took this for permission and went to the bucket. A dipper-full of water made her feel better. She turned around. Ann's eyes had followed her. Corrie May began,

"Miss Ann, I reckon you thought I was kind of crazy, acting like that. But what I meant to say was, I want to come back and work for you. If you ain't got no money that's all right, I'll work the best I can if you'll let me eat here. I'd do anything in the world for you if you'd just give me one of them muffins there."

Still Ann did not move. Corrie May reached tentatively toward the plate. As she heard no forbidding words she grabbed a muffin and began to eat.

Ann was watching her. "You're going to have a baby, aren't you?" she asked in a strange monotonous voice.

"Yes ma'am." Corrie May set the plate on the table and swallowed the scrap of bread in her mouth. Ann went on.

"And that man Gilday has thrown you out, hasn't he? Didn't you know he would?"

Corrie May wiped her hands on her skirt. "Miss Ann, I reckon I should have knowed it. Only I didn't think about it. And now—"

As she hesitated Ann gave her a funny little smile. "And now when you have your child you can imagine what it would be like to sit and watch it burning up with fever, poisoned in a summer heat-wave—" she caught her breath like a dry sob —"while other people take the ice that would have saved its life and use it to cool liquor for a party—"

Corrie May's eyes were stretching. "Why Miss Ann, what are you talking about?"

"I'm talking about my little girl." Ann's voice was like the clank of a rusty chain. "My child who died last summer because I couldn't keep her milk fit for her to drink. How does it feel to kill children, Corrie May?"

Corrie May shook her head slowly.

"I ain't never killed no children. I didn't know your little girl died. I didn't even know you had a little girl."

"Didn't you know when you bought all the ice in town there'd be children who needed it? Children screaming for want of decent food in that horrible weather? While you were decking yourself with finery we were bleeding white to pay for it—you with your satins and your peacock feathers and your champagne bottles spinning in buckets of ice!" Ann put the back of her hand against her forehead and the fingers closed into a fist. "Oh, you had a wonderful time, didn't you, while my little girl was dying! And now you come out here asking me to feed you." She began to laugh. Her laughter was dreadful; it made Corrie May's flesh creep. Ann reached across and picked up the plate of muffins and threw it out of the window. Corrie May could hear the plate break as it struck the ground outside. "Get out of here," said Ann. "I hope you starve to death."

For an instant the two of them faced each other across the kitchen table. Then Corrie May found herself answering. She gripped the back of the chair in front of her and spoke tensely and clearly, as if these were words that had been saving themselves up and now came forth without any need for direction.

"You want me to starve to death, do you? Do you think what you want makes any difference to me? I could have starved years and years ago without it making any difference to you." As she talked she felt her spine stiffen as if somebody had rammed a poker down her back. "I don't know nothing about your little girl dying and I'm sorry she died but it wasn't my fault—no more than I reckon it was your fault the soldiers shot Budge Foster for not wanting to fight your war."

Ann was hearing her with amazed anger. As Corrie May paused for breath she said,

"Foster? I never heard of him."

Corrie May began to laugh back at her. "Of course you never did. I reckon a lot of things happen that we don't know anything about and yet it seems like they're our fault just the same. Oh, you make me tired," she cried. "You with your pretty talk and your sweet ways. You did right by your husband and children and you was respectful to your elders and you had a nice disposition, and you think that's all it takes to make the whole world run itself to suit you. Didn't it ever enter your head that sometimes there's a way of doing things that's got to go, and the people that do things that way have to go along with it? And you're going, because times have changed and your way of doing things is gone." She paused. Whether or not Ann was listening she could not tell, but Ann was staring at her with fury so intense that she must be hearing.

"You got trouble and I got trouble," said Corrie May, "and I ain't concerned about whether we deserve it. I'm concerned about whether I myself personally can stand it. You can tell me to starve to death but I ain't got no notion of doing it. I'm telling you, you with your veins full of blue blood and dishwater, if there's anybody in this room gonta starve to death it ain't gonta be me."

Ann had sunk back into her chair behind the table. Now as if her throat were tight she gasped out,

"Will you for God's sake get out of here?"

"Yes," answered Corrie May, "I'm leaving."

But at the door she paused, and as she looked back at Ann the stricken whiteness of her was too much for Corrie May. She added,

"Miss Ann, I'm honestly sorry about your little girl. But it's a shame in a way to have always had things, because then when you have to do without 'em you don't know what to do. If there's another bad summer and you get worried about your little boy, you put the milk in a bucket with a tight cover and put it down the well, and it'll keep just as good as if you had ice."

Chapter Thirteen

I

WHEN she had left Ardeith Corrie May walked and walked. The road curved past the fields, shaded with moss-hung oaks that were still unchanged and magnificent like the river. She had no idea where she was going now. She just kept walking, afraid if she sat down she would not be able to get up again. Her outburst had left her with a drained-out feeling, unable to think clearly of anything except that she must keep on walking.

She was so heavy. The burden of her weighed on her legs and dragged them back. Over her head the gray moss swayed and the wind in the leaves kept whispering. There was rhythm in the wind and the moss and her steps. She swayed on her dragging legs. The road began to sway before her. It moved, left, right, left, right. She felt herself going too, now on the left side of the road, now on the right. When she tried to stop the road moved anyway. Everything moved, back and forth, with rhythm and soft sound. She put her foot down and felt herself swaying. She put her other foot down and moved with her burden, back and forth. She couldn't see straight. The moss moved, the road moved, the trees moved. Her knees began to bend. She was down on the ground. Her eyes were closed. But she was still swaying, though she caught at the ground with her hands to keep steady. But the very earth under her did not seem steady any more.

Out of the dark came a slurry Negro voice.

"Lawsy mussy. Liza! Dis here white girl—come see!"

There was a sound of feet on the ground, and a woman's voice answered.

"Why Fred, I 'spect she's drunk. Didn't you see how she was walkin' down de road?"

"Drunk, you reckon? Dis time of day?"

"Plenty folks get drunk in de daytime. You don't nebber notice nothin', you wid yo' big empty head. Didn't you see her jiggin' from side to side?"

Hands turned her over. Corrie May opened her eyes. Above her were two shiny black faces, grinning amiably. She could see them, though not clearly; it was as though they were blurred about the edges. She managed to speak.

"I ain't been drinking."

An odd tender look came into the woman's face. "Lawd, Fred, she's gonta have a baby." She put her hand under Corrie May's shoulders. "Can't you walk, honey?"

With a great effort Corrie May shook her head. "No. I just can't walk no more."

"Where you goin'?" Liza asked.

"No place."

"Don't you live no place?"

"No." Corrie May tried to sit up, her fists pressing the ground behind her. "If I had something to eat," she murmured, "maybe I could walk. I don't know."

"You po' chile," said Liza gently.

Corrie May turned to Fred. "Ain't you got a cabin maybe?"

"Yassum," Fred returned dubiously. "But it ain't no place for white folks."

Corrie May managed to sit up. The world had stopped swinging in front of her. "If I was right good," she ventured, "if I helped you around the house and all, couldn't you make out like I wasn't white folks?"

They looked at each other and back at Corrie May. "Ah, you po' chile," said Liza again.

There was more talk between the Negroes. Corrie May didn't listen. She couldn't. But she felt Fred's arms picking her up, and then she was lying on the floor of a wagon, her head in Liza's broad lap. The wagon turned into the field. Liza held Corrie May as it rumbled over the ground. The next thing she knew she was being carried into a little whitewashed cabin and Fred was yelling at a crowd of black children, telling them to get along and mind their business. He put her down on a mattress by the clay-chinked wall. Liza held her up and offered her a slab of fat bacon. "Dis here'll stick to yo' ribs," said Liza.

Corrie May ate the fat and sucked the rind. Liza brought her a big cup of coffee.

"Now you drink dis here, honey. It's good coffee."

Corrie May began to gulp it down. "It sho is," she murmured. It had been a long time since she had had a cup of coffee like this, strong and hot and invigorating. She looked over the thick mug to Liza, smiling. "I know sho 'nough coffee when I drink it," she assured her.

Liza grinned at her appreciation. "You feel better?"

Corrie May nodded. She alternately sucked at the bacon-rind and sipped the coffee smiling meanwhile at the vari-sized pickaninnies who clustered around staring at her. "You sho got plenty children," she remarked to Liza.

"Sebm head," Liza told her proudly. She was rocking back and forth in a cane-bottomed chair. "I declare to my soul," she added, "ain't nothin' de matter wid you. You was just hungry."

"That's right," agreed Corrie May. She swung her legs off the pallet and knelt on the floor to put her arms around Liza. "You's a good Christian woman," she said. "You'll go to heaven when you die."

"I's sho prayin' de Lawd, sugar," said Liza.

"I'll pray for you every day I draw breath," promised Corrie May.

She dropped her head into Liza's lap. "Oh, please let me stay with you. I won't give no trouble. I'll be all right soon's I get some rest and some eating. I'll work for you. I'll help put in your cotton or I'll watch your young uns while you's out in the field. I want to stay with you."

Liza wonderingly raised Corrie May's head between her black hands. "But sugar, you don't want to stay wid me. You's white. You's gonta have a white baby."

"You's a better Christian than any white woman I ever saw," pled Corrie May. "If my baby's as good a Christian as you I'll thank the Lord on my knees. Let me stay with you!"

"Ah, you lie down and get yo' rest," said Liza.

When Corrie May woke up it was morning. She stretched luxuriously. She still had on all her clothes except her shoes; somebody had taken those off while she slept. She felt miraculously well. Turning over she observed two fat picka-ninny babies asleep on the pallet beside her. There was a sound of shuffling feet and a moment later Liza, garbed for nighttime in a chemise made out of blue checkered apron-gingham, came over to the pallet. "How you feel, honey?"

"Fine," returned Corrie May. She reached to the floor where her shoes were standing. "I'll help you get breakfast."

Liza grinned. "Got to gib dis un his breakfast first." Picking up the smaller of the two pickaninnies she dipped inside her chemise for an ample breast. "Lawd, Lawd, dese new-bawn sho can eat."

"Where you keep your breakfast things?" inquired Corrie May.

"Fire done started," said Liza. "Coffee pot on de shelf by de fireplace."

Corrie May had no time to kneel down to pray. But when she had put the kettle on to boil she paused a moment and covered her eyes with her hands.

"Thank you, God," she whispered. "Thank you."

II

Fred was making a good crop. This piece of land had been put up at a tax-sale and he'd bought it on time. Just a little piece of land, he told Corrie May, just about big enough for a one-mule crop, but then he and Liza had been fieldhands all their lives on a plantation up near Vicksburg, so they didn't find it hard to make a living here. They'd wandered down the river when the Yankees burnt up everything around Vicksburg. With seven young ones, four of them old enough to work, they were doing fine.

Corrie May helped them the best she could. She didn't know much about field-work, but she could cook and mind the babies. Fred and Liza said she worked more than enough for her keep. They were good to her, and didn't pester her with a lot of silly questions about what was none of their business. Corrie May thought she had been misjudging Negroes all her life. She had never seen such genuinely good people.

The day her baby was born Liza stayed in from the fields the whole afternoon to help her. When Liza brought her the baby, wrapped up in a clean piece of sheeting, Corrie May murmured, "You sho is a good woman. Remember I'm gonta pray for you."

"Ah now, you got a fine big boy," said Liza. "You better pray for him."

So Corrie May obediently shut her eyes and prayed in her mind. "Please God, make my baby grow up to be a good man. Make him good as Fred and Liza." Then she added a white folks' prayer. "And please God, let him grow up to be somebody! Let him have fine clothes to wear and have folks speak to him respectful on the street."

After she had rested a little Liza bothered her to ask what she was going to name the baby. The pickaninnies had come in from work and they wanted to drink coffee to the new white boy. Corrie May hugged the little bundle in the sheeting.

"His name is Fred."

Liza gasped. "You mean Fred for my man?"

"Fred for your man," Corrie May assured her. "His name is Fred Upjohn, for your man and for me."

Liza laughed and laughed with glee. She went over to where her husband sat and slapped him on the arm. "You no count triflin' nigger, de white lady done name her baby after you."

Fred laughed too, thrilled and embarrassed at the honor. He came over to the pallet and brought Corrie May a cup of coffee to help bring her strength back.

III

Not wanting to be a burden any longer than she could help, Corrie May moved back to town as soon as she was well enough to take care of herself. She got a room in a house near the wharfs, where the people needed money so sorely they would put up with a squalling baby. The house had a back yard where there was sun enough to dry clothes, so Corrie May tucked little Fred under her arm and went to the back doors of the houses on the better residential streets asking for laundry.

Things were easing up a little and there were a good many families now who could afford to put their work out, so she got promise of enough laundry-bundles every week to pay the rent and buy food. She had to work hard and Fred was a lot of extra trouble. It was heavy walking with him on one arm and a laundry-bundle on the other. But somehow she found it was different about working when you had a baby. She had always thought a baby would be a nuisance, and so he was, but she didn't really mind, not as long as he kept well, and Fred was gloriously healthy. He shot up like a weed in the summer time. He was a fine boy. You could tell it by the way he strutted around even when he was just a little morsel of a child. He looked like a fellow that was just naturally *born* to be somebody.

Corrie May was so delighted with Fred that she did not have room in her mind to be more than slightly resentful when she observed that the great folk of the plantations were becoming prosperous again. They were raising bigger crops, and steamboat trade was increasing on the river. Sometimes Corrie May saw Ann, driving about in a new carriage with her little boy, who was very stylish in neat dark suits and striped stockings. Now and then she wondered if Ann ever saw her. Probably not, and that didn't matter. She had no wish to speak to Ann. Nobody needed to tell her more than once to starve to death. She wasn't starving, which in itself was something of a victory, and besides she had Fred, who was going to grow up educated and respected. As she went along the street, dragging him and toting the laundry, she reminded him that now the country was fixed so a man could get just about what he wanted.

"Carriages and horses like them folks?" Fred asked her.

"Sure," said Corrie May with confidence.

Fred measured his growth by the fireplace. When he got big enough to reach over the mantel, he said, he was going to work and get rich, and she would have a carriage to ride in like those ladies he saw around the park. Already he could run errands for her and help her carry bundles that were not too heavy. But when he was eight years old Corrie May told him it was time he was learning to read. A house near the wharfs, formerly a residence, had been turned into a school. It didn't cost anything except for the books.

Fred protested about going to school. "They keep them boys in all day," he said.

"But it's fine to go to school," said Corrie May. "You can't get along without knowing how to read."

"You told me you didn't know so much about reading," he countered.

"Yeah, and you see me, don't you?" she retorted. "Taking in washing, and me a white woman."

"You ain't got no money to buy a book."

"I got a dollar and thirty cents coming Saturday from a lady," said Corrie May. "I reckon that'll buy you a book and a slate."

So that fall Fred started to school. Corrie May got up early every morning to cook him a big breakfast of hominy grits so he'd have something to stick by his ribs through all that learning. Pretty soon Fred could recognize every letter in the alphabet, and one afternoon he brought her his slate, where he had printed his name. "FRED UPJOHN" in big letters. Corrie May was so proud she thought she'd break right open in the middle, and him such a little boy too.

But one day in the winter time when she came in from taking laundry home to her customers, she found Fred huddled up in the corner by the fireplace and he was crying. He wiped away the tears with his sleeve when he saw Corrie May coming in, but she rushed up to him and asked if he was sick or what.

No, Fred said, he felt fine. He wouldn't say what was the matter. But she insisted he must tell her, and finally he confessed.

She made his shirts out of flour-sacks, and the one he had on today was a new one. The lettering identifying the brand of flour hadn't washed out of it yet. The boys at school had laughed at him when they saw "DILLON'S BEST" printed right across his back, and he wasn't going to school any more.

Corrie May tried to cuddle him up, but he was too big to submit. She made him eat his supper and go to bed. After he was asleep she got into bed by him and cried a little bit too into the pillow. The next morning Fred just wouldn't go to school. No matter what she said, he wasn't going, not with "DILLON'S BEST" across his back.

Corrie May remembered there was a lady named Mrs. Price who owed her for two weeks' wash, two dollars. The ladies often made her wait for her money when it wasn't convenient to pay her, for they felt pious about giving her work anyway since she needed it so. Corrie May was too used to this form of Christian charity to be very critical of it, but today she went to Mrs. Price and begged for the two dollars, saying she needed it for something very special. After saying she really couldn't spare it this week Mrs. Price finally gave her half what was owing to her, along with a little speech about how Corrie May should be grateful to be working for nice people, seeing she had a child of sin and all.

Corrie May patiently said "Yes ma'am," to the lecture, but she ran all the way home with the dollar in her hand so she could give it to Fred.

"If you'll go to school tomorrow like a good boy," she told him, "you can have this. Go by the store tomorrow after school and for a dollar you ought to get cloth enough for two shirts, one to be in the wash while you're wearing the other one."

Fred's mouth popped open and his eyes widened with delight. He had never held a whole dollar in his hand before. Oh sure, he'd wear the flour-sack shirt another day. Then he'd have some good ones. A blue shirt and a white shirt, maybe, both new at once.

Corrie May scraped out the last hominy grits for his supper. It was all the food she had in the house. Unless Mrs. Price paid her the rest of what was owing her she didn't know what they'd eat the rest of the week, but if Fred had good shirts he oughtn't to mind being a little bit empty for a few days. The next morning she made him coffee for breakfast, which was all she had, but she felt so pleased when he scampered off that though she was hungry herself the day's work seemed hardly like work at all.

When he came in from school she ran out to meet him. But as he caught sight of her he broke out crying again like a baby.

"What on earth is ailing you now?" she demanded.

Fred came in and pitched his primer and slate on the bed and sat down on the floor sobbing. It took her a long time to get any sense out of him. He just bawled.

"Why don't you act bright?" she exclaimed at length. "A boy going on nine years old."

Finally he told her. Some of the big boys always stayed

around shooting craps after school. He never had, because he'd never before been to school with a copper cent in his pocket. But today he'd been so proud to have a whole dollar on him he had shown it to all the boys. They invited him to join the crap game after school was out. And he had joined, and they had won every bit of his money.

Corrie May was so sorry for him she nearly burst out crying herself. Then she remembered she mustn't do any such thing, because he was just a young one and she was a grownup woman. He had to have some sense put into him right now and there was nobody but her to do it. So by the time he had quit blubbering enough to notice she shook him by the arm, though it nearly killed her to do it.

"You's the no-countest, triflingest boy I ever saw in my life," she told him. "I declare, I'm ashamed you's my son. Shooting craps. Well, I'm glad you lost your money. Serve you right. And if I hear one more whine out of you I'm gonta spank you. Wearing flour-sacks is all you got a right to wear. Shut up."

Fred shut up.

The next morning she took him by the hand and dragged him to the schoolhouse. "You go in there," she said to him at the door, "and learn all they got to teach you. Lord knows you need something in your head."

But that afternoon she went back to Mrs. Price and told her they didn't have a scrap of eating in the house, and finally she got the other dollar that was coming to her. She went by and bought a loaf of bread and some beans, and then some calico for a shirt. Hurrying home, she ironed a pile of clothes belonging to another lady named Mrs. Harris, and took them around to her, though they weren't due until Saturday. Mrs. Harris told her she couldn't give her the money for them until the end of the week, but Corrie May remarked that it was time to weed the flower-garden for spring, and didn't Mrs. Harris want a good strong boy for the weeding? Mrs. Harris said she believed she did. So Corrie May said well, her little boy was sitting around most of the time doing nothing and for two bits he'd weed the garden fine. She arranged with Mrs. Harris to have him come around Saturday afternoon.

When she saw Fred coming down the street she was still sewing on his new shirt, but she hid it under the mattress. He

came in, still resentful, for the boys had continued to make
fun of the lettering on his back. She told him he was a smart
lad to go to school anyway and not to mind them, and the
trouble was those boys didn't have any manners anyhow, and
here was a good supper, beans and fresh bread. Then she told
him about the weeds in Mrs. Harris' garden, and how he
could earn two bits by pulling them up. "For a quarter-dollar,"
she reminded him, "you could get calico enough for a shirt, I
expect."

"You reckon?" exclaimed Fred, beginning to beam.

"I ain't so sure you deserve a job of work," she returned
casually. "You shooting craps and all."

"I ain't gonta shoot no more craps," he cried. "Honest,
Ma."

"Arright," said Corrie May. "Now come eat your supper."

But when he earned the quarter for one shirt, and she got
the other from under the mattress and showed him he had
two, Fred was the proudest white boy on the river. "Now
maybe you've learned some sense," Corrie May said to him.

She made him keep on at school a long time. He not only
learned to read and write, but to do sums, and he told her he
could do sums better than any of the other boys. He was the
only boy in the class who liked arithmetic, but he liked it so
much he sat up in the evenings doing the sums out of the
back of the book. Corrie May was uncertain just what good
arithmetic did even if you were smart at it, but she figured it
must be useful if the teachers said so. After awhile Fred
began coming home with his head full of the most remarkable
knowledge. He told her people hadn't always known about
America, but a man named Columbus had come from across
the ocean and discovered it. Corrie May hadn't known the
country had needed to be discovered.

"He just—found it," Fred informed her.

She looked around. "Well, I must say I don't see how he
could have missed it."

Later he told her about a man named George Washington
who had made the country free.

"Free of what?" asked Corrie May.

"The British," said Fred.

"Who's them?"

"People over the ocean."

She sighed. "Fred honey, I reckon them things is too big for my head. They didn't even know the United States was here, and then it had to get free of them after they found it."

Fred laughed at her, and she blushed.

But by the time he was twelve years old Fred was protesting in earnest about school. He didn't want to stay there all day while she worked. She told him to hold his tongue. She didn't mind working. Besides, he carried the bundles for her now on Saturdays, and helped her all summer.

"That ain't sho 'nough work," Fred insisted. "I'm big enough to make money."

"You got to get some learning in your head," said Corrie May.

"I got plenty learning. I can read good as anybody, and I can write and do number work. I ain't very good on spelling but I'm faster on sums than any of them. And Ma, they make us do such damfool things—"

"You quit saying such words. You hang around the wharfs too much as it is."

"Well, some things *is* damfool!" Fred exclaimed hotly. "They make us learn verses. I'm sorry that I spelt the word I hate to go above you because the brown eyes lower fell because you see I love you." He said it fast as thought it were all one long word. "Ma—" he got up and came toward her— "I wouldn't mind school if they taught you something reasonable all the time but if you think I'm gonta sit around and bang stuff like that in my head you got another think coming."

"Ah, go on," said Corrie May.

Fred looked away from her and smiled a funny determined smile. For the first time she noticed that he looked like Gilday. Fred was a chunky little boy with a roundish face, but with that little mirthless smile on his mouth it was as though she were seeing Gilday again and hearing him tell her, "I got to get places, Corrie May." She knew if Fred had got his mind made up now there would be no stopping him.

He spoke, still looking away from her. "I'm tired watching you scrub clothes all the time. I'm going down on the wharfs and get me a job."

His hands were thrust into his pants pockets, and she saw the pockets bulge as the hands doubled into fists. His whole attitude was so familiar that though she had an unreasoning reverence for school she could not answer him.

The next day Fred went down and started running errands and doing odd jobs on the wharfs.

Chapter Fourteen

I

IN the spring after little Denis was eight years old Ann ordered the family portraits brought down from the attic and rehung in their places. She took Denis by the hand and showed him the picture of his father.

"He was a great man, Denis," she told him. "One of the most gallant gentlemen who ever lived. You're going to be like him when you grow up."

Denis nodded gravely. Already he had heard so much about his father that in his mind the older Denis had become an inspiring legend. For a moment he looked up at the portrait as he might have looked up at a shrine that symbolized the ideals of his race. At length his eyes shifted to the other portrait ranging beside it. "Who's that lady in the big blue dress?" he asked.

Ann turned abruptly. "Why darling, that's a picture of me."

Denis' eyes went to her, wide. "You?" he asked in a voice too childish to have acquired any polite cover for astonishment.

She dropped his hand. "Yes, dear, in sixty-one I looked like that."

Without saying anything else she left him and went into the back study where she kept her confused plantation records. She sat down at Denis' old desk. Wonderingly, as if she were becoming acquainted with something hitherto strange to her, she put her hands up to her face, feeling the crease that had replaced her dimple and the little rolls of skin that were relaxing under her eyes. Sixty-one, and this was only sixty-nine. In August she would be thirty years old.

That afternoon she made Napoleon drive her to Silverwood. She saw Jerry alone and gave him the key to the

257

Ardeith liquor-closet. "Keep it," she said to him. "Don't give it back to me. No matter what I say, don't give it back to me. Not even if I tell you I only want some sherry to season a pudding, not if I say I've had a heart attack and need brandy——" she laughed harshly. "Oh, I can already think of good excuses for getting it back, can't I?"

Jerry answered simply, "I understand. I won't let you have it."

That was all he said. She looked up at his grave ugly face, wondering if he had ever wanted to drink. How little, after all, one knew about the people one knew best. Jerry was wise; he did not proceed to read her a lecture or tell her he approved of her resolution. But suddenly he bent and kissed her forehead. It was the first time she could remember his ever having kissed her.

As she drove back to Ardeith it was with a sense of relief and victory, though she knew there would be nights ahead of her when she would regret having given that key to Jerry more than anything else she had ever done in her life. She looked out at the wasted fields, thinking how like them she was. Then it occurred to her that but for the wreckage she might never have discovered even such reserves of strength as she possessed.

She thought of Denis, and wondered what it would have done to him to have had to face the ruins. Remembering Jerry's bitter, scurvy-ridden face she was glad she did not have to know. Denis would always be young; he was forever the soldier in the portrait, valiant and full of glory. She herself, worn out with defeat, did not feel capable of giving her son very much, but with such a changeless tradition as his before her, it should not be hard to make young Denis like his father.

As soon as she could afford to pay for it, Ann ordered a granite monument set up in the Larne plot in the churchyard along with the stones placed there in honor of Denis' ancestors. Cut into the monument were Denis' name and the date of his birth, and the line, "Slain during the siege of Vicksburg, 1863, and buried on the field of battle." On Sundays when they came to church they brought fresh flowers in the carriage and young Denis arranged them at the foot of the granite pillar. Their friends said it was touching to see Denis' devotion to a father he could not even remember. He was such a beautiful boy, and so jolly and clever. He must be a great comfort to his widowed mother. Ann said, "Yes indeed, already he almost takes his father's place," and she watched him proudly. Cynthia admired Denis too, though she took more interest in his skill at riding almost anything on four legs than in the pretty reverences Ann had taught him.

Two days a week Denis did his lessons with his cousins at Silverwood, under a tutor Jerry and Ann had engaged jointly, and the rest of the time he studied at home under Ann's supervision. She loved teaching him and would have liked doing it always except that she wanted him to have such subjects as fencing and Latin, which her own education had not included. Denis liked his lessons with her. Even after he was a big boy he would bring her his storybooks, saying, "Read to me, Mother," and would sit raptly, his arm across her knees, enjoying the sound of her voice.

Cynthia watched them impatiently. "He reads as well as you do," she exclaimed to Ann once or twice. "Why don't you let him do it?"

Ann resented her saying that. She could not help feeling that since Denis was all she had left she was justified in finding such joy in him. Except in her moment of confession just before Frances died she had never owned to a soul that her marriage had been a disappointment. But she could not deny it to herself; fair and shining it had been, but it had not given her the comradeship she needed, perhaps because she had hardly felt the need for that until her marriage was so near its end. But now she knew what she wanted, and she had another Denis to give it to her.

As for Cynthia, she was a great help in practical matters— such as voluntarily taking charge of the household so Ann could give all her energy to reclaiming the plantation. But when she spoke of Denis it was obvious that she could never have the same feeling about him that Ann had.

By the time Denis was old enough to be aware of economics, life at Ardeith was easier. Politically there was still confusion and taxes were still high, but no amount of chicanery could alter the world's need of the cotton, sugar and rice that grew so richly on the river acres. Ann told Denis of the struggle she had had to keep the plantation for him. She wanted him to appreciate it. "I thought I knew all about cotton and cane," she said to him. "But I found all I knew was how the fields looked at different seasons of the year."

"Then how did you find out?" he asked.

"Oh, you can learn almost anything if you have to. At first, of course, I could have been the most expert planter on earth without its doing any good. They taxed us till we were in rags. I used to cut up sheets to make dresses for you."

"It must have been a dreadful time," Denis said in wonder.

"Yes, darling, it was. But I did hold the plantation for you, Denis, and now you'll have it as long as you live. But for you I shouldn't have cared."

Denis regarded her with admiration that had in it a touch of awe.

II

As Denis grew up it seemed to him that the first thing he had learned about the world was the value of gentle behavior. Remembering, he thought the first important occasion of his life had been when he and his mother stood looking up at the portrait of his father, and she said, "One of the most gallant gentlemen who ever lived."

He thought he might have liked his father, who looked very gay and handsome in his gray uniform. Though he had been painted just before he went off to war, he looked as if he might have stood for his portrait just before a party. But his father had been the essence of nobility, kind to servants, courteous to ladies, irreproachable among his friends. When Denis was puzzled about what to do in any set of circumstances he needed only to ask himself, "What would my father have done?" His mother told him that, and she should certainly know.

His mother seemed to know virtually everything. She was a great lady, lovely in a sad way. Everybody called her a remarkable woman. It was splendid, people said, the way she was holding on to the plantation through these years, getting the taxes paid and making the land produce with a minimum of laborers.

Denis could remember his mother subtly changing with the years. His earliest recollections showed him a woman whom he never thought of as young, teaching him beautiful language and manners so insistently that he was past childhood before he realized that all boys were not taught these subjects. Sometimes she was quietly tender with him, and sometimes she would catch him to her and hold him convulsively as though afraid somebody was going to try to steal him away.

He frequently heard other women say his mother was the best-dressed woman in the neighborhood, and when he was a boy this used to surprise him, for nobody could ever tell exactly what she had on. She wore dark materials made with exquisite simplicity, and though they gave her an impressive beauty, Denis—with a guilty feeling—recalled her in the years when her faded old dresses had been somehow so soft, inviting for a child to rest his head against. He slowly began to understand that the soft old clothes had been remnants of her fluffy girlhood, and he missed the way she had seemed when she wore them. The heavy fabrics she wore later were like a shell around her. She looked like a great lady, assured and unapproachable.

In all she did she was so entirely right that nobody ever challenged her—except now and then his Aunt Cynthia, who was habitually irreverent. But even when Cynthia ventured on irony Denis' mother could quiet her with a word or two. Aunt Cynthia was often incomprehensible but always amusing. One day shortly after Denis' twelfth birthday she happened to meet him in the parlor. Denis sat by the fire doing his sums, so as to have them ready to show his tutor when he went over to Silverwood the next day for his algebra lesson. When Cynthia entered with her sewing he laid down his book and sprang up to draw her a chair by the other side of the fireplace. Noticing that though the day was cloudy there was a glarish light at that spot, he drew the curtain across one of the side windows to keep the glare from her eyes. As she sat down Cynthia murmured, "Thank you, Denis," but there was a puzzling flicker at the corner of her thin mouth.

"You're quite welcome, ma'am," Denis returned. But as he was about to go back to his algebra Cynthia reached out and detained him with a hand on his arm.

"Denis, every day I'm compelled to have greater admiration for your mother," she said slowly. "What a masterpiece she has made of you."

"I—what do you mean, Aunt Cynthia?" Denis asked.

Cynthia chuckled. "All the marks, boy, of the perfect gentleman." She leaned back, letting her workbag lie unopened on her lap. "Denis, I'm not the seventh daughter of a seventh daughter, but I can prophesy your future very well."

Denis was both confused and interested. He stood listening politely.

"You'll read the Latin poets, especially Catullus," Cynthia went on, "and you'll be fond of Byron, and you'll treat every lady as if she were in danger of breaking in two, and say the Army of Northern Virginia was the greatest bunch of fighting men God Almighty ever let get together on his earth."

"I never saw it," said Denis, rather wistfully.

"My dear child, do you think that matters? That's the ultimate test of your type, Denis—living by legends you don't know anything about."

Denis heard a step in the doorway. His mother stood there, staring at them both in astonishment. "Cynthia," she exclaimed, "what are you telling that child?"

"Nothing I can ever make clear to you, darling." Cynthia opened her workbag and began with great attention to thread a needle.

"Denis," said Ann, "a fire's going in the study. You'd better do your lessons there."

Denis gathered up his books and obeyed, though he left them reluctantly. He had an idea this was about to be an interesting grownup conversation.

When he was out of earshot Ann advanced into the room and shut the door behind her.

"Look here, Cynthia. I don't know what you've been telling Denis, but I'd just as soon you didn't fill him up with any more nonsense."

Cynthia unfolded her work. She was placing a bias band around the edge of a collar. Her eyes were on the stitches as she answered, "I'm sorry, Ann. I truly am. You're very proud of him, aren't you?"

"Yes." Ann stood by the window, looking out between the curtains at the double line of live-oaks leading to the gate. The month was December, and the air outside was cold and heavy with the promise of rain.

"I know," said Cynthia. "I won't laugh at him any more.

But maybe," she added without looking up, "maybe because I'm an old maid with nothing to do but sit around and watch other people I can understand their behavior better than they can."

Ann laughed kindly. "Don't be absurd, Cynthia. Calling yourself an old maid at twenty-three!"

"Don't *you* be absurd," Cynthia answered tersely. "I've never danced a waltz nor been kissed by a man. There must be thousands of me North and South, don't you think?—our husbands are at Shiloh and Corinth and Gettysburg, so here we are, left-overs of war. Not many of us will own up to it, but don't you think we don't know it."

Ann still looked out, at the trees gray with the grayness around them. At length she asked in a low voice, "Do you think you're the only left-overs of war?"

There was a pause. Cynthia placed several stitches before she returned, "At least you'll be remembered for creating a legend."

"What do you mean?"

"Magnolia flower with ribs of steel. And your husband the embodiment of a great tradition, when you know as well as I do he was merely a rather nice young man." She laughed shortly at Ann's startled face.

Ann turned around sharply. "I'm not creating a legend. I'm giving my son an ideal."

"It does sound better that way, doesn't it?" Cynthia returned dryly. She stitched a moment, then she added, "I'm not wise enough to say you're wrong, Ann, but when I hear all these descriptions of the fine Old South I can't help wondering if young Denis is ever going to find out how much of it was never dreamed of until after Appomattox."

Ann said, "Don't be a goose," and went out.

As time passed Denis grew to look more and more like his father. Everyone said he was a charming boy. Denis was healthy, handsome and well-bred; nobody had ever seen him rude or ill at ease. As she watched him grow to manhood Ann felt she had good right to be proud of her handiwork.

Chapter Fifteen

I

SOME days Fred earned money and some he didn't. But he was on the wharfs every day, and when the produce wagons came down from the plantations he ran up and offered to help unload for a dime, and was always glad to hold people's horses when they left them at the curb. Sometimes he got a nickel for that, sometimes as much as fifteen cents. There were weeks when he earned as much as a dollar and a half. He gave it to his Ma. She never fussed about things being hard for her, but he could see how she sometimes put her hands to her back as if she was so tired from bending over that washtub. And he could see too how mean the ladies in the big houses were, sometimes not paying her for a month and then taking it out of her wages if she let the iron so much as scorch the corner of a handkerchief.

But his mother said times were better than they used to be. She told him that if the rich people still had slaves she would not be able to get any washing at all, and Fred observed that on the wharfs he could get jobs as readily as any Negro boy his age, so evidently she was right.

By the time he had worked on the wharfs a year most of the men around there knew him. They liked him because he was good-natured and not a bit lazy, so Fred found it easy to get some sort of work almost every day. He looked forward eagerly to spring, remembering from last year how things had picked up after the winter fogs.

But that spring the river began to rise.

At first Fred thought nothing about it. The water rose every spring when the snow melted up North, then as summer approached and the snow was borne to the Gulf the water went down again. The river had risen pretty high last year, higher than usual, but the boats had gone on just the same.

But this year, the river went up and didn't go down. It kept going up.

As the water rose the steamboats all but disappeared, for only the most intrepid shippers would trust freight on such a current. The others turned to the railroads. There was no work to be had on the wharfs. Fred asked the men who sat about on crates and cottonbales what people did when the water got high. They shook their heads. It hadn't ever been as high as this, not since they could remember, they told him. But in high-water years, you just didn't do anything. Fred was astonished at such resignation. But they spoke with acceptance that had in it a sound of wisdom. No man could do anything about the river.

Puzzling about their attitude, Fred recalled that back in school his teachers had told him that in olden times the Indians used to worship the river, thinking it was God. Heretofore he had thought that was merely because they were benighted heathen, but now, though he was not a heathen and this was the year 1882, he began to understand it. The rising river was like God, silent, vast, inscrutable, going ahead without care for the little things running along its banks.

But he reminded himself God was not like that. In Sunday School they had taught him that God did care about the people in the world. His Ma was breaking her back taking in washing, and he was nearly fourteen years old and he had to do something to help her. That night after his Ma had gone to sleep Fred got out of bed and knelt down and prayed that God would not be uncaring like the river, but kind enough to give him something to do to help Ma.

The next day was bright and tangy with spring, and the sunshine seemed to be laughing at the deserted wharfs. Fred approached an old man who had worked on the river all his life and now sat taking the sun on an empty fruit-box. "Don't folks work some places, even in high water?" he asked.

The old man removed the pipe from his mouth. "Well, they work on the levees."

Fred brightened. "Oh. Up on the plantations?"

The old fellow ruminated, his mouth open and his tongue feeling one of his remaining teeth. " 'Pears like that un's getting kind of loose," he observed. "No, I don't reckon up on the big plantations. Places like Ardeith and Silverwood, for instance, they got mighty big levees and when the water gets high they just stop field-work and put all the hands on the levees, if there's any weak places. Anyway, I reckon the big plantations got levees higher than the river'll ever get."

"All the way up the river they got big levees?" Fred asked.

"Oh no," returned the old man. "Not at all." He felt his tooth with his finger. "You see, away up beyond the big plantations, folks ain't got so much money. State builds levees, but in low-water years seems like the State sort of forgets about 'em, and you know how it is with a levee, you got to keep at it or it's liable to get soft. I hear they's working quite a lot now." He sighed with the superior sort of pity folks give other people's troubles. "Tell you, I reckon there might be some floods up the river this year."

"What's a flood like?" Fred asked.

His instructor took a puff of his pipe. "Son, you ain't never seed a crevasse?"

"Crevasse?"

"Levee breaking."

"No. I ain't never seed one."

The old man shook his head slowly. "It's right bad, a crevasse."

Fred rested his elbows on the fruit-box. "Who's working the levees up there?"

"Oh, men. Levee gangs."

"They pay 'em wages?"

"Sure."

"How you get up the river?"

The old man shrugged. "Well, there's the river, and the road follows it. But it's hard work for a young un."

Fred laughed. "That don't make no never-mind. I'm tough."

He moved back from the old man and looked around the wharf. Not far away, sucking an orange, was a Negro man who lived in the alley back of Fred's house. Fred went up to him. "You Zeke, look here."

The Negro grinned affably. "Mornin', white boy."

"I got three cents," said Fred. He had been about to say four, but as he put his hand into his pocket he reflected he might need the extra penny, so he took out only three. "You take word to my Ma about me," he went on. "Tell her I'm going up the river to work with a levee gang, and I'll be back when the job's over. And tell her she ain't to worry about me. I ain't gonta get in no trouble."

Zeke promised, and Fred gave him the three cents. It was still fairly early and he figured if he kept going he could find a levee gang before night. With his spare penny he bought a cake from a Negro woman promenading the park with a tray. Pocketing this he started trudging up the road.

After awhile he met a wagon that carried him as far as Ardeith. At the gates of Ardeith he paused a moment and peered through. That place sure was pretty, like a church. Stuck-up rich people lived there. His Ma had told him that right after the war they'd been poor, but the war was seventeen years past and now they had money again. The lady who lived there had once ordered Ma out of her kitchen and said she hoped Ma would starve to death. Talking like that to his Ma, Fred reflected angrily as he started plodding up the road again and watched the little clouds of dust his bare feet kicked up as he walked. Well, he'd show them. When he got grown he'd ride his carriage along the front of their house and really raise some dust.

The day had been cool this morning, but now it was getting hot. Fred met up with another wagon that took him as far as Silverwood. After that he got out and walked again, munching his cake. It was getting toward afternoon, and he was tired. He walked on, and said "Howdy" to folks who passed him.

This was the first time he had ever been so far from home. The Silverwood fields looked pretty fine, and past the fields was a stretch of woodland. Maybe that belonged to Silverwood too. He'd heard tell how great landowners liked to keep some space for the flourishing of birds and squirrels so they could go hunting. Just as if there weren't enough poor folks like him and Ma who'd be glad to farm that land for the eating that would grow there. Past the grove he came to other fields, under cultivation but scrubbily worked. In the patches around the whitewashed cabins he could see women here and there hoeing the crops. Far across the fields was the levee, curving with the river bed, and even to Fred's inexperienced eyes it was obviously lower here than it had been farther down. The levee was like a long stretch of hill fifteen or twenty feet high, coming down toward the field in a gentle grassy slope. Fred tried to think about how fine it would be to get a job so he'd forget about how tired his legs were. It was late afternoon now, for the sun was on the other side of the river.

The road gave a sharp curve. As he rounded it Fred looked across at the levee again and saw that it was suddenly black with men.

Men were crawling all over the slope like ants. On the flat ground was a cluster of tents. In the field and along the slope the men were driving mules hitched to queer conveyances like enormous shovels, and the top of the levee, as far as he could see, was piled with sandbags. Fred turned from the road and started across the soft plowed ground toward the river.

As he neared it he stopped to watch the mules drawing the scoops, forgetting his weariness in his fascination. He could see now that the men were building a solid board fence lengthwise along the tip of the levee, about three feet higher than the crown had been, and they were piling sandbags against the fence to reinforce it. The mule-drawn scoops were bringing up tons of earth from the field to provide further reinforcement. There seemed to be hundreds of men, black and white. Nobody paid him much attention at first, but as he edged his way up one man yelled at him, "Hey, boy! Get off the levee!"

Fred tried to ask him if they didn't need one more, but the man giving orders to his mule didn't listen. He accosted several others, but all he got was a repeated "Move on, boy."

Finally he spied a Negro man pausing a moment to mop his face. The man was struggling with a heavy post about four inches thick, dragging it up the levee side. Fred went up to him. "Hey, you. Who's boss of this here job?"

The Negro turned a moment. "What you say, white boy?"

"Who's boss here?"

"Mr. Vance." He began struggling with his post again.

"Who's Mr. Vance?"

"White gentleman. Government gentleman."

Fred scrambled after him. "Where's he?"

The Negro paused again. "Up on de levee crown, by de sandbag line. Can't you see? Got on big boots."

He was off again, dragging the brace. Fred looked toward where he pointed. At the top of the levee he saw a long, gangling man who had his overalls stuffed into big leather boots reaching nearly to his knees. As Fred climbed, being ordered out of the way again and again, he had a feeling of confidence, for you could tell by his bossy gestures Mr. Vance knew his business.

At the top of the levee Fred stopped by the sandbag line and glanced over the fence. "Holy Moses!" he said aloud.

Instead of dawdling along fifteen feet below him, the river was as high as the original levee top had been and was edging toward the braces that held up the sandbags. Its beautiful golden indolence had become a brown fury; it was whirling and seething, full of eddies tearing at the levee. There were big logs in it, whole trees that somewhere upstream the river had torn down, and the trees were spinning in the whirlpools as though the river liked to play with them before dumping them into the Gulf. From here to the west bank was about a mile, and looking across that howling mass of water Fred had a blank unreasoning terror. He wanted to run.

Somebody grabbed his shoulder and a voice said, "Move off the levee, kid. Can't you see we're working?"

Fred looked up into the lean unshaven face of Mr. Vance. Getting off the levee sounded like a welcome order. But he caught the edge of the nearest sandbag firmly. "But I ain't gonta get off!" he exclaimed. "I came to work for you."

"Ah, get along," said Mr. Vance. "A kid like you."

Fred grabbed him with both hands. "Look here, mister. I'm stout and tough. I can tote sandbags good as them men!"

Mr. Vance started to grin. Under his week-old beard he had a ruddy, dirty face and a nice smile. "How old are you?"

"Going on fourteen."

"You're too little, boy," said Mr. Vance, hurriedly but not unkindly. "This is a big job."

"I can work like a man, mister. And I got to get a job. My Ma takes in washing. She ain't got nobody but me to look out for her."

Mr. Vance yelled at a man dragging up a brace. "Further down!" he shouted. "South end of the line." He looked back at Fred. "Suppose we had a crevasse? Not likely, but suppose we do. I don't want to take criticism for putting a kid on the levee." But as he saw Fred's eager face he began to grin again. "Well, Lord knows we've already got every full-grown man hereabouts. It's plenty hard work, and once on a gang of mine you don't get off till the flood crest passes. Go over to that foreman with the red hair and tell him I said put you to work. Ten cents an hour till the flood crest goes by."

Fred broke from him gratefully and ran over to the red-headed foreman. "Put me to work," he ordered. "Ten cents an hour. Mr. Vance said so."

The foreman took a notebook out of his overall pocket. He took down Fred's name, and with a glance at the sun made a note of what time it was. "See them wagons bringing in sandbags?" he asked. "You start dragging the bags up here."

Fred scrambled down the slope and grabbed a sandbag from the pile a man was unloading near the foot of the levee. The thing was heavy, a lot heavier than he'd thought. It was hard dragging it up the slope. But when he got it to the top and stood to catch his breath the foreman looked up sharply. "Well, what you waiting for? Bring some more."

Fred obediently trudged down. He knew enough to jump when a foreman spoke. But these things were mighty heavy. By the time he had brought up five or six of them the bags were so heavy he could hardly move them at all. He had walked miles that day and he'd been tired before he started to work. He observed that it was getting dark. He tugged and panted, digging his bare feet into the earth as he went. But even when it got black dark nobody seemed to be stopping. A bonfire flared near the sandbag line. Further along he could see other fires. In their light he saw the men still working. He got down to the bottom of the levee again and looked at the helter-skelter pile of sandbags. In the fitful light they looked enormous. "Well, take 'em up," said the wagon-driver.

Fred tugged at another. The slope that had looked so gentle by daylight seemed nearly perpendicular now and miles high. He closed his hands on the edge of the bag and felt his toes spreading and gripping at the grass as he strained.

"Coffee, boy?" said a woman's voice by him.

By the light of the bonfires he saw a rawboned woman in a dingy gingham apron. "Time for the coffee bucket," she said amiably. As he let go the sandbag she put a tin cup into his aching fingers, and taking the lid off a big bucket she carried she poured the cup full of coffee black as river mud. The steam rose up with an exquisite smell.

Fred sat down on the grass. "Thank you, lady."

"Sugar?" she inquired competently, holding out a piece of newspaper crumped into a sort of cup. "Just dip in."

He dipped his fingers into the pile of sugar and dropped it into the coffee. "Gee, this sho is good," he sighed.

She raised her voice. "Mrs. Lyman! Oh, Mrs. Lyman! Man over here!"

A gray, humped-over woman appeared out of the shadows, lugging a bucket in which were greens and fat pork. She gave Fred a plate and tin spoon and helped him generously. "Mighty fine of you men to work so steady," she told him as he began to gobble. In spite of his weariness Fred smiled proudly at hearing himself called a man twice in three minutes.

It was the best supper he had ever had. Even when there were times at home when there hadn't been enough to eat, he didn't believe he'd been as hungry as this.

"You done with that plate?" Mrs. Lyman inquired as he scraped up the last mouthful. "Well, give it here and I'll take it on to the next one."

She went off into the dark. Fred got to his feet, thinking how wonderful good hot food was. Now he could drag up that sandbag with no trouble at all. As he took it up he could see several dozen women, evidently the wives, mothers and daughters of the men on the gang, bringing buckets of food and coffee from the cabins in the fields. By the eagerness with which they urged the men to eat all they wanted and keep their strength, one could tell they dreaded the river with knowledge as sure as that of the men working to hold it back. Fred noticed that the men didn't loll around after eating, like those who loaded boats on the wharfs. These fellows lived in the cabins under the levee and it was their land the river threatened. They were working for a lot more than their wages.

"How're you getting on?" a friendly voice inquired at his elbow.

It was Mr. Vance. Fred could see that his whiskered cheeks were smeared with mud and his eyes were red-rimmed with weariness, but his smile was kind. Fred smiled back at him gratefully.

"Oh, I'm getting on fine, sir," he said as stoutly as he could.

"You better catch a little sleep," Mr. Vance suggested.

"Yes sir," said Fred, ashamed of how much he wanted it. "Where do I go?"

"I'll show you. I'm about to catch a little myself."

Fred followed him down the levee. At its base the tramping of men and mules had churned the earth to a gluey mud. They trudged to one of the nearby tents. Mr. Vance raised the flap, and Fred made out the dim outlines of men rolled up on pallets. They all seemed to be fast asleep.

"Where do I lie down?" he asked.

"Anywhere you can find room," Mr. Vance said. He smiled a little. "Pretty good job you're doing."

Fred beamed with delight, but before he could answer, Mr. Vance was gone into the dark to find his own sleeping-place. Fred felt cautiously along with his muddy foot till he found an empty spot. He tumbled down into it and went to sleep.

When he heard the men getting up, the inside of the tent was still dim, but a shaft of daybreak came through the flap. Nobody said very much to him. The men didn't talk much at all. They just mumbled wearily that the river sure was acting up, and they hoped it wouldn't rain. But outside the same pleasant ladies who had been on hand last night were going about with coffee and cornbread. Later on Fred saw them working the fields, helped by their children. Though the work he was doing was harder than any he had ever attempted before, Fred was glad he could help such nice folks.

The work got harder as the water rose. The laborers seemed scarcely to stop at all. They worked as Fred had never seen men work before. Three times a day the women brought food and coffee from the cabins. They brought out the buckets through the sun or the rain or the dark or whatever there happened to be, and the men ate, leaning against the scoops and wheelbarrows, and then went back to work.

They piled sandbags on the levee crown for a mile, thousands of sandbags heaped against the board fence. The women dug earth from their fields and brought it to the levee in wheelbarrows. The giant scoops worked steadily, drawn by mules too tired to give any but the feeblest responses to the lashes of their equally tired drivers. Sometimes the rain pelted them, sometimes the sun shone. The rain softened the levee and the mud clung to their shoes till their feet were heavy lumps that had to be dragged about. Most of the men took off their shoes and threw them into the fields, working barefoot.

Fred lost track of day and night and the passage of time. At night the men built bonfires to give light, but if it rained the fires went out and they worked blindly in the dark. When they were too tired to go on they stumbled into the tents, or sometimes dropped down where they were on the damp levee and went to sleep, waking up and swearing when those who were still working stepped on them, and going back to sleep again. The water crept up, inch by inch. Every morning they could see it was nearer the top of the sandbag line than it had been the day before.

In front of the levee the current gradually carried away the batture and the side of the borrow pit, and was eating under the crown. The men tried packing sandbags in the water to hold up the inner side of the levee, but the bags were wasted, for the river tore them away and carried them downstream. When the sandbags didn't come fast enough some of the men brought their own cottonbales and tried to bolster up the levee with those. Mr. Vance said to Fred that cottonbales didn't do much good, but the sight of them standing solidly there made the men feel better, so it was all right.

Meanwhile the women corralled the cattle in groups at the foot of the levee, to be driven to the top if there should be a crevasse. The foremen would not allow the animals on the levee yet, for they would impede the work. In the two-story houses everything had already been moved upstairs. Negroes from the littlest cabins brought their family Bibles or their cherished pieces of store furniture to the homes of white persons who were fortunate enough to have two stories, and they prayed that if there should be a crevasse the water would not rise that high. Children climbed the trees and hung bunches of carrots and radishes in the upper branches, hoping they could reach them if the levee broke. Little girls hung their dolls there too, and little boys their pet toys, till it looked like a travesty of Christmas.

The women and children had to take care of the property, for Mr. Vance could not spare any men from the levee work.

The wife of one of the workmen came to the levee and clung
to Mr. Vance's arm till he had to listen to her; she pled that
her husband be spared long enough to climb a tree and tie up
the bundles of clothes she had made for the baby who was
coming. Mr. Vance let the man go. It was the only concession
he made to any of them.

Those who had boats tied them to the front steps to be
ready for rowing to the levee if the water came through. They
packed provisions and put them into the boats.

But in the intervals between cooking for the gang and
putting their possessions into the safest places, the women and
children went on with their normal lives with a surprising
quietness. They hoed the fields and fed the cattle. The women
sewed on their front steps and the children played in the road.
The levee might not break. They had seen high water before,
and the levee had held.

Fred carried sandbags till his shoulders ached and his arms
were nearly numb. He built bonfires and worked by them at
night, and when it rained he worked just the same. He ate
when he had a chance, standing up or squatting on the levee
while some women dished up greens and pork for him. He
had to eat hurriedly and pass the plate on to someone else.
Sometimes he held cornbread in one hand, munching while he
dragged braces up the slope. He slept when he had to, in a
tent or lying on the ground; then he got up and worked again,
fighting the river with a fury he had never known was
possible.

He had forgot this was a job to help Ma. He did not stop to
remember he was earning ten cents an hour. This was a battle
he was fighting for its own sake, fighting so that cruel,
snarling river would have to stay where it belonged. They
would keep the flood back. They would make the levee strong
enough if they killed all the mules and half the men. But
they'd beat that river.

One day Mr. Vance met him while he was dragging up a
sandbag.

"Try making out like you're a mule and drag it behind
you," Mr. Vance suggested. "Sometimes that eases your
shoulders."

"Yes sir," said Fred. He liked Mr. Vance. It was only
occasionally that Mr. Vance had time to stop and say any-

thing personal to him, but when he did he was always mighty friendly.

"Wait a minute," said Mr. Vance. "Here comes a lady with some coffee."

Fred paused as the wife of one of the workmen approached with a bucket and a newspaper package of sugar. A dozen men clustered around waiting for the chance to dip in their cups. Mr. Vance filled his own, took some sugar from the paper with three muddy fingers and passed the cup to Fred. "Here, son. You fellows wait a minute—this kid's littler than you."

"Thank you sir," said Fred. He gulped the coffee down. It was good and hot. Mr. Vance, drinking coffee too, grinned at him. Mr. Vance's clothes were so muddy their original color was hidden, and he had not shaved in so long that his face looked like a big cockleburr.

"That sure is a help, ma'am," Mr. Vance was saying to the coffee-bearer. "Mighty fine of you ladies to help us so much."

"No trouble at all, sir, pleasure," she assured him, and Fred could tell by the heartiness of her answer that the ladies hereabouts liked Mr. Vance too. "When I bring the victuals for supper, you want me to bring 'em here or further down?"

"Here. The fellows at the end are going to get fed tonight by Mrs. Lyman and her bunch." He scrambled to his feet. "Well, son," he said to Fred, "I guess we'd better be getting back to work. Tired?"

"Oh no sir," Fred returned sturdily. "I ain't tired."

Mr. Vance smiled. "Well, try dragging 'em up from behind anyway. It's kind of awkward but sometimes it rests you."

Fred began to climb again, pulling the sandbag behind him according to suggestion. He wished Mr. Vance had more time to talk to him. It was a fine job, being boss of a levee gang; maybe when the flood crest was passed and Mr. Vance had leisure to talk, he would explain how a man worked up to a good job like that.

The men whose turn it had been to stop for coffee were going back to work. Mr. Vance was yelling at the driver of a mule-team. Fred listened with respect. Mr. Vance knew more bad words than any other man he'd ever heard. At the top of the levee Fred scowled at the tearing river. It had nearly reached the top of the sandbag line. Trees ripped from the banks farther up still came down on the current, knocking against the levee as if they too were now part of the river and shared its greed. Fred dropped his sandbag by the pile from which the men were bolstering the wooden braces and started down again. The sun was moving across the river, which meant that pretty soon it would be time for supper. He heard Mr. Vance shouting at the men.

"Tell that woman she can't bring those cows up here! Leave 'em at the base, lady. Hey, Fred! Fred Upjohn!"

"Yes sir?" Fred ran over to him.

"They're driving some more braces down yonder. You'd better bring up a few of those."

"Yes sir." Fred paused a moment and glanced across the sandbags at the river. "Er—Mr. Vance, is the river gonta get much higher?"

"Hope not, son." But Mr. Vance's face was grim. "Pretty tough flood, ain't it?"

"It sho is," Fred agreed. "Does it often get like this?"

Mr. Vance shook his head. "Highest I've ever seen, and I've been on the river twenty years. Must be damn near two million second feet going by."

"Second feet? What's them?"

"Cubic feet of water per second. You better start bringing those braces."

"Yes sir. I didn't mean to be loafing." Fred ran down the levee.

The laborers fixing the braces in place were working with a slow, dogged rhythm. Fred wondered if they were as tired as he was. He was so tired he forgot how long he had been here, and it didn't seem to him he had had any sleep at all to speak of. Dropping down like that when you were so tired you couldn't walk any more didn't seem to rest a fellow. You got stepped on and it rained on you. If it rained any more he figured they would all feel like just giving up. The rain got into the men's eyes and gave them colds. Now and then a man had to be sent off the job with chills and fever after working in the rain.

But he didn't. He was tough. Didn't anything make him sick. He was going to hold out till the flood crest went by. The ladies had promised after the crest went by and the men could quit working they would give the gang a big dinner with pork and chicken, for saving the levee. And then the government would send down some engineers from Washington to build an entirely new levee to replace this worn-out one. It sure would be fine to have a big dinner at a table, but that wouldn't be the reason why they would all feel so proud. They would be proud because they had beat the river. Lordy mercy, what a river it was! Fred was so tired he hurt all over, but he wouldn't stop. He'd beat that river if it killed him dead.

The men told him to get some boards. Then they sent him for loads of nails and more sandbags. Fred's feet were all sore and scratched and he could feel sweat running down his face and inside his clothes. Above the shouts of the men he could hear the river rushing past. That was strange. Usually the Mississippi crept down with perfect silence. Its noise now had a wicked triumphant sound. Climbing up and down Fred found that he was beginning to pray.

"Oh Lord, please don't let the levee break. Please don't let it break, Lord. We're doing the best we can. We'll work all day and all night and not mind if you won't let the levee break. Please don't let it break, Lord. If you'll let us hold the levee I'll go to Sunday School every single Sunday and not mind having no shoes and learn my Bible verses and not shoot no craps as long as I live. Please Lord, let us hold the levee. We honestly been doing the best we could. Please let us hold the levee. Please don't let it break. Please, Lord, please. . . ."

There was a shiver under his feet and a rumble deep down in the earth and under the rumble was a sucking noise. The sandbag line quivered. From the men on the levee went up a yell that was like no human noise Fred had ever heard, and they dropped their hammers and braces and sandbags and began to run, howling like wild animals and knocking each other down as they tore along the top of the levee in two directions, away from each other. Fred felt his shoulder grabbed and found he was being pushed by Mr. Vance. He tumbled down and got up again and ran. The cattle under the levee howled and the women screamed and the men shouted; and under it all was that hideous rumbling, sucking noise like something laughing. Fred ran, hardly knowing why he ran nor where, knocking into men and women and mules and cows, and everybody screamed to everybody else and to heaven—

"Crevasse!"

He fell down again, against the sandbags. He stumbled up panting. As he got the mud out of his eyes he saw the men and women trying to drive the cattle up on the levee. The cattle were howling with panic. Fred felt a kick in the pants and heard Mr. Vance shouting,

"Run, you young fool! Run, I tell you! My God, why did I ever let a kid on the levee? Run, you damned little snipe!"

Fred ran. Everything was all mixed up, white people and Negroes, mules and cows and pigs and buckets of coffee and papers of sugar and children and sandbags and wheelbarrows. The mob seemed to be slowing down. He was so out of breath he couldn't run any more. He rubbed his eyes, for they were still muddy, and looked back from where he stood on the levee top.

Away up yonder where he had come from there was a breach in the levee, and the yellow water was tearing through. The break was only about as wide as an ordinary road. But as he looked the sides tumbled in, caving faster than he could see; the sandbags they had piled fell down like marbles, toppling into the water as it rushed through the crevasse. A terrified cow kicked the end of the sandbag line and the levee caved under her and she fell into the water, trumpeting with panic. Across the widening crevasse Fred could see the men who had fled in the opposite direction from himself. Above the roar of the water he could hear them groaning and cursing as they moved backward. It was as though he stood on a world that had split in two, and he wondered if he would ever see those men again.

As he watched, the break was two hundred feet wide, four hundred, six hundred. The water was spreading over the fields in a yellow fan-shaped lake, sucking the levee under with a noise that was still like laughter, the way the man in Sunday School said God would laugh on the Judgment Day. Beyond the advancing edge of the water women were untying the boats they had made ready at their doorsteps and scrambling into them. Children were climbing into the trees where they had hung their toys. They screamed for their mothers, but their mothers could not reach them. The water pushed along the outer slope of the levee till the levee top was like a long island, twelve feet wide and reaching as far as they could see. Men and women and animals were jammed on it, moving backward in a lump, afraid lest the levee cave under them as the crevasse widened.

The two broken ends of the levee still crumbled. The crevasse was a thousand feet wide. The water had covered the fields and the road beyond and was still rising. Women and children were trying to row their boats toward the levee, but were making small headway against the current from the crevasse. Some of them were being pushed around in circles. The water had entered the houses. It rose and covered all but the chimneys of the little cabins. It was still rising.

On a branch of a tree near the levee Fred could see a nest with four little birds. The two parent birds were flying around them, screaming. The baby birds had their mouths open. The water rose to the lower branches and crept up. It crept up and up. It lifted the nest off the limb and the parent birds fluttered helplessly. The current turned the nest upside down.

"It wasn't no good," said Fred. "Our levee wasn't no good."

He was talking to nobody in particular. Everybody was making a lot of noise and no one paid any attention to him. All of a sudden Fred felt something hurt in his throat. It was a different hurt from the ache in his back and legs. He put his sleeve up to his eyes. He hoped nobody saw him. It made him ashamed, for he had not cried since he was a little bit of a kid. As he took his arm down he saw Mr. Vance, sitting on the levee, his legs hunched up under his chin as he watched the spreading desolation. Mr. Vance put the back of his hand to one eye and then to the other. At that Fred felt his own eyes smarting again. He surreptitiously raised up his arm. Mr. Vance caught sight of him and gave him a funny crooked grin. He reached out and pulled Fred to sit down on the damp earth by him.

"We won't tell on each other, will we, son?"

Fred shook his head. He was afraid to try to talk lest he was unable to swallow the hurt in his throat. But it was comforting to sit by Mr. Vance and know that even a big bossy man like him could get tears in his eyes at the sight of a crevasse.

The water had covered the smaller trees, and the branches of the bigger ones poked above the surface, thick with birds. The sun was tauntingly bright on the ripples. Here and there in the swirling lake Fred could see a chimney or the crest of a roof. The men on the levee called encouragement to their wives struggling toward them in the rowboats. Bouncing in the water were chairs, tables, mattresses, bodies of drowned cows and pigs.

After awhile Fred thought maybe he could speak.

"Mr. Vance," he said, "ain't there no way to build a levee so it won't break?"

Mr. Vance gave a long slow sigh. "I don't know, son. They say they can. But so help me God, I don't know."

Fred watched the carcass of a cow thump against the levee. Her udder was heavy with milk.

"When I get grown up," said Fred, "I'd like to build levees. Levees that can't break so people won't have to have things like this happen to 'em."

"Hell," said Mr. Vance.

Mr. Vance was mad. Fred didn't blame him. Only he himself didn't feel exactly mad. He felt defeated. All that backbreaking work, and now it was exactly as if they hadn't worked at all.

It was getting to be night. The sun went down. The day halted for a moment, with stark white light in which everything was clearer than it had been in the sun. Then, abruptly, it was dark.

The folks on the levee had built a bonfire. Fred could smell coffee. Some of the women had stocked their boats with provisions, so he guessed they wouldn't starve.

"How long do we stay here like this, Mr. Vance?" he ventured.

"What?" Mr. Vance turned his head sharply, as though his mind as well as his eyes had been on nothing but the yellow destruction before him.

Fred repeated his question.

"Oh, a day or two. The state has a fleet of boats out for relief. Soon as they hear there's been a crevasse up here they'll send for us. We won't drown. That water's as high as it's going to get."

"You know all about the river, don't you?" Fred asked enviously.

"I ought to," Mr. Vance returned grimly. "Been working it most of my life. But I reckon don't anybody know all about this river."

Fred wished he could run away. He felt he wanted never to see another crevasse as long as he lived. Bodies of animals kept bumping against the levee. Furniture and pieces of clothing floated by, all sorts of things, things people had and took care of. In spite of Mr. Vance, Fred kept thinking there had to be a way to build levees that would keep things like this from happening.

He sat there in the dark, while the bonfires glittered over the water and the refugees huddled around them. Mr. Vance stretched out on the ground, his arm under his head.

"Better try to sleep, son," he suggested.

Fred lay down too.

"Mr. Vance," he said, "before you go to sleep—"

"Yes?"

"Do you work on the river all the time?"

"Pretty much. Why?"

"I'd like to work levees. Maybe if I worked them all the time I could help think up ways to build 'em stronger. You reckon I could work with you?"

Mr. Vance reached over and patted Fred's arm. "Well, I tell you, son, if you grow up to be smarter than the river you'll be a mighty big man. I don't reckon you'll ever be that smart. But—let's see. You ever been to school?"

"All the way through the fourth grade," said Fred eagerly, though he didn't quite see what that had to do with piling dirt on a levee.

"Take arithmetic?"

"You're mighty right I did," Fred exclaimed. "I was the best in the class. We was up to problems about decimal fractions. I could do every one of 'em."

"Well, I tell you," said Mr. Vance. "I don't see why you shouldn't work regular."

"You mean it?" Fred sat up.

"Sure. You shut up now and go to sleep."

"Yes sir." Fred lay down. But even as he watched the bonfires flickering over the terrible water he felt happy. He was going to fight the river, and besides he had a regular job. Maybe Ma had been right after all about making him go to school. He hoped the rescue boats would come in a hurry so he could get home and tell her.

II

Corrie May knew she shouldn't be worried about Fred. He was a sensible boy and could look out for himself. But when she heard there'd been a crevasse up the river she was troubled in her mind. As she could not make out what the papers said about the flood, she spent as much time as she could around the wharf, asking the men there if they'd heard anything about Fred. No, they said, they hadn't, but they supposed he was all right. But she found their optimism far from satisfying.

So one noontime a week after the crevasse, when she came out of her alley with a basket of clean clothes on her arm and caught sight of Fred walking toward their lodgings, Corrie May dropped her basket right there on the street and rushed toward him, calling his name. Fred came running along the sidewalk to meet her.

"Oh, Fred honey," she cried, "I been so worried! Oh, praise the Lord you're all right, Fred sugar—"

She hugged and kissed him, too happy to remember he was a big boy now and averse to such goings-on.

Fred gave an embarrassed laugh and wriggled himself out of her arms. "Oh Ma, can't you see I'm all right? Quit kissing me!"

"But Fred, I been so upset! Was you there when the levee broke?"

"Sure, I was there," he returned like a fellow who knew all about everything and found it boresome to recount his adventures.

"Tell me about it."

"Oh, I'll tell you sometime," Fred answered nonchalantly. "Take too long now. Say, you better get them clothes. Somebody's gonta walk off with 'em."

Together they went back to where she had dropped the basket. "I'll tote it for you," Fred offered as she reached the handle.

Corrie May's excitement was subsiding enough to let her take a good look at him. "Fred Upjohn," she exclaimed, "you sure is a sight."

Her eyes went over him. Fred's clothes were stiff with dried mud. His shirt dangled in strips, one sleeve entirely gone, and the bottoms of his trouser-legs flapped like fringe about his dirty shins. Even his hair was caked with earth.

But Fred laughed at her shocked gaze. "Man does get dirty up on a levee," he said airily. "Say, it sure is getting hot. You feel like some lemonade?"

"Lemonade?" she gasped.

Fred was already strolling over to a stall where refreshments were offered for sale, and she heard him grandly giving orders for two glasses of iced lemonade. "And mind you squeeze the lemons fresh," he directed the boy.

Amazed, Corrie May followed him. Except for the year she had spent with Gilday she had never been affluent enough to buy such luxuries. She stared as Fred laid down a dollar bill in payment for the drinks and gathered up the change. He grinned, handing her the glass.

"Right nice, ain't it?" he commented. He had set the clothes-basket on the ground by him.

She nodded. "But Fred, you ain't got no business wasting your money like this. You ought to get yourself some clothes. That outfit of yourn ain't fit to be a dishrag."

"Oh, I'll get some clothes," said Fred. Corrie May was suddenly aware that she had to look up to him as he talked. Fred began to stroke the ground with his toes. "And—er—Ma," he began.

"What?"

Fred got a little bit pink. He stammered. "Er—you—I mean—you better get a dress too. Here."

He reached into his pocket and offered her a five-dollar bill.

"Fred! What you been doing?" Corrie May demanded in

alarm. She gripped his elbow. "Is you been up to something you shouldn't?"

"No, no. Lemme go, Ma. Holding me like I was a baby! you know I been working on the levee upriver! These is my wages. Ten cents an hour I got, and I worked twelve-fifteen hours a day, Sundays and all. We even got paid for the time we sat on the levee waiting for the relief boat."

Corrie May swallowed a scrap of ice from the lemonade and coughed. "Well, well," she said when she could speak. For the first time she felt almost ill at ease with him. He was so grown up. She asked politely, "Was it bad, the flood?"

"Yes. Right bad," Fred answered briefly. "But Ma, that ain't what I was gonta tell you." He set his empty glass on the counter.

"Look, Fred," she interrupted, "there comes a carriage. If they get out maybe they'd give you a nickel to hold the horses."

"I ain't holding no more horses." Fred did not even glance at the carriage. But as she set down her own glass Corrie May noticed that it was the carriage from Ardeith, so it was just as well. She didn't want Fred to have to work for the Larnes. "Listen, Ma," Fred was saying. "I got a job. I mean a real sho' enough job, regular."

She turned back to him in delight. "Honest? Doing what?"

"Learning how to be a levee man." Fred had lost his embarrassment and was talking fast. "Ma, I'm gonta work for Mr. Vance; he's the fellow that bossed the job I just been on. He knows more about levees—" Fred sounded almost out of breath with eagerness. "I'm gonta start in Monday. He's giving me three dollars a week to start with. He says if I keep on I can get to be a boss like him. I might even get to be a contractor building levees for the government."

"Why—Fred!" Her face glowed as she listened.

"And them contractors is big men, they go to Washington and everything, sometimes they even get to talk to the President—"

"My Lord," gasped Corrie May.

It was all she could say. This was too much for her to

answer. Fred was still talking, but she could hardly listen for the glorious whirling in her head. Fred Upjohn, her own son, talking to the President. Corrie May saw the Ardeith carriage come to a stop by the curb. She saw Denis Larne get out, a slender, exquisite young gentleman in a gray broadcloth suit.

"—and Ma, it's really just like you told me. Mr. Vance said didn't nobody but niggers used to work the levees. In the days when the planters all had so many slaves they just put the niggers on 'em, but now if a white boy don't mind working he can learn all about levees and get to be a real big man—"

Denis Larne held out his hand and assisted his mother to alight from the carriage. Involuntarily Corrie May's eyes followed Ann, who stood still an instant while Denis closed the carriage door behind her. How striking she was still, though she was no longer young. She had on a dark blue silk dress and a dark blue bonnet with a yellow plume across the top. Her bodice was laced to elegant fragility, and below it her skirt fell to the ground, so tight Corrie May wondered if she didn't have to tie her knees together to take a step without splitting it. And young Denis in his impeccable broadcloth was no less elegant as he took her arm with the grace of perfect assurance. The splendor faded out of Corrie May's mind. That magnificent confidence of birth! Fred might get to be the biggest contractor that ever was, she thought wistfully, but he'd never acquire such effortless charm as that. It took—oh, generations. With a sensation of resentment she remembered her father's legend that she and Ann Sheramy had an ancestor in common. Fred's voice was going on insistently in her ears.

"—now listen, Ma, if I'm making three dollars a week you won't have to do so much washing. Tell the truth, you won't have time. If I'm gonta be a regular working man I expect I'll need you to keep house for me—"

Reluctantly she turned her eyes from Denis Larne back to him. "Yes, Fred," she agreed, not wanting to spoil his pleasure, "I reckon you will."

"Sure I will. Mr. Vance says if I work good, pretty soon I'll be making lots more than that. I can learn how to build a levee from the ground up. He told me about it. Up there waiting for the relief boat he didn't have so much to do, so him and me could talk. He said I did as good work as any full-grown man on the job." With a proud grin Fred began to look around for some other acquaintance to whom he could tell his grand news. "Look Ma," he went on, "I'll deliver these here clothes for you; then I'm gonta walk around the wharf awhile and see the men. You go on home and cook supper. Get us a beefsteak. I got money for it." He jogged her elbow impatiently. "Oh Ma, quit watching them people!"

"That young man sure looks fine," said Corrie May.

"I bet he ain't never done a day's work in his life," Fred retorted contemptuously. "Now Ma, you get that beefsteak —Oh, I declare, I don't believe you're hearing a word I'm saying!"

"Yes I am," Corrie May said tensely. She put her hand on Fred's arm. This was the arm that had no sleeve on it. She felt the tough young muscles rising under his dirty skin. Her eyes went back to the Larnes, as Denis graciously assisted his mother into a shop. Her mind went back to the Larnes too. She remembered how she had fought them and how utterly they had conquered her at every turn. But she looked at the unconsciously disdainful figure of Ann's son, perfect embodiment of a tradition that no longer had any reason for existence. It came to her like a flash of glory that though her son had inherited no tradition he had the strength of which fresh traditions were made.

"Are you listening to me, Ma?" Fred demanded. "Will you get that beefsteak?"

"Sure," said Corrie May heartily. "I'll get that beefsteak. "I'll cook you the best supper you ever ate in your life."

She watched the last flicker of young Denis Larne's coattails as he disappeared into the shop, and as she watched him her eyes were full of triumph.